NATIVE GROUND

MICHAEL O'CONNOR

For Debra
There at the beginning; there at the end.

Like all the other days of Cody McPherson's life, his last one was governed by habit.

Cody was up at dawn and had taken his sweet time with a spoonful of blackberry preserves on a crust of toast. He poured himself a scalding mug of yesterday's coffee, rolled a cigarette, and sat quietly at the kitchen table, watching smoke rise and curl through his fingers.

When the cigarette was half gone, Cody pinched its ash onto a plate and slipped the butt into his jacket for later. Waste not.

Jo walked into the kitchen as Cody was headed out.

"Bacon and eggs in thirty minutes, mister."

Jo had made Cody's breakfast for sixty years, and it was always ready a half-hour after he went out to the barn.

Cody checked in on Boone before seeing to the cattle. Boone was an American Quarter Horse with a hefty brisket, two white socks, and fine legs that ran back to his Barbary lineage. His buckskin coat was halved by a line of black hair so straight that Cody always said God himself had drawn it. Without Boone, Cody couldn't have run the place—the animal was Cody's legs and lungs.

Boone was constant in a world of change, and Cody loved him. When the old man died later that day, two hearts broke.

After leaving Boone to his oats, Cody fired up the Case and moved a couple of 500-pound hay bales from the shed to the bunks.

The shed was a double-high version of a pole building, with a pleated steel roof high enough to stack bales four-up. Weather generally rolled in from the north and west, so those sides of the shed had corrugated panels against the rain and snow. Not many ranchers sheltered their bales, but Cody knew better. Bales sitting on the ground, even with a tarp over them, leach minerals and nutrients into the ground and rot from the bottom.

Cody figured that a man had the right to ranch any fool way he wanted and didn't tend to argument. His herds always got top gains per bale, and Cody didn't feel the need to crow or have himself proven right in any other man's eyes. He sure as hell didn't see any reason to change his ways.

With the bunks full, Cody walked back to the house.

Jo said, "I was thinking I'd have to stuff these eggs back into their shells if you hadn't shown up just now, old man."

"It was Boone chewing my ear off that kept me."

"You like your conversations with that animal too much, Cody," Jo clucked.

Cody stepped into the kitchen.

"Boots stay in the entry, cowboy," Jo scolded without looking.

"Women!" Cody muttered, straining against the boot pull.

"What'd you say?"

"Said I love ya, darlin'."

"You love your eggs and bacon, is what."

"And my bacon loves you, sweetheart."

"You can get that thought *right* out of your head, Mr. McPherson. Now sit yourself down and mind your manners," Jo said, smiling.

Finished eating, Cody announced his plans for the day. "I think I'll head on out to the mineral lick and see about that whiteface and her calf. She's been out a couple of days, now. Could be dead."

"The calf hasn't come in alone, has it?"

"No ... he ain't."

"That's a good sign."

"Still, I'd better check."

It wasn't unusual for a calf to remain with its dead mother—until the whelp died of starvation or was taken by coyotes. Cody would never countenance losing a perfectly good calf just because the cow was done for.

Jo began clearing the table.

"I'm going in to town to pick up some things and see Ellie. I'll put your lunch in the fridge and be back by dinner," she said.

Dinner was one of six daily meals on the ranch.

Breakfast was served about a half-hour after the animals were fed and, during seasons when there was a lot of heavy work to be done, breakfast was the second-biggest meal of the day: two kinds of meat, potatoes, dumplings, eggs, pastries, cheese, milk, toast, juice, something sweet like canned peaches, and coffee.

Lunch, the first one, was taken midmorning and was often eaten outside. It consisted of sandwiches, chips or potato salad, glorified rice or a piece of fruit, some lemonade or a soda, and coffee.

Dinner was served at noon and was the biggest meal of the day: roast chuck or rump; fried chicken; corn creamed, steamed, or on the cob; cheesy beans; round steak, sirloin steak, Salisbury steak, T-bone steak; buffalo burgers; stuffed pork chops; country and spare ribs; sauerkraut; mashed potatoes, sweet potatoes, home-fried potatoes, potato salad, hashed potatoes, baked potatoes; Jell-O; white and wheat bread; every manner of bun ever baked in a kitchen except croissants; apple butter, currant jelly, honey; fresh butter and fresh cream; home-canned plums and applesauce; sweet, dill, and bread-and-butter pickles; freshly baked cookies; apple, boysenberry and blueberry pies; cakes that made men cry; homemade vanilla ice cream—and coffee.

Lunch, the second one, was eaten midafternoon and looked a lot like morning lunch, except that there was usually something left over from dinner that found its way into the afternoon lunch, with coffee after.

Supper was at six, or thereabouts. It was a slimmed-down version of dinner.

The last lunch was put out around eight, eight-thirty in the evening. In slow months it was just a piece of cake, a muffin, or maybe some cheese. When there was company, or the work was heavy, so was the last lunch. There was always fresh coffee for the last lunch of the day—a mess of it—so there'd be leftovers in the morning.

Cody stood and pushed his chair in to the table.

"I'll be seeing you about noon, then," he said, laid his coffee cup down on the counter with a thud, turned, and was gone.

Boone knew that they were heading into trouble well before Cody sensed it. While there was no obvious reason for it, the animal shied as they approached the mineral lick.

"What's the matter, old-timer? There ain't no rattlers out here this time of year." Cody put a hand on the horse's neck to calm him, but Boone wasn't having any of it. His ears had gone flat, and he was dancing sideways.

Although Cody trusted Boone's instinct, he didn't consider riding off. It wasn't in Cody's nature to cut and run.

On the alert because Boone was spooked, Cody dismounted slowly. As his boots hit the lick, two men walked out from around the rise behind it and approached Cody.

"Doc, Sam. Aren't you boys a little far from home?"

"Come to talk to you, Cody," Sam Barker croaked.

Cody was wary now. "Come a long ways to talk, fellas. You could have just stopped at the house. Got coffee there."

Neither answered; they just kept coming. Boone started to throw his head up and down and backed away.

When they got close, Sam offered his hand.

That was when Cody knew. The air was as cold as night, but Sam Barker's hand was in a sweat.

Once he got hold of the old man, Sam pulled Cody into the mean corral between himself and Doc Jennings. Jennings' hands were hidden in his pockets until that moment, when one of them sprang out, covering Cody's mouth with a rag.

Cody couldn't make out the smell, but he figured it wasn't going to matter much. He was wiry and strong, and a better man by twice than either of those scoundrels. Still, at his age he was no physical match for them.

His legs buckled, and the three of them went to the ground together.

At least I'm going to get it out here in the open, under the sky, Cody thought.

Jennings pressed harder on the rag.

"I love you, Jo." Cody mouthed the words as best he could through the chloroform that was taking him away fast.

Then he fixed his eyes on Boone and the light went out of them.

THURSDAY

Father, to the West I am standing. Behold me.
The wind blowing in my face. I am standing.
Lakota vision quest song

———

5 A.M.

"Jesus, Tom, wake up," Kathleen Larkin growled, "and shut that fucking alarm off."

She tucked herself back under the covers, but not before giving Tom a harder-than-necessary shove in the back.

"Sorry, Kath," Tom said. But Kathy had returned to her dreams.

This was exactly how Tom didn't want to start his trip—and his extended time away from Kathy. He and Kathy had managed to speak civilly about things the night before, and now he had shot that small reservoir of goodwill square in the ass. Tom hadn't even managed to leave without getting into it with his wife.

Tom retreated from the bed and slipped into a pair of moccasins. He sneaked over to the master bathroom and eased the door shut before flipping on the light. How long he had been tiptoeing around in his own life, Tom couldn't remember.

The razor's first stroke cut into flesh, and soft, pink drops of lather and blood began to spill into the sink. With a mild curse, Tom stepped into the shower.

Out of habit, Tom ground bar soap into the cut, burning the capillaries shut. In his suit-and-tie days, a blood-stained collar would have mattered. But today, Tom was headed to the Black Hills to buy a ranch. Maybe do a little looking around for his soul, for that matter. Out West a man got dirty and, often, bloody doing an honest day's work. A little blood here and there wouldn't be noticed.

Tom had been white-collar since college, but he had grown up with dirt under his nails, surrounded by horses, cottonwoods and cornfields in a place where a man's word was his contract. People were hardworking and mostly Lutheran.

Because Tom's family was Baptist, he was regarded by the neighbors with a stubborn reservation that no amount of volunteer plowing, baling, or manure-spreading could dispel.

Tom preferred chores to church any day of the week, but especially so on Sunday. His brand of communion was roast rabbit along the banks of Split Rock Creek, slouched with his mangy dog against a tree, listening to the wind and the fat spitting in their fire.

Tom had wanted to believe in God. If nothing else, it would have been a convenient thing to tell the Lutheran neighbors. Tom faked his conversion for six months during the eighth grade before he couldn't stand the hypocrisy any longer. Since then, he hadn't wasted any daylight arguing religion.

If he had wanted an argument in those days, he had seemed to always find one in town, where he'd gotten into his first real fight.

Tom was sixteen, chore-hardened, and about as wise to the world as a box of rocks. He'd gone to see a movie with friends and found himself staring at a heavily-tattooed man waiting in line. It wasn't the tattoos that caused Tom to stare. It was the guy's habit of stretching his lips up over his front teeth and gums, chimp-like, while he talked. Young Tom was fascinated.

"Hey kid, what are you looking at?" the man spat.

"Nothing," Tom shot back. "What's it to you?"

"You'll see after the movie, kid," tattooed Townie said. "Don't you try running out on me, neither."

When the movie let out, the man, his mountainous Indian buddy and their two women were already camped in the lobby.

"Been waiting on you, boy."

"So?" Tom sassed.

"So . . . you and me, outside."

Tom and the man had marched out of the cinema abreast and silent, like an old couple who had been wrong for each other from the start but had stayed together for appearances—and now the only thing they had to look forward to was the next good fight.

In the parking lot, the older man took off his coat and laid it neatly on the hood of a car. The gesture was so prim. He'd been to this dance before.

Tom stood cow-eyed and did nothing. It was his first mistake.

One fist exploded in Tom's eye; a second landed on the bridge of his nose. Tom looked at the blood running onto his jacket and knew he must be hurt, but he didn't feel pain, and anger had replaced his fear.

"You son-of-a-bitch!" Tom hissed as he launched a flurry of wild punches. Two or three landed, but with a thud rather than the satisfying crack of knuckles against cheekbone.

The jacket Tom wore kept his arms from extending, and his gloves prevented his fists from inflicting pain. Tom took a step back to shed this outerwear. It was another mistake. As soon as the jacket was half-way off, the more experienced fighter moved in and hit Tom repeatedly in the face.

"Fuck!" Tom spat the word out in a gob of blood.

Tom's face began to swell, blurring vision in both eyes. Blood was running freely out of both nostrils, across his mouth, and down his chin. He wondered absently if his nose was broken.

Tom's advantages in height and arm length weren't going to be any match for the man's experience and speed. Changing tactics,

Tom sprang forward, launching his foot into the man's crotch with a fearful energy.

The little man seemed to jump, as if he were cheering, then doubled up and dropped into a fetal curl on the ground.

Emboldened, Tom dropped his hands.

"Had enough?"

No answer.

"You through?" Tom demanded.

Tom would have gladly let things end there. But the Indian, the two women, and Tom's three friends had appeared and formed a circle around the fighters. The thing would have to be finished.

Tom looked at the Indian and hoped like hell he hadn't come to help. His opponent was five-six or -eight and maybe 140 pounds. The Indian was a titan.

The human pile on the ground stirred, uncurled, and brought itself up on all fours. Tom relaxed a bit and waited.

That was the last mistake.

Once upright, the little man advanced without hesitation and landed three punishing blows to Tom's face.

Stirred from its dark slumber by this violence, something primordial rose in Tom and took hold of him. Tom's heart rate slowed, and the pounding in his head vanished. He noticed his breath condense and knew the night must be frigid, but he felt warm. Tom calmly cleared blood from his eyes and fixed them on the man. A smile formed on Tom's lips right before his leg lashed out for a second time. The man saw it coming and blocked with his arm.

Tom heard the muffled sound of bone cracking under muscle and skin the instant his foot connected with the man's forearm. It pleased him.

Again the man collapsed. This time, Tom moved in to finish the job, but the Indian stepped between them. He didn't raise a hand or speak. He didn't have to. Tom backed off.

The injured man righted himself, cradling the injured arm in his good one. It was ugly. A jagged bone pierced the skin and the hand hung at an impossible angle.

"Call the cops," Tom said. "The guy needs a hospital."

"No!" the loser pleaded. "No cops. We can find a doc on our own."

The man took a step toward Tom.

Tom readied himself.

"Take it easy, kid," the man said. "I just want to shake your hand. That was the best goddamn fight I've had since the pen. No hard feelings, OK?" He tilted to support the shattered wing while extending his good arm to Tom.

"Yeah. No hard feelings."

The water in the shower had cooled, snapping Tom back to the present. He had been late getting out of bed and had been daydreaming in the shower for another fifteen minutes.

He'd have to light a fire under it if he was going to be in the Black Hills by three o'clock. He stepped out onto the mat and looked at himself in the mirror.

The cut on his neck was still weeping blood.

THURSDAY, 6 A.M.

After stowing his prized Stetson in the back and putting the palm hat on the passenger seat, Tom fired up the Cadillac SUV. It roared to life, and like Tom, seemed anxious to get out of town.

He and Kathleen had built a good life despite the fact that Tom had wanted a place far from the city, while Kathleen would have preferred Manhattan. Their St. Paul suburb was middling ground they had agreed to for the sake of their careers—and for the kids.

Although the suburbs hadn't made either of them completely happy, it was a good compromise at the time. But now the kids were gone, and new choices were possible.

Kathleen was lobbying for the Bay area: opera, theater, bustle and dance.

Tom wanted a ranch.

The two agreed to explore their options, but the process had driven a wedge between them, and things became openly hostile.

Neither could quite understand what the other was feeling. Tom and Kathy had grown up five miles apart on separate farms. The Larkin farm was small, and his father leased out all of the cropland until Tom was in high school. When he wasn't on his uncle's ranch in the Black Hills, Tom was free to roam the countryside, and what he remembered were the smells of alfalfa, black dirt, and horses. For Tom, the country life was all about an open sky and living in harmony with the land. For him the land was freedom.

Kathy moved to the country when her divorced mother married into the farm community. Her memories were full of thankless chores, dirty clothes, and 4-H meetings that caused her to miss out on being in the orchestra. For Kathy, the country life was all about being miles from any kind of culture and working your fingers to the bone as a slave to land that produced only when you were lucky enough to get rain. Kathy associated the farm with her mother's divorce and leaving the Black Hills, and so she fought against any return to a country life.

Each lobbied only for his own idea, with the understanding that neither would stand in the other's way should a reasonable opportunity come along. All they succeeded in doing was to chase each other back into their separate corners, there to fume and to refuel the bitterness.

Tom felt patronized; Kathy felt used. They withdrew staggering sums from the trust and goodwill accounts held by each for the other. And still, each of them stood his ground.

Like the housing tracts and highways, Tom's marriage was closing in on him. He had no relationship to the place where he lived, and now the relationship with Kathy had gone sour.

During their early years in the suburbs, their place had been different. It hadn't been unusual to see deer grazing by the kids' play set or occasionally spot a gray fox moving through. Woods surrounded the house, and Tom's favorite place to take the kids had been a thicket of dead oak trees that housed a colony of piliated woodpeckers.

Although it stands a foot-and-a-half tall, the piliated is a skittish bird that prefers to dwell as far away from humans as possible. The male sports a scarlet crest that spills like fresh blood down its forehead and onto its bill.

The thing looks prehistoric and acts that way, too. To stay conscious while hammering away, the piliated wraps its tongue around its brain. To feed, it unwinds its tongue and slides it into the tree.

The piliateds weren't long for the suburbs, and when a developer bought the property that harbored their colony, they vanished. Tom was sad to see them go; like him, they didn't fit in anymore and had overstayed their time. At least they got to leave.

Tom was determined to buy a working ranch, not some forty-acre "ranchette" that real estate agents love to foist onto city folks. The first thing the ranchette buyer wants to do is run horses; and then he wants a goddamn tractor. Just two pleasure horses grazing forty acres turn the ground into a thistle patch overnight, and it never recovers. After fouling the ground, the thistle baron builds an extra-large pole building for the tractor he doesn't need, and of course he puts up a fence. It doesn't take long before there isn't a direction worth looking in, and folks don't leave their double-wide *ranch* houses for anything but beer, groceries and prescription refills.

Tom dreamed of landing a big place—several thousand acres—that would create a healthy buffer between himself and any rancher-ettes. His prospects were good. Black Hills land was relatively cheap—at least compared to Colorado and Montana prices. But there was still a formidable gap between his dream and his bank balance.

Tom was sitting on a short stack in a high-stakes game. The medical start-up in which he'd invested most of his money had gone south. But he was prepared to ante up everything he had left to get the right place.

As Tom drove west, housing tracts gave way to farms, and the fence posts that streamed by perforated the landscape.

There weren't as many fences cutting the land back when Tom didn't have as many years on his brow. The slicing and dicing had worsened over time and would continue, for there is no undoing the fearful calculus that demands the land be broken into smaller and smaller chunks. For every two sons who want to stay, the farm becomes smaller by half. If each of them has two sons or daughters who refuse to leave, the mitosis continues. In another millennium or two, fences won't be needed. Scions of the land will be carrying the family farm around in their backpacks.

Fences have long been central to the American way of life. Whether good ones made good neighbors was debatable. It is certain, however, that there was something in Tom that didn't love barbed wire.

After crossing over into South Dakota, the fence posts started flying by at eighty miles an hour, and the sky unfolded to twice its Minnesota size. There just wasn't much to get in the way of it out there.

THURSDAY, 1 P.M., MOUNTAIN STANDARD TIME

Tom was halfway across the Rosebud Indian Reservation when he spotted a man walking along the highway about twenty miles west of Mission, South Dakota.

Tom and the road walker were in the middle of nowhere.

Tom donned his cowboy hat, slowed as he neared the old man, pulled up alongside him, and lowered the passenger window.

"Having car trouble?" Tom asked.

"Nope," the Indian replied. "Are you?"

"Actually, I thought you might like a ride. There isn't much daylight left, and if it were me, I wouldn't want to be hoofing it out here after dark."

The Indian took his time measuring Tom with his eyes. He reached into his jacket and pulled a 12-inch sheath from his belt, got into the car, placed the knife on the floor, and pulled the door shut.

They'd traveled together in silence for about ten miles when the Indian said, "Where you going?"

"Hot Springs. You?"

"Down there," the Indian said, nodding his head to the west.

Tom nodded back. It was possible that the old man would ride all the way to Hot Springs just because that was where Tom was headed. It was possible that he'd ask to be let out at some two-track that was miles from anything marked on a map and then wander into the hills.

After another several minutes, the Indian said, "What's your name?"

"Tom Larkin." Taking a chance, Tom added, "What's your name, grandfather?"

The grizzled corners of the man's mouth rose in a faint smile. Turning his face to the windshield, he said, "Iyankapi kici sukawaka."

"Eye-on-copee ke-chee soo ... I'm sorry, I didn't get that last part," Tom said.

"You don't know what that means, do you, Tom Larkin?"

"No idea, really."

"Didn't think so. It means Runs With Horses ... my name. Why did you call me grandfather?"

"I thought it was a respectful way of talking," Tom answered.

"It is, Tom Larkin. And you may call me grandfather because I do not like to hear my Lakota name said so poorly."

Tom broke into an embarrassed smile, and the old man laughed.

"So, *grandfather*, where can I take you?"

"I'm going to a place west of Pine Ridge. I'll let you know when we get close."

"Do you live there?"

"I live here," the Indian said, sweeping his hand to indicate everything the eye could see. "Where do you live, Tom Larkin?"

Tom started to say something, but couldn't find the words. *Where do I live, anyway?* Tom thought.

"Minnesota, I guess," Tom said.

"If you live in Minnesota, why are you here?"

The way Runs With Horses put it raised a larger question.

"I want to live here," Tom said. "In the Black Hills, I mean. I'm looking to buy some land and move out of the city. I want to ranch."

"Another white man coming to carve up the ground," the Indian said, shaking his head.

"I don't mean to do any harm," Tom said. "I was raised in the country, and I'm just trying to get back."

"Why do you have to own the land?"

"To tell you the truth, I don't know any other way. If there was some other way ..."

"The chance for another way is gone," the Indian said. "Even my sister married a white man and moved into his house and owns the land. It is sad."

"I think I know how you feel," Tom started, but Runs With Horses cut him off.

"You do not know, Tom Larkin. You cannot know."

The sun fell lower in the sky, and a silence fell between the two travelers.

Tom stole a glance at the old man. The features of his face and the land beyond bore a striking similarity.

The ground was a burnt sienna identical in color to the Indian's pigment. The old man's face—and that of the land—gave the impression of smoothness despite each having endured years of contouring by the wind. The Indian and the ground blended and belonged together.

The landscape was exotic and would seem alien in Tom's world of manicured lawns and elm-lined boulevards.

As the miles passed, the land began to roil and rise, forming itself into sculptures—each new monument was more striking than the last. Like the dangerous water where two great oceans meet, this ground where the East dissolves into the West is unpredictable. For now, the arid western climate is winning its battle with the moist, cool conditions of the East. Still, blue jays congregate with mountain plovers, and elms stand side-by-side with ponderosa pine, competing for water. Bluegrass and sage mingle, each gaining or losing ground according to the annual rainfall.

Runs With Horses reached down, picked up, and unsheathed the long knife that lay at his feet. He raised the blade, and Tom flinched.

The old Indian cut several long strands of hair from his head. Still brandishing the knife, he reached into his pocket and produced a piece of leather strapping and halved it expertly.

"Are you running away or going home, Tom Larkin?" Runs With Horses asked, and returned the knife and sheath to the floor.

Tom stared at the unbroken sky beyond the windshield for several seconds. "I don't know," he admitted. "I'm just trying to find something I lost."

"I am going to tell you a story," Runs With Horses said, his old fingers beginning to weave the leather and the hair into a braid.

"A very long time ago, white men came to the Black Hills and made their camps. But they did not camp in the Indian way. They failed to place their lodges facing east, and smoke from their camp-fires choked them in their sleep. This did not seem to bother these creatures. They walked on the same path every day and ran fat animals and heavy wagons on it until the ground was dead and spoke no more. Even if the tree people's leaves still grew green and golden, the white man cut them down to make boxes to live in and never moved their camps, even if all the boxes burned to the ground.

"Their camps made the ground—our Mother—foul-smelling, and no four-legged dared to come near, because the white man would kill it even if he was not hungry.

"When the white man had finished making boxes to camp in, he kept cutting down tree people and putting them into holes he dug in the ground to look for gold. He did this over and over— cut down tree people and carried rock people away.

"*Hetchetu welo!* It is as I say!" the old man cried out. "Shall I dig under my mother's skin to look for bones? Then when I die I cannot enter her body to be born again."

The Indian did not look at Tom while he told his story. He set his gaze on the horizon and held it there without squinting. His hands worked at the braiding like two old lovers in a slow dance, each knowing the other's moves as well as it knew its own.

"Like chipmunks in the trees, our people watched the white man dishonor our Mother, and a great sadness fell over our camp.

The people no longer sang songs, and the spirit of the forest no longer visited our feasts. Soon everyone fell ill and would not come out of their tipis either by night or by day. One by one, the people turned into mushrooms from sitting on the same ground without moving.

"The last one of our tribe to have his human form was a brave by the name of Otaktay, or Kills Many. When his wife and children turned into mushrooms, he became sad and prayed to *Wakan Tanka*, the Great Spirit, to become a mushroom, too.

"As his feet began to grow soft and melt into the earth, he felt a tremendous pounding, and when it stopped, he heard singing outside his tipi.

'I am Ptaysanwee, the white buffalo! You must come and sit by my fire, little mushroom!' the voice said.

Kills Many was just able to reach his knife, and dug furiously into the ground to free his feet. Gathering his courage and his strength, for he believed that the sacred animal had come to take him to the next life, he crawled out of the tipi and lay on the ground for several minutes while his eyes remembered how to see.

"*Hetchetu welo!*

"When he could see, Kills Many looked at Ptaysanwee, who had quit singing and had squatted down on the ground and was making a fire.

"'You must go to the center of the world,' the white buffalo said, throwing sage on the fire to help Kills Many remember the sweet smell of the air before the white man arrived. 'There you will find the four powers: the plant, the mineral, the animal, and the human. They will give you *Ee-wah-kee*—the medicine—to wake your people so they may once again walk the sacred path.'

"The white buffalo finished making the fire. It burned like the summer sun in its center—no smoke, just hot, round air. It was a good cooking fire.

"'Where will I find the center of the earth?' the brave asked.

"The buffalo lifted a hoof and pointed in the direction of Harney Peak. 'You will find it in the dark hills. I cannot travel there because my feet are not as sure as those of my brother, the mountain goat. You will have to find it by listening to the wind, and you will have to ask your brother *wamblee*, the eagle, to help you. He is the only animal that survived during the time when our Mother the Earth and our Father the Sky had their differences. During that time only the sage, the cedar, the yucca, and the tobacco people covered the ground, and the center of the earth could be seen from far away.

"*Hetchetu welo!*

" 'Now,' the buffalo said to Kills Many, 'you must take your knife and plunge it into my heart, so that you will have meat and a good robe for your journey.' The brave did not want to kill Ptaysanwee, but he knew that he must not shame her spirit by disobeying.

" '*Hi ho!*' the brave shouted to *Wakan Tanka*. 'Thank you!' "

"Then he drove his knife deep into the white beast and Ptaysanwee sang out as she died, '*Hetchetu alo!*', for it was good and it was finished as *Wakan Tanka* had dreamed it."

Runs With Horses had nearly completed the braiding and stopped speaking. He reached into his pocket and produced what looked like the claws of some great bird.

The old man held it up in four directions, murmuring something Tom couldn't make out as he did so. Then, he blew his breath across the thing and, with an ingenious weave, integrated the claws with the braidwork, but left each talon fully exposed and open, as if ready to snatch prey or defend itself from an enemy.

"Kills Many butchered the buffalo in a sacred way. He offered the great animal's heart to *Wakan Tanka* first and then ate it for strength. He cut strips of meat and hung them to dry for the journey, taking only what he thought he would need and no more.

"The rest of the animal he parceled out to each of the families of his tribe, wrapping the portions and placing the bundles in each tipi, for, as I have said, the people were all mushrooms and could not walk outside to dance and thank Kills Many for sharing the white buffalo with them.

"*Hetchetu welo!* Everything that I am telling you I heard from my grandmother," Runs With Horses said. "So you can know that it is true. Listen now, and I will tell you what became of Kills Many and his people.

"Kills Many sewed a medicine bag and filled it with red willow, sweet grass, tobacco, sage, a tooth from Ptaysanwee, a pasque flower and cedar bark, and set out for the dark mountains.

"He wandered for many days and many nights in *He Sapa*, the ancient name our ancestors gave to the Black Hills. He looked and looked but couldn't find the center of the earth. The winds spoke to him, but they all spoke at the same time, and Kills Many was confused, going north one day and south the next, and so on for days as he followed whichever of the winds spoke loudest.

"Still chasing after the advice of the winds, Kills Many had not eaten in four days. He was weary and felt no closer to the center of the earth. Finding himself on a small mesa, he sat down, closed his eyes and slowly shut out everything in the world, listening only to the sound of his heart.

"He listened for a long time and learned much. Finally, he heard his heart making a funny scratching noise. When Kills Many opened his eyes, he saw that it wasn't his heart, but his brother *wamblee*, the eagle, scratching at the ground on which he sat.

"'Have you become a quail, scratching the earth for grubs?' Kills Many teased the eagle and laughed.

"The eagle didn't laugh or speak; he just kept scratching at the ground. When he had finished, the eagle came over to Kills Many and said, 'I have seen you wandering in these mountains for many days. Have you become a child and forgotten your way?'

"Kills Many had offended the eagle and apologized. 'You are right, *wamblee*, I must find the center of the earth, and I cannot find my way. Will you put me on your back and fly me there? Ptaysanwee, the sacred buffalo, has told me that you have seen the center of the earth.'

"The eagle stared into the young brave's eyes and said, 'But you are sitting in the center of the earth right now, brother. Leave your cedar, red willow, and sage as an offering and fill your medicine bag with the earth I have scratched up and take it back to your people. It is *wakan* and will free them from their illness and sorrow.'

"Kills Many did as the eagle told him and filled his medicine bag with the powdered *Ee-wah-kee*, being careful to leave some of the medicine behind. It never paid to be greedy, no matter how great your need. As a child, Kills Many had heard about a woman who was digging for medicine who dug and dug and dug and took everything she could find, and when she got to the end of the last medicine root, it turned into a snake and devoured her.

"When Kills Many got back to his people, he sprinkled some of the earth from his medicine bag onto each little mushroom person. The next day, all of the tribe had regained their human forms and put on a great feast for Kills Many using the meat of Ptaysanwee, the sacred white buffalo.

"That day, Kills Many earned a new name: Wanageeska, or White Spirit, and was a great medicine man in our tribe until he died many years later."

The Indian quit talking and the two men rode in silence for several minutes.

"Pull over here," the old man said abruptly.

When Tom stopped, Runs With Horses got out of the car without a word and walked several paces away, crouched, and began rubbing the talisman he'd braided in the red earth. The dirt turned the braid a deep bronze color that stayed fast even after the old man rubbed it in sage.

"There are many voices in this world, Tom Larkin," the old man said on returning to the car. "You must learn which ones to trust. This necklace has the voices of the four powers: the animals, the plants, the minerals and the human beings. Listen for their counsel as you search for the thing you've lost."

The old Indian handed Tom the wampum. "This is for you. It will remind you that the land you seek is our Mother. You cannot own her. But if you learn to respect her ways, she will always look after you."

"Thank you," Tom said quietly, humbled by the gift. "I will do my best."

Runs With Horses put his hand on Tom's shoulder and said, "I believe you." He turned to leave.

"Wait, grandfather," Tom said. He wanted to make a gift of his own but didn't know what to give, or if he would be insulting the old man by trying.

"I have nothing to give back," Tom said, casting his eyes down. "Please tell me there is something I can give in return."

Runs With Horses smiled. "Now that you mention it, Tom Larkin, I could use something to keep my head warm. I had to sacrifice many of my hairs for your necklace, and an old man like me hasn't that many of them to spare."

Grateful for the suggestion, Tom took off his palm cowboy hat and was about to hand it over to Runs With Horses but stopped short. "Hold on a minute," he said and went around to open the car hatch.

Tom kept his good black Stetson in its original box for protection. The hatband was a reata made of buffalo hide and silver roping. He'd searched for months to find just the right hat, with the right fit and a classic look. It had set him back over four hundred bucks, and he loved the feel of it on his head.

Taking the Stetson from its box, Tom handed it to the old man and said, "Take this. It isn't much to look at, but it'll keep your head warm and dry."

The Indian turned it over a few times and inspected it from every angle—like it was a horse he had to convince himself was sound before he paid out good money. It must have met with his approval, because he put the hat on his head and took a minute to adjust it.

"I'm going now, Tom Larkin," the old man said. "I hope what you are looking for finds you."

Tom slipped the braided necklace over his head and stood watching the old man climb the bluff above the road. At the top, Runs With Horses turned toward Tom and reached both arms to the sky, spread his fingers wide, and sang out, "*Hetchetu alo!*"

"*Hi ho!*" Tom called back, but the Indian had vanished.

Thursday, 4:15 p.m.

Tom planned to meet up with his real estate agent, Pat Burley, at the Lucky Strike bar and restaurant in Hot Springs at five o'clock sharp.

While doing research for his trip, Tom had discovered that, millennia before, what today is Hot Springs was a medical and mystical oasis for hundreds of native tribes. Clutches of near-naked hunters routinely made pilgrimages to the steaming hot pools of mineral water called *wi-wi-la-kahta*. They came to cleanse themselves of demons and viruses, of sadness, rheumatisms, fear, and uncertainty. Some came to find God.

The healing water still bubbles up from the underlying gravel at ninety-six degrees, just as it did ten thousand years ago. Today, the water is captured at its source and tumbles into a concrete, rectangular hole painted whatever shade of aqua is on sale at Wendell's Hardware. For twelve bucks a head, a person can splash around in it for a couple of hours. After mobs of four-year-olds have relieved themselves in it, the sacred water escapes through a sewer pipe that empties itself into Fall River.

Long before the natural spring mutated, five men formed the Deadwood Corporation and built a town on the site. A little more than a hundred years later, their family names—Evans, Shepherd, Jennings, Barker, and Graves—graced every important business and political office. The Hot Springs graveyard and the city phone directory were both littered with their descendants.

According to tax records, the Deadwood Corporation rarely earned a profit. But the five founding families weren't broke, and they hadn't left Hot Springs. They had money. Lots of it.

It was quarter past four when Tom walked into the Red Rock Inn.

He stopped short of the counter and studied the receptionist. She was a sight. Sorrel hair gamboled carelessly over her shoulders, her eyes shone like amber in the afternoon sun her lips were moist and flowering. She stared shamelessly back at Tom.

Desire stabbed him.

Larkin had travelled widely and was no stranger to having women of all stripe come on to him. He had not ignored all of the invitations and knew—from experience—that wagering his marriage against a moment of pleasure was a sucker's bet; but for Tom, risk was aphrodisiac.

To Tom's way of thinking, Kathy had withdrawn from him, had walked away. That was his justification for thinking about playing Eros to this clerk's Psyche, his license to scoop her up and disappear for a spell if that is how things happened to play out.

The fabric of the woman's blouse did nothing to arrest her nipples or conceal any turn of her form. She wasn't dressed, she was dipped in cream. Her lips made promises.

She evoked the earth mother, and had all the qualities of a neon bar sign.

She moved like meandering water in a dream. Tom had to hold himself back from plunging in.

Her name tag read, "Eva," and she fixed a smile on Tom.

"You got a name, cowboy? Or should we just sign you in as 'stranger?'"

"The name is Tom Larkin," he said. "Thomas Michael Larkin."

"Quite a handle you've got there, Mr. Thomas Michael Larkin. Let's see if we can find you a place to hang your hat."

Eva began tapping on a hidden keyboard, causing the buttons under her blouse to dance. Eva's eyes met Tom's, fell to her breasts, and came back to meet Tom's.

"Sightseeing?"

"Seeing about some land," Tom said.

"My cousin's in real estate. You got an agent?"

"Matter of fact, I do. I'm meeting a guy by the name of Burley over at the Lucky Strike in a bit."

"Burley, did you say?" Eva asked. "Pat Burley?"

"Yeah. You know him?"

"You could say that. I'd watch out for him if I was you," Eva said.

"That doesn't sound good . . . care to tell me more?"

"Well," Eva began, "my friend moved here from California six years ago, and they wound up in court with Burley 'cause he promised them a driveway as part of their deal, and, according to her anyway, he never built it after he took the commission on the deal, and I believe her, but anyhow, they ain't settled with Burley yet, and she tells me that Burley don't even have a real estate license in South Dakota, so I'd check it out before you do anything . . . if I was you."

"You kidding? He doesn't have a real estate license? That seems odd. But, hey . . . you can't be too careful, right? I'll check it out. Thanks for the heads up."

Dangling his room key near her breast and out of Tom's reach, Eva said, "Need more than one key?"

"One will do," Tom said matter-of-factly.

"Right," she said and thrust her hand towards Tom.

When their hands met, Eva held on to the key for a split second more than was necessary—a nibble at the end of his line—then released her hold.

"You need anything, I'm at the front desk here until six. It's no bother; not a lot going on this time of year. Anything you need, Mr. Larkin. That's what I'm here for."

22

Tom let that pass. "I need to get to the Lucky Strike at five. How do I find it?"

Eva gave her head a sassy toss, scattering her copper hair like pennies at a parade, then lifted her arms to flip the mane back. Her breasts rode up with her arms.

"Did you come in on Highway 385 or 79?"

"Came up Highway 18 through Pine Ridge."

"Well, you drove right past it. Just backtrack three-quarters of a mile. It's on the east side of the highway. Big yellow sign.

"If you don't mind me asking, how long you planning on being at the Lucky?" she asked.

"Uh ... I ... I don't know. Why?"

"I'm meeting some friends there later. Thought maybe you might like to buy me a drink, and I'll give you the low down on my cousin, or whatever. You up for that, cowboy?"

"Yeah ... well, could be." Tom picked up his bag. "Maybe see you around."

"My daddy sure was happy that you're staying with us, Mr. Larkin. He just hates it when important people like you don't stay at the Red Rock."

"Say what?"

Eva said nothing.

Tom flushed. "Did I, uh, did I get your last name?"

"Shepherd."

"Shepherd?" he repeated stupidly.

"Yeah, Shepherd. Jim Shepherd is my dad." Eva started flirting with her hair.

Tom had done his homework and knew the name Jim Shepherd. He owned half the town. Shepherd was named after his great-grandfather, who was Hot Spring's first sheriff, "Old Shep." Shep's Canyon, just south of town, was named after him. How Old Shep came into all his property on a lawman's salary wasn't clear, but Tom was sure it had nothing to do with justice.

"I'd like to meet your dad sometime," Tom offered. "Seems to me he's the important one around here."

"That's not what he says," Eva replied. "He says that anybody coming out here to look at ranches is somebody we need to take care of. He says that ..."

"How do you know I'm looking at ranches?"

"You said you were here about some land. Hot Springs is a small town. When the ranchers with places up for sale are all getting a visit from the same guy at the same time, well, it ain't too hard to put two and two together. It's not like it's a secret."

"Fair enough," Tom allowed.

Eva reprised her request. "My cousin—remember I told you my cousin is in real estate—he knows of a couple of ranches that ain't listed. Nobody else can show them. They're for sale just by him. You sure you aren't interested in talking to him?"

Tom couldn't turn Eva down. It would be an insult to her father.

"OK, Eva. Tell him to call me." Tom shouldered his duffel bag and began to retreat.

"Hey, Mr. Larkin!" Eva sang out as he rounded the hallway. "Tom!"

He turned and walked back to the desk.

"Yeah?" Tom asked.

Eva was on her tiptoes and leaning over the counter, the front of her blouse puckering. Her breasts were jammed fast against the counter and they rose like storm clouds from a canyon.

Above those clouds her hand held a prize that waited for Tom to reach out for it.

He raised his hand to hers and felt its heat.

"You left your honor bar key, Tom. You'll need it if you want some goodies later on."

Her other hand crept up from behind the counter and cradled his hand. It might have been tender under different circumstances.

Like a host, she placed the key in Tom's palm and folded his fingers around it.

"See you later?" she asked.

"Maybe so," Tom mumbled, and escaped.

Thursday, 5 p.m.

Tom's real estate agent, Pat Burley, was holding court at a bar table, fit for three middle-aged women from Wisconsin or four trim cowboys. A dozen men surrounded him, and people sitting nearby had their ears cocked his way.

Even from where he stood, Tom could tell that Burley was in the middle of a story, because nobody was drinking up anything but Pat's words.

Burley paused in mid-sentence, and his audience held its breath. Then Pat delivered the punch line, and they all laughed as if they'd been born with the same voice.

Tom hadn't heard Pat's words, but he joined in with everybody else because he couldn't help himself.

Pat spied Tom and sang out.

"That there is Tom Larkin," Burley said, pointing at Tom. "He's one of them liberals from Minnesota. He come out here to see what easy living is all about.

"Making matters worse," Burley continued, "Tom's an East River boy." Burley wagged his head in mock disapproval, and those hanging on him nodded in agreement. "On the other hand, he was born a country boy and generally knows a saddle horn from a skirt, so maybe we'll let him stay on a couple days ... providing he buys us a drink now and again."

Burley had given Tom a ringing Western endorsement, and now he instructed the man standing nearest to give up his bar stool to Tom.

"No need to get up, friend," Tom countered. "I've been sitting on my keister all day."

"Don't make no never mind to me," the man said. To Burley he added, "I'm pretty sure I already heard the joke you was fixin' to tell next—couple of times, at least." The man stood, downed his beer in a swallow, and walked off.

The rest of Burley's entourage dissolved into the bar. They had no part in this business meeting and went to drink at other tables. Not necessarily, however, out of ear shot.

While Tom took a seat, Pat excused himself, saying he had to take a piss and order up a couple more drinks.

Like the dark mountains he loved, time had taken a toll on Burley. A hell-raiser and a gamer, Pat had burned through his best years like penny poker chips.

Tom's Scotch and Burley materialized at the same moment.

"When did you get in?" Burley asked.

"Less than an hour ago. Slept in this morning. Got to have my beauty rest, you know?"

"If that's the case, I think you better high-tail it back to the hotel and get yourself some more sleep, Larkin!"

Tom laughed.

"You ready to spend a few hours getting cold tomorrow? I've got a couple of ATV's trailered up behind my truck—only good way to cover all of the ground we've got to see."

"Looking forward to it, Pat. And I figure I'll be able to survive what passes for cold around these parts."

"How about we meet for breakfast at the Flat Iron around seven and go from there ... that too early for you?" Pat asked.

"Seven is fine. We can get going earlier if you want to."

"Hell, I have to wake up at five as it is, just to get my plumbing in gear and still make it to the restaurant by seven." He laughed, then turned serious. "There's an issue with one of the ranches I lined up for you. It's the McPherson place. That's the one that ..."

"You sent me the poop sheet. About ten thousand acres, over by Edgemont?"

"Yeah, that's it. But it's eight thousand four and change."

"I may know that place. Maybe been there before, not sure."

"You don't say?"

"Yeah. When you sent me the listing, the name rang a bell. I thought maybe it might be a place I worked the summer of '67 or '68, don't rightly remember. Starting in the sixth grade I spent summers on my uncle's ranch south of here. I wound up coming out every year until he died in '70, then my aunt sold the place. Anyway, I worked at another ranch off and on one summer, for a friend of my uncle. I think it had something to do with their help leaving. Anyway, the name McPherson rings a bell. I'm pretty sure I'd recognize them if I saw them again. Good people, but I haven't been back in, what, 35 years? Could be the same ranch. Who the hell knows, right?"

"Well," Burley said, "we'll find out soon enough. Probably won't matter, anyway, because as I said, there's a bit of a complication."

"What's the problem?"

"I don't exactly know, yet. The place is up for sale because old man McPherson died a couple of months back. I met him when I got into the business in '72. One of the first big deals I ever did was to sell him a couple of thousand acres that was between his place and that old ghost town."

"Igloo. Read about it. Named for all those weird Army sheds they built west of it ... hundreds of them, weren't there?"

"Yeah. That whole set-up out there is cock-eyed. Anyway, McPherson's widow, Jo—she's near eighty I'd say—she tells me this morning that some Philadelphia lawyer called her yesterday and offered her three times the listing price."

"Life is rough, Burley!" Tom chided. Three times the listing price would be around seventeen million dollars, Tom figured, and the commission on it over a million. "That is a damn shame, Pat. Tell you what—if you have any trouble spending the commission, maybe I can lend a hand."

"Me spending a fat commission, unfortunately, ain't the problem," Pat said. "Mrs. McPherson spooked when they came at her with two thousand an acre right out of the chute. You know, what's wrong with this picture, and all that? Well, she gets her back up and tells me that, until she knows the name of the buyer offering that kind of dough for the place, there ain't any sale at seventeen million—or seventeen billion, or seventeen anything, for that matter."

"You serious?"

"As a heart attack."

"You planning to get her into counseling, or what?"

"Believe me, Larkin, I'd French-kiss a fat baby's ass to get the property moved at that price.

"But Jo McPherson just isn't the kind of person you're going to bully. Not that I'd try. When she sets her mind to something, best just get the hell out of the way."

"Well, this can't be rocket science, Burley. Check these guys out and then go get their money," Tom said.

"If it were that easy, I wouldn't be sitting here drinking whiskey with your sorry ass. I'd be in my office taking some dumb-ass Philadelphia money," Pat said.

"I don't get it."

"Look. I'm on this like stink on shit the minute I get off the horn with Mrs. McPherson. I call the law firm, which is Perez and Farmer and a couple of other no counts, and get right to Farmer, who's one of the partners. I tell him that I need to know who he represents, or no deal."

"What'd he say?"

"He says that his client isn't any of my business, and do I want to take the offer or not."

"And . . ."

"... and I say that it ain't my place to take the offer, that it would be up to my client to accept or reject it, and she said no deal unless she knows who she's selling to."

"Was that the end of it?"

"No." Pat finished his whiskey in one draw and went on. "I told him that he could call Jo himself if he wanted to, but it wouldn't make any difference. I told him all he'd do is piss her off."

The waitress came by and refreshed their drinks.

"Smart guy Farmer there tells me, yeah, he wants to call Mrs. McPherson and would I give him a number where he can reach her right away."

"Did you give him her number?" Tom asked.

"Hell, yes. I figured it would be the fastest way to hear back from him. And it was." Burley may not have known squat about lawyering, but he knew Jo McPherson. "My coffee didn't have time to chill before Mr. Big Shot calls me back."

"Let me guess. He's singing a different tune?"

"Yeah, and bumbling the lines," Pat said, pausing to swallow more whiskey. "Mr. Ambulance Chaser tells me that his clients are 'highly motivated' to buy the ranch, and he didn't think that 'details' should get in our way. I'm thinking, 'highly motivated,' my ass. His client must want the McPherson place real bad; otherwise he'd have waited a day or two before calling me back. So, I'm thinking he's in the bag."

"But ... no?" Tom asked.

"The lawyer says that he'll give me the name of their client, but—get a load of this—he wants me to sign a nondisclosure agreement before he'll tell me. I'm thinking, so what? It's a piece of paper that means something to them yahoos, but not to me. Nondisclosure? In this town? That's funny. I can tell you right now who's banging who any given day of the week, and them hotshots want nondisclosure? So I say, yeah, I'll sign it. He says Jo has to sign it, too. I tell him to fax the cotton-pickin' thing over.

"Well, Jo isn't that hot on signing, but I told her it was no big deal. She signs it, and I fax it on back to Philly right after lunch."

Burley had worked himself up pretty good. The whiskey helped. Lowering his voice and leaning in close, he whispered, "You're not going to believe this. He calls me back and says he represents Elements Corporation."

"Hey!" Tom interrupted. "Don't tell me that. You signed a nondisclosure agreement!"

"Like I told you, Larkin, it don't mean shit to me unless I'm short on toilet paper."

"Who the hell is Elements Corporation?" Tom asked.

Pat dropped into a whisper. "Elements Corporation is a quiet little mind-your-own-business kind of company that's been around longer than dirt. And the owners are ..." Pat's voice fell another decibel as he continued, " ... Dr. Bill Jennings, Sam Barker, Carl Graves, Jim Shepherd and John Evans, Jr. The Hot Springs mafia."

Tom sat forward. Carl Graves was the mayor. He had Eva to thank for the reminder on Jim Shepherd. Evans owned the Hot Springs pool and a couple of other tourist traps. He remembered reading about Barker and Dr. Jennings somewhere.

"The Elements offer don't make sense," Burley slurred. "These guys are *from here*. They've got plenty of land that they ain't doing anything with, and even if they had good reason to buy McPherson's place, there's no way they'd offer that kind of money. What the hell gives?"

Each man took a pull on his drink in silence.

"Something ain't right here, partner ... probably ain't nothing right about it. But it don't matter what I think. I told Jo who was behind the offer and asked her what she wanted to do."

"What did she say?" Tom asked.

"She said no. And she didn't mean maybe."

Burley polished off his drink. He looked every bit the salesman who had come close enough to smell a million-dollar payday just before it vanished into the blue sky.

Tom ordered another round, and the conversation turned to horse racing.

THURSDAY, *6:30 P.M.*

A hand came to roost on Tom's shoulder.

"Hi there," Eva said.

"Well . . . hi! I didn't really expect you to show up. Ah, Pat, this is, ah . . ."

"Cat got your tongue, Larkin?" Pat asked.

"No, it's just that . . ." Tom fumbled.

Putting his hand on Tom's other shoulder, Pat addressed himself to Eva. "He been giving you trouble, sweetheart? Wouldn't surprise me in the least—you know, these hotshots from east of the river come out here and think they can get away with murder." Pat gave Tom's shoulder a conspiratorial squeeze.

"What a mean thing to say, Pat Burley! Why, Tom was a real gentleman in every way, a sweetheart," Eva said, turning to face Tom, "I wish all our guests were more like you, Tom."

Ignoring Burley's presence, Eva draped her hand over Tom's and held his eyes.

Burley looked at Tom, raised an eyebrow, and doused a grin in his whiskey glass. Tom thanked Eva for the kind words and freed his trapped hand to pick up his cocktail.

The set-up was a disaster in the making, and Tom knew it: Mix several cocktails with a come-on from a stunning young woman, place everything in a bar several hundred miles from home, and stir.

Eva's get-up added more than enough spice to the mix.

Her sheer blouse barely concealed breasts swaddled in an embroidered demi bra. It was classic Old French corsetry and a stellar marriage of seduction and glamour. Tom had helped Kathy select a less racy design when they were in Paris a few years back.

Her swans were nestled in delicate lace cups and suspended in mid-flight on impossibly thin ribbons of silk. Lace flitted along the scalloped edges, and a tiny lilac bow peeked out from the place where her blouse quit plunging.

It could have been no more elegant had Botticelli painted it on her.

Less substantial than gauze, the blouse sported long, cuffed sleeves and a high, silk collar. Iridescent butterflies on its front revealed enough of Eva to render imagination moot. The bodice precisely followed her contours, and darts carved it sharply under her bust. Embroidered buttons ran from her throat to her waist, but Eva had engaged only half of them. It was her way of showing men everything they were not about to get.

It was made her tempting—and intimidating.

Eva would have fit in well in New York or Rome. No doubt she would have turned a few heads even in those places. In Hot Springs, however, even men considered her dress unacceptable. Not that they didn't grab an eyeful of her at every opportunity; it's just that people there didn't make a habit of calling attention to themselves.

Eva obviously didn't care if she looked out of place. She got noticed. Every time she stepped into a room.

Her skirt glistened with an otherworldly sheen that men and fish find fatally attractive. It was a swirl of cinnamon, sage, and pumpkin chiffon, with a glimmer of pearl. It was a passing dream woven of organza and nothing more.

A string of amber encircled her waist. A casual knot in the front gave the impression that this mooring might be undone simply by desiring it so. Below the belt, faux bone buttons marched down the front to its hemline, all but the top three undone.

Tom knelt before her and, deliberately, undid each of the remaining buttons. Each burst open at his touch, a seedpod ready to flower. Tom felt her warmth on his hand, closed his eyes, and muttered something akin to prayer. Eva reached down and cupped the back of his head.

Eva's laughing brought Tom back to the Lucky Strike.

"Hello? You go to sleep, Tom?" Eva said, turning to face Tom. "I've been telling Pat here that I intend to get your business for my cousin, and then Pat tells me you probably aren't worth a plug nickel anyway—so I could just have you. What have you got to say about them apples?"

The skirt was still buttoned and Eva and Pat were standing as they were before.

"I'm sticking with Burley," he said to Eva. "But, Pat, if you insist I wander off with Eva and her cousin, you just give me the high sign."

Eva laughed and gave Tom's cowboy hat a playful tip forward.

"I 'spose I better hang on to you as a client—for now," Burley said. "No telling what kind of trouble you'd get yourself into if I don't keep an eye on you. Especially if I was to turn you loose with this here filly."

Tom ordered a round and offered the empty bar stool to Eva. She thanked Tom, and, nudging close to him, sat down.

Tom whispered to Eva, "I thought you said that you didn't like Burley?"

"I told you what my friend told me. I never said I didn't like Pat," she said loudly. And turning to Burley, she continued, "Hey, Pat, do you like me?"

"Like the clap."

"See. He loves me."

Eva's Cointreau martini arrived. "Looks like I've got some catching up to do, boys," she said, inhaling a manly portion.

"If you love me, Burley"—she dripped sarcasm but not a drop of Cointreau—"be a doll and order me up another one. These aren't hard to take at all."

Pat left to see about their drinks, and Eva promptly laid her hand on Tom's thigh. As he reached down to remove it, she said, "A little birdie told me you're going to look at the McPherson place."

Tom's hand froze.

"What'd you say?"

Eva gave Tom a quick squeeze before her hand took flight.

"I said, Thomas *Michael* Larkin, that a little bird told me you're looking at the McPherson place. True or false?"

"Who wants to know?"

"Nobody, Tom. Everybody already knows."

What Eva said was true. Jo had told Joanne, her neighbor, that Burley was showing her place that weekend, and Joanne had told Ellie, the postmaster, and Ellie told just about anybody who'd listen.

Tom hailed Burley back to the table. "Pat ... hey, Burley! You been telling Miss Two-Fisted here about our ranch tours? She seems to know my itinerary betteran I do." Tom was starting to feel the whiskey.

"Din I tell ya? I took out an ad inna *Star* an' published the whole damn tour. You sure I din tell ya?" Burley was already in the tall weeds and just managed to slosh the fresh drinks onto the table. He'd brought a double for Eva. "Whud she tell ya anyhow?"

"Wants to know if we're lookin' at McPherson's."

"Well, seeing as how it's the biggest goddamn spread anywhere near here, and seein's how it's my goddamn listing, ya think I just might wanna show it? I gotta be more careful what I tell Multiple Listing, Larkin. They doohn keep secrets like they yewsta."

Shaking his head, Tom turned to Eva. "OK. We're seeing Jo McPherson's place in the morning ... or whenever we get around to it. What's it to you?"

"Wanna know something else, Tom?" Eva chirped.

"I'll bite."

"You might as well not waste yer time on McPherson's place, 'cause you're not ever gonna get it, Mr. St. Paul. In fact you're not gonna touch it with a ten-foot pole ... or with that other ... never mind ..." Eva tossed back half of the double martini, and continued. "Unless you're the Prince of Wales, you ain't got the scratch. And even if ya do, ya don't. Catch my drift?"

Burley had been drinking before Tom arrived at the Lucky Strike and had matched him drink for drink all evening, but suddenly appeared as sober as gray dawn.

"Old Eva here is just trying to impress the good-looking guy from the big city," Pat offered. "She don't know shit from shinola. Listen here, darlin', don't you go worrying your pretty little head about what Tom can and cannot buy. It'll just give you a nasty old headache."

Eva took Burley's bait.

"Well, guess what, wise guy? Maybe my purty little head gets itself inta places and hears things that big, tough real estate salesmen like you can't go. I'm telling you that my dad and his partners are lookin' at McPherson's, and if they want it, there ain't a snowball's chance in hell of you gettin' it, and you know it. I heard my dad and Doc Jennings and the mayor talkin' about it a while back—before you even got the damn listing. And they said it was critical, or sumpthun like that, for their new project, and you kin bet your ass they ain't gonna let Patrick Burley sell it out from under 'em." Eva paused to inhale—and drink—deeply.

"What project?" Tom asked, stepping into the fray.

"A projek that'll be yer business when it's wrote up in the newspaper for everybody else to know about—that's 'what projek.'" Eva seemed to realize that she'd been running at the mouth and went mute.

Burley steered Eva back toward the cliff she'd been skirting.

"I don't think Tom was all that serious about McPherson's anyway. It's a lot of money—even at the listed price," Pat said. "Place probably won't go that high anyhow."

Eva couldn't stop herself. "It'll go fer as high as it has ta. Take that ta the bank, too." She rose from the bar table on two wobbly but extremely well sculpted legs.

"Either a you two bums wanna buy me dinner ta go along with the 'tinis?" Tom knew that the question had been laid out for him, but didn't answer.

"Thought not. Oh well, maybe there's some *men* over at the Junction," she said. "Thanks fer the drink. Nice seein' ya, Tom."

And then, more sweetly, Eva added, "Call me." And she was gone.

"She's a piece of work, huh?" was all Tom could muster.

"She's a piece of something," Pat said.

"But she is quite a looker, ain't she? Not that it makes any difference to a geezer like me," a new voice chimed in from behind them.

Tom looked up and saw a balding man of perhaps sixty standing behind Pat. Out here, it was difficult to tell much about a man by the way he dressed. The fellow could have been a convenience store clerk for all that his clothes gave away. They weren't old clothes, they were new clothes that didn't fit the man or the times.

"Carl, you worthless rascal," Burley said. "How long have you been eavesdropping on us?"

Pat and Carl shook hands. They seemed friendly with each other.

"Tom, this here's Carl Graves. Mayor Carl Graves. He's an important man around these parts," Pat said. "Carl, this is Tom Larkin. He and I are scouting some ground out here. He thinks he might be wanting to ranch—or some other such foolishness."

"Real good to meet you, Tom. You should know that the only reason Pat thinks I'm so important is 'cause I own the bar, and he's hoping I'll buy a round." When Carl smiled, he only used half of his mouth—the other half just stayed put like it was dead.

"Well, that's damn gentlemanly of you, Carl. I'll have the usual, bring a Scotch for this young fella, and if you can spare a couple of beers for our horses . . ."

"Oh, hell. May as well, I 'spose. Jackie," Carl said, holding up one finger to the bartender, "I'm buying one, I repeat, *one* round for our guest of honor and the bum that dragged him in here."

"Huh?" Jackie asked, stunned. "Did you say you were buying a round, Carl?"

Carl dipped his chin and glared at Jackie over his cheaters: "A round for my friends—that is, if it's all right by *you*."

As a rule, Mayor Carl Graves spent as little money buying drinks for his customers as he spent time at City Hall. To be fair, there wasn't a whole lot of mayoring that needed doing, but Carl enjoyed what little authority came with the job of mayor, primarily because he could use his political position to further his business interests.

Men who are single-minded about money rarely have a sense of humor or personal charm, but Carl had both, in quantities that matched his ample girth, and folks liked him. Maybe people naturally take a shine to a man who doesn't seem threatening or different. Maybe Carl had been politicking and selling whiskey for so long that he just treated everybody like a customer, and, hell, the customer's always right. Maybe Carl had just learned that friendly works a sight better than contrary when it comes to getting along in the same small town with the same cast of characters for several decades. Whatever it was, it kept getting him re-elected.

"Been staying out of trouble, Pat?" the mayor asked.

"More or less, except your wife's been bothering me to run over to your place and keep her company while you're here keeping the drunks liquored up!" Pat and Carl laughed in the same cadence and at the same pitch and for the same amount of time, as if they'd rehearsed it.

Sporting his half-smile, Carl turned to Tom. "So ... Tom. What made you pick this area to look at?"

"My Uncle Seth, Seth Wallace, he had a place around here once, but my aunt sold it after he died."

"I remember the Wallace place ... that was a while back, wasn't it?" Carl added.

"Round about thirty-five years ago, I guess. The other thing is that my wife was born in Rapid City before she moved East River. So the area's a bit familiar."

"What's your wife's maiden name?"

"Hirsch. Kathleen Hirsch. Her mom and dad got divorced when she was little, but her dad, who's gone now, ran the municipal golf course in Rapid for years."

"Oh, sure!" Carl brightened considerably. "I knew old John Hirsch. Good man. Do you know that, at one time, we tried to get him to come down here to run our little nine-hole course? He came down and had lunch and was real nice about it, but he wasn't really interested. And you married his daughter, what did you say her name is?"

"Kathleen."

"Right, Kathleen. You a golfer?" Carl asked.

"No, I'm not. But Pat tells me that your nine-hole is about the prettiest little thing in the country."

"Well, we like to think so. Of course, so does *Golf Digest*. They named ours the top nine-hole course in America back in '99. And we get on the top ten list every year," Carl said proudly.

"I'd love to see it, Carl."

"I was hoping you'd say that ... have you got time tomorrow? 'Cause if you do, I could take you around the course and show you something that'll make our nine-hole look shabby by comparison."

"What do you mean?"

"I mean the new nine we've just finished. And I'm telling you, you have never seen bunkers like these, ain't that right, Pat?"

"True fact," Burley replied.

"Now, let's see here … I'm done with the municipal planning meeting at four tomorrow. Why don't you meet me in the bar at, say, four-thirty? The tour will only take us a half-hour or forty-five minutes. What do you say, young man?"

"Done deal. Pat, you coming?"

"No. I've got to get back and do my ironing," Pat joked.

"OK, then. Four-thirty tomorrow. Here," Tom confirmed.

"Right. By the way, let me write down my phone number for you." Carl reached into his shirt pocket and produced a ballpoint pen with an advertising message on it. He scribbled both his cell phone and home phone numbers on the back of his business card and handed it to Tom.

"Give me a call if anything changes; otherwise, I'll see you at four-thirty. We've got a lot to talk about."

Tom stared at the two handwritten numbers, thinking how unusual it was to meet the mayor of a city and have him give you his personal contact numbers after twenty minutes of idle chitchat. Carl's business card was one of those thermo-graphic, black-on-white jobs that could be purchased for ten bucks at any quick print shop, and read, simply, "Carl Graves, Elements Corporation." No phone numbers, no address, no e-mail. *Weird,* Tom thought. He looked up, but the mayor was gone.

"Christ, Burley, is there anybody in town who doesn't know why I'm here? Or who isn't standing in line to 'help me out'?"

"It's like this, Larkin: At a time when most folks are trying to cash out or just plain get out, you're bringing cash in—and in a big way. That gets folks' attention.

"Now, on top of that, the mayor and his buddies have this unnatural interest in the McPherson place, and you're a potential competitor. So watch yourself tomorrow. Old Carl may not look like much, but his bite is worse than his bark."

Pat drained his glass.

"Let's have one for the road, Larkin, and then I've got to get out of here or I'll never be able to haul my carcass out of bed in the morning."

"Shoot you a game of eight-ball to see who pays?" Tom offered.

"Rack 'em up."

Thursday, 9:00 p.m.

Stripping to his shorts, Tom took stock of himself in the mirror. He worked out regularly, held the scale at a hundred seventy-five, and had that tough-around-the-edge look of a farm kid. Although he'd be fifty in a couple of years, there weren't many thirty-somethings that could match him pound-for-pound.

Tom was nicely squared off, stood six-three in his boots, and had an untamed shock of hair he let grow well over his collar. Men took him seriously, and older folks liked him right off. Getting the second look from women wasn't unusual.

There was a time when Kathy liked the idea of other, especially younger, women making eyes at her husband; it fed her ego. It was the thought that Tom might have given in to one of them that worried her. But she liked the feel of Tom's body on hers and didn't much like the idea of trading him for a flabbier model that would be more secure from other women's prying fingers. Over the past few years, though, they had drifted seriously apart, and she was worried.

Kathy believed that she still loved Tom, but after all their time together, she wasn't sure exactly what made him tick. Given their differences about the ranch idea, she was even less certain about their future together.

As a kid, Tom had borrowed money to buy calves and sold them at a good profit. He'd been given forty acres to plant in exchange for doing the work on the other three hundred, but he paid for his own gas, seed and combining.

He made plenty of extra money trapping during the winter and had used some of it to buy his way into a work-study program in Switzerland when he was sixteen. The water-ski school he managed that summer didn't make him rich, but it was another chance to learn how to win customers, and the hotel manager had asked him back the next year.

Instead of returning to Europe after graduating from high school, Tom ran off with the carnival in his late teens.

The "show"—as it was known to carnies—was a gaudy little Neverland where men behaved like motherless boys, and a girl could pretend that it was Prince Charming who'd given her a sawdust-filled, lime-green teddy bear for sex. Maybe women were drawn to carnies because they liked the feeling of getting screwed by a complete stranger, and they'd never have to account for it. Tom had been young and didn't really give a damn. He screwed men out of their money and women any way they wanted it.

The carnival wasn't all corn dogs, blow jobs and Tilt-A-Whirls. When the carnival came to town, trouble followed.

Tom had obeyed the carny code: You were either "with it," or you were a mark. If you were with the show, you took the carny side of any fight, and anything Tom did to defend himself—or another carny—was considered fair play on the carnival lot.

A man's view of right and wrong, Tom learned from the carnival, often depended solely on whether or not he had a dog in the fight.

The carnival hadn't taught Tom to like fighting. It had taught him how to win.

After college, he learned about money the hard way—by losing a bunch of it. Tom had discovered that many of his white-collar colleagues lived by the same philosophy as his carnival buddies: If the rules got in the way, bend them or break them, just get what you came for.

44

However practical that thinking might be for a carny, Tom decided he wasn't about to live his life that way. In business, he played his cards straight up and let the chips fall where they may.

Sometimes it paid off, sometimes it didn't.

He had learned the language of business as a marketing strategist, made good money working for big corporations, and then had invested most of his savings in a medical education start-up company. Tom figured that he had as much as earned a medical degree during the thousands of hours he had spent in lectures and operating theaters.

The start-up was to be Tom's retirement fund, but it folded, along with hundreds of others, in the dot-com stock market crash. Other than that market crash, what luck Tom had in his life—good and bad—was generally of his own making.

He sat down at the hotel desk, wrote a search for "Elements Corporation" + "Hot Springs" + "South Dakota," and hit send. The search produced seven citations, four of which were garbage.

"That's impossible," Tom muttered. He rekeyed his search, without Boolean limitations, and double-checked each keystroke as he made it. He hit the return key and the search engine spat back its answer.

Same seven citations for Elements Corporation. Same four pieces of garbage.

He followed the links to the three citations that looked promising. Two of them were fluff from the local newspaper, the third was a *Washington Post* story about a Justice Department inquiry involving Elements.

"Weird," he said aloud to himself, and dialed Kathleen at home.

"Hello?"

"It's me. Did I wake you?"

"No, you didn't. It's a little late to be calling, isn't it?"

"Been busy. Sorry I didn't call earlier. Sorry about waking you this morning, too. OK?"

"Yeah, sure. What's happening out there?"

"Everything here is going great. Pat Burley and I are going out to see the first properties tomorrow morning. But something came up tonight at the Lucky Strike, and I'm going to need your help sorting it out. Will you do that for me?"

"What's a Lucky Strike?"

"It's a bar, a casino—you know, a restaurant kind of place. That's not important. It's what I heard from the mayor that I need your help on."

"You've been in a casino all night?"

"Yeah, a restaurant-kind-of-casino—like I said. What is your problem, Kathy?"

"Forget it, Tom!" she snapped. "Just tell me what you need—start with the mayor." Kathy had been a newspaper reporter her whole life, and she switched effortlessly into investigative mode.

"His name is Carl Graves. Seems like a stand-up guy. He's been mayor for ... I don't know how long. I should have asked him that. Anyway, he's involved in a company called Elements Corporation that's put a bid in on the McPherson ranch, and I ..."

"Hold on a sec. I'm going to need a notebook and pen."

Tom heard a drawer being opened.

"Spell the mayor's name," Kathy commanded.

"Graves, G-R-A-V-E-S, first name Carl. Carl is spelled with a 'C'."

"Good. I'll find out how long he's been in office, party affiliation, election results, the works. That won't be a problem. You said that he has a business ... tell me what you know."

"He gave me a card that says 'Elements Corporation'," Tom read from the crumpled card Carl had pressed into his hand earlier in the evening.

"What is their address and phone number?"

"There's nothing printed on the business card he gave me. Just 'Carl Graves' and 'Elements Corporation'."

"I'll get the details," Kathy assured him.

Flipping Carl's card in his hand, Tom said, "He did give me his cell and home phone numbers, if that will help."

"It might. Give me the numbers. You said that Elements is a corporation? What kind?"

"I honestly don't know, Kathy. I tried a web search and came up with squat—seven citations."

"You sure you didn't make a mistake?" she asked.

"Yeah, that's what I thought, too. Then I redid it and came up with the same results. That's when I knew I'd better get the Pro from Dover involved." Tom was doing his best to be upbeat, hoping to break the new ice between them that had formed during the fourteen hours Tom had been gone.

"Go on, Tom." Kathy's voice was a few degrees warmer.

"I've just told you about twice as much as I really know about this company."

"You don't know Grave's title, you don't know what his company does, you don't know what kind of corporate structure they have, don't know if it's private or public"—Kathy caught her own mistake and continued on with the same breath—"of course they're not public or you'd have gotten a ton of citations with your search."

"I know it's not much to go on, Kathy. But . . . wait . . . how could I have forgotten? Burley told me about the other guys in the company."

"Give me their names, Tom, and don't bother spelling them unless you're dead certain. You know I'll double-check them."

"Let's see. I know for sure that Jim Shepherd is one of them. I met his daughter tonight. And . . ."

"How old is she?"

"Hell, I don't know how old she is, Kathy. What difference does it make?"

"It might make a big difference, wise guy. Given the fact you're not exactly a wealth of information about, well, about anything here, I thought that if you knew the daughter's age it might help me determine the father's age and narrow the list of possibilities—which includes about everybody on the planet right now."

"I see your point. I just didn't want to hazard a guess ... could be any age for all I know."

Kathy let Tom's lame answer hang. "We've got Carl Graves, Jim Shepherd, age fifty to seventy, let's say ... by the way, how old is Carl?"

"I'm going to guess he's sixty or thereabouts."

"OK. Who's next on the list, and how many names did Burley give you?"

"He gave me four names in addition to Carl's. Shepherd is one of them. The other three are Sam Barker, John Evans, Jr., and a Dr. Bill Jennings. And no, I don't know what kind of medical doctor he is. I did a little research before I left; you might want to check a file named 'Ranches' on the home computer. It'll help get you started." Tom repeated what he knew about Graves, Shepherd, Barker, Evans, and Jennings. It didn't take long. He ended by telling her that Pat Burley had called these guys the "Hot Springs Mafia."

"Now, do you mind telling me why you're so interested in Elements Corporation and its mysterious owners?" Kathy asked.

"It's like this: Mrs. Josephine McPherson owns one of the ranches I'm going to see tomorrow; her last name is spelled M-C-P-H-E-R-S-O-N, I think, and her nickname is 'Jo.' Burley is the listing agent on her ranch. Anyway, she was offered three times the listed price yesterday by a Philadelphia law firm, and ..."

"That doesn't seem to be any of your business, Tom."

"I know. But she's not taking the deal, and guess who's behind the offer?"

"I don't know, Tom ... the Wizard of Oz. You tell me. And while you're at it, tell me where are you going with all this, and tell me what it has to do with you—with us?"

"The law firm that called with the offer represents Elements Corporation. Carl is one of the Elements' owners. As I told you, he's the mayor, and he roped me into a tour of the city's new golf course tomorrow so we can 'talk.' Talk about what I have no idea—just like I have no idea why he would take such an interest in me the day I come to town. Then Eva tells me . . ."

"Who's Eva?"

"Eva Shepherd. Jim Shepherd's daughter—the one I told you about—and now that I think of it, she's probably thirty-something."

"Early thirty-something or late thirty-something?" Kathy pressed.

"Early." Without waiting for more cross-examination, Tom kept going. "I met her tonight, at the bar, with Pat." Tom stopped. He had met Eva at the hotel, he hadn't been introduced to her at the bar.

"Actually, Kathy, Pat formally introduced me to Eva at the Lucky Strike, but I'd already run into her at the Red Rock hotel. She was the clerk who checked me in when I arrived."

"So, you've been in Hot Springs, what . . . six hours, and you're on a first-name basis with little early-thirty-something *Eva?*"

"For Christ's sake, Kathy, will you quit? Her name is Eva Shepherd, daughter of Jim Shepherd, who's involved with Elements Corporation. She happened to check me into the hotel, I happened to get introduced to her at a bar, and she said something I think is important. Do you want to hear the rest of the story, or not?"

"What, exactly, did *Eva* say?"

"She said that she knew I was going to look at the McPherson place, and that no matter how much money I had, I'd never get the ranch, and that even if I made an offer that was accepted, I'd never get the deal closed. Her words were a bit more direct, something like, 'even if you get the deal, you won't get the deal,' is how she put it, as I recall. The way she said it sounded threatening."

Tom could hear Kathy scratching notes, and waited for her to catch up before continuing.

"Burley is really stumped by this Elements offer. It's way over the top, and he says that these guys are well aware that the McPherson ranch isn't worth anything near what they're willing to pay. Then, I arrive, and I'm the most popular guy in town with the mayor, a mysterious corporation, and one of their owner's daughters."

"Why do you say that you're 'popular' with Eva? Because you were introduced?"

"I didn't really mean that being threatened by Eva Shepherd was being 'popular' with her; it was just an expression. How far do you want to take this, Kathy?"

"I don't know, Tom. How far did you take things with *her?*"

"Look, Kathy, I just happened to mention Elements and Eva together in the same breath. Let's just say that I seem to have drawn everybody's attention without having done anything yet. Does that work for you?"

"Anything else?"

"Yeah. The Philadelphia firm representing Elements is Perez, Farmer, something and something, according to Pat." Tom clipped his answer short. "Your guess on the spelling is better than mine."

"Anything else?"

"Not at the moment."

There was more to the silence between them than miles.

"I appreciate your help, Kath. I'm meeting Graves tomorrow at four-thirty. If there's any way you can get something before then, leave me a message in the hotel voice mail and . . ."

"Look, it's late. I've got to get some sleep. I'll do the best I can and give you a call one way or the other. Just don't expect too much, because I've only got my lunch hour. Can we take this up tomorrow? I'm really tired."

"Sure, I understand. Good night. I love you."

"Good night, Tom."

Click.

Tom shook his head and put the receiver down.

THURSDAY, 9:15 P.M.

As Eva cruised down Main, she conjured up one scenario after another in which she seduced Tom Larkin. She knew how to turn a man into a puppy, but this one would be hard to take home. She pulled into the convenience store parking stall, killed all 320 of her Ford Mustang's horses and stepped out of the car.

The Ford Mustang GT convertible might just as well have been one of her lovers.

The GT's standard transmission was equipped with a polished aluminum sphere shift—thick and sturdy—that Eva had strapped with leather so it pleased her hand. Its calfskin bucket seats molded themselves to her thighs and made a firm cup around her ass that felt to her like a supernaturally big man's hand. The seat was firm, but gave in just enough to spank her nicely when the car's tight suspension made the Mustang buck.

On trips to Rapid City or Chadron, she'd put the top down and leave the smooth four-lane whenever a rough and dangerous mountain road presented itself.

She controlled whether to slow down and enjoy the delicious outward tug on a curve, or to push everything to its limit, clinging to the shoulder and expecting to be flung off the edge at any moment. *She* decided when to spur the Mustang, throbbing with purpose, uphill, upmountain, up and up, ramming the gas pedal down and holding it hard to the floor while she jumped up and down on the clutch, over and over, until she was propelled downhill, lost and falling, lost in her childhood and lost in the frantic heat of summer, only to awake when her screams and open blouse were torn from her in a frenzy of speed and, half-naked, take miles to wind down, gasping for breath and laughing and crying windtears and shaking her sorrel comb in defiance, and finally, if daylight still lingered, turning the Mustang round again for one more run.

Eva stopped a few steps short of the store and reached to smooth the back of her skirt. Not to tame the fabric, but to check. She was wet.

She smiled and walked back to the Mustang. The yogurt and diet Coke would wait. Eva wanted a bit of private space, and her house wouldn't do.

She needed a new stage to act out her new fantasy.

Eva found what she was looking for behind the Farm and Home store: a service alley for lumbermen and their trucks.

Eva pulled up so that the driver's side of the Mustang hugged the back of the building. It trapped her in the car but would allow another vehicle to pass by. She turned the headlights down, the heat up, and with the car rocking her gently in idle, she pulled her skirt up to her hips and slid down on the seat.

She needed both hands. One to pull and hold that expensive thong back, the other to play Tom Larkin.

Eva relaxed and played light touching games for several minutes. As the heat rose from within, the words started to come.

"That's it, sweetheart. I waited all night for you. That's it. I want you to … to help yourself … to some of this … to all of me, baby." One leg raised itself and she helped the thong slide down and snap free. With her panties lost, the other hand was free to conjure Larkin.

His hand followed no pattern, wandering everywhere, exploring. Nape and hair and neck and nape again. Breasts and throat and under and around them, cupping and squeezing. Butterflies landing, dancing, and flirting. She rose up and let the hand knead her ass, then she wet its fingers, and they went home, and back … and home and back and back and home.

Eva touched the knobby stick shift with her free fingers and gave it light tug.

The bucket leather was hot and slick, allowing Eva to slide down further, jamming her knees against the dash. Neither hand was hers now, and each began to move with more speed and purpose.

"Yes, there. Do it, Tom." The stick was damp and warm under her hand, and reliably rigid. The imaginary Tom couldn't refuse her.

She reached out, first fumbling with the front of her blouse and then groping for the heater switch. She jammed the fan up to high and felt the Mustang's hot breath blow her hair back and warm her face and nipples. They stood up and she tugged them until they stung.

She felt the first bead of sweat form itself behind her ear, and then another broke free, and another, until they ran in a hot stream over her shoulder and breasts, down her back and front, between her ass and her legs.

She wanted to scream, but could only rasp. "Tom. Will you ... please ... I can't wait ... for you ... like this. Get your hands ... under my ass ... push it in there ... that's it. Oh, yes, yes, yes ... that's it. How's that baby, is that what you want?"

With one hand, Eva jerked on the stick shift, forcing her hips up and her ass off the seat. The other hand buried its fingers as far as they would go. "Get ... up in there ... oh! ... like that. Ohhh, Christ, yeah. That's good. That's good, Tom. That's good. Oh, I want you to, I want you to fuck me good." She was whining and pleading and demanding things now. "Oh, God that feels good. That's nice. Make ... it ... go in, Tom, please! Yeah, like that. Like that, baby. Give me some more, some more, some more, Tom, farther, more, please ..."

Eva's thighs were pressed up hard against the steering wheel, straining against it, and she imagined herself trapped under Tom—bound by him and to him.

She lost track of the hands. A voice she didn't recognize was urging her and Tom on in hoarse little yelps and whimpers. And then it came. Her ears chimed with the holy sound of nothing and everything, and ecstasy crashed over her in hot waves, sweeping her up in its arms and bearing her away. She welcomed its dominion and gave herself over to it, and she rolled, again and again and again, in its steamy, pounding froth. A primal voice burst from her lips, screaming words only Eva and God understood, until, at last, she emerged from this chaos, moaning for more of that which her imagination had stirred.

As she lay spent, heart drumming and body rocking with the Mustang, a flight of hummingbirds was loosed from the garden of her soul and were kissing every flowered part of her body, keeping on with their sweet buzzing and suckling until they reached her lips and curled them. She laughed so wantonly that it might as easily have sprung from madness as joy. She threw her head back and willed her eyes to stay closed for a few golden moments longer.

Eva flung one hand up over her forehead, and opened an eye. She saw that her right leg had freed itself from beneath the steering wheel and had hooked itself over the console and the damp calfskin stick.

She eased the leg back under the steering wheel and sat in silence for several more minutes, thinking about nothing. Then, like a colt that flounders unless stopped, Eva let her foot fall heavily on the gas pedal. With its horses straining to run full out, but held fast, the Mustang roared and shook and roared and shook until the waves came back and swallowed her up in another rush of birds and tongues.

In that dark place, Eva Shepherd laughed and wept until the sea rolled back, and there was nothing left but emptiness, and the leather was dry and cool.

Thursday, 9:20 p.m.

"Carl, it's Jim and Sam. You in a secure place?"

"No, Shep, I'm standing in the middle of the goddamn bar so's everybody in here can listen in. Yeah, I'm secure."

"Evans can't be on the call tonight. Some bullshit or another about his wife and her sister, so you'll have to patch Doc Jennings in from your phone. After you get Bill on the call, we'll dial Philadelphia. Got it, Carl?"

"Yeah, I got it ... Jim."

Sam Barker didn't say anything. He rarely had anything original to say, and he would never think of upstaging Jim Shepherd. The pecking order in Barker's world had been determined in junior high school, and Carl was at the bottom of it. Later, in high school, Barker tagged along behind Jim Shepherd because it was the only way he could hang out with Bill Jennings, who stood at the top of the order. When Jennings left for college and medical school, Barker continued to tag along behind Shepherd.

After Jennings returned to Hot Springs, he invited Sam Barker into his circle. There wasn't anything Sam wouldn't do for Bill Jennings, so great was his gratitude for having been included.

Jennings had come home to practice at the V.A. hospital, giving up a bright career in pathology. He'd graduated near the top of his class at Mt. Sinai Medical School and done two fellowships: one at Sloan-Kettering and a second at the Robert Wood Johnson Institute as the lead scientist on a blood toxicity project.

Hot Springs all but threw a parade to celebrate Jennings' homecoming. Most of the local folks explained his return as a simple desire to come back home to God's Country. They'd all stayed. Why shouldn't Bill Jennings? In the town's collective judgment, being a doctor didn't make Jennings any better than the rest of them.

Jennings' academic and clinical achievements weren't well understood or especially well regarded in his home town. But he had money and plenty of it. That was the real deal. Money is easy to measure and, therefore, to judge a man by, and every man in town treated Jennings like he was a better man.

Jennings was welcomed back as a city father, like his father before him. What Jennings did at the V.A. hospital, or in his dealings with Shep and the others, wasn't exactly clear, nor need it be. The circle remained unbroken.

Carl hit the three-way conference key on his cell phone and dialed Jennings' number.

"Dr. Bill Jennings."

"Hey, Doc. It's Carl."

"How's the ticker, Carl? You keeping up on the Bepridil? You start cutting back on the meds again and we'll be patting you on the breast with a spade, big boy," Jennings admonished.

"I'm taking them regular and feeling fit as a filly," Carl lied. He didn't need to be patronized by Jennings, who wasn't his doctor anyway and who gave him the same lousy advice he got from his own physician. *Yeah, I'm poppin' pills, Doc. And I'm poppin' my Dockers and my joints are going snap, crackle, pop and my dick hasn't popped up in a month of Sundays, so I'll just keep poppin' them pills, for all the good it does me.*

"We on with Philly?" Jennings asked.

"Hold a sec while I get Shep and Sam on with us. If I lose you, I'll call right back."

God, let me do this right, Carl thought as he reconnected Shepherd and Barker. *If I misdial, Shepherd will rub my nose in it, and the Doc will have one more reason to believe I'm nothing but a screwup.*

"Doc, you there?"

"I'm here. We on with Jim and Sam?"

"We're here," Shepherd answered, for himself and Barker.

"Anything we need to discuss before getting the Perez and Farmer lawyers on the line?" Carl asked.

"Like what, Carl?" Shepherd snorted.

"I don't know. Maybe review our game plan or whatever. Just asking, Jim. No need to go off on me." *Asshole.*

"I've got it covered, Carl, and for your information, there is no game plan, OK? And you ain't running this call, either. So I suggest you sit back and take notes."

"We paying the freight on this one?" Carl persisted.

"Don't worry about it, Carl. Qwestead Pharmaceutical is picking up the tab, same as always."

Carl went silent.

Shepherd plowed on. "Here's the score. Jo McPherson rejected the offer we made yesterday. The attorneys went back and forth with that idiot Burley, but it was the old lady who put her foot down. Shouldn't be any surprise. She's nothing but a dirt-worshipping squaw. Probably got a few screws loose, too. Remember I told you guys a month ago that we weren't going to convince Jo McPherson with dollars? But nobody wanted to listen to old Jim Shepherd.

"So, the law dogs are looking for some way to make McPherson sell to us, or at least tie her up in court until she comes to her senses. It don't really matter how long the legal wrangling takes, so long as it keeps somebody else from coming out of the woodwork and buying the property out from under us."

Carl jumped in again. "Do they have any ideas?"

"It's kind of a brainstorming session, Carl, which means you won't need to do any talking," Shepherd laughed.

We'll see who the brains of this outfit are soon enough, shithead, Carl thought, but said, "Like I was saying, I think we ought to have a little powwow before we get on the call. You know, just between us girls."

"You want a powwow, Carl? I hear they're having one over on the Rosebud next Saturday. Why don't you just go powwow with them?"

Jennings intervened. "Quit squabbling, you two, and listen to me. We'll let the lawyers tell us what they have in mind and keep our thoughts to ourselves for now. We can get back to them after they tell us whatever it is they know. I'll do the talking. Anybody have a problem with that?"

Nobody argued with Jennings.

It was Jennings who had the connections with Qwestead Pharma. It was Jennings who'd recognized the value of the mineral they'd stumbled onto while extending one of their storage tunnels. They had dug too far to the east and later discovered, to their dismay, that the mineral was on McPherson's property.

The fact that the mineral belonged to McPherson didn't matter to Jennings. Once he'd convinced himself that the deposit was worth having, he started behaving as if he already owned it ... figuring he'd get hold of it one way or another. Things usually worked out for Jennings, so nobody was surprised when he was able to negotiate a deal with Qwestead for development rights—contingent on Elements actually getting the land from McPherson. Even without holding title to the property, Elements had been able to get an agreement with Qwestead worth millions of dollars.

Early on, Qwestead had tried to buy the ranch directly from Cody McPherson. They even offered to let him and Jo stay on the ranch until they both passed. That approach backfired. Cody started asking questions and talking to people he had no business talking with and rooting around down at the lick. Slowly and deliberately—which was Cody's way—he'd gotten on Elements' trail and was closing in right before he died.

"Bear in mind that Qwestead is only dealing with us because they think we can get for them what they can't get for themselves," Jennings said. "They'll lose billions of dollars if this mineral gets into the wrong hands. They don't give a tinker's damn about how we come out or about the few million bucks they've sent our way so far. We're a pimple on an elephant's ass in their eyes. So we can't bicker amongst ourselves like schoolboys, or they'll walk away from us. We're in too deep to lose out now. Way too deep."

Shepherd dialed the Philadelphia law firm.

"Perez and Farmer. How may I direct your call?"

"Randy Hearst, please."

"May I tell Mr. Hearst who is calling?"

"Yeah. It's Jim Shepherd and the Elements Corporation Board of Directors."

"I'll put you through right away."

"Hearst, here."

"Randy, it's Jim Shepherd and the rest."

"Good evening, gentlemen. I'm here with Caroline Lesser, one of our junior partners. Ms. Lesser works in our mergers and acquisitions group and is researching the offer-acceptance issues. Although he is not on this call, we've arranged for Mr. John Bohr, who oversees our litigation in the Midwest, to superintend a review of South Dakota code. We've had no prior reason to develop our understanding of their laws, and as a result, Mr. Bohr will need a few days to come up to speed."

Lawyers! Carl thought. *All of their people are "Mr." this and "Ms." that, even if they call each other Jim-Bob and Peaches when there are no clients around. Meanwhile, we get to be Carl, Bill, and Jimmy. They can go screw themselves.*

"Randy, this is Carl. I understand that this is your show. What's up?"

Shepherd groaned.

"Our client, Qwestead, has asked us to provide you with a review," Randy Hearst began, "although it will be brief given what little time we've had since our ranch offer was refused. Following that review, we'll open the floor for discussion—brainstorming, if you will—regarding our next steps in the McPherson matter. Let's hear from Ms. Lesser first."

"In real estate practice," Lesser began, "it is more or less expected that a seller will honor his listing price, and at a minimum, give serious consideration to all offers made by qualified buyers. This constitutes, however, only an ethical expectation, not a legal obligation. In South Dakota, sellers are not required to accept any offer, regardless of its merits or denomination."

"So, what's the good news, counselor?" Shepherd asked.

"There is no 'good' news, Mr. Shepherd. Had Mrs. McPherson first signed a formal offer agreement, and had she accepted earnest money on that agreement, then we would have grounds to pursue litigation against her. Until Mrs. McPherson takes either, and preferably both of those steps, I'm afraid that we don't have any legal basis ... except that ..."

Lawyers don't fancy giving their clients clear-cut choices. Definitive choices can have the unprofitable effect of cutting short billable hours.

"... except that Mrs. McPherson's real estate agent had previously advertised the property, and fortunately for us, also advertised its price. The advertisement appeared in several publications that are circulated widely enough to qualify the ad as promotional fraud. We found just two South Dakota cases regarding promotional fraud. Unfortunately, neither concerned real estate, and the plaintiff was not successful in either case. That is not to say that we would be unsuccessful in our claims, should we pursue this strategy. Nonetheless, even an unsuccessful suit would tie Mrs. McPherson up for some time.

"On a different tack, we've been told that the property's listing agent, Mr. Burley, has some blemishes on his record. We haven't yet seen a copy of Mr. Burley's record, but, depending upon the severity of his infractions, we may be able to force him to void his listing agreement with Mrs. McPherson. This would delay any sale of the ranch considerably.

"These actions, undertaken simultaneously, would cause Mrs. McPherson more than a little distress, creating an opportunity for you—or some other group—to come in as a white knight and make her problems go away."

Now there's a brilliant idea, you twit. Involve somebody other than us! That's about as smart as slopping hogs in your four-hundred-dollar Guccis, Carl thought, but, for once, was able to hold his tongue.

"We don't anticipate any other group getting involved," Hearst quickly inserted, "and we certainly haven't broached this topic with Qwestead. Given my conversation with Mrs. McPherson this afternoon, I'm convinced that she would see through any white-knight ploy. We believe that the legal steps Ms. Lesser has just outlined will, at best, buy us time to develop an approach more likely to achieve our mutual objective. The downside, of course, is that any legal maneuvering by us lowers our standing in Mrs. McPherson's eyes. So, before we decide to take action on promotional fraud or professional misconduct, we should examine other ways to resolve our problem.

"Do any of you have questions of Ms. Lesser?" Hearst asked.

There was a long silence before Jennings spoke.

"Caroline, have you looked into the McPhersons' marriage license or into any claim on the property that an extended family member might have? Have you been able to procure a copy of Cody's will? There may be provisions in it that govern the sale of the ranch, or there may be mistakes in it that can work to our advantage. I believe that South Dakota probate law offers us recourse if there are any irregularities in the will. Is that correct, Caroline?

"Caroline?" Jennings pressed, sensing his advantage.

"Just jotting a few notes, Dr. Jennings ... " Caroline kept scribbling until she was rescued, inasmuch as rescue was possible from this embarrassment, by Hearst.

"Those are excellent questions, Bill, and I have to admit that we have not yet researched them. I can assure you that we will have people on it first thing in the morning." Hearst groveled the best way he knew how, and he knew some dandy ones.

"We don't have any further questions for Caroline right now," Jennings said.

"All right, then. Is it time to hear from your group?" Hearst asked.

"Has Ms. Lesser been cleared to discuss all matters pursuant to Qwestead?" Jennings asked.

"No, Bill, she hasn't. Sorry," Hearst said, and dismissed Caroline Lesser.

"I think we all know where things stand at the moment, so let me be clear," Hearst continued. "Qwestead will have the McPherson property, or they will have, in perpetuity, the uncontested rights to what lies beneath it. If the efforts of this law firm or the efforts of Elements Corporation prove insufficient, Qwestead will take whatever actions and expend whatever resources are necessary to accomplish that task without either of us."

"You ain't telling us anything we don't already know, Hearst," Shepherd replied. "We ain't idiots."

"I'm not implying anything with respect to your intelligence, Jim. I'm simply underscoring the gravity of this situation. Qwestead Pharma, Limited—our client—has kept faith with your group for nearly three years now. They are as committed today as they were the day you approached them about the special nature of the mineral—this montmorillonite—on the McPherson land. I'm just saying that Qwestead is committed to the mineral, with or without your firm or mine.

"The sale of the McPherson ranch to anyone unfriendly to Qwestead would be a disaster of the highest magnitude. Qwestead has patents on drugs worth nearly one hundred twenty billion dollars in annual sales. Many of them could be rendered worthless by this ... this stuff."

Jennings stepped in. "I think we appreciate the implications for Qwestead—and for you, Randy. We have a huge opportunity here and don't intend to squander it. In that spirit, we are keenly interested in hearing your alternative plans for securing the McPherson place. What have you been working on?"

"Ah ... alternatives?" Hearst stammered. "We're not actively working on anything yet, Bill. Quite frankly, we were all caught off guard by the property listing, and ..."

"You aren't paid to be 'caught off guard,' Hearst."

"Look, that's not fair. We're supposed to be in this together, and we're following your lead. You're the ones on the ground out there."

"You're right," Jennings agreed. "So maybe we're both a bit premature with our talk about alternatives. Of course we have ideas about how to proceed if the real estate can't be secured through conventional channels. Like you, we haven't had enough time to flesh them out—and neither of us wants to present Qwestead with any half-baked schemes."

"So, what do you propose?" Hearst asked.

Jennings began barking orders.

"First, get your library rats working overtime on the issues I laid out for Caroline. If necessary, we can fall back on the baloney she was jabbering about, but we both know those actions will accomplish nothing more than to piss off Jo McPherson.

"Second, go to Qwestead and tell them that we have several new legal angles that we're pursuing. Let them know we need a couple of days to prepare a comprehensive review and recommendation.

"You getting this, Hearst?"

"I'm with you."

"Good. Lastly, we need some creativity from your side, for once. So far, Elements has come up with all the ideas, and now it's crunch time. If we don't come up with a plan, Qwestead will dump us both and move on. Your boss Farmer would shit his pants if they pull their business ..."

"There's no need to get hostile, Bill."

"I'm not hostile, Hearst, I'm pissed. You called this meeting, and your big shots don't even bother to show up—which is par for the course. Farmer and Perez want us to screw an old lady out of her land and grab the goodies for their biggest client, but they think they're too high and mighty to roll up their sleeves and do some of the work."

"There's no need to bring our principals in on this," Hearst whined.

"Yeah, right, Randy. We wouldn't want your principals to have to clean blood off their retainer before they spend it—they've got us for that chore."

"What are you saying ... clean up what blood?" Hearst protested.

"Figure of speech, forget it. The point is, we're the ones who found nature's little miracle cure, and we've kept the wheels on the wagon year in and year out while you guys sat around strumming your dums—and billing Qwestead for it. So, yeah, we're a little jumpy at the moment, especially when your lackey tells us that some other group might be needed as a white knight."

"OK, OK, Jennings. Take it easy. I get the point. Caroline was off-base. We're joined at the hip, I assure you."

Jennings continued in a friendlier tone.

"This is make-or-break for us," Jennings said, "so try not to be offended when we take things seriously."

"No offense taken, and none intended on my part."

The taming of Randy Hearst was complete.

"OK. Today's Thursday," Jennings said calmly. "Why don't we reconvene Monday noon and draw up our new plan of attack? That work for you?"

"I'm sure we can be ready by then."

"That'll be great, Randy. Goodbye."

Hearst rang off the call; the Elements partners stayed on.

Carl couldn't wait to congratulate Jennings. "You really dressed that son-of-bitch down, Bill. Whooee! The nerve of them guys. Here we've done all the work, and . . ."

Shepherd cut him off. "Doc already said all that. If you've got something new to add to the conversation, Carl, now's the time. We need to get our shit together here and come up with some ideas."

"That's right, Jim, we all need to get our shit together," Barker aped.

"To be honest," Shepherd added, "I really don't have any bright ideas off the top of my head. How about the rest of you guys?"

"We could buy the old lady a one-way ticket to join up with Cody," Barker said with a nasty chuckle. No one else laughed, and he clammed up.

"I've given this some thought, and . . ." Jennings announced and let his voice drop.

"And . . .?" Carl prompted.

". . . and my thoughts are preliminary, and I'm not in the habit of running my mouth—even with my associates—until I've had a chance to convince myself the ideas have merit. So, I suggest that each of us works through his ideas, and we'll discuss them over lunch tomorrow."

Jennings' ideas—whatever they were—would be adopted as the Elements plan. None of the others would need to waste his time thinking up dumb ideas for Jennings to shoot down.

"So, are we done here?" Jennings asked.

"Well, you all may be interested in this little tidbit," Carl said. "Pat Burley is bringing a guy from Minnesota out to the McPherson place tomorrow. His name's Larkin. Tom Larkin. From St. Paul."

"How you know that, Graves?" Shepherd snapped.

"How do I know that, Jim? Because that Larkin fella and your daughter Eva was sitting with Pat Burley at my place tonight, and I went over and talked to the guy right after Eva left. That's how I know about him. And I gotta say it looked to me like your Eva was sitting more on top of Larkin than next to him—although it didn't seem to bother him any, if you ask me."

"Nobody asked you anything, Graves, so why don't you just try to keep your fat trap shut," Shepherd snarled, and slammed the receiver down at his end.

"Popular with Eva, are you, Tom? I'll bet you are. In fact, I'll bet you're racking up points right now," Kathy ranted aloud. "Well, two can play that game!" She poured herself another Scotch and dialed Greg Lynch, a co-worker of fifteen years and someone who, in the past few years, she had begun to confide in.

"Greg, it's Kathy Larkin. Did I wake you?"

"Hey, Kathy! No, I'm just sitting here by my lonesome. What's up?"

"You're going to think this is weird, Greg."

"Try me."

"You up for a cocktail?"

"Right now?"

"Right now. I need someone to talk to."

"Where's Tom?" Greg asked.

"He's in the Black Hills. But if it's too late for you, I understand. I just thought I'd give it a shot and see if you'd be willing to give up some shuteye for an old friend."

"Ah . . . sure, not a problem. Where are we headed?"

"O'Gara's. See you in fifteen minutes."

Kathy grabbed her jacket and purse, but stopped in front of the hallway mirror. *What am I doing? This is about the worst idea ever. I'm running out of the house on a work night to do what? Let Greg know that all his years of flirting with me are about to pay off? No. I'm just going to look nice for him. That's all. It can't hurt. He's doing something nice for me, after all. We're just going to talk.*

She threw her coat over a chair and dashed back upstairs. Her sweater jacket and blouse landed in a heap on top of her work khakis and flats. In the bathroom, it took several minutes to find the eyeliner she never used and a cinnamon shade of gloss lipstick. She decided that the lipstick was too much after the rouge and eyeliner were in place.

She pulled a clump of lingerie from the back of a dresser drawer and retrieved the Venetian lace underwire bra Tom had helped her select when they were in Tuscany. She shed the Maidenform and roughly situated each breast in the gift from Tom. *They'll show through. Good.*

She slid into a lightweight V-neck cashmere and a snug pair of black wool slacks. The sweater streamed over her, only slightly muting the topography beneath. She found her suede boots and pulled them up sharply onto her calves; once released, they draped themselves casually around her lower legs. The boots' silver ankle chains resembled cuffs and suggested that the woman wearing them might prefer to be shackled—and would, herself, provide the means. Tom had bought the boots for her when, after several cocktails one Friday evening, they'd jumped on a plane and spent the weekend in San Francisco. Having left without luggage, they shopped for each other all Saturday morning. She had agreed that, whatever Tom purchased for her, she would wear. The boots, she remembered, were the only things she hadn't shed later that night.

She took stock of herself a second time in the hallway mirror. *We're just going to talk. Just talk.*

The woman who stared back at her had a frightened and sad look. Kathy spun away from her image and flew into the night.

Greg was at the bar when Kathy walked in to O'Gara's a half-hour later.

"Wow! You look … nice," Greg stammered.

Kathy kissed Greg's cheek continental-style as she pressed herself against his chest. The hug was several degrees beyond collegial. *Just touch me now, Greg,* she pleaded silently, *and you can have your way. Just don't force me to make the first move.*

Like an ox, Greg stood motionless.

Kathy peeled herself away. "Sorry to drag you out so late, Greg."

"You know I'm here for you … anytime," he offered.

Kathy smiled back, and they plopped down at a table, positioning their chairs improperly close for being just friends.

Kathy pretended to need Greg's counsel, and he pretended that his only interest was in giving her some. No matter what Kathy prattled on about, Greg would say, "I see," or, "He didn't," or, "I don't think that's fair, either," while touching Kathy's hand lightly and occasionally rubbing her back. Once he even dared stroke her hair.

Kathy let Greg paw her in his clumsy way. She felt ashamed, but she needed the kind of comfort that she and Tom didn't provide for each other these days. Tom was up to something with that Eva woman. She could just feel it; she could tell by his tone of voice, by his awkward comments about Eva. That was so unlike Tom's otherwise easy manner. His confounded fumbling of her questions about Eva was, she remembered ruefully, very much like the young Tom she had first met in college, when he seemed thunderstruck in her presence.

Damn you, Tom, she thought, and reached up to rest her hand on Greg's arm.

Thursday, 10:45 p.m.

Jennings eased back into his oversized leather office chair. He'd come far since medical school and took great pleasure in the trappings of his success.

He had always been successful. In medical school, professors sought him out, offering to help "review" his research. *Review* my ass, he thought. *They just wanted to get their grubby mitts on my projects.* It still galled Jennings to think about the number of *New England Journal of Medicine* articles that were based on—but gave no credit to—his work.

Jennings had fixed the last guy who'd taken credit from him. Knowing that the professor planned to publish an article based on research Jennings was conducting, he'd jury-rigged the findings. When it was discovered—after publication—that the data was fraudulent, the professor had to relinquish his tenure and resign.

Nobody screws me. I screw them, Jennings thought with a smile.

Like his chair, Jennings' desk was oversized, framed in Black Hills cedar with an elk hide inlay, and rested on a Persian carpet. Other government employees made do with one-size-fits-all, fluorescent-green metal stuff. Jennings didn't have to make do with standard-issue anything and told the government to keep their claptrap. He furnished his office in the way that pleased him, and if the government didn't care for that arrangement, Jennings had told them, then they wouldn't be needing his services.

With an effort, Jennings sat up in his chair, shook each leg in turn and stretched. *In only three, four more months,* he thought, *there'll be no more backaches or smelly old veterans or headachy wives to deal with. It's time for me to take my place among the captains of industry and science. To be admired by men and fawned over by women. To ride off into the sunset with a bag of gold that will make my current net worth look like chump change.*

Although it was late, Jennings dialed a New York City number. It rang several times, and then he heard the receiver being dropped.

"Phil Brady," a voice croaked.

"It's Jennings, Phil. Time to sober up and do some lawyering for your favorite client."

Jennings was Brady's only client.

"Give me sec, Doc," Brady wheezed.

"Get out of bed and find your antacids. I'll wait."

Phil Brady was brilliant—and an inveterate drunk. He was on the brink of losing his job at a top litigation firm when Jennings rescued him with a fat retainer. Jennings kept Brady in whiskey and a job, and, in return, Jennings had exclusive claim to Brady's canny legal mind.

"I'm back, Doc. Shoot."

"We've got serious trouble, my friend, and I'm going to need you twenty-four by seven for the next several days. That means staying one hundred percent clean—no Rob Roys for break-fast. Otherwise, I'm down the road, and you're on the street. We clear?"

"Crystal, boss."

"Good. There's no room for mistakes on this one, Brady. I just got off a call with my partners and Qwestead's law firm. Although we haven't played all of our cards, Elements is close to losing control of the McPherson situation."

"What are you going to do?"

"My partners have become a liability and it's time for me to act independently. Qwestead is my game, and I won't allow my partners to screw it up. Starting now we're putting a new plan in motion.

"Your immediate task, Phil, is to get our guy at Qwestead to approve two things. First, I need a new representation agreement stating that my relationship with Qwestead Pharma supercedes all others, including Elements and Perez and Farmer. Second, I want an open letter of credit—exercisable at my sole discretion—for thirty million dollars."

"That's a tall order, Doc."

"Just get it done," Jennings barked, and pushed on. "I'll require both items from them—in writing—by Sunday noon. Otherwise, I take a drive down Highway One and stop at Squibb, Smith-Kline, Novartis, Merck … all of the multinationals … they know what happens if the mineral goes up for bid on the open market. The winner goes home with everything. The losers find other businesses to be in."

"Where will this new arrangement leave your partners?" Brady asked.

"If we can get the deal done through Elements, fine," Jennings began. "But if I have to sacrifice them—so be it. They're pissants, just riding my shirttails.

"I don't need partners to force Qwestead to pay through the nose for the mineral, and partners sure as hell don't add anything to my net take, nor do they contribute to the enhanced enzyme development …"

"Whoa, whoa," Brady interrupted. "You lost me on that last bit."

"Have I explained the montmorillonite's enzyme-enhancing process to you?"

"No. Never. I'd like to hear about it … but in layman's terms, please," Brady said.

"The stuff we found under McPherson's land—the montmorillonite—is a living clay. However, it is not the kind of clay you make little pots and sculptures from. It's a dry, powdery substance."

"You told me before it isn't Play-Doh. You never explained its medical use."

"Living clay makes your body produce more and better enzymes. Enzymes help your body maintain its health. When you're sick with anything, from flu to melanoma, your bodily functions aren't working as designed. Montmorillonite is a catalyst—a helper—to get your body working the way it should … especially the immune system."

"That protects us from disease … right, Doc?"

"Close enough. Diseases—like cancer, AIDS, or radiation sickness—either trick the immune system or overwhelm it. When the immune system goes down, so do you. Standard medical practice doesn't address your body's system as a whole; most doctors focus on treating just one symptom—usually with a pill. If that pill doesn't work, another is prescribed, and so on, hoping to hit the right target. Even when the pill alleviates the targeted symptom, it often causes something bad to happen in another part of your body. Living clay doesn't have any of those problems."

"Are you trying to tell me that montmorillonite is a cure-all with no side effects? Sounds like snake oil," Brady snickered.

"Far from it, wise guy. There are about a dozen tiny deposits of this mineral scattered around the globe. The first one was found in a place called Montmorillon, France, in the 1800's. There is a known deposit high in the Himalayas and another in the Andes, but it's scarce as hen's teeth: There's less montmorillonite on earth than plutonium. The montmorillonite we found has been artificially altered. Ours is the only deposit of its kind in the world.

"The Incas used a version of the naturally-occuring montmorillonite; their word for it translates literally as 'miracle cure.' Physicians in Europe have been experimenting with it for a decade. Believe me when I tell you—it's for real.

"But here's the rub. No company can patent the montmorillonite in the form that's dug up out of the ground. If the research being done on it turns out positively, there will be a slew of new therapies that use a substance that can't be patented. That means the pharmaceutical industry is in for some big changes; some companies would even go out of business."

"Yeah, right, Doc. Like Novartis is going to fold up its tent because some witch doctor in Africa is curing bunions with mud paste?"

"Let me explain how these companies work, Phil.

"Big pharma considers their customers to be little more than human pill receptacles that have to buy refills for a lifetime. The biggest pharmaceuticals actually conjure up new diseases and, using advertising, convince people that they need the companies' drugs to be cured. A patent protects the company from competition for twenty years, during which they charge whatever they please for their pill—because people who need the drug can't get it elsewhere.

"If the drug can't be patented, then everybody can produce it. Goodbye astronomical profits. So, if a pharmaceutical company can't patent the drug, they aren't interested in it. Is that simple enough for you?"

"But Doc, you said nobody could patent this mineral—at least in its natural form. I don't get it. Even if Qwestead gets hold of the stuff, they can't patent it ... right?"

"Half-right, Brady. They can't patent the mineral, but they can patent the refining process and any new compounds that use montmorillonite as part of their formulas. More importantly, though, the clay can't be duplicated. For years, Qwestead has been trying to create a look-alike substance in their lab. They're not even close.

"If we can't duplicate the substance, we have to control it— which is even better than a patent, because control never expires. We think that the McPherson land has more montmorillonite than all the other known deposits on earth combined, enough to make medicine for a hundred years into the future. Profits for the company that controls McPherson's ranch will be obscene and will continue long after a patent would have expired."

"Well, I never was one of those squirrels that thought big pharma shouldn't make money on their pills, Doc," Brady said. "I figure the profit from the successes just makes up for the cost of the failures. I don't see the basic wrong in that. Free enterprise, you know?"

"There's more to it," Jennings replied. "Drug companies don't create pills for a disease unless there are enough people sick and dying of it to make a viable market. Only about one in every hundred serious diseases qualifies as a viable market. Consequently, drug companies spend big money on little holes in your stomach, on hay fever, and on making your dick hard; very few spend their time or money on Stevens-Johnson syndrome, the Marburg virus, or other diseases that don't have millions of sufferers who can afford the pills."

"You're saying that if only a couple thousand people a year die or become disabled by a disease, it isn't worth pharma's time?"

"Exactly. So don't pity big pharma. They spend eighty percent of their research dollars on one or two percent of the disease groups—and they're all chasing the same ones. It's an unjustified duplication of effort and requires a boatload of cash to be spent on advertising so the pill-popper will demand Brand A over Brand B to treat his allergy—not knowing that both brands do the same horseshit job."

"Geez, Doc, I didn't know you cared."

"Don't get me wrong, Brady. I'm not out to save the world from big pharma, and I'm not losing sleep over the penniless saps dying of AIDS in Africa. I just wanted you to understand the connection between the money and the patent—and in our case, between money and control."

"Got it."

"If this living clay successfully addresses even two or three major diseases, the pharmaceutical industry stands to lose tens of billions of dollars per year. As a result, the industry is united in an effort to control—or destroy—any natural compound with real curative properties.

"They're already buying off scientists doing research on natural cures and paying high-profile doctors to debunk any promising results. But they're slowly losing the war, and they've changed their strategy. Now they're quietly buying up every known deposit of living clay on earth."

"That still leaves the hundred-billion-dollar question: Does it work?" Brady asked.

"Although the substance itself is very complex, it works in a simple way: Living clay adheres to and absorbs toxins. Toxins are positively charged. The clay molecules are negatively charged. When the clay gets into your system, it attracts and bonds to the bad stuff, and your urinary system discharges all of it as waste."

"Essentially, this stuff collects the body's garbage and takes it out?" Brady asked.

"Right. It attracts all kinds of toxins, so it works on almost everything. Ultimately, that means—and I'm oversimplifying a bit—that we can rely on one therapy for almost any affliction. We only need to regulate dosage."

"Now I see why you believe this stuff could destroy the pharmaceutical industry."

"That's not half of it, Phil."

"There's more?"

"As I explained a moment ago, the mineral we found is different. All other living clay on earth is child's play compared to the McPherson clay. It has the potential to eradicate most bacterial and viral diseases in our lifetime, eliminate most cancers, and cure or prevent radiation sickness.

"I'm not speculating, Phil. I've tested it. On human beings. In secret."

"You've what? How?" Brady started.

Jennings continued in the same serious tone. "I understand the legal concerns, Phil, so don't let them bother you. Hear me out.

"For the past three years, without their consent or knowledge, I've been administering the substance to patients at the V.A. hospital in Hot Springs ... with astounding results." Jennings chuckled. "I've got patients who think I'm God, and all I did was feed them McPherson clay stuffed into gel caps."

"You have got to be shitting me, Doc."

"I'm serious, Phil. I've crossed every ethical boundary in the medical profession—and those were the minor infractions. I've had to take other steps to protect my interest in the clay that can't even be discussed in the context of attorney-client privilege.

"Now do you think I'm shitting you?"

Brady was at a loss for words, and Jennings continued.

"The McPherson clay is unique in a way that raises the stakes of our game far higher than just billions of dollars.

"You know where our property is located?" Jennings asked.

"Yeah. It's between Edgemont and an old ghost town, a World War II army depot of some kind, if I recall."

"Right. The government did a lot of uranium mining in and around Edgemont from 1953 through the late '60's. Then they sold the operation to the Tennessee Valley Authority, and the whole kit and caboodle was decommissioned," Jennings said.

"What's this got to do with the clay?"

"Uranium mining produces two things—yellow cake and tailings," Jennings explained. "Yellow cake is an enriched form of uranium ore that is used to make fuel rods for nuclear reactors and ignitions for nuclear bombs. Yellow cake production leaves a U_3O_8 version of uranium as residue—called tailings—and they're about as radioactive as the yellow cake itself. When the Edgemont uranium mine closed, there was a huge pile of tailings."

"These tailings have something to do with the McPherson clay?"

"They do. Early on, they just dumped tailings into a deep pond or dug a hole and buried it. Problem is that the tailings remain radioactive for thousands of years, and the TVA buried millions of tons of tailings in the ground. They carted this crap as far away from the mine as they dared, which was somewhere near the border of the McPherson place and the land that Elements Corporation now owns."

"Don't tell me they mixed these tailings up with the clay?"

"No, but the two substances wound up very close to each other in the ground. Apparently, radiation from the tailings altered the clay's natural ionic charge, enhancing its effectiveness."

"You mean it got supercharged or something like that?"

"Specifically, radiation enhanced the ionic structure of the montmorillonite."

"The stuff goes radioactive, and it gets better?"

"It didn't go radioactive, Phil. I can't explain how the radiation caused the substance to morph because I haven't been able to duplicate it. I just know that, clinically, it works far better than the existing montmorillonites. To use your phrase, it works like a cure-all."

"You don't need to worry about me telling this story to anyone, Doc, because it's so far out that I don't think anybody would believe it," Brady said with a laugh.

"It's not funny, Phil. What makes this stuff so incredibly good as a medicine also makes it profoundly dangerous as a weapon," Jennings said.

"Now you're going to tell me you can make bombs out of it, too, Doc? Is it explosive, or what?"

"Far more dangerous than all the bombs we've manufactured in the history of warfare, counselor."

"I don't get it, Doc."

"The ultimate test of the clay is radiation sickness. As much as we read about cancer, Ebola and AIDS, it's radiation sickness—exposure to things like fallout from a nuclear bomb—that we just can't cope with. Most of the exposed die. Those who live through exposure are disfigured for as long as they survive. Survivors without obvious disfigurement usually have genetic damage.

"Since radioactive fallout from a nuclear bomb can't be controlled, using one would be just as devastating to the aggressor as it would be to his enemy. But if one country could protect itself and its troops from radiation sickness, and its enemy couldn't, it could use its nuclear weapons with impunity."

Brady was silent for several seconds.

"You're telling me that our government could wipe out whole cities—whole *nations*—without fear of reprisal?"

"That's what I'm telling you."

"Christ, Doc, you could play God with this stuff."

"That I could, Brady. You with me?"

Brady didn't hesitate. Without Jennings, he was nothing.

"I'm with you, Doc. I'll get Qwestead to come around on the letter of credit and the representation agreement. Take it to the bank. The Qwestead assignment will be ..."

"... will be done as I instructed, or you lose your job," Jennings completed Brady's sentence for him. "Get back to me by Sunday noon, Phil."

"Goodnight, Doc."

Jennings retrieved a bottle of Lagavulin single-malt Scotch whisky and a Waterford double old-fashioned glass and poured himself a dram.

As he sipped, his eyes wandered over the collection of Native American artifacts that adorned his office walls.

"Lucky for me that those savages never got hooked up with a good attorney," he chortled. "Otherwise, I'd be wearing a loincloth and sucking hind tit."

He drained another whisky and killed the light on his way out.

FRIDAY

All things come from earth,
and all things end by becoming earth.
Xenophanes 580 B.C.

———

6 A.M.

Dawn was sifting through the curtains when Tom's wake-up call came through. He tossed back the sheet, went to the desk, and powered up his laptop.

There were a couple of dozen new e-mail messages, most of them offering low-rate mortgages, discount Viagra and chats with horny, cheating housewives, but nothing from Kathy.

There wasn't any voice mail either, so Tom pushed back the desk chair, padded into the bathroom, shaved, and got dressed. Before leaving the room, he left five dollars and a note, "For Housekeeping," on the bed. Tom couldn't understand the logic of giving a doorman two bucks to hail your cab, but not leaving a dime for the person who changed your sheets, scrubbed your toilet and spent a half-hour in your room alone with your belongings. If nothing else, it was cheap insurance.

As he pulled the room door shut, Tom hesitated and took a quick inventory. The laptop screen was flipped up and glowed at him from the desk. *I should shut that thing down and hide it,* he thought. *It'll take me all of two minutes.* He started back into the room but glanced at his watch. It was twenty to seven and he wanted to get to the cafe before Burley did. That way, he could give Pat guff about wasting daylight or some such thing.

"To hell with it," he muttered, closed the door and trotted down the hall.

Burley was sitting at a corner table and cradling a cup of coffee when Tom walked in at ten to seven.

"We're burning daylight, city slicker," Burley called out loud, and laughed. He extended his hand to Tom and said, "Sit down, sodbuster, and get something warm in your belly."

"Sounds good, Pat. Sorry I'm late."

"Yeah, well, you have to get up early to get at the coffee pot before I do, Larkin."

"I can see that." Tom sat down and poured himself a cup of coffee. "What's our plan of attack, Pat?"

"Since you're headed back to St. Paul Sunday morning, we've got two days to see four ranches. I sort of figured we'd get you started off easy-like and see the Casey place first. It's the 2,000-acre place ..."

"... over near Buffalo Gap, if I recall," Tom said.

"Right. It's a pretty piece of real estate, but the grass ain't all that good—most years. Still, at 700 an acre, it's in the affordable range, wouldn't you say?" Burley said, posing his first qualifying question.

"So, you thought I came out here to *buy* a ranch. Well, shit, Burley. I thought I signed up for a two-day ranch tour, and here you are trying to sell me something already."

"Well, I'll be go to hell. You say you just signed up for the ranch tour, that right, Larkin? I better tell you right now that this here tour can get a trifle spendy ... you charging that to your VISA card, or what?" Burley grinned.

Touché.

Burley was being insistent, in his way, and Tom thought better of trying to avoid the money issue. He'd best come clean and risk Burley's displeasure. It would be better than risking his own credibility.

"OK, Burley, I'm not going make you wheedle it out of me. Let me tell you straight out where I'm at with the money. For starters, I won't be writing a check out for the full purchase price, unless your seller is inclined to accept one those rubber ones," Tom joked.

"People don't take too kindly to them things around here," Burley said, not joking.

"Seriously, Pat, I'm not sure what we can afford. Kathy and I have agreed that we'll sell the house and borrow against two life insurance policies for the down stroke. I figure we can come up with four, maybe five hundred thousand bucks.

"I know it isn't enough, so we're going to need your help putting the financials together. I promise you that we're committed to moving out here, and I guess I'm going to have to figure some of it out along the way. I'm not a first-class prospect, but I aim to buy, one way or another. Can you work with that?"

Pat took a few seconds to judge the man, not his wallet.

"I'm not your run-of-the-mill dreamer, Pat," Tom said to fill the silence.

Apparently having decided something, Pat said, "Damn, Larkin, don't scare me like that. For a minute there, I thought you were serious about writing out one of them rubber checks." Burley laughed out loud. "You been doing business with them city bankers way too long, buddy. At four, five hundred K, you're loaded for bear. If you decide on something like the Casey place, I don't think we'll have any problem with those numbers." Burley paused for a sip of joe and went on. "With the other ranches, you're looking a little light at the front end, I'd say. But, I'm thinking that maybe we can get you in at the Lucky Strike washing dishes on weekends to make up the difference."

"If they're using that mild dish soap that won't ruin my nails, that'll probably work for me," Tom quipped.

"Then I guess we're about ready to go look at some dirt," Burley said, stabbing a sausage and biting it in half.

" 'Preciate it Pat. I surely do."

They finished their eggs and headed out.

They entered the Casey place from the north, drove along a ridge that ran diagonally to the southwest, and stopped the truck at its highest point.

"Didn't I tell you this was a sight to see?"

"You weren't wrong, Pat."

"Yeah, I'm kind of partial to this ranch, Larkin. I done a lot of horseback riding here when I was a kid, and my wife and I always talked about buying it."

"Why didn't you?"

"Long story, Tom. Ask me sometime when I've had too much to drink."

The Casey ranch was shaped like a trapezoid, with the narrow end to the north, and the broader end, by double, at the south. It lost about five or six hundred feet of altitude from the north to the south and east, but only about a hundred feet as it sloped down along the western edge. Nearly two-thirds of the ranch was flat ground or gentle hills. The other third, in the north, was damn poor grazing land, but the views were spectacular.

"When they first homesteaded this place, they put the ranch house down there along Blackthorn Creek. I understand there actually used to be water in it," Burley explained. "If this ranch were mine, I'd put my house up here and let the cattle have the run of the rest of it."

"Let's see as much of this place as we can in a couple of hours, Pat. I need to stop back at the hotel over noon and check my e-mail before we get to the McPherson place. It's four times bigger than this one and I want to see as much of it as daylight allows."

"Let's get to gettin', then."

They unloaded the ATV's, checked the gas levels, and tested the winches. Burley threw a couple of bottles of water in his ATV's saddlebag and they headed out.

It was a handsome ranch, and there were several stunning home sites along the north ridgeline, but it didn't grab hold of Tom in the way he was hoping for, like he'd just met a woman who would blind him to all the others.

Kathleen had done that to him once. Blinded him with how she smelled, how she walked, how it felt to lie down beside her. Tom knew with certainty that he'd recognize the feeling when it came over him again.

As they pulled the ATV's back up alongside the trailer, Tom said, "Impressive, Burley. Very impressive." He didn't want to offend Pat by saying the wrong thing, seeing how Burley and his wife had once thought enough of the ranch to want to buy it.

Burley was an old hand at real estate and people.

"Nice, but not your cup of tea, eh, Larkin?"

"I'm not ruling it out, Pat."

"No need to mince words, partner. When people are out looking for land they intend to stick with until they die, it ain't as easy as good grass and passable views, is it?"

"You been reading my mail?"

"No . . . but I've been reading people buying ranches for going on forty years, Larkin. There are two kinds of buyers. Most are people that are looking to resell, at some time, for whatever reason. They're easy. You just need to determine what criteria they've got the most confidence in—you know, property appreciation, grazing capacity, water, subdivision or development—and hone in on property that's got lots of the thing they value most.

"Now, the other kind of buyer, well, that's your kind, Larkin. They're the porcupines. They have a general idea of what part of the country they want to look in, and they have a general idea of what they want in a piece of property, but ultimately, they don't know what they're looking for until they lay eyes on it. Hell, everything they thought they wanted when they was jabbering away and looking at pictures in my office can go right out the window when they see a piece of land that grabs them in some special way."

"I guess you lucked out with me, Pat. You got a two-bit customer looking for a dollar's worth of dirt, and you're going to have to go through hell to find what he'll settle for."

"I kind of figured that out at the Flat Iron this morning. But I got you pegged as a resourceful son-of-a-gun, and when we find your ranch, and we figure out a way for you to pay for it, your money spends as good as the next guy's."

Burley and Larkin were on their way back to Hot Springs by eleven-thirty.

"I need to talk to Kathy—or at least see if she's e-mailed me, Pat. So why don't we go our separate ways for lunch?"

"Fine by me," Burley said. "Let me give your hotel a call and order you up some grub. Won't be French cuisine, but it'll save you fifteen minutes biding time in their lunchroom."

It wasn't Eva, but some kid who answered Burley's call to the hotel. At that moment, Eva was busily engaged in room 303.

Eva glanced around Tom's room. There was no clothing strewn about, his toiletries were neatly arranged in the bathroom, two pair of shined boots looked like they had been lined up with a ruler, and three shirts—one of them ironed—hung neatly in the closet.

His duffle bag was empty and sat square in the middle of the luggage rack.

Eva rifled the dresser first. Tom's underwear was folded and stacked in one drawer; jeans, a leather vest and an Abercrombie and Fitch pullover were in a second. The third dresser drawer was empty.

"I wonder if you are as thorough making love as you are stowing gear, cowboy," Eva mused.

She proceeded to rummage through Tom's Dopp kit, looking for what, only she could say, and then turned to her appointed chore.

Tom's laptop case was empty. His briefcase yielded only a couple of files on Burley's real estate agency and the ranches Tom was in town to see.

That left the wastebasket and the laptop computer.

Housekeeping had already been in the room. That was just bad luck for Eva. Anything Tom had written and tossed was gone now.

Eva looked at the scratch pad on the desk and saw indentations. She found a pencil in the desk drawer and began to lightly smudge the top sheet.

She said each word as it emerged: "Elements Corporation . . . Graves . . . McPherson." And at the bottom, with a lot of doodles around it, the word, "Eva."

"You are a naughty boy, Thomas," she whispered. "There's hope for you yet."

She tore the page from the scratch pad and slid it into her pocket. Then she pulled the laptop toward her and moved the mouse. The screen lit up.

"You're a careless boy, too."

A quick search of his documents using the keywords "Elements Corporation, Graves, McPherson, Shepherd, and Jennings" yielded nothing. Eva opened Tom's e-mail and hit send/receive.

There was one new message from klarkin@pioneerpress.usa.

"Bingo."

It took her only seconds to see that Tom had enlisted "klarkin"—the wife, presumably—to do some research on Elements. Eva scanned the e-mail and the three attachments quickly. Larkin's wife had assembled a lot of information in a very short time.

Eva forwarded a copy of Kathy's e-mail to her own mailbox and covered her tracks by purging the copy of the forwarded e-mail; then she highlighted Kathy's incoming message, pulled down the edit menu, and hit "mark as unread."

"Perfect," she smiled.

Eva absentmindedly closed the laptop and got up to leave.

The red message light on the phone was blinking.

"The phone! How stupid can I be?"

A computer-generated voice announced that there was one new message.

Tom, it's Kathy.

I sent you an e-mail earlier this morning with some pretty interesting background on Elements Corporation. I'm calling to be sure that you got the mail and to fill you in on a bit more information I think you'll want to know.

Eva grabbed the pencil and scratch pad and began to take notes.

You were right to want to look into this crew. You'll see from my e-mail that Elements bought most of the old TVA, U.S. Army and Nuclear Commission property in the Edgemont area about thirty-five or forty years ago. All of the parcels were part of a massive Environmental Protection Agency cleanup during the Super Fund days of the 60's and 70's. I asked Gita, a documents librarian here at the newspaper, if she'd pull the EPA files on the Elements properties. Tom ... there weren't any! Gita thought that was really strange. She said that it wasn't unusual for the odd file to be missing, but when there's nothing, somebody meant it to be that way. She also said that government files from that time were all kept on paper—usually just one copy—so if no one scanned those documents, we'll probably never get any further on the EPA stuff. Sorry about that.

I also called Mel. You remember him from our South Dakota days? He's an investigative reporter at the Washington Post now. He told me that Elements has been the subject of two federal investigations, most recently by Homeland Security. Mel said that he'd keep an ear to the ground for me.

Tom, these guys aren't bumpkins. If they have an interest in you, it can't be good.

That's about it. Oh! I forgot. Elements is not a corporation. They are a limited liability, limited partnership. They shouldn't even be using the word "corporation" on their business cards, but I suppose most people they deal with don't really care.

That's it for now, but I'll stay on their trail. Speaking of which, call me when you get on the road Sunday; I'm looking forward to seeing you, you know, so we can . . .

"You can what, Suzy Homemaker? Bake him a cherry pie? Blow his nose? Blow something else? I doubt it!" Eva said with a sneer as she heard Kathleen's voice signaling that the message was about over. Without listening any further, she set the receiver back in its cradle. If the entire voice mail message isn't listened to, the voice mail system thinks that the message hasn't yet been heard at all, and the red message light continues to blink. Tom would never know he'd been burgled.

"You're good, girl." Eva winked at her profile in the mirror. "In more ways than one." She ran a hand over one breast and let her fingers linger and play for a few seconds. "Wish you were here, Tom . . . maybe next time."

The digital clock by the side of the bed read eleven-forty. Eva let herself out and slipped through the stairwell door moments before Tom stepped off the elevator onto third floor.

He sensed something the instant he opened the door.

Tom looked around but saw nothing. Closing his eyes, he drew a deep breath. There it was. Perfume. Not just any perfume, either. It was, he was sure, Serpentine, a scent he knew well.

God, I'm getting paranoid in my old age, he thought. *It's the maid, of course. She probably just finished cleaning my room.*

But he couldn't shake the odd feeling, filled both nostrils again, and was again uneasy.

"I know that scent. But from where?" The question started to nag him, in a very wifely and insistent voice.

Tom tossed his coat on the bed and sat down at the desk.

As he reached over to the laptop, he stopped in mid-motion.

The laptop screen, which he clearly remembered being open when he left, was shut.

Tom began talking himself through the possible scenarios: "Obviously, the maid has been in the room. Maybe she thought that the laptop shouldn't be on, that it might be damaged from being left on or open, so she closed the screen … no … no … that can't be it. I smelled her perfume, so she was here recently. If she entered the room recently, the screen would have already been dark—so she'd have no reason to believe that the laptop was running. Still, she obviously changed the screen position, because it was open when I left the room this morning."

He felt silly. There had to be a logical explanation. *My fault for leaving the damn thing out in the open.*

The sharp knock at his door was room service.

Tom half-expected that Eva would finagle a way to bring his sandwich up to the room herself, but it was a young man of about twenty standing in the hall with Tom's roast beef and Swiss and chicken noodle soup.

"You order a lunch special?"

"I did. Put it on the desk over there, would you please?"

The kid marched past Tom, placed the tray on the desk and turned to leave without so much as a "howdy," "hi, how are you," or making eye contact.

On any other day, Tom would have let the little twerp go on with his business without a comment or a tip, but Tom needed some answers.

"Don't I have to sign something for you?"

"Naw. We'll just put it on your bill."

"Kind of loose arrangement, isn't it?"

"I s'pose. That's the way they do it here. Ain't my decision. Ask at the front desk if you want to."

"I'll do that. By the way, can you help me out with some information?"

"Maybe. Depends on what it is."

"I'm just curious, but you wouldn't happen to know what time they clean the rooms around here, do you, as a general rule?"

"Yeah. We clean the rooms as soon as we can in the morning. That is, as soon as the guests are out. Then we can get out of here early."

"What do you mean 'we' ... do *you* clean rooms?"

"I cleaned yours this morning."

"Ah ... did you say ... that *you* cleaned this room today?"

"Right. Something wrong with the way it was done?"

"No. No. Everything is great. You get the fiver?"

"Yeah. Thanks." And with that, Room Service turned to leave.

"Hold your horses, friend. Got another minute for me?"

"I guess."

Tom knew that his next question was going to sound accusatory, but he had to know. "You didn't move the laptop computer, by any chance, did you?"

"Nope."

"Didn't even touch it?" Tom questioned again.

"What are you saying? Are you saying something got broken, or what?"

"No. Not at all. It's just that I thought I left a document on the screen this morning, and it's gone now," Tom lied. "I'm worried that I might have lost some keystrokes. Really, it's not a big deal." Tom tried his best to be folksy and reassuring.

"Look, mister, I saw that your computer was on when I came into the room to clean. As far as I remember, it had gone dark by the time I left. But I never touched it, all right?"

"I believe you. Like I said, no big deal."

Tom took a breath and asked the next-most-difficult question.

"About when, would you say, this morning I mean, did you clean my room?"

"What?" The kid was getting edgy.

"You know. What time were you making up the room this morning?"

"Why do you care?"

"I'm not trying to give you a hard time, kid. I'm just trying to get the routine down. I'll be here for a few more days, and I don't want to get in your way—but I like to have the room cleaned as early in the day as possible. I'm just trying to accommodate the way you do things around here."

"Whatever. Let's see … I came in about seven this morning. You left the hotel a little after seven-thirty, and I came up and cleaned your room then."

"You know when I left the hotel?" Tom was incredulous.

"Hey, I'm sorry if I did something to piss you off. We've got maybe six or seven guests in the whole place right now, and when somebody comes or goes, it's pretty obvious. It's not like we're watching you or something."

"Gotcha. So if I leave by the stairs, you won't see me, and you'll have to wait to clean the room."

"We go around and knock by nine o'clock if we haven't seen you leave."

"Well, I'll try to remember to call down to the desk and let them know when I leave in the morning, so you can get at things right away. That way you can get off-duty as soon as possible. Sound like a deal?"

"Good by me." The kid opened the room door to leave.

"Oh, cripes, I forgot." Tom reached into his front pocket for a couple of ones. "For the service."

"Thanks, man."

Tom shot one more question at Room Service as he walked away. "By the way, you have any help with my room this morning? You work in teams, or anything like that?"

"Are you kidding, mister? This time of year I can clean every guest room twice over and still be twiddlin' my thumbs half the morning. Nope. It was just me," the kid said and shuffled down the hall.

Tom sat back down to his soup, sandwich, and laptop.

The message light on the phone was blinking, but he decided to check e-mail first. The top message was from Kathy. He double-clicked, and it opened.

All doubt as to whether he should be troubled by the irregularities he found in his room was erased after Tom read Kathy's e-mail.

The documents Kathy sent raised more questions than they answered, if they answered any. In addition to deed information about the property Elements owned in Edgemont, Kathy had attached two reports from federal agencies investigating their company.

Nothing serious had been pinned on Elements. There were just a lot of dots that didn't connect.

One of the reports suggested that Elements was illegally dumping radioactive waste and acting as a middleman for the export of uranium yellowcake. The second report was a Department of Treasury investigation into Elements' relationship with Qwestead Pharmaceuticals. The IRS apparently had questions about several million dollars of payments Qwestead made to Elements but had not been reported as income. Tom wondered what Elements could possibly have to do with Qwestead, one of the world's largest drug companies. That had to be Jennings, Tom guessed.

Tom checked his watch. He'd be downstairs to meet Burley in ten minutes, so he pulled up and electronically faxed Kathy's e-mail to the hotel, to his own attention, so he would have hard copies of the documents.

That done, he picked up the phone to retrieve his messages.

The scent of perfume on the handset assaulted him. Someone—some woman—had been in his room and had used the phone. A troubled Tom Larkin listened to Kathy's message twice, erased it, and stowed his laptop in a dresser drawer under a pair of blue jeans.

FRIDAY, *12:30 P.M.*

Pat was in the lobby when Tom got downstairs.

"Hold on a jiff while I pick up some faxes," Tom said. As he approached the front desk, Eva stepped out of the office.

"Greetings, stranger."

"Hi, Eva. I should have some faxes; would you check for me?"

"They're coming through right now, Tom. Going to take a few minutes, though. I could just bring them up to your room when they're done printing, if you don't want to wait."

Tom moved a step closer to the counter, caught her scent, and recoiled. *Serpentine! It was her.* Tom was certain. Eva had been in his room.

"No ..." he stammered, "... I'll just wait. Something I've got to go over with Burley." Tom gave Eva a hard look and silence set in between them.

How could I have been so stupid? he thought. *I should have just burned a CD and made copies myself. Too late now.*

"The machine's stopped," Eva mumbled. "I'll go get your faxes."

She returned with the faxes and handed them over without comment.

"You going to be at the Lucky Strike tonight?" Tom asked.

Eva brightened. "Maybe. Maybe not. Who wants to know?"

"I'll be there around seven, seven-thirty," Tom said. "Meet me for a drink. We need to talk." Without waiting for her answer, Tom strode past Burley and out the door.

They turned onto a gravel road, drove north about a mile-and-a-half and entered the McPherson place from the southwest corner, right about where the ranch butted up to the Elements property.

"You've got that golf course tour with the mayor at four-thirty, right, Larkin?"

"I was hoping we'd both forget about that," Tom said.

"My advice is you better go. You said you would."

He's right, Tom thought. *I made the commitment, best I keep it. People here will remember a long time if I don't.*

"Well? You going or no?" Pat asked.

"Yeah. I'm going."

Pat stopped the truck and motioned for Tom to get out. He spread a section map as big as a blanket onto the hood, running his finger east and west along a line.

"We're coming into the ranch from the southwest corner. Here's the fence we're sitting on right now, Larkin. And here's where she turns north.

"Now, this here ranch ain't square. It's pyramid-like; we're sitting at the base, see, and the top of the pyramid points north . . . well, maybe a shade more northeast, I 'spose.

"In total, it's around 8,400 acres, or about thirteen square miles. Now, if a guy was to pretend that each square mile was a block, and then if he was to put five of them blocks on the bottom, then four on top of them, then three, offset to the east a bit, and then put that last block right at the top, why, he'd have a pretty good idea of what this place looks like."

"How are we going to see it all in less than four hours?" Tom asked.

"We ain't going to, Larkin. There's no possible way.

"I figured I'd just take you to the places that I think are kind of special. If you don't see anything to like in them places, this probably ain't the ranch you're looking for," Burley said, letting fly with a stream of tobacco juice that hit the dirt with a dull slap.

"Just remember that this place'll run you a nickel or two more than you got in your checkbook at the moment. If you think you're interested, there's no guarantee we'll be able to package it up."

"Based on what we're seeing right now," Tom said, "I doubt I'd be all that interested. This place looks like a very bad day in West Texas."

"We're looking at the working side of the ranch, boy, so pay attention to the buffalo grass, not the views. We've got to plow through a few more of these flats and some hay ground before we get to parts I think might catch your fancy. Let's jump back in the truck and head north another mile before we fire up the ATV's."

As they gained altitude, a feeling of déjà vu grew in Tom. He was deep in thought when Burley stopped the truck on the crest of a hill.

Tom gasped.

The landscape below had transformed itself from a spartan sage plain to a jungle of escarpments the color of blood oranges. Dark canyons were gouged raggedly from the earth, ponderosa pine clung to life on near-vertical surfaces, and scrub cedar danced in and out of the odd stand of aspen.

Scattered clouds mottled the light, making the gorge look like a freshly-painted canvas, spread out to dry by its artist on the floor of this secret valley.

"Pat, it's ..." Tom couldn't finish.

"I know."

"Can we just ... sit here ... for another minute?"

"Don't see why not. In fact, why don't you get out and stretch your legs? I've got to find me that other tin of chew I stashed. The old lady don't like me chewing no more, so I gotta get my fix when I'm out of her line of fire."

Larkin was already out of the truck. He hadn't heard a word Pat said.

High above, an eagle screeched, calling Tom's attention to the circles it was tracing in a sea of blue sky. The bird could hunt like that for hours, without a single wing beat, riding the updrafts. Standing on the ridge in silence, Tom believed for a moment that he could hear the great bird's feathers rustling in the wind.

The breeze at this altitude was brisk, but not cold. Tom filled his lungs with the sweet air, exhaled, and drew more in. It tasted familiar and felt good. It awakened him.

Tom felt the ground pulsing with life.

"Kind of purty, ain't it?" Pat said as he exited the pick-up.

"You can say that again. Wow! Where has this been all my life?"

"I was afraid you'd feel that way. C'mon. It gets better."

They hopped back in the truck and drove to a place on the valley floor where they could unload the all-terrain vehicles. A horse is generally the best way to look at land—providing time is no object. When time is short, an ATV is the ticket.

Like the people who lived on it, the land was rugged. Around every outcrop, another ravine or cutback revealed itself. Each succeeding rock sculpture begat and complemented the next. The unspoiled, haphazard art quieted Tom.

After a time, they made their way to the north face of the valley. Pointing to the top of the rise they were facing, Pat said, "I'll meet you up there," and took off up the hill.

Tom bumped his ATV onto a narrow plateau at the top, coming to a stop next to Pat. Pat's gaze was to the north. Tom raised his eyes in the same direction.

That was the moment that would forever separate Tom's past life from the one he was about to begin.

The ridge divided two valleys. The one they'd just passed through was closet-sized compared to what now spread itself out below and in front of them.

The land tumbled away in a medley of mesas, meadows, hogbacks, steppes, and gorges. Tom reckoned the far side of the valley to be two miles distant. A canyon splayed with primrose the color of sunrise had wounded the heart of the valley, connecting here and there with ravines that further splintered the valley into a mosaic of vermilion, jade, and adobe. Its crazy pattern would have thrilled Picasso; its sculpture would have been no less pleasing to Michelangelo.

White pine, red cedar, birch, Black Hills spruce, and juniper sprang from the soil like happy children. Aspen and cottonwood huddled in clusters around the creek's bed. Pinyon jays, mountain bluebirds, and western tanagers sang to their lovers and gave notice to their enemies. In the fracas nearby, a black-backed woodpecker drummed away.

Fast-moving clouds took turns shading and bathing the ground in light, making the midday sun hopscotch, meadow to grove and canyon to cliff, across the valley.

Lifting his eyes from the pageant below, Tom saw a staircase of hills and peaks cascading down from the northeast and plunging into the deep canyon at their feet. Far in the distance, the mountains blended and became dark.

Turning east, Tom saw the valley's maw open to a swale that escaped through Buffalo Gap to a vast prairie twenty miles distant.

Tom turned back to the valley, his face in the direction of the wind.

For a moment he thought he saw his son and daughter, as young children, running down the hill before him, their hair golden in the spring light, their little legs driving them pell-mell and carefree along the warming earth, their laughter singing in his ears. He foresaw his grandchildren tumble into existence and chase their creators down this natal slope in a river of tomorrows that swept up all of his generations and carried them away.

This land would be his love and his legacy, his memory and his hope for the future. This land would see him reborn and cradle him in death.

The silence overtook him before he could prepare for it. Larkin had seen the sun rise nearly twenty thousand times, and this day, in his forty-eighth year to heaven, he discovered at last that silence wasn't the lack of sound.

Silence happens inside a man; it's not a condition of the outside world. Silence is a way of being in the world without having to change it, without interfering with it, without needing to know what has passed on or what's in store.

The land embraced Tom in silence.

It embraced his lifetime of nurseries and lovers, angst and summer trips, kisses, college all-nighters and one-night stands; of books and seminars, lovemaking and deal-making, pain and victory, rejection, loss and conquest, drunkenness and art, beauty, sea shells, music and cathedrals; of adversaries and friends, bridges and broken promises, chemistry, physics and starlit evenings up north, salt air, walleye and campfires, graduations and funerals, wedding bands and jazz bands, children and spring flowers.

It embraced the whole of him, planting his memories and hopes in its soil.

Tom fell to one knee and filled his hand with dirt. Tears streamed forth and spent themselves on the red earth.

Pat saw that Tom was caught up in something neither man would be able to talk about and stood as still as a buffalo in a blizzard, waiting for it to pass.

At last, Tom stood.

"I know this place, Pat."

"I can understand how you'd feel that way."

The sound of the wind filled the time before Tom spoke again.

"No, Pat, I don't think you do understand. I was here before— so long ago now I hardly trust my memory of it. But I know this place and I am not ever going to leave it again."

They spent another few minutes on the ridge overlooking the glorious land that now owned Tom Larkin. Then they wound their way down and lost themselves in it.

Two hours later, Pat and Tom pulled up under the ranch gate. "Trail's End" was hand-chiseled into a spruce log as thick as a steer and supported on either side by pillars of the same girth.

Jo heard them before she saw them coming, and she was on the porch to greet them when they pulled up to the house.

She stood there like a monument, except that her hands were busy with a dishtowel.

Tom hadn't said much on the ride to the ranch house and didn't immediately move to get out of the truck, so Pat jumped out and sauntered over to the porch.

"Afternoon, Jo," he said as he reached the bottom step.

Jo didn't answer, but she'd stopped working the dishtowel.

"This Larkin fella's a live wire, Jo. Now he ain't going to make you any 17 million dollar offers or nothing, but I think you'll find him to be a pretty serious ..." Pat stopped talking. Jo wasn't paying the slightest attention to him or listening to what he was saying. She was fixed on something just over his shoulder.

When Pat turned, he saw Larkin standing stock still immediately behind him looking at Jo the same way she was looking at him.

"Tommy Larkin?" Jo said in disbelief.

"It's me all right, ma'am," Tom said in a whisper.

"You have an uncle who lived out here, don't you? Named Seth Wallace?"

"Me, again, ma'am."

"When Pat said that he was bringing a Mr. Larkin out here—from Minnesota—I was hoping it might be you, but I just knew it wouldn't be ... and now, here you are!"

"You remember me?"

"How could I ever forget? You practically lived here the summer of '68 ... Cody and I thought we'd never see you again. It's so good to have you back, Tom."

Jo eased herself down the porch stairs and marched right past Burley. A single tear escaped, ran down one cheek, and fell silently to the dust. She stopped in front of Tom, arms akimbo. She gave him a pretty good once-over.

"You are a sight for sore eyes!" she said, shaking her head with delight. "Now, come on over here and give me a big hug—if you're not too grown-up for that sort of thing."

Tom obeyed. Jo smelled like fresh laundry and apple butter.

"We have a lot of catching up to do, young man," Jo announced and took Tom's hand in hers. Tom guided her up the familiar steps and into the house. Burley tagged along behind.

By the time Pat caught up to Jo and Tom, they were sitting together on an old leather couch in the living room, chattering like magpies.

It had all come back to Tom in a rush earlier that morning. He had worked at Trail's End the summer he was fourteen years old. The McPherson's help had up and left when the work started getting heavy in late June that year. So, Uncle Seth dispatched Tom to the McPherson place now and again to help them out. Three or four times he had stayed with Jo and Cody for a whole week. His memories of that time, like the memories of most fourteen-year-olds when they think about work, were dim. But Tom warmed to the ones that were now coming back to him.

He remembered chowtime with great fondness, and there was a gelding that Cody said was "his" anytime he visited the ranch. He remembered his room in the house, and that there seemed always to be a cool breeze from his night window no matter how hot it had been during the day. Although he hadn't the faintest recollection of what they had talked about, Tom had especially happy memories of sitting around the supper table and jabbering away for hours on the nights he stayed over with Jo and Cody.

Still, he hadn't been certain that this was the place until, thirty-five years since the last time, he passed through the Trail's End ranch gate. Then it hit him. It was the McPhersons he'd known;

Trail's End was where he'd worked a good piece of one lost teen-age summer. Like lost boys, his memories began coursing their heedless ways back home.

Funny, Tom thought, *what a person remembers. I always called them Mr. and Mrs. McPherson; they always called me "son."*

Jo and Tom sat for an hour talking of nothing but what each remembered of the other, broken only by the occasional update about where life had taken Tom over the past decades. Jo seemed to remember every little detail about his time at Trail's End, and Tom was happy to let Jo be his memory of that summer.

Pat finally came in from the kitchen, where he'd been reading a magazine, and asked Jo if he might help himself to a slice of the pie that was cooling on the counter.

"Look at us going on, won't you?" Jo asked of no one in particular. "Tom and I have so much to talk about, Pat. I'm sorry for letting you sit out there in the kitchen with that pie staring you in the face. Me going on and on is a fine way to welcome Tom back to Hehaya O Ihake ... shame on me! Now you boys follow me into the kitchen, and we'll all have a nice piece of pie."

"Hey-hey-ah ... hockey? What does that mean?" Tom asked.

"Why don't you tell him, Pat?"

"Uh ... yeah! It, ahhhh, I believe it comes from an old Lakota saying about ... uhhh ... about elk hunting. That's how I heard it." Pat flushed. "I get that about right, Jo?"

"Don't tell me you don't even know the name of the place?" Jo pretended to scold him.

"It's the name of the ranch?" Pat sputtered.

"Oh, go on, Pat, you know what I'm talking about," Jo said, letting him off the hook. "But let me explain it to Tom."

She had Tom by the arm and was walking him into the kitchen, explaining that "Hehaya O Ihake" was Lakota for Trail's End. Like most Lakota phrases, it didn't have an exact translation in English, but generally meant the place where all trails end.

"The true Lakota meaning is a bit more elegant than 'Trail's End,' Tom, but you get the idea. Try saying it again." She repeated the ranch's Lakota name slowly: "Hehaya O Ihake."

"Heh hay yah oh eh hoc kee," Tom repeated after her.

Jo smiled in approval.

At the kitchen door, Jo let go of Tom's arm and clucked at herself. "Good lord, will you look at the time? Why, I'll bet you're both half-starved. Have you boys had lunch yet? Of course you haven't. I'll pour you some hot coffee to go with that pie ... or you can have chocolate cake, if you prefer. Cake or pie. What'll it be?" Her head wagged as she talked, making her two silver braids dance.

"Tom's got to meet the mayor at four-thirty, Jo, so we can't ..." Pat started.

"We'd be delighted," Tom interrupted, finishing Pat's sentence.

Pat and Tom trailed into the kitchen behind Jo, sat down, and requested pie. Jo set the plates out for them, sat down next to Tom, and touched the eagle claw necklace that Runs With Horses had given him.

"Where did you get this, Tom?" she asked.

"Oh, an old guy gave it to me as thanks for giving him a lift."

"It's beautiful," Jo said quietly. "Do you know what it means?"

"The man who gave it to me said something about voices I should learn to listen to. You know that he made this thing while we were driving along, while he told me a story about an Indian brave who went to find some medicine at the center of the earth."

Jo hadn't let loose of the talisman.

"Where were you giving this old man a ride to?"

"Somewhere down on the Rosebud. He got out of the car in the middle of nowhere and just wandered off. Why do you ask?"

"Oh, I don't know, Tom," Jo said, the eagle claw still in her hand. "It's just that I've only known one person who braids like this," and she pointed to the loops around each talon.

"You never know, Jo, could be the same guy," Tom said.

"That would be something, Tom, it surely would," Jo said, and gently laid the necklace back on Tom's shirt. "When you've got the time, if you like, I'll tell you more about what this golden eagle claw means to the Lakota people," Jo said, and reached down to take up both of Tom's hands. "Whoever gave this to you thought you were someone special." She sat holding his hands and looking straight into Tom's eyes, like she'd seen something that took her by surprise and wanted to be sure she'd seen it right.

Tom looked at Burley, who just shrugged.

"We'll talk about this later," Jo said abruptly, releasing Tom. "I'm going to make some sandwiches, and, Tom, you can tell me all about where Pat took you today and what you remember about it."

After ten or fifteen minutes of running on breathlessly, Tom realized that there was just too much to say and too much to hear and too much to see and too much getting reacquainted to be done to wrap anything up on this day.

"I'm sorry. I haven't let anybody get a word in edgewise. I'm just, I don't know, I don't have all the words, Jo. After everything that's happened today, being back here, seeing you again. I know I'm not doing a very good job of describing how I feel."

"I think I know exactly how you feel," Jo answered. "I love this place, too, Tom, and the thought of leaving it is almost more than I can bear. But I can't run the ranch on my own, and I don't have any children or other family to take it over. There just comes a time when a person has to stand aside and let another step in."

"Well, maybe there's a way for you to keep the ranch, hire somebody to run the cattle, or let the grazing rights out, I don't know ..." Tom offered.

This was the last kind of discussion any real estate salesman wanted one of his buyers having with one of his sellers. But Burley did not interfere.

"That's sweet, Tom. But it's time. Even though I've been an everyday part of this ranch for sixty years, it'd make me feel worse to be hanging on here with no purpose.

"Oh, listen to me!" she cried. "I'm starting to cluck like an old hen, aren't I?" Jo's cupped hands sat in her lap in a way that made Tom think she'd just lost whatever it was she was holding in them.

"Jo," Tom said in a very quiet but clear voice, "I want to make Hehaya O Ihake my home." He stopped to collect his thoughts, and his courage. "This is only the second ranch we've looked at, but I know this is the one. I think I have known it for a long, long time." Tom paused for second, clenched his jaw, and continued.

"I'd do just about anything to live here, but ...but I don't know if I ...," he hesitated, then forced the words, "I don't know if I can afford to buy it."

Jo searched Tom's face. She seemed to be looking for something. She reached out and put one of her hands on his.

"I'm sure there are lots of things for us to discuss before we get to the mathematics, aren't there, Patrick?" Jo gave Pat a stern look that made disagreement impossible.

"Got that right, Jo. Besides, Tom here hasn't got the faintest idea of what he can afford or not afford, because I haven't told him, yet!" Pat said brightly.

"Jo, I want you to know the truth, right up front," Tom insisted. "Now I know that this other offer you've got is confidential, but Pat told me it's something like seventeen, eighteen million dollars."

Jo glanced sharply at Pat.

"My wife, Kathy, and I aren't sure how we're going to handle the listing price yet, let alone triple that number. We're just not in that league."

That set off a storm.

"That is true, Tom. You are definitely not in their league. And don't you never, ever go near their league." This was a different Jo talking, and she rolled on like a July twister.

"That other offer will not be accepted." Tom didn't recall ever having heard the word 'not' said with such finality.

"The people who made that offer will not own this ranch. They will not set foot on my Cody's ranch," Jo stormed on. "They will never, ever, own one clod of dirt . . . not today, not ever . . .

". . . not over my dead body."

The ticking of the wall clock was thunderous.

Pat was busy picking at his boot heel, hoping like hell somebody would say something.

Tom, at a complete loss for words, was trying not to stare at Jo.

Jo's eyes were fixed on something distant.

The wall clock thundered on.

Abruptly, Jo snatched up a fistful of skirt in each hand, fluffed it once, and said as nonchalantly as anyone ever pleased, "Now, Pat. Did I hear you say that our Mr. Larkin has a date yet this afternoon with Carl Graves at four-thirty?"

"By golly, I did mention that."

"Well, then, young Tom, it seems that you've got to be on your way. Can't keep our mayor waiting, can we? I expect you both back here tomorrow, and we'll take up right where we left off today. That'll give you, Patrick," and Jo looked straight at Burley, "time to figure out what's to be done about all this money business. Can you boys do that?"

"That'd be great, Jo," Tom said, jumping in. He was afraid that Burley would tell Jo about the two conflicting ranch tours they'd arranged. "What time is best for you?"

"When was the last time you had dinner on the ranch?"

"Dinner on the ranch? Oh, about thirty, thirty-five years ago—and I'm still kind of full!" Tom said, delighted.

So was Jo.

"That's that, then. I'll be seeing you boys back here tomorrow noon time."

"Should we bring anything, Jo?" Tom knew that her answer would be no just as certainty as he knew he should ask.

"Bring your appetites or you'll break an old lady's heart. And Tom ..."

"Yes, Jo?"

"Welcome home."

"**I** want you to see the mineral lick where Cody died," Burley said as they drove away from the ranch.

It didn't seem like a good use of time to Tom.

"But, I've got to meet Carl at four-thirty."

"Don't worry. He'll wait."

"He'll wait? He's the freaking mayor, and he'll wait—for *me*?"

"Yeah. He'll wait," Burley repeated. "This'll only take us another fifteen minutes, Larkin, and it's important."

"If you say so. What's the big deal?"

"It's important to Jo that you've been to the lick. If I had thought of it earlier, I wouldn't have ever brought you back to the house without having gone over there. I ain't making that same mistake tomorrow."

"Why can't we just swing by there on our way to dinner?"

"We could, but what if we don't have time? We're scheduled to see them other two places tomorrow ... and you went ahead and agreed to dinner with Jo ... and that'll take us two hours if it takes a minute ... and since we're within spittin' distance right now, I figure that right now is the best time to take care of it."

Burley didn't give Tom time to protest; he just plowed on. "Now, even though it may not have occurred to you, Mr. Rockefeller, you're going to need financial help from Jo to have any chance of buying Trail's End. So, what's important to Jo is important to you. End of lecture."

"Point taken," Tom said. "Show me the lick."

"You're a farm kid, Larkin, so you'll appreciate it more than most."

"As far as I remember, there aren't any natural licks back east. We mostly had to provide minerals in block form, but it did the same thing."

"No," Pat said.

"No, what?"

"No, mineral blocks do not do the same thing for livestock that this lick does. In fact, it ain't even close."

"What're you getting at, Burley?" Tom asked.

"It's like this: Cody was always saying how his animals never went bad on him, you know, got sick and so forth. Well, one day he tells me he'd only lost about a dozen head of cattle in over forty years of ranching."

"By any chance was Cody partial to smoking weed during working hours, Pat? I mean, no disrespect to a dead man, but give me a break … who's going to believe crap like that? Lost a dozen head in forty years?"

"That's what Cody told me. And, to tell the truth, what you just said was exactly what I was thinking. So, I just nodded like I believed all that malarkey and checked it out for myself."

"And …"

"… and I talked to a bunch of the old boys around here, and they pretty much said the same thing about McPherson. He just didn't lose stock. And I mean he didn't lose stock to a point where it was downright unnatural."

"And now I bet you're going to tell me it has something to do with this lick," Tom sneered.

"I am. It kept them cows healthy, and on the rare occasion one of them got scours or black leg or whatnot, Cody would turn it out to the lick. Ninety-nine times out of a hundred, that damn cow would walk back in, as fresh as a spring calf in a couple a days. And it's the lick that done it."

"Yeah, whatever," Tom said, still thinking the story was a lot of hogwash. "I guess it was nice for old Cody, though, not having to haul minerals from town."

"I told you, Larkin. These ain't any minerals you're going to find in town!"

The topic had run its course—at least as far as Tom was concerned—and neither man spoke until Tom asked, "What was Cody doing out there the day he died, anyway?"

"That's a bit of a difficult question."

"Meaning what?"

"You going to listen to what I've got to say, or blow me off like you did with the last bit?"

"Let's just say the story stuck in my craw. Now, about Cody?" Tom asked.

"Apparently, Cody never made it home for dinner the day he died. According to Jo, he saddled up Boone right after breakfast and came out here looking for a cow that had just calved but hadn't come in for a few days. When Cody didn't come in for dinner, which was damned unusual, Jo got in the truck and drove out to the lick and found him laying in the ground, Boone standing over him.

"Jo says that she knew driving out to the lick that something had gone bad. Said she could feel it. Anyhow, she could see right away that Cody was gone even before she got out of the truck, but she went to him and put her arms around him because there wasn't anything more to be done.

"When Jo lifted Cody up, she seen he'd got a cut on the back of his head, but there wasn't hardly any blood on it. Then she sees this rock sticking out of the ground that the dirt hadn't settled in around naturally. Somebody had put that rock in the ground, and damned recently, too."

"Jesus, Pat, you saying that Jo thinks Cody was killed?"

"I ain't saying nothing, Larkin. I'm telling you what's going around town."

"Sorry, Pat. Go on."

"Well, as I heard it, she also said that there were lots of human tracks on the lick. It didn't seem right to her. And if it looked wrong to Jo—I'm here to tell you—it was wrong. She's a damn good rancher *and* she's Oglala Sioux. People say she was any man's hunting equal—even mountain lion—before she married Cody."

"Jo's Indian?"

"Half Indian, Larkin, and she was born and raised on the Rosebud Reservation.

"Anyway, back to my point. Jo just sits there next to Cody's body studying the situation. After a spell she notices that his right hand is in a fist.

"She tries to pry the fingers apart, but can't, you know, because rigor mortis had set in. So she leans down close and makes out something in Cody's hand, something shiny and round. She tries to pull it out but can't. At least that's what Ellie down at the post office says that Jo said."

Pat stopped the truck and killed the engine. They were at the lick.

"So Jo drives back to the house and calls the sheriff, figuring he'll do his job and let her know what it all means.

"But get this—the sheriff comes out to the ranch with a god-damn cast of thousands ... and doesn't even stop to say 'Hi, how are you?' to Jo. Just roars on out to the lick and starts fouling things up."

"Like ... fouling up what?"

"Like running a mess of people in, over, around and through the lick ... wiping out any trace of the track Jo said didn't look right to her. And they just picked up Cody's body from where it was laying, straight off without no photographs or whatever they do—and put it in an ambulance and took him off to town."

"For an autopsy, I hope," Tom added.

"Yeah. For an autopsy. Done by Hot Springs' one-and-only, mucky-muck MD, Dr. Bill Jennings."

"*The* Doc Jennings? The Elements' Jennings?"

"You catch on fast, city boy."

"What the hell is he doing autopsies for?"

"Apparently because he wants to—he volunteered to do them. The County loves it because it don't cost them a penny. Course, I don't *really* know why he's doing autopsies. He don't have to be doing autopsies, and he don't have to be working at the V.A., or working at anything else that he don't want to, for that matter.

"So . . . you tell me, Larkin. Why is Doc Jennings doing autopsies?"

Burley wasn't looking for an answer.

"By the time the sheriff gets done mucking things up at the lick and stops back at the ranch house, Cody's body is already at the hospital being poked and prodded by our man Jennings. But all the sheriff does is give Jo his condolences and leaves. He never even asked for her side of the story.

"Next morning Jo hears that Jennings said Cody must have fallen, hit his head and suffered cardiac arrest from the trauma, loss of blood, or whatever."

"But . . . that just doesn't make sense, does it Pat? You said that Jo noticed that the head wound wasn't bleeding much."

"Exactly. That was one of the things that was bothering her about the whole deal. She's seen enough head wounds in her time to know how they ought to look, but she don't know nothing about cardiac arrest. So, she just asks the sheriff what about that thing that was in Cody's hand."

"And . . ." Tom prompted.

"And the sheriff says to Jo that he didn't know squat about Cody having something in his hand.

"So Jo tells him to ask the Doc, since he done the autopsy. Sheriff goes to Jennings and Jennings says there wasn't nothing in Cody's hand when he got the body. Not that he doubted Mrs. McPherson or anything, he said, it's just that there wasn't nothing in the hand when he got the body.

"Of course, there ain't no way to prove anybody right one way or the other, because the nitwit sheriff didn't take no pictures, and apparently nobody took notes, either. They all just assumed that an old man went out to the pasture and fell off his horse and killed himself—like Cody would be falling off any horse, much less Boone."

"What do you make of all this, Pat?"

"First, I'd take Jo McPherson's word over what Jennings and Sheriff Barker had to say any day of the week. And second, ..."

"Did you say Sheriff *Barker*? Sam Barker? The Elements guy?"

"No, not Sam—his half-baked brother Sheldon. He's a piece of work. You know what they say about being a sandwich short of a picnic? Yeah, well, old Sheldon's short the cole slaw and the chips, too.

"Like I was saying, I don't think anything that Jennings or Barker says is worth a plug nickel. And number two, I think Jo suspects something, and she's afraid to come out with it. Not like she's scared, mind you. I just think she doesn't want to say anything because people would chalk it up to an old woman's grief and wouldn't take her seriously. She already got the brush-off from local law enforcement, and Doc Jennings said there ain't nothing unnatural about the way Cody died. So, I think Jo is biding her time, waiting for the right opportunity to ask more questions. That's what I think."

"Seriously, Pat. What do *you* think happened out here?" Tom pressed.

There was a long pause.

"My two cents worth? Cody's dying wasn't God's doing."

Tom got to the Lucky Strike at twenty minutes to five. He would have preferred to go back to the hotel and dress more appropriately for a meeting with the mayor, but he hadn't had time. Tom figured it was better to be more on time than more fashionably dressed.

Turned out he would have looked pretty foolish in a pair of Dockers.

Tom walked in and saw Carl perched on a stool, decked out in a pair of OshKosh duck-hunting bibs and a camouflage hat. Carl waved Tom over with a long-neck beer.

"You ready to see the purtiest little golf course in the Hills, Tom?"

Tom extended his hand. "Sure am, Mayor. Don't take my lateness for lack of interest. We had to race back here from the McPherson place because ..." Tom caught himself and stopped short.

Carl took a long pull from his beer and set it on the bar top. "Hows about a short one before the tour?"

"Don't have to ask me twice, Mayor."

"Call me Carl."

For the second time in as many days, Carl bought.

"So, you've been out looking at property with Pat Burley. How's that going?"

"Well, Carl, it's a bit early to say." Tom lied.

"Did you like the McPherson place?" Carl said, cutting to the chase.

Tom decided to see how far he could bullshit Carl.

"Well, it's like this. I'm no expert when it comes to deciding what's good ranch land in these parts, you know? I'm a sodbuster from East River, and I figure it's going to take me a good long while to learn the ropes out here—real estate-wise, that is. We saw a couple of places today, and they both looked good to me. But what the hell do I know?"

"Which one of them places did you like the best?"

No way out of or around that question.

"If I had to choose, you mean?"

"That'd be exactly what I mean, Tom."

"If I had to choose, it'd be the McPherson place, I guess."

"You guess?" Carl was relentless.

Tom took one of those long, satisfying first pulls from the cold beer that had materialized in front of him and decided to shift gears.

"No bullshit, right, Carl? Fine. I'm no ranch expert, but I know what I like. If Jo McPherson were to hand me the keys to her place, you know, for a song, I'd quit looking at ranches right this minute."

"Go on," Carl said.

"I liked the place. There isn't anything not to like out there as far as I can see, except maybe the price tag. Got to tell you, though, it's a bit rich for my blood. You know what they're asking?"

Carl just glanced up and took a sip from his beer, but said nothing.

Tom leaned forward. "We're talking seven bills, Carl. That's damn near a thou an acre. What do you think of that?"

"Well, Tom, it don't matter much what I think, now does it?"

"Fair enough, Carl. After all, you're not buying the place, so why would you give a good goddamn?" *How do you like them bananas, Mayor?* Tom thought.

"Who said I'm not interested in buying the McPherson place?" Carl replied.

Tom choked on a mouth full of beer.

"Come on, Tom. Tell me that Burley didn't fill you in on our offer for the ranch."

Damn it! Tom thought. Carl had him over a barrel. Again.

"OK, you win, Carl. Burley told me that you'd made an offer."

"What all did he tell you?"

"You trying to get Burley in trouble, or what?"

"You mean because he talked to you about our offer? The confidentiality thing?"

"Yeah. That," Tom said.

"Oh, hell, no. That confidentiality agreement was cooked up by one of our East Coast lawyers. It don't mean shit."

That's exactly what Burley said, Tom thought, smiling.

"Anyway ... what did Burley tell you about our offer?"

"He told me you and your company had made an offer. A big one."

"He tell you how big?"

"Yeah. Something like three times the asking price ... that about right?" Tom replied peevishly. He was tired of playing cat-and-mouse with Carl.

"All of that and a couple of bucks more, to be honest, Tom," Carl admitted. "I suppose Pat also told you that Jo McPherson turned our initial offer down?"

Initial offer? Tom thought. "Yeah, he told me that, too."

"Now, Tom, tell me, this McPherson ranch ... are you serious about pursuing it?"

"Yeah, Carl, I'm damned interested in the McPherson place," Tom said, throwing back the last of his beer.

"Good," Carl said, downing his own beer. "What do you say we head out to Whispering Pines, rustle up one of those little carts, and talk golf for a while? Sound like a plan? Good. I'll drive."

Carl plopped down from the bar stool, leaving a stunned Tom to gather his wits, his hat and his gloves and follow Carl out the door and into the parking lot.

THEY HAD BEEN on the course for a half-hour, and talked nothing but golf. Carl did most of the talking—which was mostly bragging.

Carl came by his bragging rights honestly. The golf course was special.

"Got to hand it to you, Carl. I've never seen anything quite like this."

"We like it."

"I bet you do. Who's the genius behind it?"

"Well, it's one of those things that gets going, and everybody jumps in with an idea, and then, nobody knows when to stop. Takes on a life of its own, you know what I mean?" Carl said. "At first, all we wanted was a nice little ol' nine-hole course, so's we wouldn't have to drive into Custer or Rapid to play. Then we kind of let people in town come up with ideas for each hole, and volunteer labor and materials and so forth, and before you know it," Carl continued, "we decided to go whole-hog with another nine. That's where the real fun started."

Carl had been going on for another twenty minutes when he pulled the cart up on a high overhang and stopped. Without turning to face Tom, Carl rested his meaty forearms on the steering wheel and leaned forward, as if the point he was about to make was far off in the distance, and he needed to strain to make it out.

Tom had said something earlier that had given Carl an idea: Elements might just be able to get hold of the McPherson place a lot easier—and a sight cheaper—than what was happening under Jennings' plan. Carl knew his idea was risky, maybe a little wild—but it was *his* idea. An original Carl Graves idea. He smiled to himself. *Won't all the boys be surprised come next Monday noon when he, Mayor Carl Graves, lays out his plan to save their hides and get the ranch from old lady McPherson?*

Carl turned and faced Tom.

"Back at the bar, you said the price on the McPherson ranch was a little rich for your blood. Isn't that what you said?"

Tom hesitated.

"Tom? Isn't that what you said?"

"I . . . did. Why do you ask?"

"Well, frankly, that surprises me," Carl replied. "You mean to tell me none of those big city banker buddies of yours will step up for you?"

"Listen, Carl, you know as well as I do that the bank wants the buyer to kick in twenty percent—in cash—on a big land deal like this. On seven million, that's a stretch for Kathleen and me. To say the least."

"I don't mean to pry, Tom. Really, forgive me. It's just that, well, we're real anxious to get new blood in the area, and as mayor, I figure it's just part of my job to help new folks out where I can."

"What are you getting at, Carl?"

"I'm thinking that maybe, and I said *maybe*, I'm just thinking out loud now, but maybe there's a way for the City of Hot Springs to help you and your wife out if you're serious about the McPherson ranch." Carl paused to gauge the effect of his words on Tom.

"When you say 'help,' are you talking money?"

"I most certainly am talking money."

"I don't know what kind of a program you've got going here, Carl, low-interest money for ranchers, or whatever," Tom said, "and I appreciate any offer of financial help, believe me. But you need to understand that, even if the city could loan me money for a down stroke, I couldn't make payments on a second loan for several years."

Carl could plainly see that he'd instilled hope in Larkin, and he chuckled. "We don't have a program, Tom. Nothing that organized. I'm talking about a special loan . . . just for you. Because of your special circumstances."

"What special circumstances?"

"I'm not going to blow smoke up your skirt, Tom. You know that me and my partners are interested in buying the McPherson place, and it doesn't take a rocket scientist to see how much you'd like to own it.

"The special circumstance I'm talking about," Carl said, "is that you're in a position to buy the McPherson place. It appears that all you need is financing. I'd like to think I can help you with that."

Now it was Tom's turn to stare into the distance.

"No offense, Carl, but do you mind if I speak plainly?"

"Please do."

"What gives here?" Tom demanded. "You and your business partners offered Jo McPherson three times the listing price—and you got turned down. Obviously you guys want that ranch bad—bad enough to pay about anything to get it. Fair statement?"

"Go on."

"So I wander into town, stars in my eyes, looking for a ranch. You don't know me from Adam, but you're offering to help me buy the ranch out from under your business partners. It doesn't make a lick of sense to me. What am I missing here, Carl?"

"You done, Tom?"

"I'm done for now."

"You want to hear what I've got to say, or have you already made your mind up that I'm some kind of shyster?" Carl's jowls twitched at the edges, but his eyes were hard.

"I'm all ears."

"*Of course* we want the ranch, Tom."

"What for?"

"If you'll let me finish ..."

"Sorry."

Carl swallowed hard. If his plan failed, and if Jennings or Shepherd or any of the others found out what he'd offered Tom, they'd make his life miserable. But the idea that he, Carl, would be the one, for once, to have an idea that made Elements money was intoxicating. He felt certain that he could use Larkin for his own purposes, and if it didn't work out, well, he'd figure out how to cover his tracks.

"Yes," Carl began. "We want the ranch. It is very important to our company.

"Elements Corporation is already one of the largest land owners in this part of the state. We've spent the better part of fifty years acquiring parcels of land that suit our particular business interests. Sometimes the land is purchased for speculation or development, sometimes for grazing or crops, sometimes for the water rights, and sometimes for what lies below the ground."

"You telling me there's gold on the ranch?"

"If there is gold on that ranch, I'll personally eat all the ore it sits in." Carl smiled as if to show Tom what a silly notion that was.

"No. There's no gold on the McPherson place. And the grass ain't much, either. You'd be lucky to support one cow-calf unit per forty acres on an average year. Can't make money on them numbers."

"Why are you telling me this if your company wants the ranch so badly?"

"It's simple, Tom. We think you're interested in what's above the ground, not what's below it, and if we can help you, perhaps you can help us. You scratch our back, we'll scratch yours."

"How can I help you? We can't both own the ranch."

"We don't need to own the ranch to get what we require. We're only interested in exclusive mining rights to property. That's it."

"Exclusive mining rights ... for what?" Tom asked.

"For whatever the ground yields," Carl answered.

"Whatever is a pretty big category, Carl. Besides, I didn't think you could do that. Aren't all the mining rights divvied up by type of mineral ... and aren't most of those rights already assigned to somebody other than the landowner? I heard that big companies like Homestead own most of the rights around here."

"Everything you say is pretty much true, Tom."

"So I'm saying that I probably won't own those rights even if I was able to buy the ranch," Tom countered. "Where does that leave us?"

"We know that ranch deed quite well, Tom. There are a few restrictions on the water, but the mineral and mining rights have been preserved with the deed ever since the property became part of the Dakota Territory back in the nineteenth century. I'll grant you it is unusual for the landowner to have retained so many of these rights over time, but it just so happens that McPherson owns all of the mining rights to the property. So, to answer your question, yes, you'd own those rights if you own the ranch."

"Let me get this straight. You'd want me to hand over all of the mineral and mining rights to Elements, that right?"

"That's right."

"Blind?"

"In a manner of speaking, I guess. Is that a problem for you, Tom?"

"I don't know if it's a problem."

"What do you know about mining around here, Tom?"

"Why?"

"Because, generally speaking, you ain't going to find much of anything in this here ground—excepting gravel and sand. Now, you will find some beryl and muscovite here and there, but usually not in quantities that make it worth taking out. Bottom line is, there just ain't much out here."

"OK, Carl. I'll admit I don't know much about mining rights, but you're asking me to believe that you'd pay three times the asking price for a ranch, on the incredibly small chance that there's something in the ground? Frankly, Carl, it's a bit much to swallow."

"If that was all there was to it, I'd be as skeptical as you are. Of course, it's more complicated, and I think—if you'll let me explain—that our actions are very logical."

"Fire away, Mayor."

"Elements owns a large piece of land adjacent to the McPherson ranch ..."

"It's near Igloo. Burley filled me in. Got all those goofy-looking structures that look like Eskimo houses on it," Tom said.

"Right. Eight hundred and two of them, if you're counting."

"At any rate," Carl said, "we provide a certain service to a select group of multinational companies that requires an extensive system of underground tunnels and chambers. Our Igloo property looks pretty normal from up top, but underneath, well, it's more like a prairie dog town.

"Thing is, we are required by the government to own the mining rights simply to dig holes in the ground, even if—strictly speaking—we aren't really mining."

"That's interesting, Carl, but what does it have to do with the McPherson property?"

"Simply put, we've run out of room. The tunnels have reached our property line. In order to grow our business, we have to expand the tunnels east. That means digging into the McPherson ranch."

"But why the McPherson place, Carl? Why not go some other direction—go north, or west, hell, go anywhere but into the McPherson's? Jo obviously doesn't want you there, and it seems like it'd be a sight cheaper for you to buy anybody else's land," Tom said.

"Believe you me, my partners and I wish there was an option other than the McPherson property."

"What's so special about Jo's ranch?"

"We tunneled as far north as we could on our own property before we hit a layer of granite about seventy feet thick, with an aquifer below. Going any further that direction would cost us about twenty million bucks a mile. North isn't an option for us. Most of our western and southern property lines abut National Forest Land. If getting a permit from a government agency were the only issue for us, it would already have been done. While it would be time-consuming, it is doable. We have friends in high places."

"What's the problem, then?" Tom asked.

"There are two, Tom. Every time a private party wants a lease on public land, the tree-huggers and environmentalists come out in force to question the transaction and gum up the works. That is something we can't control, so it could be very time-consuming with no assurance of success."

"What's your other problem?"

"The other problem is actually the deal-killer. We can't have anyone broadcasting what we do or for whom we do it. Anything we did in conjunction with the government would become public, one way or another, and that simply won't work for our type of business," Carl said. "So that basically leaves the McPherson place. It's our only option."

"Just exactly what kind of business do you guys run, anyway?" Tom asked.

"As I said, we're kind of 'low profile,' and I'm not at liberty to share details with you. What I can tell you is that our business is a lot more profitable than grazing cattle or scratching out a wheat crop every other season. A whole lot more profitable. That's why we can afford to pay three times the asking price per acre. For us, the math works. To anyone else it looks like we've completely lost our minds."

Carl paused to judge the effect of his lie on Tom. It seemed to be working, so he barreled ahead.

"Now, Tom, are you beginning to see why we have a legitimate interest in the ground at a much higher price than anyone else would be willing to pay?"

"I don't know what kind of business requires underground tunnels and such secrecy, but, yeah, Carl, I have to say that your reasoning sounds logical.

"Here's a problem, Carl. Since I don't know dick about mineral rights and mining, you could say anything, and I'd have no reason to dispute it. So, I'm concerned about signing away mining rights without knowing what I'd be giving away. Hey, what if there is gold down there?"

"I understand why you'd be hesitant on that point, Tom. Tell you what. It would take months and months to completely assay the property—and several hundreds of thousands of dollars to boot. Neither of us has that kind of time, and I'm going to assume you don't have that kind of money. Am I right?"

"Amen to that, Carl."

"Here's what I propose. Why don't you just name whatever minerals you are concerned about giving up, and when we write up our agreement, we'll exempt those minerals from the rights you sign over. That way, if we do find gold, for example, it's all yours. Would that satisfy you?"

Carl knew that he had Tom in a box. Why wouldn't Tom sign over the rights under these conditions? Larkin had no intention of mining anything. Tom needed down-payment money, and he must need it badly, Carl guessed.

"Carl, what you say sounds pretty good to me, but there are issues that would have to be ironed out."

Carl's heart leapt. The kid had bought his lie. The side of Carl's face hidden to Tom rose in an involuntary smirk.

"First, there's the issue of how much these exclusive mining rights are worth to Elements. Next, there's the fact that I can't make two payments simultaneously—as I said before—on the principal and the down-payment loans. And finally, I'd have to be convinced that the arrangement between me, the City of Hot Springs and Elements was kosher. I don't want to get myself entangled in something that lands me in court."

"Is that it?" Carl asked. "Anything else that might be a prob-lem?"

"Not that I can think of."

"What if we were to structure the down-payment loan as 100% forgivable? You know, you'd never have to pay it back? Would that ease your concern about making two payments?"

"You'd just give me the down stroke?" Tom asked, dumbfounded.

"Essentially," Carl said as nonchalantly as he was capable.

Tom broke into a goofy smile. "Ah ... yeah ... I guess that pretty much takes care of that issue."

He's acting like a sappy kid. That's good for me, Carl thought.

Tom added two caveats. "Assuming the City Council approves this in writing and assuming the mining rights are structured *exactly* as we discussed, I am inclined to accept. Hell, I'd be crazy not to accept. Put it that way."

Carl nodded sagely.

"I'm sure we can get those details worked out to your satisfaction, Tom. That just leaves the issue of how much we'd be willing to pay you for the mining rights. Correct?"

"That's right. How much?"

"I know you're a businessman, Tom, so I won't insult you. You know how much we were prepared to pay for the property, so you know we can pay a good deal for the exclusive mining rights and still come out ahead financially."

"You read my mind, Carl."

"On the flip side, of course, we wouldn't actually own the land, which could cause us any one of a number of problems in the future. So, having only the mining rights is a far cry from actually owning the land. Do you see my point?"

"Go on," Tom said.

"Now remember that I have to run this by my partners ... as I said earlier, this is just a discussion right now, no guarantees, right?"

"I understand that, Carl. How much?"

Carl was sure he had Tom now and moved in to close him.

"How does $1.5 million sound to you?"

"One point five million? Dollars?" Tom said, stupidly.

Carl simply repeated the number, "One point five million ...," and just to emphasize his control of the situation he added, "... dollars."

Tom sat as still as a cat. He didn't look at Carl. He just sat there in that golf cart staring straight ahead at nothing.

Tom's silence worried Carl. *Have I misjudged the kid? Could my offer possibly be too low? An idiot would jump at one and a half million bucks. Maybe Larkin really is a tough negotiator. Should I have started lower and wrangled with him?*

Tom finally found his voice. "Did you say I could exempt any minerals I chose from the agreement?"

"You may exempt any minerals you like," Carl said.

"I'll want to run this by my attorney, you understand?"

"Is that a 'yes,' Tom?"

Tom paused again and finally said, "That's a 'yes,' Carl."

"Oh, and I'm sure you can appreciate that our arrangement must be kept strictly confidential until the actual contract is executed. That means you are not free to discuss it with anyone—including any of my partners or your Realtor. This is important."

Tom exhaled.

"I can live with that."

"Good," Carl smiled and extended his hand. "Do I have your *word* on it?"

A man's word without a signed piece of paper wasn't worth siccum in the city, but out here, it was how a man was defined. If your word wasn't worth a damn, neither were you. If a good man gave his word, he'd never try to weasel his way out of it later. A man kept his word. Period.

"Do you have my word on what, Carl?"

"Do I have your word that you won't discuss this arrangement with anyone?"

"I will have to discuss this with my wife, Kathleen, and with my attorney. Other than that, I will not discuss our arrangement with anyone. On that you have my word," Tom vowed.

"Then we have a deal," Carl said.

"No, Carl, we don't have a deal yet. We have an understanding as to terms, and you have my word that I won't discuss those terms with anyone other than Kathy and my attorney. We'll have a deal when the agreement we draw up matches what you and I discussed just now. If the agreement is everything you've promised, then we have a deal."

"No problem, Tom. That's what I meant."

Tom extended his hand while his eyes sought out Carl's. Out West, a man looks you in the eye when he makes a promise.

Carl's eyes flicked up to meet Tom's for an instant and then darted away. His hand was soft and damp, and he pulled it away from Tom's hard grasp a little too quickly.

THE SUN HAD settled itself behind the mountains. Tom and Carl, each blinded by his own desire, managed to find their way back to the clubhouse together, in the dark.

When Tom entered the hotel lobby, Eva was at the front desk, but busy with a check-in. She looked up at Tom as he came through the lobby. He pointed to his watch, mouthed the words, "be there," and kept walking.

Once in the room, Tom cracked open a beer, sat back on the bed, and dialed Kathy.

"Hi Kath. It's me."

"Tom? Tom, be careful of those guys."

"Say what?"

"I said be careful of those Elements guys. I mean it. I talked to Mel and Gita again this afternoon, and . . ."

"Whoa down there. What happened to 'how was your day,' and 'how are things,' and all that happy horseshit?"

"Sorry, Tom. I'm a little nervous about what I've found out."

"I can tell," he said, and laughed out loud.

"What's so goddamn funny, Tom? I took a half-day of vacation today to do your research, thank you very much. You want to hear about it, or what?"

"Jesus, Kathy, take it easy. I appreciate your help, I need your help, and I want to hear every last detail, believe me. I only laughed because you're so damn cute when you get mad."

"Thank you, I think."

"I didn't mean to interrupt you, Kathy. It's just that, well, I've got good news. Do you want to start with the good news or your news? Your call, sweetheart." He hadn't called her that in a long time.

"You go first, Silver Tongue."

"You're not going to believe what happened today. I hardly do myself."

"Is this tall tale going to require a single or a double whiskey?" Kathy asked.

"Double. I'll wait while you pour yourself one ..."

When Kathy was back, Tom dove into his pitch.

"We saw two ranches today. I don't think I'll need to see any more. I fell head over heels for the second place, Kathy. It is the most beautiful thing I've ever seen. It's ..." Tom went on for fifteen minutes describing the McPherson ranch, not letting Kathy say anything other than an occasional "really?" or "wow" or "that sounds terrific, Tom."

"Oh, crap! I forgot the coolest part. You remember that I spent some summers back in junior high school out on my uncle's place in the Hills? Well, you're never, ever going to believe this ..." and Tom went on for another fifteen minutes about Jo, and getting reacquainted, and he shared with Kathy what Jo had remembered for him.

Back in St. Paul, Kathleen Larkin sipped her whiskey and listened, a smile forming itself on her lips and spreading warmly to the rest of her being. It had been a while since she'd heard Tom talk like this. It was scary, and exciting. She was so happy for him. She loved his passion and seriousness, his boundless energy in pursuit of a cause, his sense of wonder and beauty.

God, I seriously don't know if I can go through with this, she thought as Tom raced on. *He won't take no for an answer sitting down.*

Kathleen snapped out of her private thoughts when she realized that the other end of the phone was silent.

"So ..." Tom's voice finally said. "What do you think?"

Kathleen quickly said, "I think it's wonderful, Tom, and I think you're crazy, and it sounds like you've got your heart set." Bringing her own serious misgivings into the conversation at that moment would have sparked an argument, and things would end badly. "Give me the nitty-gritty, and let's see if this is something we both really want to do."

Kathy heard Tom catch his breath at the other end, and his next words broke a bit.

"I knew you'd understand, Kathy. Thank you for that."

"You can thank me when I've put my stamp of approval on it, Tom. Which, as yet, I haven't done."

"You would love this place, Kathy. I promise you. It is so amazing. The ..." Tom was launching round two of his ranch gush when Kathy cut him off.

"Save it for tomorrow ... or Sunday. OK? I think you painted a pretty good picture already. Let's just say that you have me sold on the concept. The concept, Tom."

"Fair enough." Tom said, gulping the last of his warm beer and breathing an audible sigh of relief. "So ... on to the bad news?"

"Not quite yet," Kathy answered. "Just one more teeny, tiny detail on the ranch. What are they asking for it?"

Tom said nothing.

"How bad is it, Tom?"

"Pretty bad."

"How bad?"

"You mean the listing price?"

"No, I mean the in-your-dreams price," Kathy swatted Tom's flip answer back at him. "I thought I was the one with the bad news, not you. Now just tell me what the ranch is going for."

"They want 800 an acre, which I think is fair, and there's 8,400 acres total, so that means the ..."

"Eighty-four hundred acres, Tom? What are we going to do with 8,400 acres, assuming of course that we can afford it? Jesus, Tom, that's ... that's like ten or twelve square miles of land!" The moment the words were out of her mouth, Kathy regretted them.

"I'm sorry, Tom. You caught me by surprise; I didn't mean to jump all over you. How much does it all add up to?"

"It's OK. I should've told you up front. It's roughly 6.7 million dollars, all told."

"Did you say 'million' dollars, Tom?"

"I did," Tom said soberly. "Six point seven million."

Kathy burst out laughing at the other end. Tom started giggling, too.

"That's a good one, Tom," Kathy laughed uncontrollably. "Six point seven …," and before she could say "million dollars," she started cackling again.

"Listen, Kathy. I'm serious here," Tom said, barely able to speak. "I told them that we couldn't …" he said as laughter began to overtake him, "… that we couldn't go a dime over six point six!" He finished the sentence and broke into hysteria.

Neither of them could muster a word without provoking a new ruckus, and several seconds passed before the howling subsided.

"Oh-h-h-h-h," Kathy finally managed, "what am I going to do with you, man? Have you lost all of your marbles?"

Tom was about to answer when Kathy shrieked, "Oh shit!" She had spilled her drink in her lap, and they were both back in stitches for another several minutes.

As they both calmed, gasping for air, Tom said, "I know, I know. You're thinking, what the fuck am I thinking? Am I right?"

"No, Tom. I'm thinking what the fuck are you drinking!" That set them both off again.

It took another minute or two to find their bearings.

"OK, Kathy, you've got me there. That kind of money—for us—does sound kind of ridiculous. I'm glad we were able to laugh about it and get it out of our systems. But I am serious about the ranch, and I believe that there is a way to make the financials work. I've been working on the numbers and have a plan. That's the good news I was talking about earlier."

"You aren't kidding, aren't you?"

"I am not."

"Well, then, just give me the top line for now. That will give me a chance to absorb this preposterous number. We can argue the details later," she said. "How much is the first mortgage?"

"Thirty-two thousand."

"Thirty-two thousand a year? We pay that much on our house, Tom."

"Thirty-two thousand a month, Kathy. A *month*."

"How are we going to pay 32,000 dollars a month, Tom? I mean, really." Kathy laughed one of those not-*even*-funny laughs of hers. "Are you totally nuts?"

"Just hear me out, Kathy."

"Ohhh-Kaay, your show."

"Look, this is a working ranch. Grazing contracts should bring in about twenty dollars per cow-calf unit per month per acre, and the timber is ..."

"I don't have any idea what you're talking about, Tom. I'm already in shock, in case you hadn't noticed. Just give me the big picture so I won't feel like I should send some little men in white jackets out there to bring you back home—or commit you there."

"Grazing and timber are worth about $210,000. That leaves us short $174,000 per year. We've got $300,000 equity in the house. If we sell it, and put the money in bonds, we would have just enough to make the first mortgage payment for two years."

"Then what?" Kathy said.

"We could set aside a thousand acres on the southeast corner of the ranch and sell it off as vacation and retirement acreages. I know that I can sell 50-acre parcels for a minimum of $150,000 a pop, which will raise, averaged out, about three million, give or take.

"You still with me?"

"Barely."

"We put the three million in the bank and draw it down over time to cover the difference between the grazing and timber income. Voila! The land supports itself and it is ours, free and clear, in thirty years." Tom waited for Kathy to respond.

Kathy's words were calculated, so as not to either anger Tom or give him any false sense of hope.

"Suppose for a minute, with the emphasis on suppose, that your numbers work. Add to that the assumption that I would be willing to let the house go. That leaves the two small matters of the down payment of over a million, and the matter of how we expect to pay our living expenses at the same time. I'm hoping you're not thinking of living on tomato soup and beans for thirty years to make this work."

"You're right. The down payment is $1.3 million. Now, like to hear the good news?"

Tom paused.

"Well?" Kathy hated surprises and wasn't enjoying this drama.

"You remember yesterday that I said that the mayor—Carl Graves—invited me to take a tour of the golf course?"

"Of course I do—I spent several hours getting familiar with the mayor and his shady friends, do you remember that? So what's the golf course tour got to do with making a down payment of over a million dollars?" Kathy demanded.

"Carl offered to loan us money for the down stroke."

"You're kidding?"

"Not at all. I can fill you in on the whole conversation later, but Carl says the Hot Springs City Council has got a slush fund that they will use to underwrite our down payment. Something about bringing new blood into the community."

"Sounds bogus to me, Tom."

"Look, Kathy. The goddamn mayor laid it out for me in black and white. I'm just telling you what he told me. And that wasn't even the good news. Hell, I could get some hard moneylender to go the twenty percent down, but we'd still have to make a payment on it. The mayor says our loan would be one hundred percent forgivable. We don't have to pay it back! How's that for good news?"

"Are you absolutely sure you have this right, Tom?" Kathy couldn't hide her skepticism any more than Tom could hide his enthusiasm.

"Kathy. What more can I tell you than what I heard? Mayor Graves is willing to put together a forgivable loan for the down payment. I'm guessing that his company is going to underwrite it—at least that's what he gave me to believe."

"Elements is underwriting it? Why would they do that? Aren't they the ones who tried to buy the place and got turned down? Isn't that what you had me running around all afternoon trying to help you figure out?"

"I'm not trying to tell you I've got this all figured out yet. I just left the mayor an hour ago," Tom explained. "When I first heard him offer us a loan, I had the same reaction you did. But his explanation, on the surface anyway, sounds credible. I think you'll see the logic in it once I explain it to you. You want to hear it?"

"Not at the moment. First tell me where we get the money to live on once we've sold the house and given up our jobs to live in the Garden of Eden."

"Just ... don't start with the sarcasm, Kathy. Can you do that?"

"Whatever. Just tell me where the money comes that we'll need to live on," Kathy groused.

"Elements wants exclusive mining rights on the McPherson ranch. And believe it or not, they don't seem to give a good god-damn about actually mining. They've got some hush-hush business that requires them to dig tunnels under the ground, and they've run out of room on their property. Apparently, they make a piss-pot full of dough on whatever it is they do, and so Carl said they'd pay us one-and-a-half million dollars for the mining rights, and we can stipulate in the contract any minerals we want to exempt from that agreement.

"That's one-and-a-half million bucks to live on. In a moderately aggressive portfolio, that would earn a hundred, hundred-and-fifty grand a year. Think we could scrape by on that if we didn't have a mortgage payment? And if that isn't enough, we can spend down the principle and figure things out again in fifteen or twenty years. Or, God forbid, one or both of us could get a job outside the ranch," Tom spat back and went silent.

Again, Kathy measured her words. Tom was deathly serious about the ranch, and she realized that she would have to prepare herself to make some serious decisions. "You've done a lot in a very short period of time, Tom. I am impressed. Please don't be so irritated with me for asking questions. Presumably, this is also my life we're talking about. And you know my feelings about moving back to the country."

"I realize that. It's just that you always think my big ideas are pie-in-the-sky and you immediately start picking the fly shit out of the pepper. It's disheartening."

"Let's not do this, Tom. I have a right to ask as many questions as I feel necessary."

"Whatever you say, Kathy."

"Now, you really have had a day, haven't you?" Kathy offered, hoping to get the discussion and their attitudes about each other, if not on track, at least back to cordial. If the ranch deal went forward, Kathy thought, there would be a lot more at stake than a bunch of numbers on a napkin. She opted for a lighter tone. "I've only heard tell of one other person who went into the wilderness and created miracles in less than forty days and forty nights."

"OK. You can call me God if you'd like," Tom joked.

" 'Oh, God, please' is more like it, if I know you," she said, and was able to coax a chuckle out of Tom.

"Anyway, I did take good notes while you were explaining the financials, and I promise I'll go over them before you get home on Sunday so we can discuss this in detail."

"One more thing, Kathy. I gave Carl my word that I would not discuss this financial arrangement with anyone except you and our attorney."

"Why did you do that?"

"Because it was one of Carl's conditions, Kathy. Is that such a big deal?"

"I don't know, I'm just asking. So I guess I won't discuss this with anyone. Does that include the kids, too?" Kathy asked.

"It includes everybody—the kids, your mom, my parents, the dog."

"Are you ready to hear the not-so-terrific news about the guys who are about to become your best financial buddies?"

Tom winced. "Give me both barrels."

"Do you remember what I said in the voice mail I left earlier today?"

"Yeah," Tom said. "The land Elements owns out by Edgemont, next to the McPherson place, was a Mining Authority site, and they dumped a bunch of tailings that the EPA cleaned up in the early '70's, right?"

"Right."

"Then, the land was sold off privately, and the Elements guys bought most of it. You also said something about a Homeland Security investigation," Tom added.

"That's about it, except that we couldn't find any documentation on the Mining Authority activities or the EPA clean-up," Kathy added.

"Right, I do remember that bit."

"Let me bring you up to speed on the rest.

"Sometime before the business with the tailings, a lot of the land was purchased by the United States Ordnance Department to house ammunition during World War II. They needed a place that was remote, high and dry, and had good rail access. The land that Elements now owns fit the bill perfectly. You won't believe what they built to store the munitions in."

"Eight hundred and two bunkers and a town called Igloo," Tom said. "I came across that when I was doing my ranch research, and Carl mentioned the number of bunkers during our golf course tour."

"Right. The bunkers are mostly underground; what you see from the surface is just a portion of each structure. Apparently, they were built in one hell of a hurry, since we were at war. The few construction records that we found didn't give us much relevant information. However, one of the papers mentioned a now-defunct construction company out of Philadelphia, Perez Construction ..." Kathy paused to see if Tom would pick up on this connection.

"Did you say Perez Construction?" Tom asked.

"I most certainly did."

"That's the same name as one of the partners in the law firm that represents Elements!"

"Not only is it the same name," Kathy added, "it appears to be the same family. Since you told me about the law firm, I asked Gita to see if she could find a connection between the two. Sure enough, daddy Perez's construction bucks funded junior Perez's prestigious law firm."

"But you found nothing about those bunkers?" Tom asked.

"Gita did find one engineering document in the archives. It was a description of the landform at Edgemont before and after all this bunker construction took place."

"So ... what's the point?" Tom pressed.

"Most of the information in the document was Greek to me, but I could see that there was a huge net addition to topsoil volume. At the time, I just figured it was from digging out all those bunkers.

"Now I find out from you that Elements has a network of underground tunnels in which they conduct some unknown business. Maybe the government dug more than bunkers out there ... I don't know. Since you're much better at these things than I am,

I'll fax you a copy of the document. Maybe you can figure out if there's more new dirt on top of the ground than just the bunker spaces would produce."

"That is one hell of a good idea, Kathy. If nothing else, it would help me determine whether or not Carl is lying about Elements having to dig tunnels on their land. If the government dug all of those rat holes fifty years ago, he's lying through his teeth. Send me the document; I'll do the math. I need to know the exact dimensions of the bunkers to reconcile the numbers," Tom said. "Do you have that by any chance?"

"Sorry. Nothing doing on that count."

"No big deal. That's information I can dig up here."

"You're not going out there yourself, are you? That's private property!" Kathy warned.

"No, no. Nothing like that. I'll just ask around. I'm sure somebody knows. In fact, I'll bet Pat Burley can tell me off the top of his head. What else have you got?"

Tom checked his watch. It was six thirty. "Time's a wasting."

"What's your hurry? Going to look at ranches in the dark tonight?" Kathy said.

"I'm meeting Pat at quarter past seven to talk money," Tom lied. You know, to go over all these new developments with Carl and so on."

"I thought you couldn't talk to anyone about that."

"Well, I'm not going to tell Pat what Carl said; I'm just going to go over the numbers on the ranch to be sure I've got the financials correct, and to reassure Pat that we can cover the payments and the down stroke. I don't intend to give him any details. OK?"

"Then what's the point of the meeting? I don't get it."

"If for no other reason, Pat has to feel that I'm—that we—are qualified buyers. Otherwise, I'm just wasting his time," Tom said.

"Well, if he hasn't already decided that you're a legitimate buyer, he isn't much of a real estate guy, if you ask me," Kathy countered.

Don't bullshit me, Tom Larkin. Kathy thought. *Just what the hell are you really up to tonight?* Kathy buried that thought and said, "Let's get back to Elements, shall we? According to Mel, Homeland Security is involved because of a connection with a guy named Abdul Khan.

"Khan is a Pakistani scientist who sold uranium-enriching technology to Iran several years ago," Kathy explained. "Something about centrifuges. Then, about a year ago, guess who shows up to have coffee with Khan in Istanbul?"

"Who?"

"Jennings."

"No way! What was the meeting about?"

"If the Feds knew that, they probably would have arrested Jennings or dropped their inquiry. Mel says that the only link they've got between the two is that one meeting in Istanbul. That isn't enough. Jennings is a physician, Khan is a Ph.D; they could have any one of a number of professional reasons—or alibis—for having made contact. The reason Homeland Security put Jennings in their crosshairs has to do with some of Khan's e-mails they've intercepted.

"Seems that our friend Abdul Khan had been having a very interesting conversation with somebody about building a centrifuge farm," Kathy said.

"What the hell is a centrifuge farm?"

"It's a whole lot of centrifuges being used in tandem to enrich uranium," Kathy explained. "It seems that natural uranium isn't of much use for anything. It has to be enriched before it can be used in either industrial or military applications. Apparently, and I'm just quoting Mel here, natural uranium is converted into a gas and then fed into these centrifuges. The gas is spun at high speeds to enrich its potency—don't ask me how. Low-level stuff can fuel a reactor, for example, and the really high-potency stuff is used to make bombs.

"The point is, you need a lot of these centrifuges working twenty-four hours a day to produce even small amounts of high-grade uranium."

"What does all that have to do with Jennings?" Tom asked.

"Two things," Kathy said.

"First, the Feds can't seem to find out who's communicating with Kahn about the centrifuge farm. E-mail is somewhat easy to track, but not in this case."

"All they have to do is find out who paid for the e-mail account and backtrack," Tom protested. "It's simple."

"It isn't. Whoever is communicating with Khan by e-mail is pretty cagey. All the e-mail accounts have been paid for by check. Every one of the checking accounts the Feds tracked down had been closed. It seems that the accounts were set up for only one purpose—to write a check in payment of an e-mail account," Kathy explained.

"It gets more interesting. All of the Social Security numbers on the checking accounts are from dead people. And, get this, all of the checking accounts have the same mailing address—a post office box from which no mail has ever been retrieved!"

"What kind of banker opens an account with a post office box?" Tom demanded.

"You're going to love this part, Tom. All of the checks used to pay for the e-mail accounts were drawn on family-owned banks in small towns in western South Dakota and eastern Wyoming."

"Bingo!" Tom exclaimed.

"No kidding, 'bingo'," Kathy agreed.

"You said there were two reasons—other than that one meeting with Khan—that Homeland Security had put Jennings on their radar. What's the other?" Tom asked.

"A shipment of specialized magnets that Standard Electric lost in transport. Guess where?

"Don't tell me—Hot Springs," Tom said.

"No. Edgemont," Kathy corrected him. "Right down the road from the Elements property."

"What have magnets got to do with Khan and uranium … I'm getting lost," Tom confessed.

"The lost shipment included a number of very specialized magnets which can be used to build those centrifuges we were talking about. When it dawned on our boys at Homeland Security that a giant defense contractor lost centrifuge magnets in the same area where uranium was mined for twenty years, and where they also suspected a bunch of local businessmen were exchanging electronic postcards with a rogue Pakistani nuclear physicist, they thought maybe somebody ought to look into it."

"How the hell does Mel know all this?"

"You know Mel, he knows a guy who knows a guy. Washington is the ultimate insider's town."

Tom exhaled. "There is no way these yahoos could be involved in something like this ... could they?"

"I'm not trying to sell you a story," Kathy said. "I'm just telling you what I found out, and that I think the information is credible. Make of it what you will.

"Elements may or may not be doing anything illegal on their property—there's no way to tell from the available information. But it smells bad to me. That's why I cautioned you when we got on the phone tonight."

"Yeah. I get your drift," Tom said.

"What are you thinking, Tom?"

"Just trying to make heads or tails of what you found, is all. What they do on their land isn't really any of our business ..."

Kathy cut him off. "It's our business if it makes us glow in the dark living next door to them, Tom, and it's our business if we sign some kind of agreement linking us financially to their company. Don't tell me it's none of our business!"

"Calm down, Kathy; supposedly, we're on the same side, remember? And I'm not trying to pick a fight here. All I meant was that I'm no federal agent, and I think we ought to stay focused on information that is directly relevant to the financial agreement they've offered us."

"Well, you can start by exempting uranium from those mining rights and see how bad they squirm. That ought to tell you something."

"Great idea. What else do you suggest?"

Kathy was feeling drawn into the process and it bothered her.

"The truth? I suggest we find another way to finance this ranch, or look for another property that we can buy without involving Elements. But I suppose that you're not interested in that line of thinking, are you?"

Tom said nothing.

"Back up and look at this from my angle, Tom!" Kathy implored. "You go out West and get your heart set on a huge ranch that we can't afford. A bunch of local business guys that are being watched by the Feds have tried to buy that same ranch every way they know how, and failed. Out of the blue, these same guys offer us a deal that sweeps away all our financial problems—so that we can buy the ranch they want. Don't you see anything wrong with this picture?"

"Say it, Kathy."

"I don't trust them."

"Do you trust me?"

"Of course." She was thinking about telling Tom all of the reasons why she shouldn't, or didn't, trust him, but then thought better of it.

"Then you know that I won't do anything illegal or anything that will harm us financially just to get this ranch."

"I'm sure you won't. That's not what concerns me. I'm worried about what they might do to you if they don't get what they want. These aren't good people, Tom. They're not like your neighbors back on the farm."

"I know. So, let's not try to figure all of this out at once, OK? Let me go over the basic numbers with Burley in a few minutes, then let's see if Carl actually comes through with an agreement that's worth anything. Then, if you're still convinced we shouldn't have anything to do with these guys, we can discuss walking away. Let's take one step at a time."

Kathy was silent for a long time before saying, "All right, Tom. I'll go along with this ... this idea, to the next step."

"That's all I'm asking, Kathy. Now, I have to run."

"Where are you meeting Pat?" Kathy asked.

"Lucky Strike."

"Isn't that the bar?"

"Well, it's more like a bistro," Tom mumbled.

"A *bistro*? In Hot Springs?" Kathy sneered. "Don't make me laugh. Is Eva going to be there?"

"What?"

"You heard me. Is your friend Eva going to be there?"

"How in hell should I know, Kathy. For Christ's sake, are you still on that?"

"On what?"

"You know what."

"Whatever."

"Listen, Kathy, half the town could be there, maybe even all of them, maybe none of them. How should I know? I'm going to meet Pat Burley to go over financials and maybe feed my face if the opportunity arises. That is, if we're done here."

"Oh, we certainly are done here, Tom. So, you better be getting along to the bistro. You don't want to keep Pat—or whomever—waiting."

"What do you mean, whomever ..."

Kathy cut him off with a curt, "Love you," and the phone clicked dead.

Tom stared at the handset for several seconds, and then returned it to its cradle.

"Yeah, right. Love you, too, *hon*."

"Hey, cowboy!" Eva sang out as Tom walked into the Lucky Strike. "I'm over here defending your bar stool."

"Sorry I'm late, Eva. Bad form on my part."

Eva hopped down, took Tom by the arm, and patted the seat next to hers.

"Forget about it. Nothing else I'd rather be doing. Now, sit down and tell me why you desperately needed to see me."

Eva gave Tom a toothsome smile and steered him onto a bar stool. When he was seated, she placed one of her hands squarely on each of his shoulders and leaned in slowly toward him, as if she were about to give him a kiss.

She held her lips short of his, but her face was indecently close.

"Obviously you're irritated with me about something, Tom," she whispered. "So let's get whatever it is on the table, and if I've done something wrong, at least hear my side of the story. Whatever it is, I hope it won't spoil the evening. I know you didn't ask me out on a date here, Tom. You're married and all that. But does that mean we can't just have some fun? Do you think I'm bad for saying that?"

"Eva Shepherd, you are totally impossible," Tom said, shaking his head. "What am I going to do with you?"

"What are you going to do with me, Tom? How about a cocktail or two and something to eat, for starters?" she purred.

"You want the truth, Eva? I figured on a cocktail—as in one drink—and no more. Supper is definitely not in my plan," Tom replied, less sternly than Eva expected. "I came here because I've got something to ask you, and, well, it didn't occur to me that either of us would have an appetite for each other's company when we were done talking."

"That doesn't sound nice, Tom."

"It's not nice, but I'll play nice if you will. Let's have that cocktail, and I'll tell you what's on my mind. Deal?"

"Deal!" Eva exclaimed with enthusiasm. "Put her there." Eva extended her hand to Tom as if they'd just agreed on the price of a good bull. There was nothing for Tom to do but take her hand and wrap it up in his own.

Her hand was smooth and hot and firm. He gave it a steady squeeze and held on to it longer than he should have.

"Don't hurt me, Tom," she feigned, letting her hand fall onto his thigh and linger there.

Without removing her hand from Tom, Eva turned to the bartender and bellowed like a sailor, "Need some whiskey for this cowboy! Pronto!"

A firestorm swept through Tom, ignited at Eva's touch. He knew he ought to brush her off, but Tom was suddenly weary of fighting his feelings, tired of turning away from affection ... and having affection turn its back on him. A longing he hadn't felt in years was awake and dancing in his head. Tom tried to convince himself that it was infatuation, but he knew better. It was more. He had quickly reached that place where he had to back away from the edge or dive in.

He surrendered himself to Eva.

"Thanks," Tom managed to say, "for taking care of our drinks."

"At your service," Eva smiled back and gave his thigh a gentle squeeze.

Tom made a half-hearted attempt to remove Eva's hand; instead, she grabbed his and held on. Rather than wrest himself from her grip, Tom tugged down on her hand and she sat, facing him. She worked one of her knees between his, and he let her do it. He was her prisoner.

"If you're trying to prove that I'm attracted to you, you win," Tom whispered. "The answer is yes. I'm married, but not blind—or perfect. Where does that leave us?"

They sat without speaking, and when the drinks arrived the waitress took her time arranging their cocktails on the napkins.

"I don't know how to do this," Tom finally said, holding Eva's hand out from where he still held it under the table. He leaned forward and gave her a kiss on the forehead, his blessing on the things to come.

"What do you think we are doing?" she asked, letting her eyes fall.

The way she said it shamed Tom.

"I don't mean to insult you, Eva; I . . ."

"I'm not insulted, Tom. To the contrary, if you want to know."

They both picked up their drinks and sat without speaking and without looking at each other for a few minutes. Eva spoke first.

"Why did you ask me here, Tom?"

"Somebody was in my room this morning."

"What's that got to do with me?"

"Eva," Tom said, turning to face her, "Was it you? Did you go into my room?"

Eva raised her glass to her lips and drank, with her eyes closed, until it was empty.

She put her empty down quietly and deliberately, as if she had expected that question but wasn't ready to answer it just yet. Ignoring Tom's question, Eva motioned to the waitress for another round.

"Who said I was in your room?"

"I did. Were you in my room this morning? It's a simple question. Yes or no?" Tom demanded too harshly.

Eva looked away from him, and her chin began to tremble. She had conjured tears and it wasn't long before she had a pretty good stream rolling.

"I'm ... I'm so ashamed, Tom. I'm ... sorry. I'm so sorry. Please forgive me," she said between sobs.

Tom watched tears plunge into Eva's lap. She'd changed from her work smock into a china-blue, body-hugging little shift made of a soft tissue that seemed to dissolve into her skin, her shape entirely responsible for the fall of its fabric. She had shinnied further along Tom's knee and the shift's scalloped hem was halfway up her thighs. The flapper-style sash that should have been slung low on her hips was heaped up at her waist. Like the unsettled leaves that clothe an aspen, the materials of her dress exaggerated Eva's every tremor; when she whimpered, the gossamer burbled from her shoulders to her knees. She was a fountain, and Tom drank deeply with his eyes.

He was unprepared for Eva's bold admission and her appeal for forgiveness.

He reached up and put a hand between her cheek and her mane, his fingertips coming to rest on her neck.

"I didn't come here to hurt you, Eva. It was wrong of me to accuse you outright like that. To put you in a corner. It's just that I feel sure you came into my room. I just don't know why."

Eva continued to shake, her head bowed.

"I'm not angry with you, Eva," Tom said softly. "This was a bad idea; I should have spoken with you privately."

Eva was saying something too faint for Tom to make out, and he leaned his face in close to hers.

"No, this is my fault. It's all my fault," Eva sobbed.

"Take it easy now, girl. This isn't the Inquisition. I'm not angry. OK? Really, I'm not," Tom murmured, feeling the heat of several pair of barroom eyes at his back. Ignoring them, he stroked Eva's hair, in the same way one might comfort a frantic child.

At his touch, Eva leaned forward into Tom, burying her face in his neck.

He stood and allowed her to come inside his embrace. He had fallen overboard in a wild but welcoming sea and was borne further out with each heave of her breast.

He began to rock her.

Eva raised her arms to Tom's waist, and pulled herself up full against him. She buried her face in Tom's shirt for a minute longer to keep him close. When she finally pulled away, his hand fell and rested on her shoulder.

Her body was flushed and buzzing.

Tom had demonstrated, beyond any doubt, that he was hers for the taking.

With one hand, she found a napkin to dry her cheeks; with the other she took Tom's arm and pulled him down into his seat.

"Thank you for being so kind, Tom. I feel like a fool," she said without looking at him.

"I'm the fool, Eva. I had no business coming here and making accusations. Forgive me."

There would be no more difficult questions from Tom. He had set her free, and now she was free to admit to anything.

"If anyone acted foolishly, it was me," Eva moaned. "Yes. I went into your room ... what was I thinking? But I swear I didn't take anything, if that's what you think ..."

"No, that's not what I was getting at," Tom cut in. "There's nothing missing. I just noticed that someone had tampered with my computer. I probably wouldn't have given it a second thought, but you'd left tracks. I knew it was you."

Eva looked up at Tom. He was smiling.

"What tracks?" she said warily, drying one eye.

Tom leaned toward her very slowly, inhaling deeply, and scooped at the air around Eva's head. "Ahhhh. The air is filled with the scent of ... of ... is it a forbidden fruit? No ... wait! It is the serpent!"

"Oh. My. God. You have got to be kidding!"

"No. I'm. Not," Tom boasted.

"You *smelled* me?" Eva said, and burst into laughter.

Tom laughed, too. Anyone who didn't know them might have believed that they were long-lost friends, or even lovers, to see them, heads together like conspirators.

"Yeah, I smelled you. I didn't figure there'd be two women in town wearing Roberto Cavalli's Serpentine. It had to be you."

"But how did you know?" Eva gaped.

"I just told you how I knew it was you," Tom replied.

"No, how do you know the scent of Serpentine?"

"Oh, that." Tom's eyes fell. "I was in New York City last month and bought a bottle of it in one of the Trump Tower shops. Saw an ad for it in the *Times*, so I brought some home. You know, for ... Kathy."

"Your wife?" Eva said as if she didn't know.

"Yeah. Kathleen. My wife."

The mention of home and Tom's wife dulled the edge of their conversation.

"If you're such an amazing detective, Tom," Eva said, quickly changing the subject back to herself, "why don't you tell me why I was in your room? Think you can figure that out from the air you breathed, Sherlock?"

Her sassiness quickened Tom's pulse and dissolved his thoughts of Kathy.

"As a matter of fact, Miss, I did. I figure you were in my room to freshen the air for me."

Eva brightened at his silliness. "Close, but no cigar, funny guy. Guess again," she squealed with delight. "Guess again!"

"OK. OK, I actually have a theory." Tom cocked his head slightly and narrowed his eyes as if he were about to deliver some very serious clinical news to a patient. "You are obsessed with strange, especially good-looking men. This obsession causes you, beyond your better judgment, to sneak into their rooms and weave fantasies about them while you change their linens and towels. Of course, you are in therapy for this, but thought that this one time wouldn't cause you to relapse, and you figured you wouldn't get caught …"

Eva interrupted, laughing. "No. No, no, no. Bad boy! You've got this all wrong. If I had been fantasizing in your room, Tom, believe me, I would have stayed, hoping to be caught."

"Well, that would have improved your tip!" Tom countered.

"You a big tipper?" Eva goaded.

"Very big," Tom replied. "Impressively big," he emphasized.

They had arrived at a place very different from the one Tom intended they go. Eva's transgression—and the reason for it—had become their private joke. Eva had as much as invited Tom to sleep with her. Tom hadn't said yes, but he hadn't said no, either.

While Tom still had his reasons to distrust Eva, and she her own to keep her distance from Tom, the uncertainty only added fuel to their fire.

After another round of cocktails and casual touching, Tom took one last stab at setting things back on the straight and narrow.

"Seriously, Eva, I was spooked about the deal in my room. It seems like every time I turn around, somebody's in the middle of my business. My interest in the McPherson place has stirred up a hornet's nest. Truth be told, I'm beginning to feel a bit paranoid.

"I actually thought you had something to do with those guys who are trying to get in the middle of my ranch purchase! I wouldn't blame you if you thought I was about half nuts, Eva. I'm beginning to think so myself."

Eva looked relieved but said nothing.

"So, Eva, for the record, tell me. Why were you snooping around my room? Tell me and we can forget about it. Scouts' honor."

She dropped her head and stared at her hands, stalling again. Then, fixing her eyes on Tom, she began to spin her lie. "Tom …

I was … you're going to laugh if I tell you, and I'm going to be embarrassed."

"I promise I won't laugh."

"After you and I and Pat had drinks last night, well, my curiosity just got the best of me. You know? I just wanted to know what made you tick, and thought that I could find something out that would, you know, help me get to know you a little better; give me some, I don't know, some advantage with you. Don't make me say it out loud, Tom. Why do think I wanted to find out about you?" She'd dropped her head and pretended that she might start crying again.

Tom went soft. "All right," he conceded. "I'll take you at your word. Just don't go rummaging around in my room again—at least without my permission. Are we good?"

Eva raised her face and met Tom's gaze. "We're good, Tom. Thank you. Really. Thank you for not embarrassing me."

Eva had dodged the bullet. For Tom, things were getting dangerous.

"Now that we're not going to be angry with each other anymore, Tom, do you think you might want to keep a girl company for supper?" Eva asked.

Tom rattled the ice cubes in his empty glass, let them go still, and rattled them again.

"What the hell. Why not?"

FRIDAY AT MIDNIGHT

After four hours with Tom, Eva floated out of the Lucky Strike on a cloud. She was radiant, and hope burned hot in her soul. As she closed her eyes to replay their amazing tryst, her cell phone began to chirp.

She stared woodenly at the caller's I.D. number and believed for an instant that she had the strength to ignore the call. But she answered. She had to.

"In case you hadn't noticed, it's midnight," she hissed into the receiver. "What do you want?"

"Get over to my office, and I'll tell you," Doc Jennings said.

"Now?" Eva whined.

"Now. Side door. Be here in ten minutes," he said and hung up.

Eva would rather have been rolled in chicken shit and paraded down Main Street than meet with Jennings right then. But she did as she was told.

Jennings was waiting inside the service entrance to Building C at the Veteran's Administration Hospital when she pulled up a few minutes later. He glared at her and marched down the hallway without a word. Eva traipsed along behind until they were ensconced in Jennings' private office.

"So, what's the big deal, Bill?"

"Have a nice supper?"

He knows! she thought. "What did you say?"

"You know what I said, you tramp."

"It's none of your business, asshole."

"Don't make me ask again. I want details!" he demanded.

There was no future in trying to hide from Jennings: he always seemed to know precisely what Eva least wanted him to know.

"Yeah, it was a nice supper. Satisfied?"

"Not even close, Eva. Perhaps you've forgotten that we have an understanding, yes? I provide you with certain resources, and in exchange, you provide me with certain information." Jennings smiled.

Eva wished she was a man and could just clock the bastard and be done with him.

Jennings turned his back to her as if to say he had nothing to fear, ambled over and lowered himself into the calfskin couch.

"Tell you what, *sweetheart*. You can start by telling me everything you found out this morning. Then, we'll move on to your little date with our friend Tom Larkin."

Jennings motioned with a pat of his hand for her to come and sit next to him.

She sat down obediently. Jennings busied himself with a hangnail on his thumb, waiting for Eva's report.

"I went through his stuff, like you asked," she droned.

"And . . ."

"And I didn't find out anything important, I can tell you that."

"I'll decide whether it's important or not. Get to it," he commanded.

Eva hung her head like a child and mumbled. "He's curious about Elements. He got his wife . . ."

"Speak up, girl. And look at me when you're talking!"

Eva hardened her heart, lifted her eyes to meet Jennings', and continued.

"I said, he got his wife involved. Apparently she's a reporter or something . . ."

"We already know that," Jennings interrupted. "We have the basics on Larkin, including his financials. And by the way, gold-digger," he added out of meanness, "Lover Boy isn't sitting on much cash. Thought you might be interested."

"I'd be interested in you going to hell, Bill."

"Tell you what, Eva. If that's how you feel, maybe we should just forget about our arrangement and go our separate ways. Is that what you want?"

She'd never escape him, and she knew it.

"You want to hear this, or are you here just to show me how fucking smart you are?" Eva snapped.

"Such language from a girl. Tsk, tsk, Eva. If we do still have an agreement, why don't you just get to the details and spare me any further outbursts?"

Words tumbled out of Eva's mouth haphazardly, like weeds before the wind.

"Tom must have asked his wife to do some research, 'cause she called him back and sent him an e-mail with three attachments with what she found. Most of the stuff is old news, like who owned the Elements' property before you and my dad and the rest of you guys got hold of it. She found out that a bunch of EPA records had been destroyed—whatever that means—and said it looked like somebody done it on purpose. She was pretty suspicious about that bit."

"Now we're getting somewhere. Do you have a copy of this e-mail?"

"Yeah. I just didn't have time to send it over to you yet. I'll do that in the morning."

"Be sure you do."

"Then, she said something about some investigations, I think."

Jennings sat up with a start. "What investigations, Eva?"

"I don't remember. I'm not good with details."

"Well, think! What about the investigations?"

"I think Tom's wife said that there were a couple of investigations," Eva continued, "and that one of them, I think it was

Homeland Security, is still going on, but they've never pinned anything on Elements."

Jennings sprang to his feet. "She said that Homeland Security was investigating Elements? Are you sure?"

"Yeah, I'm sure. Why don't you read her e-mail for yourself if you don't believe me?"

"If I'd had it, I would. What else did she say about this investigation?"

"Nothing on the investigation, that was it. I'm sure you know what she's talking about, right, Bill?"

Jennings didn't answer.

Despite her shame in betraying Tom, Eva kept talking. "One other thing. She said you guys weren't really a corporation. That you were a limited something or other, and that she was going to get your legal papers from the State of South Dakota."

"What about those e-mail attachments?" Jennings demanded, pacing the room.

"I didn't read them. Read them yourself when I forward her e-mail."

"Which you should have done already."

"Get off my back, Bill. I'm doing a lot for you … a whole hell of a lot. I'm the one who put my ass on the line breaking and entering Tom's room. A few more 'thank yous' and a little less 'what've you got for me now, bitch' would be appreciated."

He let that go and pressed for more detail. "Anything else … anything at all?"

"Only that his wife told Tom to be careful of you guys, said she thought you were hiding something. That's it." Eva slouched down on the couch, not noticing her dress ride up as she slid forward.

It didn't escape Jennings' eyes.

"Larkin's wife is sharp; I'll give her that," Jennings said. "But why would Larkin be so interested in us? He couldn't have known anything about us until he got to town, or he would have done all this homework before coming out here."

Jennings continued to pace while Eva thought about Tom, her eyes closed.

"It has to be that moron Burley. Yeah, it's Burley. I'm sure of it!" Jennings concluded. "Burley showed Larkin the McPherson place today, and he must have told Larkin all about our offer. Do you think Burley told him, Eva?"

Lost in her thoughts of Tom, Eva slid further down on the couch. Her eyes were closed, her breathing even and peaceful, her dress nearly at her waist.

"Eva! Do you think so?" Jennings barked out, arousal now propelling his anger.

Eva opened her eyes slowly and asked, "Do I think what?"

"Do you think Larkin's interest in us came from Burley?"

"Yeah, whatever. I don't know, Bill. I don't know about your offer and, frankly, I don't really give a shit. Can I go now?"

"No."

Jennings eyes lingered on Eva's long, bare legs.

Eva saw his eyes on her and sat up, yanking her dress down as far as it would reach. But it didn't provide adequate cover. She had selected the dress as a feast for Tom's eyes, not Jennings', and it was a liability to her now.

"Why can't I leave?"

"Because I haven't heard about our little supper with Larkin, dearie. Do tell. And don't spare any of the juicy details."

You bastard, she thought.

"What do you want to know?"

"Same as the room search. I want to know everything. Start with why you were there with him in the first place. That wasn't part of the plan."

"He asked me."

"Why?"

"Maybe because he thought I'd fuck him. Why don't you go ask him, Bill?"

"Let's try again. Why were you having supper with Tom Larkin?"

He's never, ever going to let me go until I tell him, she thought.

"OK. He suspected I was snooping around in his room, and wanted to talk to me about it. Satisfied?"

"He what?" Jennings was angry. "He knows you were searching his room?"

"That's right. He knows, and I handled it. It's over. It's not a problem," Eva said.

"I don't really care what you think is a problem. If I think it's a problem, it's a problem. Got it?"

"Whatever."

"How, exactly, did you *handle* it, Eva?"

"I admitted it to start off with—'cause he'd already figured it out. Said he smelled my perfume when he came into his room. Said some things had been disturbed. He didn't go into a lot of detail; he just put some odd bits of information together that pointed to me. Anyway, he figured it out. He's smart. Don't underestimate him."

"So he finds out you've been in his room, and ..."

"So I tell him, yeah, I went up to his room 'cause I liked what I saw when he checked in and thought maybe I'd find something that would help me, you know, get close to him ... get to know him better, like that."

Jennings exhaled. "Good. For once your base instincts worked out well for me."

"What do you mean by that?" Eva demanded.

"Let me spell it out for you. You're a slut, and I'll bet Larkin had no trouble believing you were in his room looking for a way to get in his pants, did he?"

"Tell you what, doctor know-it-all, why don't I spell it out for you? I cooked up the story about wanting to get personal with

him because he was barking up the right tree. He was nervous
about the ranch deal. He remembered that I'd told him my cousin
was in real estate, and Tom thought I was up in his room trying
to find something that would help my cousin get the business
away from Burley. On top of that, he tells me that he's gotten a
little jumpy with people coming at him from all sides on *his* ranch
deal. Get it, Bill? He was putting two and two together real fast.

"So I figure Tom didn't need to be thinking about anything
connected with real estate, that it would be a whole lot better to
have him thinking about what's inside my dress than what's inside
that conniving, crooked mind of yours," Eva snarled. "Pretty
good thinking for a *slut*, wouldn't you say, Bill."

"OK," Jennings conceded. "You might have done right, for
once. What else did you learn from him?"

"Well," Eva continued, "he pretty much dropped the subject
of the ranch during supper. But there was one thing he said that
will probably be important to you, since you've made such a big
point of how you're going to buy old Jo McPherson's place and
how nobody else has a snowball's chance in hell of ..."

"What about the McPherson place? Spit it out!"

"Tom said he's decided to buy it."

"That pissant? He doesn't have the money. He's dreaming."

"Oh, yeah? Well, he looked me straight in the eye and said,
'There have been developments in the last twenty-four hours that
have convinced me I'll be able to buy the McPherson ranch, no
doubt in my mind.' That's what he said, word for word."

Eva loved it when Jennings got bad news, or news that he
wasn't prepared for.

"I think he's bluffing," Jennings said, "to impress you. He
hasn't got the dough to pull this thing off."

"Personally, I hope he does buy that goddamn ranch out from
under you."

Jennings took a step toward Eva, then backed away, fuming.
"You have no idea what a disaster that would be, you little twit.

Not even the faintest idea. Nonetheless, I'll check it out. I can find out for certain whether Larkin can walk the talk.

"Now, keep going. What else came out at supper?"

"About the ranch, about Elements . . . what?" Eva asked.

"Yeah, about the ranch or about Elements," Jennings said impatiently.

"Nothing more about those things, really. We just ate and talked about other stuff. It was pleasant. Tom's a nice guy—a good guy. We had fun. I like him."

"Oh, now *Tom's* nice, is he?" Jennings ridiculed. "Tom's *nice*. I *like* him. Tom and I had a *very pleasant* supper. *Tom and I* are going on a cruise together next month. Tom *loves* me. He's going to get a divorce, and we're planning to get *married*. Jesus, Eva. Spare me."

Jennings was pacing and came to a stop directly in front of her. "You're not to see him again . . . other than a 'hi, how are you' at the front desk. Got that?" Jennings ordered.

"I'll see who I choose, when I choose. You don't run my life."

"Listen to yourself, Eva. You sound like a teenager in love. It's pathetic."

"You're pathetic, you prick."

"Watch your mouth."

"You watch my mouth," she said and clenched her jaw.

Jennings stood over her for what seemed a long time and then sat down next to her, resting his hand on her bare thigh.

She swatted it away and crossed her legs.

"What, no love for the father of your child?"

"Fuck you, Bill."

"Exactly what I had in mind."

"Well, get it out of your mind. That's not happening."

"You can't refuse me, girl!"

He was right. She'd fooled around with Jennings years ago, and she'd been paying for it ever since. She'd slept with Jennings to show her dad that he didn't control her life, she remembered, and it had backfired. She wound up with a child and had to spend a year "working in Omaha" to hide the pregnancy—and the child—from her father and the rest of them.

Little Shelly, Eva thought painfully. *Jennings is the only one who knows about her, and he could care less; my parents will never know about Shelly, and they want grandkids more than anything in the world.*

Shelly tied her to Jennings. The child had to be readmitted to the hospital within a few weeks of birth because she was born with Crohn's disease, a rare calcium disorder. By the time the doctors got her diagnosis correct, the child had developed Reiter's Syndrome, an early onset of arthritis that caused her to hobble and limp like an 80-year-old.

Shelly would never play tag with other children, or skip along the sidewalk just because it was sunny, or run after an errant spring kite.

Eva had returned to Hot Springs, telling everyone that the job didn't work out. Shelly was admitted to a long-term care facility in Nebraska. Jennings paid for everything.

Eva kept her mouth shut, did favors for Jennings when he asked, and ran off to Omaha every chance she got. Everybody in town had a theory about why she went out of town so often. Most of them believed she was having an affair with a rich married man.

Truth was, about the only sex Eva got anymore was an occasional bout with Jennings, and it was as disgusting to her as it was unsatisfying.

But how can I refuse him? she asked herself miserably.

"Look, Bill, I'm tired. Can we just not do this? Please?" She tried to get up off the couch.

Jennings pushed her back down.

"If you want everybody in town—including your father—to know that we created a little bastard together, fine with me. Go ahead and walk away; see what happens."

"You're the bastard, Bill, and if my dad ever found out he'd kill you."

"He might kill you, but he can't touch me and you know it," Jennings snorted.

"Piss off!"

"If I do, you'll be stuck paying for the little runt's medical bills, which amount to a bit more every month than you make all year working as a suck-up in your dad's hotel."

"Just leave Shelly out of this, you creep."

"You don't make the rules in this relationship, Eva. I do."

"This isn't a 'relationship,' it's slavery!" she bawled.

"Well, cry me a river, Eva. Just lose the panties while you're doing it, because Daddy's horny."

Eva panicked. *Oh god, why now*, she thought? He hadn't made her do this in months. *Why did he have to choose this night to torment me with sex. I can't do this. Not after being with Tom. I can't.*

She tried a different approach, forcing her voice to be calm. "Look, I just don't feel like it, Bill. Not tonight. Maybe tomorrow."

"Since when don't you feel like it? Well, I didn't feel like it either until you started flashing the goods in my face, but I do now." He knelt on the floor in front of her like a man about to propose marriage, and shoved her dress over her hips in one violent motion.

"No, goddamn it! I said no!" She was shouting and pulling her dress back down.

"Lower ... your ... voice ... right ... now." Jennings face was in an ugly twist that Eva had seen too many times before. There was no use fighting him.

She closed her eyes and waited.

His sour hands pushed her on her back and he climbed between her legs. She couldn't be sure that he'd entered her; his dick wasn't much bigger around than a pencil, and half as long. It was a miserable thing, even when it was hard, which was rare. She knew from experience that it would be over quickly and squeezed her eyes tighter, willing herself away to a world where just she and Tom and Shelly existed; where her dear little girl was happy and healthy; where the three of them could live together in peace.

"Tom," she whispered his name aloud. "Tom, hold me, Tom . . ."

Eva's fantasy ended with the slap of Jennings hand against her cheek.

When she opened her eyes to the pain, there he was standing over her with his little dick wagging as he ranted.

"Get out, you bitch! And if you sleep with that asshole, Larkin, then you better make it worth my while, you hear me? You better make it worth *my* while!" He continued to scream at her as she ran out of his office, down the silent green corridors of Veteran's Administration Building C, and into the frigid night.

SATURDAY

He's a walking contradiction, partly truth and partly fiction,
taking every wrong direction on his lonely way back home.
Kris Kristofferson, Pilgrim Chapter 33

———

7:20 A.M.

"Early bird gets the worm, Larkin," Burley chided when Tom entered the lobby.

"Keep the worms for yourself, Burley; I've already had an omelet and coffee," Tom said, grinning. "I'm good to go. How about you?"

"Let's hit the trail," Burley said.

Once in Burley's pickup truck, Tom asked, "Remember that ghost town we were talking about the night I got here?"

"Yeah, Igloo. Why?"

"I've got a hunch about Elements—Kathy and her reporter buddies are on to something, and I want to follow up on it, seeing as how Elements might try to cause us trouble if we make a run at the McPherson place."

"What do you need?" Burley asked.

"I need to know if those old Army bunkers out there are all the same size."

"Far as I know they are."

"Good. Now, I know this sounds a little crazy, but I want to go out there and measure one of them."

"Measure one of them bunkers?" Burley said with a laugh. "What the hell you want to do that for?"

"I just do. I can fill you in later if it turns out there's anything to it."

"You're serious."

"I am."

Pat turned west out of the hotel driveway, rather than north.

"Thanks, Pat. I'm indebted."

"Don't mention it. And, Larkin, I *mean* don't mention it. This ain't no national park we're visiting; it's private property. They come to arrest us, I'm telling them I was hijacked." Pat laughed, picked up his cell phone, and dialed the ranch owner they were supposed to meet that morning.

"Hank? It's Pat. Say ... that city slicker I got coming 'round to see your place this morning ... well, he's got some fool errand he wants to run before we head over to your place ... so we're running a tad late. See you 'round eight-thirty. That be any trouble for you?"

Burley laughed at whatever the ranch owner said and hung up.

Fifteen minutes passed before they reached the gates of the deserted and mostly disassembled ghost town of Igloo. Two hand-painted "No Trespassing" signs hung on either side of the stone gate that marked the edge of town.

"Are we going to be OK?" Tom said, pointing to the signs.

"Yeah, that don't mean nothing," Burley said. "It's just there to keep the tourists out. The real trespassing starts about a half-mile down this here road."

"How illegal is this, really ... going out there without permission?"

"It's kind of legal, and kind of illegal. Hard to explain."

"Mind giving it a whirl?"

"Most of the Elements property, including all but a half-dozen of them 800 bunkers, is surrounded by a ten-foot chain link fence with razor wire at the top. Makes it mighty unpleasant to climb over, but it keeps the riff-raff out.

"We aren't going to cross that fence. That's honest-to-God trespassing, and I ain't risking it. We might actually draw fire trying something foolish like that.

"However, there's a half-dozen or so of them bunkers out in the open on this side of the fence. We'll go take a look at one of them and hope that nobody takes exception. If anybody shows up and makes a fuss, I'm going to tell them I got some dumb shit client from East River who's wanted to see one of them bunkers his whole life, and I was just trying be accommodating. Sound like a plan?" Burley said.

"Let's be quick about it," Tom answered.

"No argument here."

Igloo is an eerie place. The only things still standing are a church, part of the school, and what looks like an office building. Block after block after block of empty foundations define a sad grid of lost opportunities.

As they neared the west side of town, Tom spied a cluster of 1950's style ramblers that looked to him like they were occupied.

"I thought you said this place was deserted," Tom said.

"It is—excepting a couple crazy old coots who come and go occasionally. Don't think they got running water, but there always seems to be electricity out here, so it attracts a certain kind of person that don't like the limelight, so to speak.

"Could even be that one or two of them folks works for Elements. Hell if I know," Pat continued. "People who live out here don't talk, and if anybody else knows something, he don't talk either."

The road split around a dilapidated brick sentry station at the far end of town. There had been no guard on duty there for decades. Still, Tom couldn't shake the feeling that, at any moment, a toothless guard, wearing tattered khakis and sporting a rusty

M-16, might spring from the shell of bricks and demand an explanation from them.

But there was no one there to challenge those who, by mishap or miscalculation, might pass along this road where nobody came and nobody went, except for this morning, when two men who had no business being there eased past, hoping that the crunch of their tires on the pitted asphalt wouldn't be heard and draw unwanted attention.

A quarter of a mile past the sentry station, the security fence cut across the road, barring any vehicle without a gate key from proceeding farther.

Beyond the fence, Tom could see scores of the bunkers, each identical to the others, nestled into ground that was more moonscape than Earth. Burley wheeled into the ditch, bumping up next to one of the strange buildings that stood just yards off the road.

"Get what you need, and let's get," Burley said.

"Dammit! I forgot to bring a tape measure."

Burley hopped out of the cab, opened a chrome toolbox that stretched from one side of the truck bed to the other, and tossed a fifty-foot tape measure to Tom.

"Need help?"

"I'm good!" Tom shouted back, already at the bunker wall.

While Pat strolled up to the structure, Tom took the outside measurements: length, width and height from the dirt berm to the roof line.

There was just one opening to the bunker, and it had no door.

"I'm going inside. Is it safe?" Tom called out.

"Let me go with you. I haven't been inside one of these little devils since I was a kid. I'm kind of curious to see it, myself," Pat said, and both men disappeared inside.

They stopped just inside the opening on a small platform overlooking a concrete floor several feet below them. After negotiating the corroded iron stairs, they found themselves engulfed in dust and shadows.

"Should've brought a flashlight," Burley said.

"Not really necessary," Tom answered. The bunker opening shed just enough light to make out the interior features.

Most of the bunker was below the surface, and there wasn't much of anything to see except what looked like two highly reinforced doors on opposite walls, about fifteen feet below ground level.

"Where do those lead?" Tom asked.

"Beats me. I don't remember nothing like that from when I was a kid."

Tom walked over to one of the doors and attempted to open it. Not a chance. It had been welded shut. He had the same luck with the other one.

"I don't care about the doors, Pat. Help me get the inside measurements. That's all I need for now. Then we can beat a path out of here."

As they made their way back past the empty guard station, Tom looked over at the ramblers they'd seen on their way in. In front of one, a man was holding both hands to his face as if he were shielding his eyes from the sun. *Or maybe,* Tom worried silently, *he's got binoculars. Hard to say from this distance. Best not tell Burley. It'll just get him worked up.*

SATURDAY, 8:30 A.M.

"Did you get the license plate number?" Jennings asked. "Good. Hold on, let me get something to jot that down."

Jennings instinctively reached for his jacket pocket, but it was empty. *Damn it,* he thought, *what became of that Parker?* The pen was a gift from the governor, inscribed with the Jennings family name. Jennings father had presented it to him at medical school graduation, and Jennings had carried the thing with him ever since. The pen didn't have any sentimental value to him; it was the idea of having misplaced—or lost—something that drove him crazy. Even a tiny disruption of Jennings' tightly-controlled world dogged him until he could reorder the situation.

He snatched up his prescription pad and a pencil.

"OK. Give it to me," he said to the person on the other end of the line. "And remember, don't say a word to anybody about this. Got it?"

Jennings hung up and dialed the state highway patrol headquarters.

"Hello? This is Dr. William Jennings, Veteran's Administration in Hot Springs ... Fine, thank you ... Yes, you can. I need the registration for South Dakota license plate number 4-1079 NL; can you get that for me? ... Yes, I realize it's Saturday, but this is a medical emergency ... Would you rather I call Governor Round's office and have them run the request over to you? ... I thought not. How long will it take? ... All right ... No, I'll wait."

Jennings scribbled down the vehicle owner's name and address on the slip of prescription pad, thanked the operator, and walked over to the window. He stood there, alternately staring at the name and staring out the window, for several minutes. Finally, he lit the piece of paper on fire, dropped it into an empty wastebasket, and called his attorney in New York.

"Brady?"

"Yeah, Doc."

"Lots of new developments, Phil. But first, tell me if you've made any progress on the Letter of Credit and the representation agreement with Qwestead."

"What have you got on their CEO, anyway, Doc?"

"What are you talking about?"

"Fifteen minutes after I left a message with his assistant, Qwestead's CEO personally returns my call, asking how he can help me. Unbelievable!"

"No, Phil. It's not unbelievable. Tell me what he said."

"He fell all over himself to be sure I understood that he wasn't turning your request down. He said he couldn't authorize a thing like that over the phone, that he had to run it through channels—but not to worry." Brady paused to catch his breath.

"It was cool, Doc."

"What happens next, Phil, and how long will it take?"

"You're really not going to believe this."

"Try me."

"He said he wanted to talk to you first, but that he should be able to get the LOC fired up by end-of-business on Monday, meaning you'd have the thing in hand on Tuesday, and that a draft copy of the representation agreement would be on your fax machine by tomorrow morning. Sunday, for Christ's sake."

"Good work, Phil. Now, let's move on. I need a work-up on a Thomas Michael Larkin of St. Paul, Minnesota. His wife, Kathleen, is a newspaper reporter. You getting all this?"

"Yup."

"We've already run a credit report on him, so get me the deep background—and I mean everything down to his shoe size."

"What'd he do to you, Doc?"

"He wants to buy the McPherson ranch, and so he's in my way. The putz and his wife aren't financially qualified to do it, but according to my sources, he's determined to make a run at the place. I don't think he's got a chance in hell of making it happen, but I'm not going to ignore him.

"Find something we can hang him with, Brady. One way or another, I'm going to take him out of the McPherson deal."

" 'Take him out,' Doc? Do you mean ..."

"No, you idiot. I don't mean kill him. I mean neutralize him using whatever tactic best suits our purpose and takes the least amount of time."

"Got it, Doc."

"Ready for the next item?"

"Shoot."

"My sources in Washington, D.C., tell me that Homeland Security is starting to sniff around Elements. If they are, it's a distraction we don't need at the moment. I need to know everything they know, and I need to know the name of the person there who can call off the dogs," Jennings commanded.

"Why would Homeland Security have any interest in the low-level bullshit you guys do out there?" Brady asked.

"That's what you're to find out. How long will it take?"

"This isn't something I can do; I don't have the juice. I'll have to go to a partner. I know you don't like me involving other members of the firm in your business, so ... it's your call."

"Do whatever you need to do. Just get me the information."

"Can you give me the name of your source, Doc? That might speed things up on our end," Brady said.

"No. I can't."

"I'll meet with a senior partner first thing Monday. Anything else for me?

"One last thing. You know that child, Shelly, that I'm paying for in Omaha?"

"Of course. What happened, they didn't get their check this month ... I sent it out like always ..."

Jennings cut him off. "No. Nothing like that. I want you to draw up custody papers for her."

"That's not my area, Doc. Can I get an associate to do that?" Phil asked.

"No associates on this one. Learn what you need to know from someone outside the firm. Then put the papers together yourself, and call me when they're ready for my review. Can you handle that?"

"Whatever you say, boss. Who's the lucky couple?"

"There is no lucky couple. I'll be taking custody of the child."

Brady quit scratching notes and stared blankly at his computer screen.

"Brady, you there?" Jennings barked.

"Doc? ... what are you going to do with a kid?"

"Your job is to get me custody. Why I want custody is none of your business. Are we clear about that?"

"We are, Doc."

"Put together two different custody packages. One of them will transfer sole custody to me through a voluntary release from the mother, Eva Shepherd."

"And the second package?"

"The second package must have all the documentation necessary for the State of South Dakota to declare the mother unfit to maintain custody of the child and to automatically remand custody to the biological father."

"Do we know who the father is, Doc?"

"It's me, Phil. I'm the father."

Brady was too stunned to comment.

"Now, pick your jaw up from the floor and get to work. I'm running out of time."

As they rolled into the yard at Trail's End, Pat turned to Tom and said, "You ain't interested in the place we saw this morning, are you?"

"It's a good piece of land, Pat, I think . . ."

"I got no time for bullshit, Larkin. Yes or no?"

"No."

"Thought as much. Same for the first ranch we saw yesterday?"

"Yeah, I'm spoiled after Trail's End," Tom admitted.

"That's just how I had you pegged, too, but we've got ourselves a problem—you can't afford this ranch. Am I right?"

"Fair statement," Tom said.

"We're going to take a run at this puppy anyway, Larkin. You with me?"

"Hell yeah! I'm lost without you, Burley."

"That you are, greenhorn. So, listen up. I've been kicking around a financing idea. If you like it, I want to go over it with Jo at dinner. And, please, let me do the talking."

"Whatever you think is best, Pat."

"Jo already told me she don't want Elements getting the ranch," Pat said, beginning to explain his plan, "so there ain't no way I'm ever going to see that big commission. The next best thing for me is to find another buyer who'll take this place at or near the listing price. That way I still get to cash a healthy check.

"Problem is," Pat continued, "it could easily take me several months, or a year, to find another buyer if you can't swing this deal.

"Every month I spend dickin' around trying to find a buyer is another month them Elements boys have to finagle a way to get the ranch. I'm in this business to make money, Tom, don't get me wrong. But I go back with Jo and Cody a long way. I intend to do what I think is best for Jo, even if it ain't the best for yours truly."

Tom looked at Pat with admiration.

"Jo's going to come busting through that door any second now, and we'll have missed our chance to talk," Pat said. "So, I think we ask Jo to sell the ranch on a contract for deed. You familiar with those?"

"You bet."

"Then you know that a contract for deed requires only ten percent down, rather than the twenty percent needed for conventional bank financing," Pat explained. "The owner loans you the balance of the selling price. There ain't no need for bank qualifying, the deal can get done in an hour if all the parties agree, and the whole thing happens under the radar. You follow?"

"I do. The downside is that if I can't make the payments, I could lose everything I've paid in without earning a dime of equity. That about the size of it?"

"Balls on, Larkin, but it's a risky way to buy and sell property, especially ranch or farm land. On your side of the ledger, if you default early, odds are you'll lose everything you've saved up over the past twenty, twenty-five years. On Jo's side, well, she ain't gettin' any younger, and she may have some plans for the ranch money that don't include waiting around another thirty years to collect it all.

"Then there's me. I have to find a way to get paid—and it's a tricky proposition in a deal like this here one. Who should pay the commission, the buyer or the seller? Should it be paid out of the down stroke? That'd eat up a goodly portion of it, which is why it usually don't happen that way. Should it be paid out pro rata, a little bit each month? That don't make the real estate guy too happy, 'cause it ain't certain he'll ever collect it all, and it dilutes the value of the commission."

"So what are you recommending?" Tom asked.

"I'm telling you that, if Jo McPherson is willing to take a contract for deed, you sign it and run, Larkin. It's your only hope. You can make the ten percent down stroke, can't you, Larkin?"

"No problem, Pat," Tom said, thinking that, even without Carl's money, he could sell the house, cash in the 401K's and get a personal loan to fill in any gap. If all of that were required, it would be the biggest risk he had ever taken in his life.

"What about your commission, Pat?" Tom continued. "I need to know that you're going to get paid, or I swear to God I'll walk away. I mean that."

"I believe you, Larkin. And that's why we're going to make this work. I'll tell Jo that you're each responsible for paying half my commission, which will now be eight instead of six percent. You each have five years to pay me your half of it, and you can set your schedule of payments any damn way you like. As for you, Larkin, you're going to write me into the contract for deed as a lien holder to cover my butt. You comfortable with that?"

The arrangement was more than fair. It was a gift. Tom couldn't really see Jo agreeing to such a drawn-out arrangement, but it was worth a try.

"All Jo can say is no, Pat. Let's give her a rip!"

"Thank God all my clients aren't like you, Larkin," Burley said with a grin. They shook on the deal and got out of the truck.

As they mounted the porch stairs, Pat said, "Just remember to let me do the talking when it comes to the money, Larkin, and we'll be fine."

The smell of dinner filled the porch.

"Somebody in there fixin' to feed a couple of hungry cowboys?" Pat yelled.

Jo appeared at the door, phone in hand, and motioned them in. When they'd cleaned their boots, hung up their jackets and put their hats on the tree in the hall, Jo put her hand over the phone and said, "I'm awfully sorry, boys; I'll be just another few minutes. Just make yourselves to home," and went back to her conversation.

"We'll be in the dining room," Pat called back.

Jo's voice could be heard over the rattle of cooking lids on the stove, and both men fell silent, listening.

"Yes, Henry," Jo said, "I'm quite certain of the changes to the will. Don't bother going into all your legalese, now. It's what I want done. It's what Cody would want done. Can you get those changes made and bring them out here this afternoon?

"I know it is Saturday, Henry. Are you telling me you don't work on Saturday these days?

"Well, then, please make an exception this one time. I'm an old lady and I like to have things my way. So if you'd just be a dear and write those things up and come on out to the ranch later today, we can be done with it. Will you do that, Henry?

"Thank you so much. And yes, I'll call Ellie, and you can just pick her up on your way out here. I'm sure she won't mind taking time to witness the changes. See you soon. Bye-bye."

Pat and Tom started making small talk the instant Jo hung up so she wouldn't think they'd been doing something rude, like eavesdropping.

"So ... Tom ... what do you think about the Pederson place? They'll be expecting us around two," Pat said, to be saying something.

"Well, Pat, I expect we'd better ..." Tom started to say, but Jo walked through the door and interrupted.

"Did you boys get the gist of that?" She smiled.

"Get what?" Pat said.

Tom looked at his fingernails.

"Patrick Burley, you know exactly what I'm talking about," she said with a smile. "Did you hear what I was talking to old Henry Finn, my lawyer, about?"

"Well, yeah, I guess I picked up a few bits and pieces there at the end. Sounds like you're making some changes to your will?"

"That's right. I'll tell you boys all about it over dinner. Now, if you're planning to eat yet today, get off your hindquarters and give me a hand in the kitchen."

With Jo directing traffic, the roast and a half-dozen side dishes were out of the kitchen and on the table inside five minutes. Steam from the feast hung in the air like pond fog in the early morning, and the room took on the feel of a memory.

Jo stood surveying the banquet, working her hands in the apron she still wore. Things must have met with her approval, because she took the apron off, tossed it on the sideboard and said, "Now, sit yourselves down, both of you! Go on, sit!"

Of course, neither Tom nor Pat did. Tom stepped up behind Jo and held her chair. "After you, Mrs. McPherson."

In mock sternness Jo said, "I hear another 'Mrs. McPherson' out of you, sonny, and you'll have no dessert!"

"Yes, *Jo*."

Pat held the roast out for Jo to help herself first, and dinner was underway.

A few minutes into the meal, Jo turned to Tom.

"Now, about that conversation I was having with Mr. Finn. It's important that I tell you what I've done; then we can get on with whatever business matters Patrick has in mind."

Tom stopped eating and folded his hands on his napkin.

"No need for you to starve while I rattle on, Tom. You go right ahead with your meal; it'll upset me if your food gets cold before you eat it.

"As I was saying, I've asked my attorney to make some changes to my will. I did a lot of thinking about things after you and Pat were here yesterday, and I wanted to get some things done while they were fresh in my mind.

"For example, what would happen to this ranch if I up and died suddenly?"

"You're too ornery to die, Jo," Pat managed between bites, "You'll still be kicking hind end at bingo when they're pattin' me on the breast with a spade."

"Isn't he a sweet boy?" Jo said to Pat, and went on speaking directly to Tom.

"Cody was the only son of an only son, and we have no children—no direct heirs. Although Cody has two sisters, they're married and both doing quite well for themselves. I've got a brother that I don't see so very often anymore. He's older than me and lives alone somewhere on the Rosebud. So, when I die, the McPherson name—*Cody's* name—dies with me." Jo's voice caught and she couldn't go on.

Tom put his fork down and reached over to put his hand on top of Jo's. "I remember Cody," Tom said quietly, giving Jo time to recover her composure. "He was a good man."

Jo reached up to clasp Tom's hand. She gave it a light squeeze, said, "Thank you, Tom," and released his hand.

"Now where was I? Oh, yes—the will. Cody and I didn't exactly see eye-to-eye about what we should do with the ranch when we were both gone," Jo said. "Of course, we agreed that whichever one of us survived the other should stay on and work the place as long as possible, but after that, we were of two different minds.

"Cody had a notion of donating the ranch to a medical school; he wanted it to go to the one run by the Mayo Clinic over in Minnesota. I told him that if we were going to be donating the ranch, or the money from selling the ranch, that I wanted some of it to go to the church, and the rest of it to go to either Sinte Gleska University over on the Rosebud, or to set up scholarships in our name for local ranch kids who want to continue on after high school.

"While Cody and I had some general agreement on giving money for education, we weren't of one mind as to what institution, and Cody didn't have the slightest interest in giving money to the church."

"Then how did you settle things?" said Pat.

"We didn't settle anything; Cody died before we got things squared away. So I've decided to just split things up fifty-fifty. I'll decide how half should be donated, and Cody's half will go to the Mayo Clinic.

"I'm also changing the will to state that, if I die before the ranch is sold, all mineral and mining rights will be separated from the property and deeded to the federal government."

"Why give the mineral rights to the government?" Pat asked.

"Because it's the only way I can think of to keep them safe."

"What are you talking about, Jo, 'keep them safe'?" Pat asked.

"It's not something I want to get into just now, Pat. I can only tell you that I will have to be convinced that I can put my trust in whoever buys this ranch, or the mineral rights go to the government."

Tom chewed in silence.

"However," Jo continued, "if young Tom here makes up his mind to take over the ranch, I'll tell him my concerns, and he can have the mineral rights—or not have them—as he sees fit." She reached over, took Tom's hand in hers, and held it tight.

Pat took this comment as his cue.

"I don't know what you're referring to with the mineral rights and all, Jo, but seeing how you brought it up, maybe we ought to talk about Tom's interest in the ranch," he said. "Maybe that'll help clear the air a bit."

"That's a good idea, Patrick." Jo began to pick at the food on her plate. "You talk now. I'll eat."

"Tom wants to buy the place, Jo. No question. Even if he can't buy it, I think you're going to play hell trying to get rid of him.

He said he'd work as a hired hand for three squares and a bunk just to stay on here."

Jo looked at Tom and smiled. "Somehow, that doesn't surprise me."

"Tom wanting the ranch isn't the issue, Jo, so I'll come right to the point. He and his wife can get a bank loan, no problem. Just about anybody will loan money at 80% of value—the problem is that that kind of loan would require them to come up with twenty percent down. They're short at that number."

"Knowing you as long as I have, Pat Burley, I'm guessing that you already have something in mind to remedy the situation," Jo said.

"Do you know what a contract for deed is, Jo?"

"Passing familiarity," she said. "Is that what you have in mind?"

"I do."

"Give me the specifics ... and in plain English, if you don't mind," Jo said.

"First, you don't get much money at sale. Contracts for deed normally call for ten percent down, and that's all you get up front.

"Second, you are the bank for the buyer. Tom makes monthly payments to you until the balance of the purchase price has been paid.

"How long does that take?" Jo asked.

"There's a lot of ways to set that up, Jo. Tom can only afford a payment based on a 30-year mortgage. For you, of course, thirty years is too long a payout term. So, we propose a ten-year balloon on the note."

"What does that mean, Pat?" Jo said.

"That means Tom makes payments for ten years as if he were paying on a 30-year note, and at the end of the tenth year, he has to completely pay off whatever remains of the balance on the note," Pat explained.

"What if he can't do that?"

"Worst case? He loses everything he's put into the deal and you get the ranch back," Pat said.

Jo was silent.

"The risks for Tom are fairly obvious, but there are risks for everybody in this kind of arrangement," Pat said. "You can always take the ranch back if Tom stops making payments, but then you've got the ranch to deal with again. Plus, things can get messy in a default."

"What about you, Pat. What's your risk?"

"I'm your listing agent, and a contract for deed makes it tough for me to collect my full commission."

Jo smiled. "Tell me your plan to take care of the Burley children, Pat."

"First, Tom pays the listing price, and that's what we figure my commission on. You each owe me half my commission, and you can pay me any way you want to, just have it paid by the end of five years. In exchange for these concessions on my part, my commission rate goes from six percent to eight percent. How does that strike you?"

Jo sat in silence and said nothing. Tom's heart was pounding so hard he felt sure Jo would notice. He didn't dare look at her, but he didn't dare stare at his boots either. He was in agony.

More seconds ticked away while Jo fiddled with a few stray peas on her plate.

"There'd have to be a couple of conditions—if we do this," she said, her eyes locked on Tom.

Tom drew in a sharp breath and didn't wait to hear Jo's conditions. "I am so grateful, Jo. I will take care of your land, I swear it. Thank you."

"Well, you haven't heard my demands yet, young man. If I was you, I wouldn't be so quick to agree until you hear what I want."

Jo turned to Pat.

"You know I'd probably just hand the place over to Tom if I'd had a glass of wine or two," she said, "but there are some things that, as a practical matter, we have to get right."

"What do we need to do?"

"First, it's good that Tom has agreed to pay the listing price, because Henry says he's already gotten a good deal of grief from Jennings' lawyers about turning down their offer. I'm afraid that if I sold at anything less than the listing price, I'd be asking for trouble. Lord knows I don't need all that money, but we don't need any more legal high jinx from Elements, either.

"I'd be happy to settle for far less than ten percent down, but I suspect that'd give those fellas from Elements reason to cry foul, too. So, ten percent is more than plenty. You put any interest rate on the note you think is fair, Pat.

"I told you about my will because it has bearing on what happens to this ranch. I will tell Henry to attach a copy of the will to the contract for deed. That brings me to the first condition.

"Tom will agree not to transfer mineral or mining rights to the ranch to anyone under any conditions," she said. "He may exercise his own right to mine, if he chooses, but it must be done by Tom or under Tom's direct supervision. If Tom sells the ranch, the mineral rights revert to the United States federal government."

Tom's thoughts were not on the contract with Jo, but were racing ahead trying to figure out how he would be able to honor Jo's request on the mining rights and keep his deal with Carl intact at the same time. A million and a half bucks was riding on Tom's ability to come up with an answer to that question.

"Agreed on the mining rights?" Jo asked.

Pat looked to Tom. "Agreed," Tom said.

"Good," Jo said, and stood up abruptly and left the room.

She returned to the dining room with a notebook in her hand and set it down in front of her plate as she seated herself back at the table.

"This is a journal that Cody kept," she said. "I know you're wondering what all the fuss is about the mineral rights. Cody showed this to me a couple of months before he died, and he told me that he'd been looking into some things about the cattle lick out there by the southwest fence. He said somebody was interested in it, 'cause he'd seen tracks other than his and Boone's out there for going on two years now, but he couldn't figure out who they belonged to or what they were doing. He also said he was suspicious of those men who run the Elements company in Hot Springs. Said they were up to no good.

"For the past couple of years, Dr. Jennings had been after Cody to sell him the ranch," Jo continued. "Cody wouldn't hear of it. If he told me once, he told he a hundred times that he wouldn't sell our land to Jennings if he were the last man on earth.

"I've looked at the journal, Tom. And I can't make much of it, other than I know it was serious to Cody." She stopped and made an effort to keep her tears in check. "He died out there, Tom. So, I'm giving this to you. If you can figure out what it means, it'd mean a lot to me."

Jo slid the journal over to Tom.

"I'll do my best, Jo."

"I know you will."

She brushed a wisp of gray hair from her forehead and continued on with the contract conditions. "So, you must agree not to sell this ranch to Dr. Bill Jennings or to his company, the Elements Corporation." She looked to Tom.

"That is a promise, Jo," he said.

Jo cast her eyes down for a moment and breathed out deeply.

"Third," she said, looking more herself, "the balloon payment can be set at fifteen, rather than ten years. I want Tom to have as much time as possible to get refinanced. If I should die—and there is a distinct possibility of that happening at some point—

I can't trust that whoever will be executing my estate will be as fond of Tom as I am. I'll assume that this condition is not a problem.

"Fourth—and this one may be a bit difficult, I know—but if I should get very ill or have an accident, and the medical costs run more than what Tom is paying me each year, then you'll have to pay up on the contract right away. Can you figure something like that out, Pat?" Jo said.

Pat was impressed. Jo had had all of ten minutes to absorb the entire concept of a contract sale before agreeing to it and devising conditions that would protect her in a worst-case scenario.

"Tom," Pat started, "This could be a serious problem for you if …"

Tom cut him off. He clearly saw the risk in agreeing to such a condition. In his mind, however, the deal was done. No obstacle was too high, no unknown too risky. He was all-in.

"Agreed, Jo. I agree to everything with the single caveat that my wife Kathy has to sign off on this—or the whole kit and caboodle goes up in smoke."

"That's just as it should be, Tom. I'm anxious to meet Kathy."

Turning to Pat, Jo said, "How long it will take to get a contract like this drawn up?"

"Hardly any time at all, Jo," Pat said. "A contract for deed can be very straightforward. We don't have to get any banks involved, which cuts out ninety-nine percent of the bullshit that we'd otherwise have to slog through.

"Hell, I could write the damn thing up myself in an hour," Pat boasted. "Another thing that's in our favor is that we don't have to register the agreement to have it be completely legal and binding."

"Well, I hope you have been paying close attention, Patrick, because my fifth request is that we get the contract signed immediately," Jo stated. "Today would not be too soon for me."

Tom and Pat exchanged a quick glance. "I'm fine with whatever we come up with, as long as it's Burley that writes it up," Tom said.

"What else, Jo?" Burley asked.

"That's about it ..." she said, winking at Tom, "... except ... well ... I'm not all that happy with the eight percent commission ... seems a mite high to me—what do you think, Tom? Are we going to let Patrick get away with this highway robbery?"

The negotiation, such as it was, was over.

"Could be a deal killer, couldn't it, Jo?" Tom said in mock seriousness. "But, I'll tell you what. Burley is starting to grow on me. If you can see your way clear to paying the four points, even though I think it's sky-high, I'll do the same just to get him out of our hair and keep him from whining. What do you want to do?"

"I think I'll dust off that old bottle of sherry in the china cabinet, Tom, don't you think?"

Tom got up, took Jo by both hands, raised her to her feet and swept her into his arms. "I think you're wonderful, Jo, that's what I think!" Tom didn't know whether to laugh or cry or do a jig. So he hugged Jo McPherson close and danced her right on into the kitchen.

A HALF-HOUR LATER, they were back in Pat's truck.

Tom let out a war whoop and gave Burley an awkward hug that left his cowboy hat tipped at a comical angle.

"Yes! Yes! Yes!" Tom shouted, his head bobbing up and down. "You are—without a doubt—a goddamn genius, Burley!"

Laughing while he righted his Stetson, Burley said, "Yeah, well, now you know why they pay me the big bucks, my fine-feathered friend!"

When they'd tired of congratulating and complimenting each other, Tom asked, "So, what's the plan, now, Pat?"

"I'm headed down to the Century 21 office in Hot Springs. They've got all the contract forms on their computer, and that's all I need to get this thing whipped into shape. If you're not coming with me, I need to know how to reach you with any questions."

"Drop me off at the hotel. I've got to call Kathy right away, of course. I can't wait to tell her everything. And I suspect that she'll have to sign the agreement—so I need her approval, right?"

"Right you are, Larkin."

"Contact me on my cell phone if you need me. If I don't hear from you, I'll drive over to Century 21 when I'm done talking to Kathy. We can send a fax right to our house, so getting her signature won't be a problem."

"What if the cell signal isn't good today?"

"Just call my cell phone; I'll explain later," Tom said. "By the way, did Jo look all right to you, this afternoon?"

"Now that you mention it, she did seem a mite peaked, didn't she?"

"Understandable … I suppose," Tom said, "given what we put her through in a few short hours this afternoon. Still, she looked tired."

"She's about to sell the place she's lived her entire adult life," Pat replied soberly. "She's obviously thrilled about you being the next owner, but selling the ranch has got to take a toll on her. So don't spend too much of your energy getting overly anxious about Jo. You've got hell's own half-acre of cats to herd, now that you're taking over Trail's End from Jo."

You don't know the half of it, Burley, Tom thought. *You don't know the half of it.*

SATURDAY, 1:30 P.M.

"**Y**our motor's running a mile a minute, Tom. Slow down and start over from the beginning," Kathy said soothingly. "You said that you negotiated a deal for the ranch? Isn't this a bit ... " Kathy caught herself. She knew that if she started criticizing before Tom had a chance to deliver his news, they'd be in for a nasty confrontation. "I mean to say, Tom, isn't this a bit of a *miracle*, in such a short time?"

"You're damn straight it's a miracle, Kath! You can't believe how well it went. I was there and can hardly believe it myself!"

Kathy laughed despite her reservations. *Don't pretend to be neutral,* she reminded herself. *I've definitely got a dog in this fight.*

"OK. Lay it on me, Tom. What happened out there today?"

"Give me one sec, Kathy," Tom said.

Kathy sensed that Tom was lining up his key arguments and calculating the most advantageous way to present his information. It hurt Kathy more than she let on when Tom chose to give her a sales presentation rather than simply share information—and his feelings—with her.

"Just tell me how it went, Tom, and spare me the pitch."

"Right," Tom said. "The big news is that Burley concocted a financing plan that eliminates the bank and lowers our down payment."

"This doesn't involve more Hot Springs 'mafia' money, does it, Tom?"

"No, it doesn't. It involves Jo McPherson financing us with a contract for deed. Are you familiar with those?"

"That's owner financing, right?"

"Right."

"And isn't it true," Kathy continued, "that if you miss any payments, or default in any way, the owner can take the property back and you lose everything? Would it work like that?"

"The shit you know amazes me, Kathy."

"Just answer me, Tom. If we were to buy the ranch on a contract for deed, would we lose everything if we default?"

"Well, technically, yes, we could," Tom began. "Is it asking too much of you to hear me out before you jump to a whole slew of conclusions that'll take me an hour to untangle?"

"Sorry, boss," Kathy mumbled to herself.

"Yesterday, you and I agreed that we can handle the mortgage payments for the first two or three years, so there is very little that can go wrong during that time. Now, let's just say, theoretically speaking, that in the fourth year, we find that we can't make the monthly payments anymore. That would be a default.

"After a default, there is a remedy period, usually sixty days, to correct it. If it isn't corrected, the owner has to foreclose on the contract holder, that's us, and that usually takes three to four months, minimum. If a foreclosure is successful, the contract holder—again, that would be us—has what is called a 'redemption period' of six more months to correct the default and reclaim the property. So our worst-case scenario is to put the ranch back up for sale, pay off the balance of the contract, and walk away with our equity."

"That is assuming there is enough time to get the ranch resold, and that land prices remain the same or rise, correct?" Kathy asked.

"Correct. And to that last point, the raw land values in this part of the country have been rising at an average annual rate between two and three percent every year for the past fifteen years. That means, in three years, the ranch will be worth roughly $600,000 more than it is today.

"I think, all told, that's a reasonable risk."

"I really appreciate that full explanation, Tom. This is a huge decision, and I can't go along for the ride unless I thoroughly understand what we're letting ourselves in for."

"No argument, Kathy. I'm sorry I snapped at you. You have every right to know the details down to the gnat's ass. What do you want to know next?"

"Are we really going to get the down payment from your buddy Carl?"

Short time and overreaching desire are often sworn enemies of the truth. Having both in excess, Tom lied.

"Yes, Kath, Carl gave me his word on it. I expect the City will be underwriting the down payment."

"But we won't know for sure until he meets with the City Council, right?"

"That's right."

"When does that happen?"

"Carl said it'd be Monday afternoon," Tom lied again. "What else?"

"I don't really know enough to ask detailed financial questions, but I do think we should talk some more about whether we're really, truly ready to live on a ranch in western South Dakota, don't you think?"

Tom sat at his end of the phone line silently, clenching his teeth and staring at the wall.

"Tom, are you still there? Don't you think we should talk about this some more?" Kathy asked again.

Tom began to speak slowly and softly. "Kathy, do you remember how many nights we sat up together over a bottle of wine discussing this very thing? And how, at first, you were dead set against moving out of St. Paul? And then, I was unsure about it, and you were encouraging me to stick with the idea of buying a ranch? And how we have gone over and over each other's concerns . . . and hopes . . . every way from Sunday?

"And now, it isn't just pillow talk anymore—it's real. It's possible. Now we have a real decision to make with real consequences for how things go the rest of our lives."

Kathy appreciated Tom's tone and the fact that he remembered their discussions with fondness. His last comment about consequences, though, sounded ominous to her. "Yes, of course I remember what we said, Tom. What exactly are you getting at?"

"Not so much what I'm getting at, sweetheart, but where you and I seemed to arrive at together."

"Which was where?" Kathy asked.

"You tell me, Kathy."

"Well," Kathy stumbled, "I guess, honestly, we thought that, if everything lined up as we discussed—you know, so that we both were satisfied—it would be a good thing to try. We also agreed that there was no way we could be absolutely sure that this kind of thing would work out."

Tom remained silent.

"We knew it would be a big financial risk, but we weren't going to take one that was likely to be a catastrophe. So I guess the McPherson ranch is OK on that count because of what you just said about reselling and all that."

"Kathy," Tom whispered, "You and I both know that things haven't been good between us for a while now. I think that we would have a chance to build something new out here, a chance to restart. It isn't just the ranch I want, Kathy."

While Kathy couldn't be completely sure that Tom wasn't just using their relationship to his advantage, he sounded sincere to her, and she knew that if she and Tom didn't find some way to begin rebuilding their marriage, it wasn't going to last.

Kathy closed her eyes, exhaled, and gave herself over to the conclusion to which Tom had artfully steered her.

"We've pretty much said it all, haven't we, Tom?" she said, seeing his purpose now. "It boils down to whether the McPherson ranch is *the one*, doesn't it?"

"It does, Kathy."

"Is this the one? Tom, is it? The one for us?"

"Yes, it is, Kathy … and you are going to fall in love when you see it. I promise you'll never want to leave. So when you come out here, darlin', pack what you need for the rest of your life."

Tom sat silently, waiting. Kathy sat in St. Paul, her love for Tom in a furious battle with her instinct for doing the safe thing, which did not include buying a multi-million dollar ranch in the Black Hills, sight unseen.

In the end, she followed Tom's instincts rather than her own.

"What do we do next, Tom? Wait until Carl and the City Council make up their minds and then sign the contract?" Kathy said.

"Let me ask you this, Kathy, are we together on this?"

"We are, Tom. Let's buy the ranch—or at least try," Kathy vowed. "How soon after we hear back from Carl do we sign on the line?"

"Pat is working on the contract as we speak. I'm going over to the local real estate office to meet him as soon as we are off the phone. For whatever reason she has, and I'm sure they are good ones, Mrs. McPherson would like to execute the contract just as soon as possible, preferably today."

"Today! Are you serious, Tom? I haven't even seen the ranch!" Kathy protested.

"I know, I know. Please don't get yourself all worked up about this before I have a chance to explain."

"Sorry, Tom. Go ahead."

"First, and most importantly, I don't want this opportunity to slip through our hands," he said. "Elements made a huge offer on the ranch, and I don't want Jo to have time to change her mind, or have someone talk her out of selling at a third of what she could otherwise get. Things happen in a void, Kathy. I would regret not signing this contract until the day I died if someone else got the ranch.

"Second, the only thing we have at risk is the earnest money, and I'll write a clause in the contract that says if we can't come up with the down payment, for any reason—including that you just don't like the place—we can get our earnest money back and the deal is off.

"Can you go along under those conditions, Kathy?"

Tom makes a good argument, Kathy thought, *as always.* "All right, under those conditions, it seems like all we're doing is preserving the opportunity without putting anything at risk. I can live with that."

Tom breathed a long sigh of relief.

"We can discuss this at length when you get home tomorrow, or Monday if you get in late," she added.

"That's another thing. If we can't get this signed off on today, I don't think it'd be wise for me to come home. I think I should just stay in a full-court press until the deed is done," Tom said.

"But you promised you'd be home Sunday."

"And I will, if we can get through this conversation so I can help Burley finish drafting the contract for deed. Otherwise, I'll just have to stay over."

She was cornered.

"Oh, Jesus, Tom, all right. How do we get it done today?"

"Two things. You stay by the fax machine at home. As soon as Pat and I have the details worked out, I'll fax you the contract and then call to discuss any questions you have."

"And the other thing?" she asked.

"Call the online brokerage firm that handles your stock plan and have them transfer ten grand into our joint checking account. This is critical."

"Why not just call them yourself, Tom? You know how these things work much better than I do."

"I'd be happy to, Kathy, but the account is in your name and they won't talk to me; otherwise, it would already be done."

"Oh."

"It's easy enough to do, Kathy. Just get your account number from that three-ring binder above my desk. The brokerage answers their phones seven days a week. Sell some of the stock if you don't have enough cash in the account—they'll walk you through the procedure. Are you clear on that?"

"I think so."

"Fantastic! We're set then," Tom said.

"Is the ten thousand dollars for the earnest money?"

"Yeah. Pat and I haven't discussed the exact amount, but I figure we can get by with as little as twenty or twenty-five thousand dollars, and we don't have that much sitting in the joint account at the moment. Sure you're OK with the transfer?"

"I said I'll get it done."

Tom indicated that it was time to hang up. Kathy wanted to talk.

"What else did Jo say? I mean, was she excited, or sad, about giving up her ranch? You can't leave me hanging like this; give me some juicy details, mister!"

Kathy loved to pore over the details long after the main topic had been decided, just like she loved to cuddle and kiss after making love. She figured that she'd given him everything he wanted; he owed her fifteen minutes of small talk.

"Juicy details, eh? Hmmm . . . let me see." Tom spied Cody's journal on the bed next to him. "I've got something for you," he cried, snatching up the journal.

"What? Sounds exciting!"

"Mysterious is more like it."

"Oh goody," she cried. "Do you mind waiting one sec while I fix myself a drink? This sounds like fun!"

"Make it quick, you lush. Sorry I'm not there to get you really drunk and take advantage of you," he teased.

"Me too," she purred. "Back in a jiffy."

The rattle of ice cubes signaled Kathy's return. "What about the mystery?"

"OK. Here's the weird thing. Jo was saying that I couldn't sell the mining and mineral rights to anybody . . ." Tom stopped in mid-sentence and froze.

"Wait a minute, Tom," Kathy said. "If you can't sell the mineral rights, where does that leave us with the Elements' offer, which, as I recall, was what we were going to live on for the next thirty years?"

"Not a big deal," Tom sputtered. "We can still pursue any kind of mining we choose, we just can't sell the rights. I'll work the deal through with Carl so that it conforms to the contract for deed and it gives him what he wants. You with me?"

"Isn't that twisting Jo's intent?"

"Maybe it is, Kathy, maybe it isn't. All I know is that we will not violate the letter of the contract, and right now, that's the important thing. Remember, we're just preserving an opportunity this afternoon; we're not signing on to anything that we can't undo. We OK?"

"Yeah. We're OK, I guess."

"Kathy. Are we OK?" Tom insisted.

"Yes, Tom. We are OK." Kathy snapped back.

"Good. Now, do you want to hear some inside dope from the late Cody McPherson's personal journal that's sitting in my hot little hands? Or, do you want to talk about those boring mineral rights?"

Kathy brightened immediately.

"You've got Cody's personal journal? What's in it?"

"Well, I don't rightly know," Tom said. "I just got back from the ranch, and I haven't so much as cracked the spine. But as I was saying, after Jo got me to agree on the mineral rights, she placed this journal in my hands like it was the Holy Grail. Then she tells me that Cody had been looking into some calcium or whatever for a couple of years, and that she wanted me to find out what it all meant. Is that mysterious enough for you?"

"Quit teasing me. Open it up and read some of it!"

"We really don't have time. Let me call you back tonight."

"Oh come on, Tom, I caved on all this legal and financial mumbo jumbo for you; just read me two or three pages, you bum."

Tom flipped through a couple of pages and stopped arbitrarily. "Listen to this," he said, and began to read verbatim from Cody's journal:

> *June 10, 2001* Got *The Miracle of Druid Medicine* book in the mail. Sounds like they were using something like what's out in the lick to cure stuff from tooth decay to pneumonia. Need to check that article about using calcium medicine in France. Maybe that stuff is useful for something other than cattle.
>
> NOTE TO MYSELF: Send a soil sample in to the County Extension Agent.

"At the risk of sounding stupid, Tom, what's a 'lick'?"

"I'll remind you when I get home ..."

"Now be serious!" she scolded sweetly.

"OK ... a cow lick. More to the point, a mineral lick. Remember the mineral blocks we set out for the horses when we were on the farm? On the McPherson ranch, there's a naturally occurring deposit of minerals that the livestock use for that purpose; it's called a lick. Don't know if I told you or not, but that's where Cody died."

"Are you kidding me?"

"No, why?"

"Just a wild thought. Read some more."

Tom flipped through another couple of pages and stopped at one that had a document marked "Extension Office" clipped to it. "Here's something that might be interesting:"

July 31, 2001 Test from the County Extension inconclusive. They say it's mostly normal stuff in the lick, but found some kind of unusual chemical bond thing. They said it had higher than normal radiation—but don't seem a bit concerned about it. Said it was probably just leakage from all the uranium mining activity over at Edgemont in the fifties.

NOTE TO MYSELF: Get another opinion on this stuff.

"Why would they test for radiation?" Kathy asked.

"I'll bet they routinely test every soil sample from around this part of the county for radiation," Tom said.

"Good point. I'm sure that's true."

Tom flipped the page and exclaimed, "Listen to this one, Kathy:"

August 4, 2001 Doc Jennings called again, wanting to buy the ranch. Sounded pretty irritated, more than usual. I told him to quit dogging me, I ain't selling at any price, and I ain't selling to him never. Guy won't quit, been after me for a year. I wonder what's put a burr under his saddle?

NOTE TO MYSELF: Next time Jennings calls asking to buy the place, ask him if he wants to buy just the lick. See what he says to that.

"Stop, Tom." Kathy's voice had a serious edge to it. "You said Jo was adamant about not selling off the mineral rights to the ranch?"

"Yes," Tom answered, wary.

"Well, I'm guessing she's talking about whatever is going on at that—what did you call it—cow lick?"

"Yeah, a cow lick."

"Well, it seems pretty clear that Cody was on to something out there. And it's equally clear that neither Jo nor Cody wanted Dr. Jennings and his bunch to have anything to do with it . . . regardless of what it turns out to be. You reading the situation the way I am?"

"Now what?" Tom asked.

"Well," Kathy said, "now you better start working on some creative plan to pay our living expenses, because I'm not signing any mining rights over to Elements. Period. I don't care how many millions of dollars they give us; it's as plain as the nose on your face that Jo doesn't want Elements Corporation having *anything* to do with her ranch."

"I gave Carl my word, Kathy."

"You gave Jo McPherson your word, too, Tom. You can't honor both."

"What am I supposed to do, choose sides? I can't do that."

"Well, I know whose side I'm on, and I don't know either side from Adam," Kathy vowed. "You have to choose, Tom, and you have to do it right now!"

"I'll tell Carl the deal's off," Tom said. "It's the only way."

"Good. That's settled. And don't come back to me with any agreement that asks me to fudge on this issue, because I won't sign. You know I won't."

"I'm on the same page, Kath. Don't worry. I agree with you," Tom insisted, sounding more like he was trying to convince himself than Kathy.

"Well, then. It seems you've got quite a good deal of work to do and precious little daylight left, Mr. Big Shot Rancher. I suggest you get that nice little butt of yours in gear."

"Be sure you transfer the money and stay close to the fax machine."

"I'm here, waiting for your call, lovey lamb."

"Talk to you in about an hour or so," Tom said, and hung up.

SATURDAY, 2:00 P.M.

Tom would have preferred to escape the lobby without being noticed, but Eva had her eyes on him and motioned him over to the front desk.

"Hey, stranger. Where're you headed so fast?"

"Meeting Burley. Big doings," Tom clipped off, signaling his haste. "You get home all right last night?"

"I got home, put it that way," she fudged. "Got a minute?"

"To tell the truth, I really don't," Tom said, all business, and kept walking. The abruptness of his comment, or perhaps its tone, doused the sparkle in her eyes and they fell away from his.

Tom saw that he'd hurt her and it stung him. He walked back to the counter and leaned in to her.

"Of course," he said softly, "I've got a minute. What's on your mind?"

Eva's adoring eyes jumped back up to meet Tom's.

"It was wonderful of you to stay with me for supper last night ... and to forgive me. I'd like to return the favor. Would that be OK?" she asked shyly.

"Are you asking me out on a date?"

"Call it whatever you want to, Tom; I consider it a peace offering."

Tom didn't have time to be diplomatic or negotiate. He was in a hurry and said the first thing that came to mind.

"How about the Lucky Strike at, say, sevenish?"

"That would be OK, Tom, but I was just thinking that you might prefer a little home cooking, instead." Without waiting for Tom to respond, Eva continued, "I get off work at three, and I'll need to stop by the grocery store. So ... why don't we say eight o'clock at my place. Four-oh-four Sherman, right as you come into town from the north," she said, writing her address down on a hotel pad.

Tom's reached out to accept the slip of paper. He knew that there were plenty of reasons to stay away from Eva Shepherd in the light of day. Being in her house at night, with her bedroom just a step away—and his several hundred miles distant—wasn't the only reason he felt conscience-stricken about accepting her invitation. It was just the most obvious.

"What can I bring?" Tom asked, folding his paw around Eva's address.

"Everything's on me this time. Just show up."

"All right, then," Tom said, and he was out the door to meet Pat. On the way, he stopped at the Carnegie Library to use their online U.S. Geological Survey database.

FIFTEEN MINUTES LATER, Tom burst through the door at Century 21, marched past the receptionist without a word, and slapped two color prints on the table in front of Pat.

"The hell are these, Larkin?"

"Satellite photos. You can download a non-classified aerial photo of just about anyplace on earth for five bucks. Look at them," Tom ordered.

Pat studied the photos for a few seconds and said, "Infrared, right?"

"Exactly. How'd you know that?"

"This may be news to you, but some of us bumpkins saw a good deal of the planet, care of Uncle Sam. I served two tours in the Navy with COMSUBRON One, Pacific Fleet, on a nuclear-equipped submarine. I learned a thing or two between ports, hot shot. You can call me lieutenant if you like, seaman."

"Fair enough, *lieutenant*; look closer, and tell me what you see."

Pat retrieved a pair of cheaters from his jacket and looked the pictures up and down.

"Tell me that this isn't them … "

"Damn straight it is."

"You're shittin' me," he exclaimed. "It's the bunkers we were looking at this morning, out near Igloo, ain't it?"

"You got it. Notice anything unusual?"

Pat set the two photos down side by side. "Let's see. The ground color is different, so I know there's a difference in temperature between the two photos," he said, continuing to study them.

"One was taken in January and one in July," Tom confirmed.

"Well, lookee here!" Pat pointed to a web of straight lines running between the bunkers. The lines were so faint they looked more like shadows. "Is that what's got you all riled up?"

"It is," Tom said. "There is something out there whose temperature is different enough from that of the surface to show up both in the winter and in the summer. But it's underground. That's why those lines are just barely visible in both photos."

"Why the hell would the ground be a different temperature in straight lines?"

"Tunnels," Tom answered. "Lots of them. I'm guessing they are air-conditioned in the summer and heated in the winter."

"Who'd do a fool thing like that?" Pat asked.

"Somebody who's using them, my friend. Don't know what for, but you can bet your bottom dollar they're using them year round."

"So, you think them doors that we saw lead into these tunnels?"

"What else could it be?"

"Make anything of it?"

"Not yet, but I intend to."

"Well, good luck, buddy. Meanwhile, unless you're getting bored with it, I suggest we focus on this here six-million-dollar real estate transaction," Pat answered. "You can spend all the time you want on them gopher holes after we get our business done."

"You're right. First things first. But I'm telling you, Burley ..."

Pat cut him off. "Tell me later. I ain't got time for this now."

"All right. How's the contract coming?"

Pat had finished a draft of the document and was going through it a second time.

"I think we're about there, Tom, but you should review it before we send it to Kathy."

Tom picked up the document, pen in hand, while Pat got up to pour some coffee.

"Black or sissy?" Pat called out to Tom from across the room.

"Sissy," Tom replied.

When Pat returned with their coffees, Tom said, "I notice you set earnest money at sixty thousand bucks."

"One percent is the usual."

Tom flushed. "I can't write a check for $60,000 this afternoon."

"You mean to tell me, Larkin, that you expect to close a six-million-dollar deal and you can't write a check for a measly sixty K?" Pat boomed, sporting an impish grin.

"Keep it down, Burley! Everybody in the whole damn town doesn't need to know I'm on thin ice here," Tom whispered, taking Burley's ribbing to heart. "Give me a day or two; I'll get the sixty K. I just can't write the check today."

"Well, what can you write a check for ... one that ain't made out of rubber?" Burley said, continuing to needle Larkin.

"I don't know ... twenty, twenty-five K?"

"Well, Scrooge, that'll just have to do then," Burley said with a laugh, and slapped Larkin on the back. "Hell, Jo would've been happy with a hundred bucks, if you ask me. I was just trying to see how much I could get off of you."

"Don't do that shit to me, Burley. In case you hadn't noticed, I'm a little keyed up," Tom growled.

"Lighten up, Larkin, I'm just having fun with you," Pat said.

"When do I get to have fun?" Tom shot back.

"When you own the ranch," Pat said, turning to the keyboard. "Now, what do you say we put twenty thou in here for the earnest? Jo don't need it from you, I just don't want anybody from the outside looking at this deal and finding a bone to pick with it, know what I mean?"

"Good thinking. Whom do I make the check out to?"

"The Burley Family Children's Fund," Pat said without missing a beat.

"Very funny. To whom?"

"To my firm—Country Real Estate. I don't intend to cash it; I'll just show it to Jo. I'll give it back to you when you deliver the down stroke. And, speaking of which, when are you planning on doing that?"

"Can I get ten days? Is that too much?" Tom asked.

"Let's make it an even two weeks. I don't want to have to redo this thing if you're a day late. Anything else we got to fuss with?"

Tom slid the contract back to Pat and said, "I don't think so, Pat. And if I haven't mentioned it twenty times already, thanks. You did a whale of a job."

"Ain't any too difficult, nowadays," Pat said. "Like I was saying earlier, ninety-nine percent of these contracts are boiler plate, and this here fancy software does all the work. Hardest part for me was having to type on these itty-bitty keys with my big, fat fingers."

Pat had the receptionist fax the contract to St. Paul. Tom had promised to give Kathy thirty minutes to review the agreement, but after just fifteen minutes, the fax machine in Hot Springs clicked into gear and spit out a single page from Kathy.

She had signed.

Everything went smoothly at the closing. The contract was passed from hand to hand around the kitchen table and each signer speechified a bit before he signed. Jo's friend Ellie had shown up as a witness, and Henry Finn, Jo's attorney, had taken the whole, blessed stack of papers to town to make copies while everyone else helped polish off Jo's sherry.

Tom was feeling his oats and raced back to Hot Springs. He was going to celebrate tonight.

Tom didn't call Kathy and implore her to find a flight to Rapid City, ninety minutes north of Hot Springs—and join him. She was the one who had supported Tom's plan today, and he was grateful as hell for that. But grateful, Tom rationalized, wasn't passion.

His head was full of Eva. Even as they were finalizing the contract for deed a short while ago, Tom hadn't given Kathy's legitimate concerns or the lies he'd told her a second thought. Other than the ranch, Tom was temporarily blind to anything but Eva Shepherd.

Tom no longer cared if Eva had lied to him about the hotel room. Now that the ranch was his, he could not see what difference Eva's lies might possibly make. That bit with the hotel room was nothing more than a footnote to the most glorious day of Tom's life.

Tom conjured a picture of Eva lying next to him, her arms a girth around his waist. Eva had given him his bit; Tom was eager for more. As far as Tom was concerned, any time he might spend with Eva—and didn't—was time wasted.

Tom put on his game face and dialed Kathy. She picked up immediately.

"Tom?"

"You can call me 'Rancher Tom,' darlin'," he boasted. "Or, you can call me Land Baron Bob, Warbucks Willey or just plain Daddy if you like. Just don't call late, and don't hesitate; I'm a man on the move!"

"Jesus, Tom!" Kathy giggled. "You are in rare form."

"Feeling good, looking good, and raring to go!"

"Well, I'm thrilled for you, Tom. For us, I mean. But, I know how special it is for you."

"Kathy, you have no idea how incredible this is for me."

"I probably don't. But I do have a sneaky suspicion that you're about to go buy rounds for everybody and his brother down at the Lucky Strike, so do me one favor, please?"

"Shoot."

"Find a ride back to the hotel, OK? Don't drive drunk."

"Kathy? Hello? It is two blocks to the Lucky Strike from the hotel. I promise, that if I can't find my car keys at closing time, I'll crawl back to the hotel on all fours. How's that for a fair deal?"

"Don't make fun of me."

"I'm just *having* fun, Kathy. Cut me some slack. This is a big day and I intend to enjoy every last minute of it."

"Oh, all right," she replied with a touch of exasperation. "You and Pat have a good time, but try to keep things down to a dull roar."

Tom paused before answering. He wasn't planning on having a good time with Pat. He was planning on having a good time with Eva.

"I will, Kathy. See you tomorrow night."

"Call me when you get on the road."

"I will."

"I love you, Tom."

"Love you, too," Tom recited.

"Bye."

Tom next set about laying the groundwork for an alibi, if needed. He dialed Pat and arranged to meet him at the Lucky Strike for a pop. He could now honestly tell Kathy that he had gone out to celebrate with Pat Burley.

Tom stopped at the edge of town to pick up two bottles of Shiraz. The guy behind the counter gave Tom directions to Fall River Floral, which was a few blocks from the Lucky Strike.

Tom waited while the florist arranged daffodils, daisies, iris and a sprig of baby's breath in a crystal vase, stopped in to toss back one highball with Pat at the Lucky Strike, and then hightailed it back to the hotel.

EVA HAD LEFT the hotel hours earlier to prepare.

She had proposed home cooking but was none too handy in the kitchen and wasn't about to attempt anything tricky. A simple success always trumps an elaborate failure. If the meal were to turn out badly, Eva surmised, Tom might gallantly suggest that they go out. That would ruin everything.

Eva believed that if she cooked within her skills she could keep Tom inside her house, where, just down the hall from the kitchen, her finer arts could be demonstrated.

She decided on beef stroganoff with baby asparagus as an entrée. Strawberries and fresh cream would suffice as dessert, should they get that far along with the meal.

She'd read about the baby asparagus online at www.epicurious. com. A little balsamic vinegar, butter and lemon made the vegetable taste delicate and French.

The beef would, of course, be local. Dave, the Safeway butcher, had been a friend since high school. If she leaned over the meat counter far enough and batted her eyes, he'd cut her the finest batch of sirloin tips this side of Kansas City. He also sold a stroganoff sauce behind the counter that was every Hot Springs homemaker's secret weapon. She knew he'd press her to take a container of it at no charge.

Cooking dry pasta, she knew, is nearly impossible to screw up.

The wine would be more difficult than the meal. She expected that Tom's taste in wine was sophisticated, and she was no sommelier. She'd have to ask for help from Jeff, the lecher at the liquor store. He was always pawing at her, but he did know his grapes. She reminded herself to buy the most expensive bottle of Scotch that Jeff had on hand. That, she assured herself, would cover her bases.

Eva fretted most, however, about what to wear.

She knew that showing up at the door in a pair of high heels and a baby doll dress would leave Tom with no doubts about what she wanted. But as much as Eva wanted to have sex with Tom, she wanted his admiration more. Her outfit would have to be that casual-but-elegant, exotic-but-not-aloof, homey-but-stylish, sexy-but-demure look.

So Eva painstakingly inventoried every garment in her closet and came as close as she'd ever come to getting her clothes to perfectly match the occasion—and her intent.

Each garment Eva considered caused her to fabricate a new scenario. In one, Tom helped her with a fallen strap; in another, her nipples brushed up against Tom's back and stood up for him; in the next fantasy, Tom was admiring her profile from the living room; finally, she imagined Tom helping her, again and again, in slow or frantic ways, to remove her outfit, his fingertips caressing her skin or raking her breast as he freed her. She told herself to wear nothing that was complicated to remove.

Still in a quandary, Eva began to dress.

She stepped into a thong the color of saffron and no more substantial than pollen. She'd found it in Omaha. The woman at the boutique said it would take on her color and all but disappear once deployed. It had the feel of warm breath on her skin and twinkled like flax, even in the faintest light. Eva hoped it wouldn't be the last thing she took off.

A bra, she decided, would create too much distance between her and Tom when the moment arrived. She didn't want to make a spectacle of her breasts, but she wanted Tom to be able to feel her when she put her arms around him. And she wanted to be able to feel him, too.

What she had in mind was a periwinkle Versace t-shirt with raglan cap sleeves and a crew neck that smacked of propriety. She discarded it after trying it on. It clung to her curves in a lewd, rather than imaginative, way.

Her eyes came to rest on a jersey wrap dress, hanging open at the back of her closet. She'd put it on the day it arrived from New York, but never since. It was Christian Dior and the color of a timid lilac.

She laid it out on the bed. The V neckline, soft shoulders and three-quarter sleeves were modest, but the microfiber fabric—if she dispensed with a bra—was anything but. It would give her a veneer of modesty, but quietly promise her flesh.

The sash in front was fixed, but appeared loosely tied, almost as an afterthought. It made the dress conform to her curves and define her hips rather than her waist; it would dare Tom to tug on it and lay bare the woman beneath.

The hem stopped an eyelash shy of her knees, and the cloth hugged her legs like sheen on Italian marble. It made an elegant statement and could be as easily shed as a kitchen apron.

It was Paris Hilton cum June Cleaver. It was perfect.

She fished out a pair of low, cork sandals with calfskin ankle straps. They were plain enough to suggest that she might have worn them to pick tomatoes in the garden. Her bare legs easily supported such fantasy; they were as fresh and firm as a school-girl's.

Eva knew that, however exquisite a piece may be, too much jewelry would be tacky, and she decided to simply wear earrings. She selected a pair she'd bought on the Rosebud Indian Reservation. Each featured a pounded copper disc hung from a tiny gold hoop that pierced the ear. An Indian trade bead dangled below each disc, and a crystal stalactite swung on each bead. Their design would direct Tom's eyes to wander down and over her body.

She was ready.

She carefully disrobed and put on a pair of jeans and a t-shirt.

With plenty of time to shop and prepare in the kitchen, Eva allowed herself to spend most of the afternoon bathing and fussing with herself, curtains drawn and candles lit.

Eva and Tom had launched themselves into a common orbit, from which there could be but one outcome—collision. Nature had put this in motion, and, being helpless to prevent it, God stood by and watched.

Saturday, 8:00 p.m. sharp

Tom didn't have to agonize over what to wear; he didn't have that many choices.

Other than a stack of work shirts, the only thing he had with him was a deep blue, long-sleeve crew-top the color of his eyes. He pulled it on, slid into a pair of stone-washed jeans, dusted the ranch off his boots, and gave them a spit shine. A western-cut leather jacket was his one concession to style. Tom had given his Stetson to Runs With Horses and didn't think the palm was a worthy substitute. So, he splashed his face with Eternity and was out the door, bareheaded.

The woman at the lobby desk gave Tom a big smile.

"Have a nice night, Mr. Larkin," she said.

"Believe I will, darling."

"Who's the lucky girl?"

Tom stopped.

"Excuse me?"

"The lucky girl," she said, still wearing a smile that was beginning to make Tom feel uncomfortable. "The flowers. You've got flowers in your hand."

"Oh. These," Tom said stupidly, holding up the bouquet.

"They're for an old friend. She's not feeling well. Elderly lady, you know," he said lamely.

"Hope your *friend* is feeling better, Mr. Larkin. Good night." Another big smile.

She knows, Tom thought. *Well, so what? If she knows where I'm going, she can fantasize herself into a puddle if it makes her happy.*

Eva was standing behind the door when Tom knocked. She waited for him to knock again before opening it.

With a plain white dishcloth draped purposely over one lilac-colored shoulder, earringed and backlit in the threshold, Eva Shepherd was a vision.

"You're the prompt one, Mr. Larkin," she cooed.

Tom's eyes drank deeply of her.

"The earrings are stunning, Eva; they complement you."

"Oh, thank you," she said, lowering her eyes, "but they're just some old Indian beads."

Tom reached up and brushed a stray wisp of hair away from her eye.

"There, now you're perfect again." He held the flowers up to her as an offering.

"How sweet! For me?"

"Let's just say they're in appreciation of the chef."

"They're beautiful, Tom. Thank you. Now, get in here before the neighbors see you and have something to gossip about."

She nodded to the bottles of wine. "I thought I told you not to bring anything ... you don't mind very well, do you?"

"I guess I don't," Tom said with a smile. "But I thought it would be rude to show up empty-handed. If it isn't the right wine for supper ... "

"I'm sure it will be lovely." Eva cut him off, put her hand on his shoulder, and reached behind him to close the front door. She pushed into his chest as she pushed the door closed.

"Let me take your jacket."

Eva stepped behind Tom and helped him out of his coat, the fingers of one hand trailing along his shoulder and arm as she slipped it off and tossed it on a chair.

Tom closed his eyes as Eva worked.

His desire for Eva and his love for Kathy crashed like waves over each other, sending the little boat that was Tom caroming across the chop. He'd set sail on a lark, and now found himself, without compass, on a fully developed sea.

How can I love Kathy and be so taken with Eva? I know it's wrong to be here alone with her. But I want to be here. Tom fought on with himself. *What's wrong about being friendly with a woman, anyway? Do I have to choose between Kathy and having a female friend? Why must I choose?*

As Tom had no intention of answering his own torturous questions, he anchored himself to the idea that his infatuation had been quick in arriving and would just as quickly dissipate. *Nothing will come of it,* he argued to himself. *I'll stay for supper and glass or two of wine, and then I'll go back to my life.*

"Come in, Tom," Eva said softly. She had set the wine and flowers down on the entry table and was standing close in front of him, within kissing distance.

They stood that way for a moment, unwilling to have it end.

Eva held his eyes and took both of Tom's hands in hers.

"Come on in, Tom, and tell me all about your day." She kept hold of his hands, and backed him wordlessly into the kitchen. Tom followed like a colt drawn into fresh June clover.

She had arranged the chair an hour earlier. It sat facing the stove and sink, so that Tom would have an unobstructed view of her while she prepared their meal. She led him to it and said, "Welcome to Chez Eva!"

She released his hands, but not his eyes.

"Would you like me to pour you a glass of wine, or would you rather have a tumbler of what Hot Springs has to offer for Scotch?" she called as she went to fetch the flowers and Shiraz.

Grateful for an easy choice, Tom said, "What are you having?"

"I'd like to try what you brought, if that's OK by you."

"Absolutely. I'll have wine, too. Shall I do the honors?"

Eva reached into a drawer and handed Tom a corkscrew.

"Nice to have a man around the house when you need one."

"So that's what you think men are good for ... screwing corks?"

"That's not what I said, Tom Larkin. And for your information, that's definitely not what I meant." The smile she gave him said otherwise.

While Tom opened the wine, Eva busied herself with the pasta.

"Tell me, Tom, should a Shiraz be given time to breathe before you drink it?"

"Not at all," Tom replied, "Let's go for it."

"Oh, goodie," Eva said and turned her backside to Tom, opening the cupboard where earlier in the day she'd relocated all the wine glasses to the topmost shelf. She had practiced her move several times before Tom arrived so that, no matter how far she stretched herself out, the wine glasses would be just out of her reach. She took her time reaching first with one hand, then the other, then with both.

Hands still grasping for the glasses she had planned never to reach, she turned her head to Tom and said, "Help?"

He was out of his chair and behind her in one motion. Eva didn't move. She just pointed to the top shelf and said, "There."

To get the glasses, Tom had to press Eva into the counter with his body. With a wine goblet in each hand, Tom lowered his arms on either side of her. Before he could back away, she turned, put both hands on his shirt and began fiddling with the fabric.

"Thank you, Tom. You're such a gentleman."

Tom stood fast and silent. He was fighting an urge to uproot Eva from the kitchen and plant her straightaway in the bedroom. He'd fantasized about her, but it wasn't until that moment, with Eva pressed up against him in the kitchen, that he finally admitted it to himself. They would make love. In five minutes, perhaps, later that evening, maybe tomorrow.

Eva picked up one of Tom's silent, goblet-holding hands. "Let me take these. You sit back down and relax."

The first bottle of wine disappeared in a flurry of small talk about Tom's purchase of the McPherson ranch. The deal had been inked, and Tom felt no compunction to hold back the good news. Getting the ranch was his joy, and he shared it without reservation.

She oohhed and ahhed over every detail of the negotiation, and saw to it that their glasses were always amply prepared for the surprising number of toasts they found necessary to propose to each other.

If someone had peeked through the kitchen window as Tom and Eva helped each other put supper together and get it to the table, he would have guessed that they were lovers who had known each other long and had a great fondness for each other.

"Oops, I'm sorry, Tom," Eva would say, wiping an invisible speck of something from his shirt.

"Forget, it, darlin'," Tom would reply, "You keep spilling on me, and hell, I'll just eat my shirt for lunch tomorrow," and Eva would put her hand on Tom's shoulder so they could laugh without having to lose touch with each other.

"Do you want clean wine glasses for the meal?" Tom would ask.

Eva would then sing out, "If you can remember what shelf they're on ... need help?"

The dance had begun.

The first bottle of wine melded into a second, and midway through the stroganoff, it was time to break out the Chianti Eva had bought. By the end of supper, Tom had told Eva everything there was to know about the McPherson deal, excepting the business with Carl. He'd given Carl his word.

Eva was glowing.

There wasn't a moment of dissention or disappointment. The air was electric with their attraction for each other. Eva laughed and cooked and shared secrets. Tom was happy just to be with her.

As Eva stood to retrieve more wine, Tom swept her into his arms. A tidal longing bore them to her bed. Although Tom wanted to ravage her, to take her in giant gulps and make her jump with the force of his pleasure, he was gentle, unbridling his passion slowly for fear she might spook and run.

His fears were groundless. Their appetites were equally fierce. They feasted on each other with abandon. He was hungry for the fresh and unexplored, she for the chance to exist in a world, if only for a few precious hours, that she had never known.

Tom shared his day's joy; Eva shared her body, holding nothing back, finally collapsing with her head on his stomach and both arms wrapped about his waist.

Tom felt her body heave and hot tears stream down his abdomen and hips. He felt certain that Eva was crying because she was happy. *Then again,* he thought, *you can never tell with a woman.* It could just as well be that something sad had suddenly occurred to her. Or that she was sad because she hadn't always been as happy as she was right then. Knowing that he couldn't know why she cried, Tom drifted off to sleep.

When he woke, Eva was lying in the same position, but now she was breathing in and out in a steady and peaceful rhythm. He wondered how long he'd been in her room. He'd lost track of time, and of himself.

Eva's chestnut hair lay tangled across his chest. Tom reached down to pet her and drifted away again, this time to the country and the horse farm of his youth. There, it was always summertime, and the breeze always carried with it the fragrance of freshly baled hay.

He dreamed again of the horses.

It always began with a walk to the pasture, the sun merely a kiss on his shoulder. After a time, maybe an instant or maybe an hour, the sweat would be running because there'd been a chase and some coaxing and perhaps even a handful of oats, and he would lay his hands on the animal and put his nose to its neck and fill himself with the sweet air next to its skin. Then he was on top, his soul given over to the beast because his life depended

on the animal's trust. His shoulders and the horse's rolled forward
and back in a rhythm he must have carried with him at birth;
breast heaved on breast and hips rocked back and in and back and
in as one. Their rhythm made him forget: Was he riding or carrying; was he the domestic one or the feral?

Sometimes, in the dream, the hard run surprised Tom, and,
having lost the reins and being unable to restrain the beast, he
would wake, half-drained, his heart throbbing.

Other times, they worked up to the hard run together, the filly
and he, starting gently and slowly. Then there'd be a git-up that
was more hint than come-on, but both man and animal knew that
the hard run was beginning. They'd break into a canter that made
the grass and their fear melt, and then fall away. With short, hot
snorts the animal begged to be loosed to the wind and its desires.
With its froth slathered on his bare chest and legs, and the animal's rowdy mane in his eyes, Tom urged it on with whispers and
reassurances that the animal didn't as much hear as feel. And then
the hard run overwhelmed them with the suddenness of a dam
broken. The animal surged and snorted and rose in the air, suspended, then hooves flailed the ground. Tom clung on desperately
and precariously and joyously, while they raced along in a blur
of pounding, an orgy of pounding, a breathless, breakneck of
pounding that shook them to their souls and was, for all its danger and risk, blessed healing. Tom pushed the animal to its brink,
over and over and over the thistle-littered turf. Tom had his knees
to her withers and urged her on, squeezing and releasing, squeezing and releasing, squeezing and holding until he didn't think
the animal could take more, but it was beyond stopping and flew
over the pasture at a pace madly out of control. Their furious and
urgent pace forced breath into each chest; exhilaration ripped it
back from them.

And then, suddenly, the sound and the color and the chaos
crystallized like lightning in a black sky, and the universe slowed
around them. They lifted away from the earth, borne up by their

love, without effort or the will to stop, and lost themselves in the stars.

Nature allowed them to exist in this harmony only briefly before their pace wound down, their heartbeats slowed, and the world reformed around them. But in those precious minutes, there was poetry and clarity. No tomorrow. No yesterday. No calculus. Just desire, given full rein.

Hot breath on his cheek woke Tom from the dream.

He put his lips to Eva's, and the beast with two backs set off again, making poetry in the place where dreams are born.

SUNDAY

The truth shall make you free.
John 8:32

———

6:45 *A.M.*

Half a world away, Tom Larkin's daughter, Anne, was fighting a stubborn and potentially deadly fungal pneumonia and had been checked into London's St. Andrew's Hospital. Kathy had called Tom's room every hour, on the hour, all night long.

She was frantic because of the thing she knew and, at first, sick with worry over what might have befallen her husband. After several hours of unanswered phone calls, worry became anger as her imagination filled in the details of the thing she suspected.

Just before sunrise, Tom crawled out of Eva's bed and made his way back to the hotel. Tom saw that the night clerk wasn't at the front counter.

"That's lucky," he muttered to himself.

Tom ducked into the stairwell and climbed up to third floor. As he unlocked the door to his room, he could hear his phone ringing. *Christ,* he thought, looking at his watch, *if that's Kathy, this is my lucky day.* He didn't notice the envelopes on the floor just inside the door as he ran to the desk and picked up the phone, feigning sleepiness.

With a yawn he said, "This is Larkin."

"Where have you been?" Kathy demanded in a shriek. "I've been calling all night. Jesus Christ! Where have you been, Tom?"

Oh shit, he thought. Instead of dodging a bullet, he'd been nailed dead-on.

"What do you mean?"

"You know exactly what I mean, I mean where in the hell have you been, because you haven't been in your room," she shrieked.

"Kathy, calm down. I just came up from breakfast."

"Breakfast where?" she demanded.

"Downstairs," he glanced at his watch. "They open at six."

"Well, that's fine, Tom, but where were you before breakfast? I've been calling and calling every hour since about ten o'clock last night, and you didn't answer your room phone or your cell phone. I even sent the front desk clerk up twice to pound on your door. Didn't you get the messages when you went down to breakfast? Don't you check voice mail? What in hell is going on out there?"

Tom looked over to the door and saw the envelopes on the floor. The red message light on his phone was flashing. He'd left his cell phone on the desk last night as a precaution. Its message light was blinking. Tom knew there was no way he'd be able to claim that he was in his room last night and tried to change the subject.

"Kathy, you sound terrible. What's wrong? Why are you calling me at this hour?"

"There's a lot wrong, starting with where were you all night? Just answer the question, Tom. Where were you?"

Tom started to weave a story.

"Look, Kathy, it's no big deal. I got back to the hotel less than an hour ago, and went right into the breakfast room to grab some coffee and cereal. I was just walking into the room when you called." He offered no further explanation.

Tom's admission that he hadn't been in the room all night had a calming effect on Kathy. If he'd denied what she knew to be true, it would confirm her worst fears.

"So what kept you away from your hotel all night? And why didn't you answer your damn cell phone?"

"You're going to be angry with me," he said.

"I'm already angry with you, Tom. So there's only a couple of things I can think of that you could say to make things worse. Where were you?"

"At the bar," he said.

"No, you weren't," Kathy fired back, her anger rising again quickly. "I called the Lucky Strike around midnight when I couldn't find you at your hotel. They said you'd been there and had left early. So try a different line of bullshit."

"I didn't say I was at the Lucky Strike, Kathy."

She had assumed that, if Tom were at a bar, it would be the Lucky Strike.

"Oh!" She said, and backed off a half-step. "OK. What bar were you at all night long, Tom? Do tell."

"We went to a place in Edgemont with some people Pat and I met at the Lucky Strike. It was chicken-roping night," he said and paused.

"Chicken roping?"

"Yeah, you try to throw these little lassos around chickens they've got caged up in the bar, you know, like in the rodeo, only with chickens." Tom was grateful to be explaining something that bore some resemblance to the truth.

"Chicken roping, are you shitting me? Jesus, Tom, you need to grow up," she said.

"It was fun," Tom said.

"Was it fun all night long? You aren't going to tell me you were up roping chickens until dawn, are you, Tom? Why didn't you come back to the hotel?"

The perfect answer dawned on him.

"Because you told me not to drive drunk, that's why, and I was three sheets to the wind at two in the morning and decided to hole up there. Besides, everybody at the bar told me that the highway patrol routinely sets up roadside D.U.I. checkpoints between Edgemont and Hot Springs, and it would have been risky as hell to drive back in my condition."

Tom's explanation was beginning to sound plausible. Stupid, but plausible.

"How did you occupy your time between two and six, then?" she asked.

"I know you'll think this is asinine, too, but I decided I'd be better off just toughing it out in the Caddy. There aren't any hotels or motels in Edgemont, Kathy."

"You slept in your car, in this weather? Are you nuts, Tom?"

"First off, no, I'm not nuts. Sleeping it off in the car is a damn sight smarter than running the risk of being picked up or getting into an accident. Second, the weather here in March isn't anything like it is in St. Paul, so I was in no danger of freezing to death. And third, to put your mind at ease, I parked a couple of blocks down from the bar, left the engine running, the heater on and cracked open a window for safety's sake," he added, before Kathy could ask.

"I woke up around a quarter to six with a sore back and a headache, spent ten minutes looking for my cell phone before I remembered I'd left it in the room, and drove back to the hotel." Tom was impressed with his fib. "I went out on the town, and, well, things just got a little rambunctious ... sorry."

Kathy had no practical alternative but to accept Tom's explanation. Still, Tom knew she hadn't fully bought into it.

"I am so sorry, Kathy. I just didn't want to make a bad situation worse," he said, looking for sympathy he didn't deserve.

He got it from her, anyway.

"Jesus Christ, Tom, I was worried sick. About you ... and about Anne."

"What about Anne!" Tom said with alarm. "What about Anne?"

"Tom, she got so sick, they had to take her to a hospital. It sounded serious, and she was too sick to even talk on the phone—they called from London for Christ's sake, and it scared me. I needed you to be there. You're the one with the medical background, Tom. I needed you!"

"I see that, Kathy. I'm sorry," Tom said, and meant it.

"I don't need you to be sorry. I need you to be here," she said.

"Kathy," Tom said in the softest tone he could muster, "tell me what you want me to do but first tell me about Annie."

"I want you to get in that goddamn Cadillac of yours and come home. That's what I want you to do."

"That's what I'm about to do," Tom said. "Now calm down and tell me how Anne is doing and give me the number of the hospital. I'll call London as soon as we hang up."

"Don't bother," Kathy replied, resigned. "I talked to the doctor—and to Anne—about an hour ago. Apparently she contracted a fungal pneumonia."

"That can be serious," Tom said, interrupting.

"I know, they told me. But they caught it—and thank God she is in London and not some third world hellhole. They did some DNA detection something or another and were able to figure out what it was in time."

"Fungus can move like wildfire—that much I remember from the continuing medical education stuff we did with Doctors Hospital in Cincinnati. Fast diagnosis is key. What did they tell you about her condition?" Tom asked.

"They did something surgical, debri … "

"Debridement," Tom said.

"Yeah, debridement. And her fever broke, and she's out of danger. The doctor told me that the best thing for her now is to sleep, which is presumably what she's doing now."

"Thank God," Tom said. "These past several hours must have been hell for you, Kathy. I know that I keep saying I'm sorry, but I am sorry that things just happened this way. That, you know … I wasn't there … to help."

"Where were you, Tom, really? Where were you?" Kathy asked in a small voice.

Tom could hear her crying.

"Kathy, I told you. I'm sorry."

"Get home, Tom. We can try and talk about it when you get here."

"I'm on my way. I just have to pack up and shower and stop by to let Jo know what's going on. I'll be on the road in two hours and home in ten."

"Call me when you get out of town," she said and hung up.

Tom showered quickly, stowed his gear, and headed west out of town, toward Trail's End. He would never just fly the coop without telling Jo why he was going and when he'd return, and he didn't think Jo would appreciate having that conversation over the phone.

When he pulled into the ranch yard, Jo's banged-up F-250 was sitting exactly where it had been parked the previous afternoon.

All of the downstairs lights were on.

He bounded onto the porch, opened the screen, and rapped sharply on the oak door.

Nothing.

He waited several seconds and knocked with some authority.

Nothing.

He looked around the yard at the outbuildings, wondering if she was doing chores. There was no sign of movement, so he pounded on the door heavily with a closed fist.

Nothing.

He turned the knob, and the door swung open.

An acrid stench made him recoil, gasping for air.

"Jesus Christ!"

He yanked a glove from his pocket, put it over his mouth, and dove into the house.

"Jo!" he screamed. The foul smoke hung down two feet from the top of the ceiling.

"Jo!" he shouted into the dining room as he ran to the kitchen, keeping himself in a defensive crouch, like a man taking enemy fire.

On the stove, a coffeepot sat smoldering on a lit burner. Tom figured it'd been that way for a long time because the coffeepot had begun to melt, and steel was dripping onto the gas jets.

Tom grabbed a dishtowel, wrapped it about his hand, and gave what remained of the pot a sharp blow that sent it bouncing off the stove and onto the floor. Spying a rolling pin on the counter, Tom hooked it through the opening of the pot, kicked open the back door, and tossed the thing into the yard. Jamming the door open with an overshoe, he raced back through the kitchen and into the dining room.

"Jo! Where are you? Jo! It's Tom! Are you in here?"

He checked the stairs, the coat closet, and the half-bath, then found her in the living room, laid out on the couch.

Tom fell to her side.

"Jo! Wake up! You've got to get out of here right now!"

She didn't stir.

"No!" he cried, shaking her. "No!"

He put his ear to her chest and made out a shallow breath.

He slid an arm behind her neck, and as he slid the other under her legs, he saw it.

A magazine with words scrawled across both pages lay open in her lap. She'd signed her name in an unsteady hand across the bottom, tearing through several pages from the effort.

Tom jammed the magazine between his belt and shirt and brought himself upright, Jo in his arms.

"Stay with me, Jo, stay with me, honey," he said, not knowing or caring if she could hear or understand him. "You are not going to die, do you hear me? I will not let you die!"

He folded her limp body into the passenger seat of the Cadillac and reclined it fully. She wouldn't be able to roll off, and he could keep his eye on her all the way to town.

Tires spinning and dirt flying, Tom tore out of the yard. Careening onto the gravel road, he almost lost it on the shoulder and forced himself to slow down.

Once on the highway, he pushed the needle to a hundred-and-forty. Dreamlike, the miles seemed to crawl by.

He started to pray and stopped himself.

"I will not pray to any God that would allow this to happen!" Tom vowed through clenched teeth. "God be damned!"

Tom laid on the horn as he skidded to a stop at the emergency entrance to Hot Springs Municipal Hospital. He jammed the car into park and tumbled out the door. Someone was coming out of the hospital, and he yelled for a gurney. A minute later, Jo was inside.

There was no need to fill out paperwork. Jo was a fixture in the community, and they took her away immediately, leaving Tom alone.

Tom knew that he needed to notify someone, but he couldn't remember Ellie's last name. So he flipped through the directory and found a home phone number for Henry Finn, Jo's attorney.

"Hello," a woman's voice answered.

"Get Henry," Tom barked.

There was a pause, and the voice said, "Who's calling?"

"Just get Henry. Now!"

A moment later, Henry was on the line.

"Henry, Jo's had a terrible accident. She's in trouble. You've got to get over here right now."

"Jo McPherson?" Henry asked.

"Yes, Jo McPherson. Now get over here!"

"Who is this?"

"Sorry, Henry," Tom said. "This is Tom. Tom Larkin. I found her. She's barely hanging on, and I didn't know who else to call."

"OK. I'm on my way. Are you at the ranch?"

"No. No. We're at the Hot Springs hospital."

"I'll be there in five minutes."

Turning from the counter, Tom noticed the magazine he'd stuck into his belt. He sat down on a plastic chair the color of a pumpkin and opened the magazine to the place where Jo had scratched her words, making them out only with difficulty.

Make Henry finish CFD. Don't let Doc J get ranch. Under these words, Jo had signed her name.

Oh my God, Tom thought. *Jo must have thought she was dying, and her last thought was to complete the ranch sale? And she even added that bit about Jennings and felt that she needed to sign it.*

Tom didn't know what it meant, but he promised himself that if it were the last thing he ever did, he'd see that Jo's wishes were carried out. "You've tangled with the wrong polecat, Jennings," Tom growled under his breath. "Before this is over, you're going to wish you'd never heard my name. And if Jo dies, I'll . . ." Tom didn't exactly know how to finish that thought and left it hanging.

Tom was still slumped in the chair, magazine in his lap, when Henry arrived.

"Tom. What's going on?"

"Thanks for getting here so quickly," Tom said. "I went to the ranch this morning on my way out of town and found Jo on the couch and she was barely breathing and the place was full of smoke and about to burn up."

"Slow down, man. One thing at a time. Where's Jo now, and what do you know about her condition?"

"She's in with the doctors. They haven't told me anything yet. But she was breathing when I got her here." That was all Tom could muster. Every time he thought about Jo dying, his voice caught.

"It was damn lucky for Jo that you stopped out there this morning. You sit tight, Tom. Let me see what I can find out," Henry said, and left the room.

Tom opened the magazine in his lap and reread Jo's words. He still staring at the pages when Henry returned.

"I think we've got good news," Henry announced soberly.

"They've got her on oxygen and stabilized. She's had a pretty severe stroke, they say, and must have been where you found her for several hours. She's got extensive paralysis, which is why she couldn't get to a phone. The doctors won't know how much of it is permanent until she regains consciousness, and they have a chance to put her through rehab," Henry said.

"But she's going to live?" Tom pleaded.

"She's still in danger, Tom, so I don't want to be telling you something they didn't tell me. But they are optimistic. Put it that way."

"Thank you, Henry. Thank you," Tom said, and dropped his head into his hands. He kept it there for a couple of minutes after he felt Henry sit down in the chair next to his. A moment later, he felt Henry's hand on his back.

"It's all right, now, Tom. You did everything possible. Jo probably owes you her life."

Tom was exhausted. Between last night with Eva, the go-around with Kathy, and the business with Jo, he'd spent everything he had, mentally and physically. He sat up slowly and rubbed his eyes for several seconds.

"Sorry, Henry. I'm just completely wiped out."

"No need for apologies, son."

"There's something you need to see, Henry," Tom said, and handed him the magazine. "I found it on Jo's lap. Out at the ranch this morning. Read it and tell me what you make of it." Tom opened the magazine to the place where Jo had left her message.

Henry read the words slowly, and then read them again.

"This is serious, Tom."

"I know. I just don't really see what's behind it."

"Nor do I, Tom. But if you're asking me if I intend to stop the sale of the ranch now that Jo has been incapacitated, the answer is no. We took care of all the important matters yesterday at the ranch, and as you know, I have Jo's durable power of attorney and can act on her behalf. This note makes clear what she wants done."

"I don't want you to get the wrong impression, Henry. The ranch sale isn't the most important thing right now. Jo getting well is," Tom said.

"I feel the same way, but it appears that the most important thing to Jo is making sure you get the deed to Trail's End ... and that Bill Jennings doesn't."

"What do we do next?"

"As a practical matter, you are the legal owner of the ranch right now. However, you need to produce a down payment on the contract within two weeks or what happened at the ranch yesterday means nothing.

"After I am in receipt of the down payment, you gain several important ownership rights—and responsibilities. As long as you perform according to the terms of the contract for deed, you may physically move onto the ranch premises. You have the right to conduct operations, buy and sell parcels, exercise water and mineral rights, let grazing and timber contracts, and the like.

"You would not be free to sell the ranch for a dollar, for example, and then declare bankruptcy. The terms of the contract forbid any unauthorized sale of land that does not generate enough net cash to meet or exceed any remaining balance due," Henry said.

Tom started to ask a question, but Henry interrupted him.

"There is one other thing that you'll want to consider carefully," Henry warned, emphasizing his last word. "The contract states that the balloon accelerates if Jo contracts any illness or suffers any trauma that causes her financial needs to exceed your annual payments to her. Do you understand the implications of that, Tom?"

"Spell it out for me, Henry."

"Listen closely, because you'll want to understand what you're getting into if you give me the down payment. If what happened to Jo last night winds up being god-awful expensive, you may be facing payment of the contract balance within a year. I probably don't need to remind you that if you are unable to finance the balance elsewhere and pay Jo off, you will forfeit your down payment and all monthly payments made up to that point. The land, of course, would revert to Jo," Henry said.

Tom hadn't had time to think things through that far, and was gratified that Henry was painting an unvarnished picture of the situation.

"You're right, Henry. I need to give this some thought. Do I still have two weeks to make up my mind? I mean, Jennings can't weasel his way into the middle of this, due to what just happened, until I make a decision, right?"

"Right on both counts, Tom."

"What happens if I decide that it's too risky and back out?"

"You've the right to do that without penalty, Tom."

"If the ranch goes back on the market, and Jo is in no condition to make decisions, would you sell the ranch to Jennings if he offered to buy it?"

"That's a very tricky question, Tom."

"Why?"

"First, I am well aware of Jo's wishes. She made it clear to us all and even included language in the contract to the effect that she doesn't want Elements to have the ranch—or to have any other involvement, like mining. This note," Henry said, holding the magazine up, "is further evidence supporting that position."

"Then what's so tricky about my question?"

"Holding power of attorney obligates me—from a legal standpoint—to act as a fiduciary in Jo's best interests if she is unable to act on her own behalf," Henry began.

"So," Tom broke in, "what's that got to do with selling to Jennings if Jo doesn't want it done?"

"Let's say, because we know it's true, that Jennings is willing to pay three—or even four—times the price anyone else is willing to pay for the ranch. Let's further stipulate ..."

"No need for the legalese, Henry. Just give me the bottom line."

"What if the stroke Jo had last night winds up costing her a half million dollars a year in healthcare expenses? Adding in living and other incidentals, let's just say that the current six million dollars she would receive from selling the ranch at the listing price would buy her about eight or ten years of good quality care—in short, life-sustaining care. Do you see where I'm headed?"

Tom did. "Every million dollars you get over and above the current listing price more or less buys Jo a couple of years of life. That about the size of it?"

"Exactly. And because it would be my decision to either prolong her life or abide by her 'intent' not to sell to Jennings makes it problematic.

"Forget what Jo wrote in your contract or on that magazine," Henry continued. "I am legally obligated by the State to act in Jo's best interest. I don't think I could convince anyone—certainly not the attorney general—that acting to shorten her life was in Jo's best interest. And that, my friend, is what it would boil down to."

It was a painful thing for Tom to hear. He saw the dilemma Henry faced and knew in his heart that he would do the same thing Henry was prepared to do.

"I'm going to need some time with this, Henry."

"I should think so."

"Who is legally responsible to make decisions about Jo, now that she's not able to make them for herself?" Tom asked, and then added, "For the time being."

"That would be me," Henry said.

"Well, then, I have a request."

"Shoot."

"I don't want you to think that I'm casting aspersions on any of the staff here at the hospital, but I'd like you to have Jo taken to Rapid City Regional—by air ambulance—as soon as she is stable enough to move."

"Why is that?" Henry asked.

"It has nothing to do with the quality of care. I just think she should be as far away from Doc Jennings and any influence he might be able to exert here. Call me paranoid if you like. Just get Jo away from Hot Springs ... and Jennings.

"I'll pay whatever it costs for the air ambulance and any difference in the cost of care. Don't let money be the deciding factor."

"That's a generous offer, Tom, but not necessary. Jo has plenty of cash, at least for now. I just need to think through what you've said. I can't give you an answer off the cuff, but I promise, by the time Jo is stable enough to move, I'll have made a decision. I know what you're saying—and Jo would probably agree with you.

"Now, there's no sense you hanging around here all day, Tom. You look terrible, if you don't mind me saying so. I'll call Ellie and ask her to come over and stay with Jo; she'll be upset if I ask anyone else. When we know something more, I'll contact you. Where can I get hold of you?"

It suddenly occurred to Tom that he should be halfway home by now.

"Shit, Henry. I was on my way home to St. Paul when I stopped at the ranch."

"Should I call you at home in Minnesota, then?"

Tom made his decision on the spot. "No. Call me at the hotel. I'm checking back in. There's no way in hell I'm leaving with Jo the way she is and everything up in the air. I'm staying in Hot Springs."

"Where?"

"At the Red Rock Inn. Downtown. And one other thing," Tom said as he stood up to leave. "Be sure you leave orders for the staff here that no one from Elements, especially Jennings, is to see Jo under any circumstances. Will you do that?"

"I can do that."

"It means a lot to me. Thanks, Henry."

"No problem. Get some sleep, Tom."

Sunday Noon

After checking back in at the hotel, Tom drove back out to Trail's End.

He felt compelled to be there. He busied himself checking on the gas stove, opening windows to air the joint, and dousing the still-smoldering coffee pot with water. Having secured the premises, he wandered into the dining room and stopped in front of a bookcase. "The Miracle of Druid Medicine" caught his eye.

That's the one Cody mentioned in his journal, he remembered, removing it from the shelf. Tucked inside the front cover, he found a magazine article about montmorillonite calcium. Tom took both items, left the front door open to keep air circulating in the house, and went back to the car.

With Jo down, Tom thought he might just drive around and check things out. He headed into the heart of the ranch and soon found himself on the same road that he and Pat had taken two days earlier: a two-track that ended at the mineral lick. When he reached the lick he got out of the car.

It was one of those perfectly clear mountain days that happen when the ground is damp enough to keep dust out of the air and the temperature brisk enough to keep moisture at bay. The muted clatter of wind in the cottonwoods was accompanied by meadowlarks singing from every direction. Tom lifted his eyes to the north and peered into the high, dark peaks. Turning his gaze east toward Buffalo Gap, he closed his eyes and was overcome by a feeling that he had been there forever.

Tom felt the earth spinning and fancied himself being borne on the wings of time into the heavens above. The landscape below rewound itself a billion years in a heartbeat, and then another billion. Looking down, Tom saw an ellipsis—125 miles long and 65 miles wide—rise from the abyss below.

The Black Hills had cooled ten miles below the surface and first glimpsed daylight when a juvenile Mother Earth gave birth to them even before the continents had formed.

Before these dark mountains were born, the entire history of the planet lay embedded in sediment and rock under a boundless ocean. In one violent moment, long before the Rocky Mountains appeared, the primeval mud was aroused in fire, driven from its bed in the sea, and thrust into the sky. Like ribbons flung into the air, the seabed came crashing back to earth in bunches miles deep and froze at sharp and nearly upright angles. Molten granite and boiling mud pushed up and filled the crevices and fissures, creating a crystalline artery that stretches to the center of the Earth.

And then, the violence ended.

For over two billion years, the Black Hills stood their ground while continent-sized sections of crust slid under each other, destroying ninety-nine percent of Earth's fossil record.

In the time it took these ageless mountains to draw a single breath, all of the Caesars came and went, Jesus was born and was crucified, Mohammed resurrected the faith of Adam, the Crusades—all of them—failed, and the Dark Ages gave way to da Vinci. In another breath, Cortez annihilated the Incas, Columbus claimed ownership of half the world for a clutch of Italian investors, the Black Death came and went a dozen times, and mankind twice failed to destroy itself in world wars.

Over the eons, the Black Hills were both tropic and tundra—several times merely an island surrounded on all sides by ice. They saw the rise and fall of vast prairies and grasslands. When the oceans swallowed the prairies, the Black Hills again became a rainforest. These mountains witnessed the migration and extinction of exotic camels, woolly mammoths, sea serpents, lions, fear-some lizards and creatures in the sky that cast shadows the size of houses.

Horses rose from amoebas in the primordial soup that once lapped at its base. The animal thrived and crossed over to Asia before its kind was wiped out in North America by the ravages of ice. Only after Europeans returned did the Black Hills again see the animal it had nurtured in prehistoric times.

Having been so long outside Earth's womb, the granite is humble and round. Peaks that once could have looked Everest in the eye are now called "hills."

Bear Mountain, Harney Peak, the Needles, and Mount Rushmore are eroded outcrops of a massive granite dome once covered by layers of sedimentary rock. A mile thick at birth, the Deadwood, the Englewood, the Madison, the Minnelusa, and the Minnekahta limestones sheltered the crystalline core. Over the course of a billion years, each layer gave itself up to erosion and washed away. Their remnants formed the Badlands sixty miles to the east.

The eroding limestone left behind a legacy of underground caves, caverns, lakes, springs, and interconnected passageways. Because of this labyrinth, the Black Hills gives up no water—its rivers and streams flow back into the ground before the water can escape and make a run for the sea.

There is a staggering amount of wealth in its honeycombed ground: gold, silver, tin, mica, and bauxite are sealed in granite vaults. Other precious things were concocted from bubbling mud, mineral froth, rotting vegetation, and cycle upon endless cycle of desert air.

Thousands of millions of years of persistent wind and water exposed these treasures just in time for humankind's arrival.

Indigenous tribes understood the ground's wealth and its secrets. They stepped over nuggets of pure gold to heal themselves in water that boiled to the surface in hot pools and springs.

They journeyed to the top of the crystalline core to feel the mountain breathe. Silver was just a shiny thing used to decorate their spears. The nomads believed that the ground itself gave life, and they came to Paha Sapa—the dark mountains—to pray and to heal.

Primitive human beings did not tunnel into or scar the earth looking for shiny stones. They could not turn ore into an atom bomb. Mankind's small, brown ancestors did not steal or hoard the secrets and wealth.

Then Yellow Hair—General George Armstrong Custer—"discovered" the Black Hills.

Within fifty years, the miracles were sullied and most of the secrets forgotten. Springs that gushed medicine were sealed; ore spewed from mines stabbed willy-nilly into the mountainsides. The Yellow Hairs took gold and left rubble; destruction defined their existence. After having survived three ice ages, the buffalo was forced to the cusp of extinction—the flesh of tens of millions left to rot on the open plain while native humans wept and died alongside this sacred beast.

The mountains were dynamited and the storehouses of metal wealth plundered, but in their haste and ignorance, the Yellow Hairs left the most valuable treasure behind, unnoticed, unknown, and untouched.

That was about to change.

SUNDAY, 1:00 P.M.

Tom opened his eyes. In the distance, he could see the security fence around Elements' land. It was an ugly thing and as out of place in the landscape as the several hundred bunkers it hemmed in.

"What are those lowlifes up to?" Tom asked the wind. "How did they get Cody so rattled?"

Tom wandered over the edge of the lick and stopped behind a rise several dozen yards beyond. He had woven a plan to buy the ranch out of whole cloth yesterday, and overnight his carefully threaded scheme had unraveled.

"Damn it, anyway!" he snorted in frustration, and gave the ground a mighty kick that dropped him like a bag of feed.

"Owwww! Jesus H. Christ, that hurt!" he moaned.

He tore off his boot and sock, grabbed the offended toe, and applied pressure. The nail was already turning a deep red. *That puppy'll be gone in a week*, he thought.

Tom reached over to pick up his sock where he'd flung it aside and caught a glitter in the buffalo grass. He crawled over to it on all fours.

It wasn't a rock, but it was just odd enough to make Tom curious. He flipped his Sheffield open and started uprooting the thing.

Tom worked the knife under it and pushed down. Whatever it was exploded from the ground in a hail of dirt and pebbles, landing a few feet away.

It was a fountain pen.

Damn nice one, too, Tom thought, picking it up. He turned it over and, seeing an inscription, squinted to make it out. He gasped and dropped it in disgust, recoiling back onto his hands and heels.

"What the fuck is that doing out here?"

Tom made no move to retrieve the pen. He remained on his haunches and rocked back and forth, back and forth, sometimes staring to the west for several minutes, sometimes staring at the ground and using his knife to draw aimless patterns in the dirt. A minute turned into five, and five into fifteen.

When he finally got up, he got up slow, stopping halfway to rest a hand on each knee and keeping his head bowed low. Anyone who'd have seen him from a distance would have guessed he was an old man, he was stooped over so.

Tom straightened himself and, taking a step toward the pen, picked it up gingerly—like it might bite him. He turned to the inscription and spat out the word bitterly: "Jennings!"

"You're going to pay for this, you bastard," he promised himself and the sky. "You are going to pay."

TOM DROVE STRAIGHT through the ranch yard without stopping at the house and was at the gravel when he turned back. *Cody's horse, what's his name? Boone, that's it,* he thought. *Wonder how he's fixed?*

Sure enough, the old horse was in the barn and needed seeing to. Tom opened the stall door and stood quietly with the animal for a few minutes before beginning to speak in an easy, soothing voice. Then he turned, and, leaving the door open, walked over to the oats bin and scooped two handfuls into each outside jacket pocket.

Being a horse and naturally curious, Boone poked his head and shoulders out of the stall door to see what the human being was up to.

Tom took his time walking back to the stall, approaching Boone from the side, not looking at him, so as not to scare the animal or appear aggressive. When he was a couple of paces away, Tom crouched down so he was sitting on the back of one boot. He reached slowly into his pocket and offered a small handful of oats to Boone.

Boone was a great deal larger and more powerful than any human being, but when Tom got down low like that, it gave Boone even less to fear.

The smell of oats was coursing into Boone's nostrils now, and he took two cautious steps toward Tom and stopped.

Tom turned his head just the slightest bit and looked at the oats in his hand, being careful, again, not to look at Boone.

Boone put his head down and stretched it out almost enough to reach the man's hand. Nares aquiver, the animal took stock of the man. Then, erring on the side of caution, Boone began snapping at the oats with outstretched lips. Most of the feed slopped onto the ground.

Tom soundlessly reached back into his pocket and produced another, smaller clutch of oats. Boone was likely to squander several handfuls before he'd let Tom get close, and Tom didn't want to run out of oats before he'd gained Boone's trust.

This routine went on for fifteen minutes before Tom stood, pockets empty, and returned to the oats bin. This time Boone followed him on over and accepted four or five two-handed helpings from Tom. *That'll have to do,* Tom thought. He didn't know Boone's diet, and didn't want to upset the animal's stomach.

Still talking to the horse about anything and nothing, Tom stroked Boone eight or ten times on the neck, scratched him behind the ear lightly to see if he liked it, and walked away. Boone turned his head to watch Tom go, hesitated, then fell in line behind him.

Normally, it would only take about ten minutes to clean Boone's stall, refill his hayrack, and bring fresh water. Tom took an hour. He wanted to spend time with Boone.

Tom didn't know the horse's routine, nor did he know where Boone was turned out. Could be an adjacent pasture, could be the paddock. Tom wasn't about to turn Boone out into a pasture that he didn't know anything about, so he and Boone spent a half-hour chatting and walking the paddock fence, checking for loose wire and other things that might be hazardous.

The outside water tank was working fine, and Tom put half a bale of hay in the mow. When Tom was ready to leave, he said to Boone, "I'll check back this evening to put you up. And don't worry, Boone, you and me, we're going to nail that Jennings bastard to the side of this barn, and you can kick the shit out of him every day of the week and twice on Sunday if you please."

The animal came to him and put his muzzle in Tom's jacket, and the two just stood there together, neither making any effort to leave.

At last, Tom leaned down and breathed some of Boone's air, and Boone breathed some of Tom's. He put his hand under Boone's lower lip, rubbed it, and closed the paddock gate before walking back through the barn.

When he was outside the barn, Tom took out his cell phone and dialed Kathy.

"Shit, no signal," he cursed, and hopped into the car where he could hook into his extended range antenna.

He started the car and dialed Kathy at home. He got their voice mail, left a message, and decided to try her cell phone. *For all the good it'll do me,* Tom thought.

Kathy's idea of a cell phone, in Tom's experience, was a device that she turned on and used only when she needed to contact someone. She was always a bit put off when Tom didn't answer his cell phone but rarely turned her own phone on. Reaching her on her cell phone was an exercise in futility.

He tried anyway, just to be able to say that he tried. She picked up on the second ring.

"Tom?"

"Yeah, it's me."

"Where are you now?"

"I'm still in Hot Springs. Let me explain before you fly off the handle."

"Now what?" she asked, exasperated.

"I stopped by the ranch to see Jo, just as I said I was going to do on my way out of town," he started.

"And?" Kathy said.

"When I got there, Jo didn't answer the door, and all the lights were on downstairs, and I could smell something funny coming from inside the house."

"Just get to the point, Tom."

"I opened the door, and the place was filling up with smoke, Kathy. I found Jo unconscious on the living room couch and rushed her to the hospital. She had a serious stroke sometime last night and apparently was unable to get to the phone to call anyone."

"Oh my God, Tom! That's terrible. How is she? Is she going to live?" Her questions quickly filled the space that her sarcasm had vacated.

"They are optimistic that she'll make it, but she's not out of the woods yet. I left the hospital a couple of hours ago and came out here to the ranch to check on the house and Boone, to see that everything was under control."

"Who's Boone?"

"Boone is Cody's horse," Tom said.

There was a long silence on Kathy's end of the phone.

"What are you going to do now, Tom?"

"I'm not exactly sure, Kathy, other than I'm not coming home today as planned. I'll probably be out here another week or so. I'm sorry about that, but what happened to Jo changes things … in a very big way, I'm afraid."

"What do you mean?"

Tom explained the situation about the contract for deed and the accelerated balloon payment in the event of a healthcare catastrophe. He told Kathy about the magazine he'd found in Jo's lap and the message on it. He told her about wanting to get Jo to Rapid City Regional Hospital and out of Jennings' immediate sphere of influence.

"I offered to pay for the air ambulance. Wanted you to know in case we get a bill for it at home," Tom said.

"Of course, Tom, of course. It's the right thing to do," Kathy agreed.

"There's something else."

"What, Tom?"

He was unsure of how to begin and didn't say anything right away.

"Tell me," Kathy said.

"I went back to the ranch today because I needed some time to myself, to think things through, and to digest what Jo's attorney told me."

"That's understandable."

"Anyway, I wound up out at that mineral deposit, the cow lick I was telling you about yesterday when we were reading Cody's journal."

"I remember," she said.

"Do you remember that Cody died out there?"

"Right," she answered slowly, her guard up.

"Anyway, I was just wandering around and stumbled onto something stuck in the dirt. It was a fountain pen, Kathy."

"And so what? Jesus, Tom! You found a pen in the dirt. This means ... oh, I don't know ... this means what, Tom?"

"It had Jennings' name inscribed on it," Tom continued quietly.

"What does that mean, Tom?"

"I'm not exactly sure. But I've got plenty of suspicions, none of them very pleasant, I'm afraid. Did I tell you that Jo thinks Cody was murdered?"

"Good grief, no, you didn't. What does that have to do with a fountain ..." Kathy caught herself in mid-sentence. "Tom, you don't really think that ..."

"I don't honestly know what to think, yet," he replied without letting her finish her thought. "If there was foul play out here— and I'm not saying that there was—but if there was, I'd bet the farm that Jennings was in the thick of it. I spent a lot of time out there trying to figure out how an expensive fountain pen—with Jennings' name on it—manages to be stuck in the mud in exactly the spot where Cody died.

"Only one answer made any sense to me."

"You need to take this to the police, Tom. This is none of your business or our business. And if, as you suggest, there is something suspect going on, it's the last thing you want to get involved with. In fact, it could be dangerous."

"I'm already involved. Can't help that now."

"You most certainly can help that now. You can give that contract for deed back to Pat and get our check back and come home and start over with another place at another time."

"No, Kathy, I can't do that."

"Why can't you?"

"Two reasons. First, Jo. Jo doesn't have any kin out here, or anywhere close, as far as I can tell. She's old, and in her condition she doesn't stand a chance against the likes of Bill Jennings and his crew. I won't abandon her, Kathy. I just won't.

"Second reason is the ranch. It's the one, Kath. I want to grow old there. I'm not giving it up," Tom said with finality. "I need your support on this."

"I don't know what to say, Tom. You're asking me to take a hell of a lot on faith."

"I know. And I know it's not fair. And I don't blame you for hesitating. But I can't wrestle this thing to the ground without your help," he said. "Before you give me your answer, I want you to understand that this isn't going to be as simple as me hanging around in Hot Springs to look after Jo and rustling up six hundred thousand bucks for a down payment.

"I have a plan that's a bit far out on the edge, but, if it works out, we'll have our ranch, and Jennings and his company will get whatever it is that they have coming to them … I hope."

"What in the devil are you talking about, Tom? You're scaring me!"

"I won't ask much of you, but you will have to sign the documents I need signed and play along in exactly the way I ask, even if that means some sleight of hand here and there, OK?"

"You're not getting me to lie to …"

Tom cut her off. "Please. Listen to what I have in mind. When I've had my say, it'll be your turn to talk. Now, it's my turn. Agreed?"

"Go ahead."

Tom pulled over at the next gravel road and stopped. Cell reception was good right there, and he didn't want to risk losing Kathy in the middle of this conversation. "First, we've got to smoke these guys out …" he began.

AN HOUR LATER a very nervous but resolute Kathy Larkin told her husband, "All right. Let's give it a try."

Tom closed his eyes and let his head drop to his chest.

"Tom, are you still there?"

"I'm here, honey. Thank you for being so brave," he said.

"You're the one who's going to have to be brave, Tom. Please, please, please be careful with those men. And if anything looks like it's going haywire, just drop off the contract for deed and come home. I don't even care if they keep our money," Kathy said. She was close to tears.

"It's not going to come down that way, Kathy. It's going to happen the way we just discussed." Tom sensed that if he allowed it, Kathy would open the whole thing back up for discussion, and it would cost him another hour or two getting her back on point.

"I've got a long, long list of things to do and not much time in which to get them done," he said. "Just do me a gigantic favor this week, will you, Kathy?"

"You mean other than what I just agreed to?"

"Yeah. Keep your cell phone charged and turned on at all times, OK? That means twenty-four by seven."

"I promise," she said.

"I've checked back into the Red Rock Inn. I'll call you as soon as I can."

"Tom? Be careful."

SUNDAY, 3:30 P.M.

The Veterans Administration campus is situated on a limestone escarpment overlooking the town of Hot Springs. Aside from the obvious symbolism of being up high and mighty, the United States government had a special purpose for selecting that location: the limestone bedrock was porous and relatively easy to blast through.

Those who study governments soon discover that what is put forth for public consumption is like that portion of an iceberg above the waterline. Gleaming white, castle-like and pure, the visible ice is the stuff of dreams, and taken at face value, can even seem a thing of beauty.

A behemoth lies hidden below. And like the grim ice that undercut the Titanic and took her down in 160 minutes, it is the unseen government that poses the most dangerous threat to its citizens.

Above the escarpment, Veterans Administration Building C reaches up three stories to heaven. Below, it plunges six stories down into the limestone, original purpose unknown.

The modern-day Building C, with its three stories of sunshine and six of darkness, devotes the three daylight floors to patient rooms and practitioner offices. The first two underground floors are for x-ray, CT, and MRI scanning; blood labs; film rooms, and other activities for which sunlight is either unnecessary or detrimental. The next three floors down are storage.

Jennings had requested approval to occupy the sixth and last underground floor as part of his agreement to join the Veteran's Administration. He had allowed one workman access to the sixth floor to clear away fifty years of neglect; to restore electrical, heating and phone service; and to repaint. The workman in question suddenly found it within his means to retire in Aruba the following year at age forty-three.

Since the day the work was finished, no one had set foot in the sixth floor below ground—except Dr. Bill Jennings. It was unclear whether any of the custodial staff even knew there was a sixth floor. There was elevator service only to the sub-basement, and the stairwell ended abruptly at a locked door on level five, a door to which no one seemed to have a key. If, from time to time, an inquiry was made about sub-level six, it was referred to Jennings. After a time, no one asked anymore.

Jennings took out his key ring and opened the door to sub-level six.

His set-up was austere, but only because he'd had to haul everything down himself, usually in the middle of the night or on weekends. It had taken him a couple of years to get everything set up, and there wasn't anything down there that wasn't absolutely necessary.

Jennings needed to be alone and to think. He needed to derail—or at least confound—the Department of Homeland Security investigation that Larkin's wife had stumbled onto. Jennings knew that Homeland Security could cause him serious trouble, and he didn't intend to wait around idly for them to act first.

What incredibly bad timing, Jennings thought. *I've got the calcium within my grasp, and now this shit hits the fan.* Once in hand, Jennings knew that the montmorillonite would provide him with enough money and political muscle to sweep all of Elements' past sins into a bureaucratic corner in Washington, soon to be forgotten.

Jennings turned on the lights and fired up the lone computer. *I just need to keep everybody off my scent until the calcium is in play, and I'm home free.*

Jennings had carefully prepared a lamb he could sacrifice, if push came to shove.

"You're the one, Sam Barker," Jennings cackled.

Jennings planned to expose Barker as Cody McPherson's killer. Accusing Barker would throw everything into disarray, distracting the federal boys, and giving him time to figure out how to deal with Larkin. If he was lucky, Jennings thought, it might even cause old lady McPherson to put the ranch deal on hold for the time being, which would play right into his hand.

Jennings knew that once he turned on Sam, Sam would respond by accusing him of masterminding Cody's murder. That would be uncomfortable, he reasoned, but not a problem. Jennings had evidence that proved his innocence and Sam Barker's guilt.

Long before he and Sam murdered Cody, Jennings had set up his alibi and Sam Barker's frame-up. It was a simple lie and would be easy to remember under pressure.

Two months before the murder, Jennings had gone to Sam's office and used Sam's computer to send himself an e-mail. The message said that Sam knew about little Shelly, Doc's and Eva's kid, and that he was going to blow the lid off if Jennings didn't agree to changes in Elements' ownership. A few days later, Jennings stopped by Sam's office, again unannounced. When Sam went out to take a leak, Jennings used his cell phone to send Sam an e-mail message saying that he'd do whatever Sam wanted if he'd just keep quiet, because the little girl meant so much to him. When the message showed up on Sam's computer a few seconds later, Jennings opened it, put a copy of it in an obscure folder in Sam's e-mail archives, and trashed the original message. These messages would be evidence that Sam Barker was blackmailing the good doctor, and that he had forced Jennings to withhold the true results of Cody McPherson's autopsy.

For good measure, while still on Sam's computer, Jennings did Internet searches on "chloroform," "lethal injection" and "potassium chloride," and filed bookmarks to the sites in a folder marked "CM." That would give the prosecutor plenty of reason to seek a charge of premeditation.

Posing as Cody McPherson on the morning of the murder, Jennings had called Sam's secretary as soon as the office opened.

Jennings-as-Cody told the secretary that he wanted to talk to Barker immediately. The secretary said that Mr. Barker wasn't in, and Jennings said that was no problem, that he'd be seeing Barker later in the morning anyway, and then he hung up.

That would place Barker at the scene of the crime. Jennings didn't figure Barker had the foresight to arrange an alibi for himself.

Since Barker would claim that Jennings was also at the scene, Jennings had Eva sign a patient consent form that placed her with him in the clinic the morning of the murder. Jennings' calendar matched the story, and Jennings' nurse was on vacation that day and wouldn't be able to testify one way or the other.

Jennings figured that the first thing a sharp prosecutor might claim was that Eva had falsified the document to protect the father of her baby. He also assumed that Eva would immediately come clean and would say that she had falsified the document. The beauty in that, Jennings anticipated, was that the jury would have to decide which Eva they believed. Was she the one that had signed the patient form, saying she was with her doctor the morning of the murder, or was she the Eva who saw an opportunity to get rid of Jennings by changing her story?

By saying she'd falsified the consent form, all that Eva would establish was that she was a liar.

And, Jennings guessed, Eva would dress like Eva, which would raise eyebrows, but not her credibility. Jennings was counting on the jury to think the worst of Eva. They would naturally think well of a medical doctor—it was his sworn duty to do no harm.

From a file drawer, Jennings produced the authentic autopsy report he'd compiled on Cody McPherson, replete with toxicology report, photos, x-rays, dissection details, date and estimated time of death, along with his opinion as coroner that Cody McPherson had died from cardiac arrest due to potassium chloride poisoning delivered by injection. The blow to the victim's head, the report documented conclusively, was delivered post mortem.

Leaving nothing to chance, Jennings had preserved Cody's kidneys and the traumatized brain section in formalin and made slides of his heart tissue and blood. The report left no room for doubt as to the real cause of his death.

Jennings planned to testify that he had created a true autopsy on Cody and kept it hidden because he intended to expose Barker at some point in the future. It would be perceived, Jennings calculated, as a credible step that an otherwise honest doctor might take to counteract his blackmailer.

The metal button Cody had torn off Barker's coat was an unexpected bonus. The old man had put up a struggle and apparently had got hold of a button and tore it off during the proceedings. Neither he nor Barker had noticed it at the time, but Jennings found it during the autopsy. It would be the most damning evidence of all. There would be no explaining how a button from Sam Barker's coat had found its way into the hand of a man who had died of potassium chloride poisoning.

Once they find somebody to take the fall for Cody's murder, he thought, *everybody will breathe a big sigh of relief, and that will be the end of it. They'll have their pound of flesh and be glad nobody had to work too damn hard to get it.*

Jennings placed the Barker file back into its cabinet.

Now that Homeland Security was sniffing around their business, all his planning was starting to look like genius. "If I do say so myself," he muttered.

Jennings had also set Barker up as his shield on the centrifuge business, and Jennings was going to get a twofer, right when he needed one. Once Barker was proven, or even assumed, guilty of Cody's murder, it would be simple to convince people that Barker was behind the whole centrifuge business as well.

Jennings had persuaded Barker to unload the centrifuge magnets alone, since Jennings had to be at a Veterans Administration dinner party honoring him for his research, and, coincidentally, the magnets had to be unloaded that same night. Barker's prints were all over the shipping cartons. Jennings had been accepting an award in front of a hundred people when Sam Barker was unloading stolen goods.

In the end, it would boil down to his word against Sam's, and no one was going to believe a killer's word against a medical doctor's, Jennings rationalized.

That meeting in Istanbul could be a problem, Jennings thought, *if anyone ever finds out about it … but I can put that on Barker, too. I'll just say that Barker asked me to meet with this scientist as a favor since I was already going to Istanbul for a medical conference.*

Jennings had it all figured out.

Pat Burley was in his boxer shorts, remote in one hand and beer in another, when his cell phone rang.

"Burley, here."

"Pat, it's Tom." Tom could hear the late game between the Vikings and the Packers in the background and felt a twinge of longing for the routine things in his life that now seemed would never, ever return to normal.

"How's life back in the big city, partner?"

"I'm not in St. Paul, I'm still here. You in Hot Springs, too?"

"Yeah, I'm still here—over at the Super 8. Thought you headed out this morning?"

"Change of plan, Pat."

"Well, come on over and tell me about it. I'll buy you a beer," Pat offered.

"Have you heard about Jo?"

"No! Heard what?" Pat asked, alarmed.

"She's at Municipal Hospital; she's had a stroke. I'm heading back down there right now, myself. I found her unconscious at the ranch this morning when I stopped by on my way out of town."

"Jesus, Larkin! Why didn't you call me right away?" Pat didn't sound accusatory, he sounded confused, like the words had just jumped out of his mouth.

"Nothing you could have done at the time, Pat. But now I can use your help."

"Well, shit, man, I'm in for anything you need," Pat replied. "You can count on it."

"You got any beer in your hotel room?"

"Sure as hell do, buckwheat."

"Put it on ice. I'll be there in ten minutes."

"Glad to have the company. See you shortly," Pat said, and rang off.

The door to Pat's room was ajar, and Tom marched right in, threw his jacket on the bed, snagged a beer without even a "hello" or "what's the score," sat down at the desk, and chugged half his beer. Tom then rattled off all the details about finding Jo and answered Pat's questions about Jo's medical condition as best he could.

"You said you needed help. What's on your mind?" Pat asked.

"It's about the ranch."

Pat clicked off the game. "What about the ranch?"

"Before Jo lost consciousness, she scrawled a message on a magazine that I found in her lap. It said, basically, that Henry should finish up the contract for deed; then she added, 'Don't let Jennings get the ranch'."

"Don't let Jennings get the ranch?" Pat repeated.

"That's right. She knew she was dying, Pat, and the most important thing to her was not to 'let Jennings get the ranch.' Because she didn't die—or at least she's not dead yet—there is a good possibility that Jennings will get the ranch," Tom explained.

"What you talking about, Tom? Your sale is under contract; all you've got to do is come up with the down stroke."

"Not that simple anymore, Pat," Tom said, and reminded Pat of the balloon acceleration clause and what that could mean in the short term.

Pat let out a whistle and took a long pull off his beer.

"If that ain't a kick in the ass," he finally said. "But Henry's right. Things work out like you say, he'd have to accelerate the contract, or he'd have to sell the place to Doc Jennings 'cause he couldn't reasonably turn down that much money, given Jo's condition. What're you thinking of doing, Tom?"

"I have a plan—that's why I'm here." *I also need to look you in the eye when I ask you the tough question,* Tom thought to himself, *and I can't do that over the phone.* When it came down to it, he knew Pat would give him an answer based on what he saw in Tom's eyes, not the logic of his argument.

"I can't tell you everything I plan on doing because, first, I only need your help for one piece of it, and, second, because you won't want to know all the details if something should go wrong," Tom warned.

"Sounds like you're planning on robbing a bank, or something," Pat laughed.

"You're not far off, Burley. And I need an accomplice."

Pat quit joking and started listening hard.

"For reasons I can't go into just now, it's going to be important to me—and to Jo—that Elements Corporation be named in a felony indictment, and soon. The only way I see that happening is to break into one of the bunkers on their property and gather evidence that can be used to force just such an indictment."

"An indictment for what, Larkin? Storing sewage ash, which is what they unload off them trains and put in the ground out there?" Pat said.

"No. Unless I'm way off the mark, Pat, they're unloading more than sewage ash. And I'll wager the ranch that most of the stuff you think is sewage ash lights up on its own pretty good."

"You saying they're storing radioactive shit out there?"

"That would be the least of their problems, but yes, my guess is that they are running an illegal disposal site for radioactive commercial waste. There's lots of that stuff in the country, it would be an easy operation to run under the guise of sewage ash disposal, and it would make them a shitpot full of money. In addition, nobody really cares about it—as long as they're doing it safely. They'd get no more than a slap on the wrist if they were caught.

"So, no, that's not what I'm looking to find. I'm looking to find evidence that they plan to help a Pakistani national build a uranium-enriching centrifuge farm using those bunkers on their property," Tom said.

"Whoa, whoa, there, Nellie. Back her up a piece and give me the Presho, South Dakota, High School graduate version."

"Bottom line? Jennings has had contact with a Pakistani scientist by the name of Abdul Kahn who is known to have sold certain nuclear secrets to Iran."

Pat interrupted, "This Abdul a terrorist?"

"I have no idea, to tell you the truth. If I had to guess, I'd say he's about as big a terrorist as Jennings. Which is to say, probably not. I don't think either Jennings or Kahn give a damn, really, about any cause other than what causes them to make money.

"I think they plan to make money enriching uranium, using centrifuges. A centrifuge is a pretty simple device that needs little or no supervision once you put it in motion, but you need hundreds of them working in concert to make it pay. You with me?"

"So far."

"As you might guess, building and running that kind of an operation is strictly regulated, and the U.S. government keeps close tabs on who is enriching uranium and for what purpose. That's why black market prices for enriched uranium are sky-high. Emerging governments, industry, terrorists, hell, everybody is willing to pay whatever it costs to get hold of the stuff.

"So what I'm telling you, Burley, is that I think Elements has hatched a scheme to enrich uranium on the cheap and sell it to the highest bidders, whoever they may be. I don't think that they've thought about anything beyond the fact that they'll make a ton of money. Those jingoes probably consider themselves the biggest patriots in the state."

"Jesus, Tom. You realize what a serious accusation that is?"

"I do, Pat. And I've got more where that one came from. Maybe even more serious," Tom added.

"Do I want to hear about them?" Pat asked.

"You sure as hell don't. But I need help coming up with some proof for this one. If I accuse them with nothing to back it up, they'll destroy or move every shred of evidence. So it wouldn't make any difference if I were right. And if I'm wrong, I'd have so goddamn much egg on my face that I'd never be able to live out here."

"I see your problem, Larkin, and I'm willing to help you try and work it out, so long as you give me one good goddamn reason why it should matter to you—or Jo—what those yahoos are doing out in them glorified farrowing sheds," Pat said.

"I think what they're doing out there is a felony. And if Elements gets indicted for it, they will never get Jo's ranch—I will. Anyway, let me ask you a question that might help you understand the pickle I'm in."

"Ask away, pard."

"Your word worth anything?"

"Worth its weight in gold, Larkin. You oughta know that by now."

"Don't be insulted, Pat. I know damn good and well that I—or anybody else for that matter—can take your word to the bank."

"Then why did you ask?"

"Because I want to know if you've ever given your word to somebody who later turned out to be kind of a scoundrel. Did you keep your word, anyway?"

That stopped Pat. "That's a bit of a sticky question."

You have no idea, Tom thought.

"I got to say, yeah, Larkin, I kept my word in them instances," Pat admitted.

"I figured you would have. And that's my problem. You see, I gave my word to a guy I think is basically a scoundrel, told him I wouldn't talk about a deal I made with him, so I can't tell you why a felony investigation will end Elements' bid for Jo's ranch. I'd have to tell you about the deal I said I wouldn't talk about. I know you'd agree with my reasons in a heartbeat; I just can't tell you what they are.

"What I can tell you, Pat, is that if Elements is wrapped up in a felony investigation, they won't be getting the McPherson place. I can also guarantee you that if my plan works out, I'll go ahead with the contract for deed and will easily be able to get financing on the balance of the note if Henry is forced to accelerate the balloon clause. What Jo wanted done will get done.

"On the other hand, if Elements is free to pursue the ranch, then I'll be out in the cold, and Jennings will be right back in the driver's seat—and better situated than before I arrived. So, I need your help breaking into one of those bunkers to get evidence or be proven wrong.

"Before you give me your answer, there's one other thing," Tom said.

Pat was rolling an empty beer bottle on his knee.

"This," Tom said, reaching into his inside jacket pocket and placing Jennings' pen onto the bed so that the inscription was clearly visible.

Pat leaned over to pick it up.

"Don't touch it, Pat," Tom warned. "You don't want your fingerprints on it. Can you read the inscription?"

Pat turned his head sideways, looked at the inscription and turned back to face Tom. "Jennings?" he asked.

"Yeah. I found it in the dirt. Behind the berm at the mineral lick."

Burley didn't need any more explanation.

"You find this today?" Pat asked.

"Yeah." Tom had set his jaw so tight he could hardly utter the words. "After I brought Jo in. I went back."

"And you found this at the lick?" Pat repeated, finger pointing at the pen.

"Yeah. Remember you told me that Jo thinks Cody was killed? And you said you thought so, too? Well, now, so do I. And I think it was Jennings that did it."

"I reckon," Pat said. His eyes hadn't moved from the pen.

Tom took a deep breath. "One way or another, Jennings has got to be involved with Cody's dying. I can't prove anything yet. But I think I know how to smoke his ass out, and lighting a fire under Elements is the first step.

"Remember what Jo said, Burley? 'Don't let Jennings get the ranch.' Jo had to have good reason for writing that down. Even if I don't get the ranch, I'll be damned if Jennings will. That's why I didn't leave today."

Pat sat there as silent as the grave, rolling the empty beer bottle on his knee.

"Going into one of those bunkers is trespassing, breaking and entering and I don't know what else. You'd be sticking your neck out a country mile.

"You in or out?"

Pat got up and uncapped another beer, then gave Tom a long, hard look.

"In, Larkin. Count me in."

When Tom arrived back at Municipal Hospital, he found Jo strapped onto a gurney, her face covered by an oxygen mask. She had been made ready for the air ambulance, which was on its way from Rapid City. Henry had been good for his word.

Jo's long-time family physician was seated by her side. He leaned over, put his ear next to Jo's lips, then sat up and motioned for Tom to come over.

"You must be Tom," he said. "I'm Dr. Faber. From what I hear, Jo owes you, young man."

Seeing that Jo was conscious and her eyes were open, Tom dropped down on his knees next to the gurney. "Actually," he said, "it's going to be me that owes Jo as soon as we get that contract finished."

Jo managed a weak smile, and Tom took one of her frail hands in his strong ones.

"Can you stay with her while I go check on the air ambulance?" Dr. Faber asked.

"Not a problem," Tom replied. "I'm here for the duration."

A single tear spilled from one of Jo's eyes. She reached up with her free hand and pulled the oxygen mask down around her chin so she could speak. "I've caused quite a stir, haven't I, Tom?"

"Oh, hell no, Jo. You made their day. The hospital people here haven't used any of their fancy-Dan equipment in ages. Henry says he's going to see about getting you a training discount on account of all the practice you gave them."

Tom beamed at her, and she whispered back, "Tom, you're all I've got to depend on now."

Fighting for breath and her hand in Tom's, the tears welled up again.

Tom released her hands and put one of his on her forehead, stroking her hair.

"Now don't you worry about a thing, Jo," Tom whispered back. "I'm not going anywhere, even after you're back on your feet."

He admitted something to himself in that moment, a decision he knew he'd already made, but hadn't yet said out loud.

"I'm going through with the ranch, Jo. Kathy and I are going to live there. And you, you and Boone, you're going to have a home there as long as you like. Jennings will never again set foot on Trail's End." He said the words as solemnly as if they were a marriage vow.

He wiped her tears with the soft gurney blanket.

"Did you say that Jennings will never *again* set foot on Trail's End, Tom?"

"I did, Jo."

Her eyes opened wide. "You know, then, boy?"

"I think I do, Jo. I think I know what you meant about Cody's dying now. And I aim to get to the bottom of it."

Jo closed her eyes for a moment and squeezed Tom's hand as hard as she was able. "Come closer, Tom," she said, rasping now.

Tom put one arm around the top of the gurney and leaned in close to her face. Alone at the ranch, Jo had fought off death all night, he saw that it had taken most everything she had to do it.

"I never did tell you where I buried Cody's ashes, did I?"

Tom leaned in closer, as he could hardly make out what Jo was saying. "No, you didn't."

Jo gathered her strength for another sentence. "Cody's ashes are up on that ridge overlooking the house, by the big rock. You know it?"

"I do, Jo. Pat and I stopped there the first day we were out."

"That's where Cody is." She was sounding rough now. "So the sun will rise and set on him. So he can wait there for me until it's my time, and we can go off together again."

"It's not your time, Jo. Don't talk like that," Tom said in a soothing voice.

"Promise me, Tom." She didn't have much left in her, and Dr. Faber was coming back into the room.

"Anything, Jo. Promise you what?" Tom leaned all the way in to her lips, and the talisman that Runs With Horses had given him fell out from under his shirt and onto the gurney.

Jo reached for it, and Tom put it in her hand. "Read Cody's journal. All of it."

Dr. Faber stopped a few steps away from them, seeing that Tom and Jo had their heads together and were whispering.

"I will, Jo. I promise," Tom said.

"Doc Jennings ... " Jo was really struggling to find enough breath to form words now.

"Doc Jennings what, Jo?"

"He killed my Cody ..." her voice had become alarmingly rough, and Dr. Faber approached them.

"She's got to put the mask back on, Tom. She's not strong enough for this."

Jo clutched at the eagle claw as she struggled with the last few words, "... Doc killed him to get the ... the ..." She fell back on the gurney unconscious.

Dr. Faber knelt down, replaced the mask, felt Jo's pulse, and gave Tom a stern look.

"Is she OK?" Tom asked.

"She's OK now. She's just gone back to sleep," Dr. Faber assured him, his brow furrowed in rebuke. "I hope your conversation was worth it."

Tom thanked Dr. Faber and left the hospital.

He planned to meet Burley at Trail's End around midnight, so Tom had six hours to burn. *If I were smart*, he thought, *I'd just go back to the hotel and get some shuteye.* He was far too keyed up for sleep, though, and pulled out of the hospital parking lot having no clear idea where he was headed.

Tom was on Elm Street, about a block from Eva's house, when he pulled over to the side of the street and turned off the engine. Cody's journal and the Druid medicine booklet stared up at him from the passenger seat. He hit the steering column release to give himself some space, opened the journal to page one, and began reading.

As the day wore itself down to dusk, the weather turned cold and then got downright bitter. During the time Tom sat parked, the outside temperature dropped over twenty degrees.

Inside the car, Tom was oblivious to the changes in the outside world. Cody's journal, the article about medicinal clay, and the booklet on Druid medical miracles painted a fascinating picture.

The article was about the history of something called montmorillonite calcium. French country physicians had used it for centuries, and before them the troglodytes, and before them medieval apothecaries, and before them tribal healers, prophets and visionaries. Although called by a different name, the source of the so-called Druid medical "miracles" was essentially the same thing as they used in France: a pure medicine dug straight from the earth and administered without processing, pasteurizing, palletizing—and certainly without profitizing.

Cody was convinced that his cow lick contained the same kind of special mineral—clay or calcium—that might be important to human medicine.

"That's why Doc Jennings and his crew want the ranch," one of Cody's last entries read. "To get at whatever's in the lick. Got to figure it out before one of them boys does something crazy."

Tom read that Cody couldn't get Jennings—or any of the other Elements partners—to flat out tell him that they only wanted what was in the lick. The more Cody tried to get them to fess up, and the more they didn't say anything about it, the more he became convinced that was precisely what they were up to.

The last journal entries described phone calls Cody had received from Bill Jennings. Jennings was demanding that Cody sell him the ranch, and he wasn't making any more offers. He was making threats.

By the time Tom finished reading, it was below freezing in the car, and a layer of rime had formed inside the windows—an icy rampart that separated him from the world. From the outside, there was no seeing in; from the inside, no seeing out.

Tom sat thinking and watching his breath dissipate for several minutes.

Having made up his mind, Tom started the car and flipped on the heater. He made a portal in the window frost with the butt of his hand and saw dogs on either side of the setting sun. *Now there's a Minnesota postcard,* Tom thought, and rubbed his hands together to get the blood flowing.

Within minutes, the windshield had cleared. He was ready to roll. Everything logical argued against it, but he had to see Eva.

SUNDAY, 6:30 P.M.

Eva's eyes lit up when she opened the door. "Tom!" she exclaimed. "What a pleasant surprise. Come in!"

Tom hesitated. "Is now a good time? I'm not interrupting anything, am I?"

"Anytime is a good time for you. Come on in. It's freezing out there," she said, grabbing him by the arm and pulling him into the front hallway.

Eva was still in her silk sleep shirt, and the frigid air that swept in with Tom sculpted her nipples into hard buds that gave her the look of Psyche. Tom's gaze was fixed on these sculptures. She put her hands to her breasts and slowly smoothed the fabric over them as he watched.

"What's on your mind?" she purred. "Or, did you just happen to be in the neighborhood?"

"Truth is, I came here to ask you some questions."

"You here to interrogate me?" she said, mocking him. "And do all sorts of nasty things to me to get me to talk?"

Tom was aroused, and they hadn't made it out of the front hall yet.

"Look, Eva, last night was great ... I mean, it was spectacular, but ..."

"It was wonderful, Tom," Eva murmured.

He took her by both shoulders. "I would love to take up right where we left off last night, but I have some serious things to discuss, so can we take this into the living room—rather than the bedroom?"

Eva looked disappointed. "Sure, Tom. If that's really what you want. Let me take your coat."

She turned him around began peeling off his jacket. There were several photographs of a child on the wall that caught Tom's eye.

"Who's that, Eva?"

"Shelly." Her voice softened when she said the name.

"Who is she?"

"My niece."

Tom looked at Eva and back at the photos.

"I should have guessed she was family. Damn close resemblance."

He looked at the pictures more closely. "*Damn* close."

Eva said nothing but turned on her heel and marched off.

"Want a drink?" she yelled from the kitchen.

"What're my choices?" Tom yelled back.

"Whiskey, tea, or me," Eva laughed.

"I'll take the whiskey." Then he added, "For now."

She put the drinks on the coffee table and plopped down next to him. "Well now, good-looking, what can I do you in for?"

Tom picked up his drink.

"I'm not exactly sure where to begin, other than to say I've got questions about Elements and Jennings. I know I have no right to come here asking you questions just because we slept together, and …"

Eva darkened at the mention of Jennings' name and wriggled away from Tom so that their legs were no longer touching. "Are you saying you had sex with me so you could ask me questions about my dad's company? Nice."

"Please don't go there, Eva. I came over here last night because I am attracted to you. I had sex with you because you swept me off my feet—in every possible way. I loved every minute of last night. Can we please just leave last night out of this? Eva?"

"Yeah, Tom, we can. You came over here to ask me about my dad and his company? And about that S.O.B. Jennings?" she spat back. "Well, don't bother. I don't know nothing about whatever it is you want to know about."

Eva sat sipping her drink, keeping her eyes from Tom's.

He reached over and gently put his hand on hers. She pulled it back, although not completely out from under. His hand crawled back over hers, and she let it stay.

"Look at me, Eva," he said quietly.

She raised her eyes to Tom. Instead of contempt, her eyes were full of worship. She had given herself over to trust, and it scared the hell out of her. Tom saw how vulnerable she was and calmed himself, bending to her need.

"Eva, you are a wonderful woman, and I want to get to know you, and make love with you, and see what happens with that. But I came here tonight because things are happening around us that put lives at stake." Tom was whispering to her. "One life has already been lost."

Her chin was quivering.

"I need you to help me. I don't know where else to turn, and I trust you, Eva."

The moment his last words reached her, she burst like a rain cloud in June and collapsed into Tom. Her sobs came in great, jagged gasps.

"I am a very bad person, Tom," she said, convulsing, "a very, very, very bad person. You don't even want to know me. And you cannot trust me. You can't!" Her lungs heaved frantically, unable to gulp enough air, like a thoroughbred run too hard and too far.

"You're not bad, girl. You're not bad. You're not." Tom felt himself slipping from his purpose, and from a lot of other things he once thought were dear to him.

For twenty minutes, they sat on the couch, she clinging to him, and he making quiet sounds to reassure her. The sobbing stopped, and Eva's breathing had been even for several minutes before she finally loosed her grip on Tom and sat up.

Her eyes were rimmed red, and tear tracks painted her cheeks.

She looked at Tom and searched his eyes for hope, or for a sign, and then took his hand in hers and said, "I love you, Tom." And then again, "I love you."

She was as fragile as a snowflake at sunrise.

Tom knew that the wrong words at that moment could cause a lot of damage, and he said nothing. He gathered her up in his arms like a foal, drew her onto his lap, and began rocking her, rocking her, rocking her away from despair, loneliness, and the unholy mess she had made of her life.

Eva laid in his arms like that for an hour before stirring. Reluctant to leave her cocoon, she tried snuggling in further, couldn't, and finally surrendered to consciousness.

"How long was I asleep?" she said into Tom's chest.

"You? I'd say about an hour. My arm? About half that time."

She sat up with a start. "Oh, God, Tom, I'm so sorry."

"Don't be, sweetheart. It was delightful. You're delightful," Tom said, "Thank you for loving me."

Eva blushed and hid her face. She seemed helpless, with no clear way forward and no way to take back what she'd said.

"I do love you, Tom. I'm sorry. I can't stop it."

"I understand, Eva. It's all right. It took a lot of courage for you to say that. I believe that you mean it, and that means a lot to me." Tom cradled the side of her face with his hand.

She took his hand from her cheek and placed it in her lap without letting go. "I'm OK now. What do you need to know, Tom?"

He spent the next hour telling her everything he knew about Elements and Dr. Bill Jennings and everything he suspected. He told her about Jo. He told her about the radioactive waste storage and the centrifuge farm he thought they were planning to build, and the mineral lick and medical practices as old as the mountains around them. And he told her about the Department of Homeland Security investigation, ending with Cody's journal and his suspicion that Jennings was involved in Cody's death.

The only part he left out was the deal with Carl Graves. He'd given his word, and somehow, an ethic absent while he was breaking his marriage vows to Kathy prevented him from breaking his word to Carl.

When Tom produced Jennings' fountain pen, Eva recoiled.

"That's Bill's pen," she said. "Definitely."

"Bill?" Tom asked. "You and he close?" Thinking better of his reaction, he said, "I'm sorry. That is not a fair question and doesn't have anything to do with this."

"Yes, it does. It has a lot to do with this." Eva bit her lip so hard it started to bleed.

Tom reached over and tended to her lip with the cuff of his shirt. "Whatever it is, Eva, I cannot imagine that any of it is your fault."

She clouded over again, but it passed. Instead of a downpour, there was an outpouring.

She told Tom about the baby, Shelly, and how Jennings had used the child to blackmail her. She just let her tears come and go during the confession, like so many spring showers that clear the air with their passing.

When she'd finished telling her story about Shelly, they sat together in a blanket of silence, holding hands and sipping their drinks. They were forever bound by what each had revealed to the other.

Finally Eva broke the spell and began talking again.

She confessed her purpose in Tom's hotel room, and told him that she'd done it at Jennings' behest. The business with Cody had been tearing her up inside, so it was difficult for her to admit the part about Jennings making her sign the appointment form. She had since figured out that it probably had something to do with Cody's death.

Finally, she asked Tom if he wanted to know about the bank accounts.

"What bank accounts?"

"It seems kind of stupid, actually," she said, "considering everything else he made me do."

"What did he have you do?"

"Every so often, about once a month I'd say, he'd give me a thousand bucks in cash and tell me to go open a bank account in some small town or another, and every single time, he'd give me a different Social Security number to open the account with. I figured what the hell, you know, whatever trips his trigger. I got to keep half the dough every time," she explained.

"Anything else?"

"You interested in this?"

"Very. Go on."

"Well, that's about it, except ..."

"Except what?"

"Except that occasionally, instead of tracking me down or calling me over to his office, he'd leave me an envelope with the money and a note saying what bank, what town, and the Social Security number on it, then stick the envelope under the door. On the porch. You know, the door's a little off and there's a pretty good gap by the frame," she said, and picked up her drink.

Tom spoke slowly and deliberately. "Did you keep any of those notes?"

She didn't hesitate. "I've got all of them."

Tom fell back onto the couch, exhaled, and then sat straight back up to face Eva again.

"Are you absolutely, positively, certain you have those notes?"

"Yeah. I kept them, figuring Bill was up to no good one way or another, and thought that maybe someday I'd be able to use them to fuck with him," she said brightly. "Want to see them?"

Eva went to her bedroom and was back in two shakes.

"Here you go, Sherlock," she said and handed Tom three pieces of paper.

He studied the notes. They were everything Eva had said they were—and more. Each of them bore the signature, "Bill," at the bottom, presumably in Jennings' hand. To top it off, all three notes had been scribbled on the backs of prescription pad sheets.

"You wonderful, beautiful, incredibly intelligent girl!" Tom beamed. He pulled her over to his side, spilling both drinks in the process, and kissed her jubilantly.

After being released, she said, "I never thought I'd be grateful to Bill Jennings for sending me on a fool's mission." She laughed and made Tom give her a longer, less exuberant kiss before allowing him to continue the conversation.

"Can I borrow these?" Tom asked.

"Each one will cost you a kiss, and they're all yours," she answered.

He folded the notes and tucked them carefully into his shirt pocket as Eva crawled on top of him, a long leg on either side preventing his escape, and collected her due.

Tom clearly didn't mind being overcharged for this last bit of evidence. Eva was still receiving payment several minutes later. Her robe was in a heap on the living room floor along with Tom's belt and shirt.

Abruptly, Eva withdrew her lips from his and said, "There's something else."

"What is it, Eva?"

She started to quiver again.

"Tell me, Eva. You've told me everything else."

Her body crumpled and her words erupted, "He raped me, Tom. Friday night, he raped me! You and I had our beautiful supper, and then he raped me!" Tom held Eva closer. "Oh, God, Tom. He raped me, he raped me, he raped me," she confessed over and over, her voice a whimper and her body dissolving in tears.

Rage swallowed Tom; he wanted to find Jennings and tear him limb from limb. Inflict pain. Dig out his heart with his bare hands. Humiliate him. Destroy him. His ears rang like sirens.

When the violence in his head subsided, he was washed with compassion for Eva. And then hatred took compassion's place. And then sadness, and then more viciousness, and then remorse for having not followed her when she left the bar Friday night, then frustration and helplessness, until there were no more feelings that made any sense at all, there was only a space defined by Tom's arms and crammed full of Eva. He promised himself that, if only for that one night, he would stay and hold her and make her safe and keep the demons at bay.

Tom stood, collected Eva, carried her to the bedroom, and laid the china doll down. She drew her knees up to her chest and clutched the comforter to her chin.

Her back was to Tom.

"Don't go, Tom."

"I'm here."

"Hold me?"

Tom placed his hand lightly on Eva's huddled shoulder. As cautious as a frightened animal, her hand crept out from under the covers and entwined itself in Tom's.

Her hand stayed with Tom's, idly squeezing and releasing it. The rest of her body lay motionless, a jumble of resignation, waiting for Tom to unbraid her from the sheets and bring order to her life.

She needed clarity, and it had materialized in the form of Tom Larkin.

From the instant they met, Eva sensed that she had, at last, found a companion, but one with whom she could not travel long.

Tom undressed and snuggled in behind her, wrapping her curled form with his long frame, his lips resting in her hair. Eva could feel him pulsing against her back and lifted one leg to accept his welcome shape.

Tom continued to nuzzle Eva until she relaxed, uncoiled, and melted into him.

"Do you want me, Tom?"

"Yes, I do."

"I want you so much, Tom. I want you inside of me, and holding me, and kissing me."

She took one of Tom's hands and caressed his fingers, starting at the tip and running down the untamed length of each one, stopping at random to kiss a spot here and there, like she was trying on shoes, each new pair more delightful and deserving of her attention than the last.

Eva remembered how Tom's hands looked when he signed his name at check-in the first day he'd arrived in Hot Springs. She remembered how his hands felt the first time he'd held her, at supper, at the Lucky Strike. She saw his reliable hands reach up to retrieve the wine glasses in the kitchen and come to rest on her hips.

She remembered how angry and ashamed she'd felt skulking about in his room, and how she had flushed with envy listening to Kathy's voice message to Tom.

Her shame and envy dissolved when the hand she had been kissing turned itself over to caress her face. It was graceful, and she felt cleansed by it. His hand would always hold the memory of her.

After a time the other hand joined in, and they began to love her.

Tom caressed and chanted, "Shhhhh, shhhhh, shhhhh ... shhhhh, shhhhh, shhhhh, ... shhhhh, shhhhh, shhhhh ..." It sounded to Eva like the waves of a gentle sea washing ashore, exhausted, but home at last.

Her hopes for Tom's love rose and fell with the cadence of his voice.

Eva drifted into his arms and received a kiss, a hot, steady, mouthful that pressed her into the sheets and made her forget any need for breath other than his. She wanted nothing more than to be consumed entirely by him, to be lost and reborn in him, to discover what it is to be loved.

The needy child begged for more of Tom's kisses. He showered her with them willingly and coaxed her tongue out to play. Tom kissed her eyes, her cheeks, her temple. His lips stayed themselves so long on her neck that Eva believed they had always been there and would always be so.

Their legs and arms had knit themselves together, shackling each to the other and both to the welcome bed. Tom's soldier drummed a sacred rhythm across the length of her belly and caused Eva's hips to begin moving to his music.

Eva lost all sense of the world outside of Tom's arms. She wanted to be filled with him, to be so fully stuffed that loneliness would be driven out, to have her ears roar like the sea and to awake redeemed, the past a secret buried as deeply in her as she desired Tom to be.

Eva wrapped both hands around Tom and squeezed and stroked him until her fingers could no longer fully encircle his girth.

"I have to have you now, Tom. *Now.*"

He reached down to her, and she convulsed in his honored hand. Tom remained in that holy place, where the first eruption had started, and encouraged the orgasm that gushed and ripened into a throbbing, blinding light.

When she was able to find herself some moments later, Eva felt relieved of some awful burden and began to laugh uncontrollably. She wanted to tell God that he was wrong and that he was right; she wanted to share with someone the feeling that belonged to her and to no other. But she was overcome by the impossibility of it all, buried her face in Tom's neck, and wept for joy.

"Oh, Tom," Eva sobbed. "Oh, Tom."

Tom eventually stirred, sliding down alongside her, kissing her chin, neck, shoulders, arms, hands, and belly. He pulled her over to the side of the bed and knelt there. Like a goddess, she awaited his tribute. Tom began to stroke her hair, then her cheek and neck, finally letting his hand trail down and rest under one breast.

He lifted it and partook. As Eva felt her nipple grow longer and harder with his attention, she understood for the first time in her girdled life that some miracles are born of the flesh.

Tom kept on with his kissing and licking, as relentless as a freshly dropped calf. He nosed and tugged on her with his teeth just enough to excite her and just enough to suggest pain.

Eva felt a few errant jolts arc between her nipples and clit; then Tom bit down on the nipple, and hot current snapped her into an arch, anchoring her to the bed by her head and heels. She fell back on the sheets, quivering.

Eva whimpered, and Tom eased off, bathing her ache with his tongue and loving kisses.

She guided his worshipping mouth to her other breast and urged him to suck harder and harder until he was at a furious pace. He rose up a second time, pointing her breast to heaven. His hand collared her mound and began to massage it. Her belly became hot before the holy bells of Kingdom Come rang out in her soul, and she was borne on a wave of shuddering light to her death.

Resurrecting herself some minutes later, Eva rose onto all fours. She hungered for him. She thirsted for him. She intended to devour this man who had unleashed her so he would never leave.

Eva anointed his bishop with her mouth, thrilling to the beat of his heart against her palate and tongue. A beholden supplicant, she took in his full measure, held fast, and let Tom choose his own gait.

She loved feeling the thud, thud, thud, thud, thud of his organ's lowest notes echo in her chest, as if she were hearing its music underwater. She knew how much he longed for her by the way he quickened the tempo, allowing her only short, ragged breaths. Just when it seemed that she could not further accommodate Tom's abundance, Eva was filled with a syrup as sweet as maple and as fresh as the sea, and she nursed greedily, sucking until Tom was spent, and sucking still as he retreated from her throat, from her mouth, and her hand.

Cool air crowded into Eva's lungs, arousing in her a fresh appetite.

She crawled back up and lay her face on Tom's chest, listening to his heartbeat as it slowed. After it was pulling steady, she dragged Tom over on his side, pressed her body fully against his, and lost herself in a kiss that went on and on because Eva could not think of any reason why, or any way how, it ought to end.

The light outside Eva's window had died, but Eva was aglow with possibility: He wanted her; he needed her; he held her close; he hadn't rolled over to sleep or gone to shower or just gone away. He was there because there was no place he would rather be. She was sure of it.

Eva pulled his arms tighter around her waist and locked herself in.

Her movement stirred him.

Resurgent, Tom eased Eva onto her back. She introduced him gingerly, spreading her slick wax along his length. She carried on like this for several minutes, dipping and milking him, putting a portion of his cock in, feeling it stretch her, then pulling away.

Tom shook under the burden of holding back while Eva worked herself up to a boil. She felt full of him, but more waited in the sheath of her hand.

She reached around Tom's ass and pulled him fully in. There was a deep pressure and something new unfolded inside her, like another pair of legs spreading. It was as if Tom had opened a window and slipped into her soul; it was so unexpected, so pleasurable, so alien.

As their ritual gained purpose and speed, Eva felt time moving faster and faster, and everything that might once have been in her grasp was slipping away. With no way to slow life down and no way to stop anything from happening, she forgave herself for everything in one blazing and sacred moment.

Somewhere in that magnificent chaos, Eva heard a woman laughing like a banshee. It was her voice, she realized, and her climax. She gave herself into its divine rush and allowed herself to be fully possessed.

Tom continued feasting on Eva, and she urged him on, urged him to gorge himself, to lose himself, and lose all control. Thus driven by her, he unloaded his marrow in one ferocious and blinding salvo.

Eva was crying and kissing him, and he was laughing and trying to breathe.

They clung to each other for another hour, unable to imagine that the world existed beyond the edge of their cradle. In darkness, they had reached the limits of their flesh and now held each other close against the coming of the light.

TOM SPOONED EVA, memorizing her scent. He stayed until her breathing slowed and became even, until he felt certain she was asleep. He then slid quietly out of bed and dressed.

Eva would never understand his leaving, but it was eleven-thirty, and Tom had to meet Pat at midnight.

Tom went into the kitchen to leave Eva a note, telling her that he had left to meet Pat, but giving no further details. He failed to sign the note "Love, Tom," but added a postscript under his name telling her he'd call her tomorrow, adding that he couldn't wait to see her again and that he missed her already.

He checked to be sure Jennings' notes were still in his shirt pocket and pulled the front door closed.

WHEN SHE HEARD the door latch click, Eva got up and pulled on her robe and slippers. From the darkness of the living room, she watched Tom pull away and drive down the street. When he rounded the corner, she went to the phone in the front hallway and picked up the receiver.

It felt cold and leaden in her hand as she punched in Jennings' cell phone number.

Before the call could register even one ring, she slammed the receiver down and stood in the dark, shaking. She picked up the phone and put it back several times before putting it down one last time and going back to the living room window.

"I'm scared, Tom. I don't know what to do."

The living room was dark, the world outside frigid. What Eva wanted, and what she had to do, was as slow coming as a winter's dawn. When it finally arose in her consciousness, her heart filled with resolve. Still, she wasn't sure that she could get hold of it and hang on.

When her feet were too cold to remain standing at the window, she went back into her bedroom and rocked herself to sleep.

SUNDAY AT MIDNIGHT

Pat was waiting when Tom arrived at Trail's End.

"Cold enough for you?" Pat said.

"Could be worse."

"Hell, Larkin," Pat shot back. "It couldn't really be better! Won't nobody be prowling around out here on a night like this. Even them junkyard dogs over in Igloo will be huddled up tonight. Damn fine weather for a break-in, if you ask me."

"You get the stuff?" Tom asked.

"Got the biggest goddamn bolt cutters this side of Denver, one battery-powered baby arc welder, a couple sets of coveralls, brand-spanking-new Georgia boots for the both of us—don't know why we need them 'cause it sure as hell ain't going to be wet out here tonight—two pair of gloves, a nylon backpack, compass, two LED low-beam flashlights, a 14-inch pry bar, and, my personal favorite, two black ski masks." Pat laughed and pulled one of them over his face.

"Good look for you, Burley."

They finished suiting up in the new gear and piled into Pat's pickup for the drive out to the mineral lick, their staging area for the assault on Elements' bunkers.

Tom had asked Pat to go to Rapid City—seventy miles distant—and pay cash for the arc welder and other gear. Tom intended to burn all of the outerwear in the ranch's garbage pit as soon as they were done with the job. He was certain that there would be security cameras somewhere along their route.

Standard-issue farm and ranch clothing wouldn't provide any clue to their identities. Footwear could be very identifiable, thus the Georgia boots—they were nondescript and half-rubber, so they would burn easily. They wore the ski masks for obvious reasons. Tom had even insisted that neither of them carry anything of their own inside the fence. That meant no jewelry, including wedding bands; no watches; and no identification, not even their own belts. It was probably overkill, but Tom didn't want get caught because someone looking at a videotape could identify Pat's belt buckle, or Tom's buffalo ring, or the like. Bare hands not only leave fingerprints, they are like faces. With gloves on at all times, there would be no way for a camera to ascertain even the ethnicity of the intruders.

Tom considered, and quickly ruled out, using his own camera. He'd registered its serial number to validate the warranty coverage, and if he and Pat had to run—and dropped the camera—it could be traced to him.

Tom had Pat pay cash for an eight-megapixal digital camera, a spare battery, and a one-gigabit memory card. They would be no second chance, and pictures were critical. A little overkill on the batteries and memory were cheap—and lightweight—insurance.

Tom also had Pat buy a box of blackboard chalk, which turned out to be the hardest item to find. Pat had gotten a huge kick out of that. "What're you planning to do, Larkin?" he'd said. "Leave a little cowboy graffiti?"

As a last precaution, Tom had Pat conceal the make and model of the camera with duct tape, so even that couldn't be determined if a security camera got a good image of it.

When they got to the mineral lick, Tom checked everything out one last time. It was midnight and time to move.

"You charged both of the camera batteries, Pat?"

Pat nodded.

"And you handled it only with gloves on?"

"Yeah, and I put a rubber on each finger before putting the gloves on, to prevent my DNA from crawling out and giving us away," Pat laughed.

"Just checking, wise guy. LED flash lights?"

"One for you and one for me. And so you don't have to ask, I got the clip cords, too." Each man attached one end of his cord to his LED light and the other to an outer ring on his coveralls.

Tom scraped the label off the pry bar and stuck it into one of his boots, being sure it was lodged between the boot and the sock, but not against his ankle.

"Jesus, Larkin. You fixing to kill somebody, or what?"

Tom ignored the comment.

"We're about ready. Got that box of chalk?" Tom asked.

"Right here."

"Open the box and put a couple of sticks of chalk in your pocket," Tom ordered, and did the same himself.

"You going to tell me what the chalk is all about now, Larkin?"

"I don't know if there are tunnels, as we suspect, or if we'll be able to gain access to them. But if we do get into a tunnel system, we will number each turn sequentially and draw an arrow that points back in the direction of the previous number," Tom explained. "We obviously can't afford to get lost inside, and if we have to make a quick getaway, I don't want to have to stop and think about which way to turn. Make sense?"

"I'm the one with the military training, Larkin—you're just an old Boy Scout." Pat said. "Where in Sam Hill do you come up with this shit? You sure you don't work for the CIA?"

"No more bullshit until we're back on our side of the fence, OK?"

"You got misgivings about this, Tom? We can still abort."

"I'm concerned about three things, if you really want to know," Tom said.

"You're damn straight I want to know."

"In order of importance, my first concern is that we won't find anything. Next, I'm worried that we may expose ourselves to radiation of some kind. And last, of course, is getting caught. Are you still on board?"

Pat gave Tom the thumbs up.

Tom checked to see that both his and Pat's ski masks were securely pinned down to the inside of their coverall collars, picked up the back pack with the arc welder, reached into the cab of the pickup where the digital camera was keeping warm, and motioned to Pat to grab the bolt cutter.

They were off.

The perimeter fence was not electrified and had no sensors. The fence's chain links yielded to the bolt cutter like wheat to a scythe.

We've committed our first two criminal offenses: trespassing and malicious destruction of property, Tom thought, as they slipped through the fence.

The closest bunker was about a hundred yards from the fence. The door was secured with a latch and padlock: the arc welder wouldn't be needed. It was a serious padlock that took both men on the bolt cutter to overcome, but it gave way, and the bolt cutter held. They were inside the bunker.

Tom scanned the bunker's interior with his flashlight.

"Shit!" he muttered.

"What?" Pat whispered.

"It's empty."

"Want to try the next one?" Pat asked.

"Not quite yet. Close the door, Burley."

This bunker differed in two ways from the open one he and Pat had inspected early Saturday morning.

"The ceiling of this bad boy is lined with something," Tom said. "Look."

"Sure as hell is," Pat replied. "What is it?"

"I have a sneaking suspicion it's lead. Let's find out." He retrieved the pry bar from his boot and drew it hard across the ceiling where it met the wall behind them.

"Yep," Pat confirmed. "It's lead."

Tom took pictures of the ceiling before they descended to the bunker floor.

The two side doors down below didn't look much like the ones they had seen in the bunker by the road. These doors were the same size and shape, but looked to be in excellent working condition. The floor of the bunker wasn't cracked and dirty, like the other one. It had been finished with an epoxy sealant and was spotless.

They walked over to one of the side doors.

"Double shit!" Tom cursed.

"Yeah, double shit is right," Pat said. The door didn't have a hasp and padlock; it had been retrofitted for key entry and a dead bolt.

"We're going to have to cut through, Burley. Hope you didn't forget how to use a welder."

"There ain't a self-respecting ranch kid who can't weld, Larkin."

Pat fired up the arc welder and went straight to work on the door hinges.

"Looks to me like the lock is on the other side of the door, Pat."

"Thought I'd cut where there ain't likely to be any sensors," Burley replied. "That I learned in the Navy. Plus, I figured these two exposed hinges would take about a tenth the time to cut through as that door and dead bolt. We've got no goddamn idea how thick the door is, or what the lock's made of. Then, we got the issue of battery life on this putt-putt welder.

"Now, you want to let me finish this baby up, or would you rather tell me how they do this in the big city ..."

Tom's approach could have been a disaster.

"Tell you what, Larkin," Pat said, moving on to the second hinge. "You just keep the big picture in focus, I'll take care of these nasty little details." He finished off the second hinge and stood up.

"Get that pry bar out of your boot, Larkin," Pat said. "It's show time."

The door moved no more than an inch or two away from the cut hinges and the frame.

"I was afraid of that," Pat said. "The lock turns a rod inside the door that anchors in a sleeve in the frame and probably in the floor, too."

"Now what?" Tom asked.

"We keep cutting and pray."

Burley set back to work. As he had suspected, the door bolt anchored itself in the frame and in the floor. It took Pat twice as long to cut through it as it had taken him to cut the hinges. But time wasn't their biggest problem; battery life was.

"Let's give her a try now," Pat said.

This time the door gave way easily, and with a loud snap the handle latch popped out of its catch and the door popped open.

Tom pulled the door away, and Pat stood looking into the space beyond.

"You had this one pegged, Larkin."

It was a tunnel, all right, and it was being used by somebody—it was spic and span. The floor was finished with the same sealant as the bunker. And, like the bunker, its ceiling was lined with lead. A single row of recessed, low-illumination lights ran along one side.

"Let's go," Tom said.

Twenty yards down, the tunnel turned to the right. "No need to mark this, there's only one option," Tom said, and continued deeper into the maze.

About a hundred yards in, they came to a junction. The tunnel directly ahead was barren and looked exactly like what they'd just passed through. To the left, Tom could see that the finished walls and ceilings ended, and the tunnel continued on as a smaller shaft, whose walls were timber. Bare light bulbs hung loosely from the cross timbers that formed its ceiling. On a hunch, Tom took out the compass and was reading it when Pat called out.

"Better take a look at this shit, Tom."

Pat was staring to the right, where canisters were piled two-high all the way down to where the tunnel ended at a door. Each of the stainless steel containers was labeled "Sewage Ash."

"Bingo!"

"Is this the bad stuff we're looking for?"

"I think it's bad stuff, but it's bush league compared to what else might be down here. Anyway, let's see what we've got," Tom said, pulling the pry bar from his boot.

"You ain't going to open them, are you? What if they're radioactive?"

"Then you and I are already cooked," Tom explained. "Look, Pat. There are no warning labels, and the canisters are stainless steel. Even low-level radioactivity would seep through them like water through a sieve. So quit whining and give me a hand, will you?"

The canisters had been spot-welded in three or four places and were easily cracked open. When Pat gingerly lifted the lid off the first one, Tom peered in and let out a long, low whistle.

"OK. We've got them on the first count."

Inside the stainless steel outer container was a lead canister with the distinctive black pinwheel on a yellow field indicating radioactive material. Just in case some nincompoop might still be thinking of prying one open, the words "DANGER—EXTREMELY HAZARDOUS MATERIAL" were printed in bold red ink, and there was a skull and crossbones under that.

Pat helped Tom to pry open another three of the outer canisters, all with the same things inside. They lined them up and took a dozen photographs.

Re-stowing the camera in his pocket, Tom said, "Let's move on."

Pat thought that they should try and get the canisters resealed first, but Tom convinced him there was no additional danger in leaving them open, and that every one of them was probably going to be uncapped in the near future anyway.

They traversed another half-dozen tunnel segments, each lined with hundreds of the same type of canisters piled neatly along the walls. Tom took pictures as they went, and Pat made chalk marks at every turn, until the tunnel leg they'd taken ended at a door.

"Probably leads into a bunker," Pat surmised.

"No doubt," Tom agreed. "Time to fire up the arc welder, ace."

"I don't think so," Pat said. He was standing in front of the door fiddling with something Tom couldn't see.

"And why is that?" Tom asked.

Pat stepped aside as the door swung open. "That's why."

"How'd you manage that, Burley?"

"I turned the deadbolt and pushed on the handle. Pretty freaking' complicated …"

"Shall we, wise guy?" Tom said, and they stepped into the black interior of an Igloo bunker, topside location unknown.

They trained their flashlights at their feet and began to sweep the area when both stopped at the same instant. A stack of wooden crates lay in the center of the bunker.

"*This,* Burley, is what we came for."

"This shit radioactive?" Pat asked.

"I don't think so, but I don't know," Tom replied. "Before we start busting up these crates, let's see if we can find a light switch. I'm guessing that these guys don't work in the dark."

Burley found the switch at the top of the guardrail leading to the outside door and the bunker was flooded with a pale fluorescent light.

Tom had the lid off of the first crate by the time Pat returned.

"This is it, Burley, this has got to be it!" Tom was practically shouting.

"Keep it down, partner," Burley said. "We ain't exactly here by invitation. Let's see if we can keep the owners in bed while we bust up their merchandise, you think?"

"Right," Tom said, and lowered his voice.

"Look at this, Pat! We've got them dead to rights!"

Pat looked into the crate and saw two long poly boxes with the words "Tesla 70" stamped on the outside. The boxes also had the word "DANGER" stamped in bold and he recoiled.

"I thought you said this shit wasn't radioactive?"

"Calm down, Hoss, it isn't," Tom said. "It's only dangerous to people if they have metal in their bodies, and only if the magnetic field is turned on, which this obviously is not.

"Now get over here and bust open as many of these boxes as you can while I get set up to take photos," Tom ordered.

Tom took pictures of Tesla magnets, titanium tubes, and other component pieces, while Pat broke into the crates and lined the materials up on the floor.

After he'd taken several dozen photographs, Tom said it was time to skedaddle.

"I'm guessing you don't want to put this stuff back in the boxes," Pat said.

"We don't have time. We're not going to have time to erase the chalk marks, either. The most important thing right now is not getting caught. We have to hope that the Feds will move fast, or that Elements moves slow, once they find out someone's been down here."

"Your show, Larkin."

They started back down the tunnels they way that they had come. Every turn looked exactly like the previous one. Without the chalk marks, they could have been in serious trouble.

They arrived at the place where Tom had seen the crude tunnel extension earlier and stopped.

"What's up?" Burley inquired.

Tom pointed to the timber-lined shaft ahead. "We're going down there."

"Don't look any too safe."

"They use it. It'll hold," Tom said, and he was off, Burley on his tail.

As they stepped off the finished concrete floor and onto the dirt, Pat asked, "What do you think is down this here tunnel?"

"Trail's End."

"You're pulling my leg, Larkin! Why do you say that?"

"When we first went by here, I took out the compass. Although this tunnel isn't exactly straight, it pretty much heads east. That bunker we entered was only about a hundred yards inside the fence, right?"

"That's about right."

"Well, then, once we've gone a hundred yards down this sucker, we'll be well onto the McPherson property, and I'll wager that's where this tunnel leads."

"What in tarnation are those guys digging into Jo's land for?" Pat asked.

"To get to the mineral lick, I reckon."

"Now, what would those shysters want with that old cow lick?"

"That is just exactly what we're headed down this tunnel to find out."

There wasn't nearly as much light in the makeshift portion of tunnel as there had been in the concrete sections. They were moving slowly and keeping a good eye to the ground, as the shaft had been dug more or less freehand. It zigged and zagged like a snake track in the sand, offering no clear view of what might lie ahead.

After about 150 yards, the texture of the ground under them suddenly changed, and they were making loud crunching sounds with each step.

Tom bent down, brushing the stuff on the shaft floor with his gloved hand.

"Help me take off the backpack, Pat."

Tom stayed on his knees and threw a handful of the stuff into the backpack after Pat had lifted it off Tom's back. The gravel made a loud clanking sound as the pieces of rock hit the arc welding equipment.

"What is that shit, Larkin?"

"I don't know."

"Then why are you bagging it up?" Pat asked.

"Since I don't know what anything is, anything might be important." Tom threw another couple of handfuls into the backpack and pressed the Velcro straps shut.

"Suit yourself, Larkin ... if you like hauling rock, then, haul all the rock you can eat!"

"I'm not hauling rock, Pat."

"You're not?"

"No," Tom said, handing the backpack to Burley. "You are."

Tom walked on down the tunnel, leaving Burley to stew.

They'd been in the makeshift shaft a good twenty minutes when the tunnel turned sharply and opened up into a room.

The domed ceiling was ten feet high. The room itself was round and about fifteen feet in diameter. Halfway into the chamber, the wall color changed from a dull reddish gray to a creamy white. It looked like someone had painted the room, leaving half undone.

Several round containers, each about the size of a big pickle jar, were lined up on shelves erected along one wall. The canisters were identical in size, but each bore a different number on its cover. Tom began to read the labels aloud to Burley.

"15.00 m, 14.75 m, 14.50 m, 14.25 m, 14.00 m, ..."

"They're in order," Pat said.

"In depth order. Meters," Tom said, and opened one of the cans. It looked like the white stuff from the far half of the carved out room. He opened another, and then another. It all looked the same.

He stood for several seconds by the shelves, thinking. Then, he walked over to the far end of the room, where the wall material looked exactly like the stuff in the cans.

Tom pulled the pry bar out of his right boot and tossed it on the ground. Then, he lifted his left foot and started hopping around in a small circle, tugging at the boot until he pulled it free and tossed it aside. Still hopping, he started to pull on his sock.

"That some kind of St. Paul rain dance?" Pat asked, starting to laugh.

Just as he got the sock free, Tom lost his balance, and his bare right foot made a nice clean print on the floor.

"Damn it!" he cursed. "Get your dead ass over here and help me, Burley," he said in the same pissed-off tone.

"All I asked was if you were doing some kind of dance, Larkin. Don't get your shorts in a bunch."

By leaning on Pat, Tom was able to get his Georgia boot back on and proceeded to scrape out the footprint he'd left.

Burley didn't know what Larkin was up to, but it was amusing.

Tom picked up the pry bar and started scraping the room's wall, letting the stuff that came loose fall into his sock. He wasn't getting much of a collection.

"Why don't you just take a couple of them cans full, over there?" Pat asked. "Be a sight easier than what you're doing."

"When we find out what this stuff is," he said, "I need to know with absolute certainty that it came from this wall in this little cavern. I don't know where the stuff in those canisters came from. Now, lend a hand, will you?"

Pat stretched Tom's sock wide at the top, and Larkin scraped away until he had a pound or two of the wall in the sock.

"Grab any one of those canisters, Pat, and let's get out of here," Tom said.

"You had enough rock collecting for one night, I take it?"

"Yeah. I've had enough of about everything for tonight."

Thirty minutes later, they stepped out of the bunker and into the moonlight. During the three hours they'd spent underground, the temperature had risen twenty degrees.

"Welcome to the southern Hills," Burley said. "We'll be in our shirtsleeves tomorrow afternoon."

Somewhere in the distance, dogs were howling up a storm. Tom looked in the direction he thought the noise was coming from. He saw first one, then a second, and then a third light blink on.

Pat had seen it, too. "That's our cue, brother. Double time," he said smartly, and took off toward the perimeter fence at a trot.

"What are those lights?" Tom shouted after Burley.

"Igloo. The houses!"

They slipped back through the hole they'd made in the fence and repaired it enough to keep any dogs from busting through and chasing them all the way back to the ranch house.

They high-tailed it back to Jo's place. Pat said he'd stay and burn their tunnel clothing. Tom headed back to the Red Rock Inn with the backpack full of gravel, a canister and a sock full of something, and a digital camera full of bad news for Dr. Bill Jennings and his cronies.

Once inside his room, Tom fell face first onto the bed, but sprang back up immediately. He knew that if he allowed himself even thirty seconds in a prone position, he'd be dead to the world, and there were things that still needed doing before he could sleep.

Tom sat down at the desk, opened a Word document on his laptop and began to type up the Elements story, giving as many dates, times, and other references as he could remember.

He stopped typing only once to find the topsoil figures Kathy had given him earlier and make a few quick calculations. His numbers showed that, without question, there had to be lots of tunnels out there. The bunkers couldn't possibly have displaced the number of cubic yards of dirt enumerated in the construction document.

The last thing he did was download the digital pictures he'd just taken. He chose a dozen that best illustrated the points he'd made in the written commentary, giving each photo a number. Then, he went back to the written document and matched each photo's number with its corresponding written explanation.

It was very rough and very short, but it'd have to do.

Now the tough part, he thought. I'll have to wake Kathy to get a home e-mail address for that reporter friend of hers, Mel, at the Washington Post.

He glanced at the desk clock. It was three-thirty in Hot Springs, four-thirty in St. Paul. Oh well, he thought, at least she'll know I'm in my room, and dialed their home number.

It rang five times, and he got their voice mail. *She's a sound sleeper,* he thought, and redialed. Same result. Five rings, no answer. After several more attempts, he tried her cell phone. He got her voice mail three times running.

Tom sat and watched the cursor blink on his computer screen for several minutes.

Whatever she's up to, Tom felt, was his fault.

He called home again and left a message saying he urgently needed her friend Mel's home e-mail address, then composed an e-mail to her saying the same thing. Tom mentioned that he'd tried calling, but didn't mention the fact that it was three in the morning. He didn't have to. Both voice mail and e-mail had time stamps—she'd get the message.

A powerful loneliness set in on him. The desk seemed to shrink in front of him, and things got hazy outside his immediate field of vision. He sat, lacking the will to move, staring at the scratch pad on the desk. "Red Rock Inn," it read. "Your Home Away From Home."

He let out a rueful laugh, turned his cell phone off, and fell into a shallow and fitful sleep.

MONDAY

It is useful when something happens to try and look at it from
different angles to see the positive or beneficial aspects.
The Dalai Lama

———

6:45 A.M.

Groggy, Tom awoke three hours later to the sound of his phone ringing. His hand felt thick and heavy, and the phone fell out of it when he attempted to answer. He rolled out of bed onto all fours and retrieved the handset, holding it to his ear with both hands.

"Hello," Tom croaked.

"It's Kathy."

Silence from Tom.

"It's Kathy, Tom. Are you there?"

"I'm here," he said at last. "Where are you?"

"I'm on my way to work," she said. "Thought I'd wait until the last possible minute to call, so you could get the most sleep possible. How'd it go last night?"

"According to plan," Tom said the words quickly, as if there was nothing more to say about his and Pat's foray into the tunnels. He wasn't about to bring up the subject of Kathy's whereabouts last night. He knew he could force her to bring up the subject simply by not answering her questions and being difficult.

"Well, go ahead and give me the details, Tom," Kathy said, but didn't really seem interested. There was a dullness to her tone, and it didn't sound right to Tom.

"I'm not sure that this phone is private anymore." Tom said the words like he was giving shipping instructions to a clerk: all business, no feelings. "I'll fill you in sometime later when I've got cell phone service." That ended Kathy's line of inquiry, and Tom went mute again.

"OK. Sure," Kathy replied.

Tom stayed mute, waiting.

"Well, it was nice chatting with you this morning, Tom. I'm at work. I've got to go," Kathy finally said, her own voice clipped and unfeeling.

"Didn't you get my messages?" Tom asked.

There was a long silence on the other end of the line. Kathy was a horrible liar. She simply had no technique when it came to creating cover. Tom waited her out.

"No."

"I left a voice message on the home phone and sent e-mail messages to both our home address and your office address," Tom said, and stopped.

"When?"

"Oh, about three, three-thirty this morning."

"What was so urgent at that time of the night?" she stammered.

"Speaking of urgent, you must have had something pretty urgent going on at three-thirty this morning, yourself, Kathy," Tom said, without any joy.

"What do you mean by that?" she demanded.

"Why don't you just guess what I meant by that," Tom goaded. Kathy was smart but not cunning.

"I take it you called more than once," she said bitterly.

"Oh, about five, six times," Tom reported. "Tried your cell phone, too. You really must have been *sleeping* hard because I couldn't seem to wake you."

"What are you saying, Tom, that I wasn't home? That I was out screwing some guy while you're out of town? Is that what you're saying?" She was getting angry.

Not a good sign, Tom thought. *She probably was out screwing somebody. Otherwise, she'd laugh. She only gets angry when she takes things seriously.*

"I'm saying I called our home at three-thirty in the morning and let the phone ring its full sequence five times in a row. Nobody answered, so I'm guessing nobody was there. Next thing I'm saying is that you haven't picked up either of the messages I left for you at home, which is highly unusual for you, and you're calling me on your way to work. On that count, I'm guessing that you haven't been at home since sometime yesterday. That's what I'm saying. How am I doing, Kathy?"

Kathy was cornered.

"You're right. I wasn't at home last night. It was stupid not to call you. We can talk about it tonight or at noon if you insist. Now, why were you calling me in the middle of the night?" She sounded tired.

"It was stupid of you not to call me, or you did something stupid and that's why you weren't home?" Tom pressed his case, smelling blood and not knowing it was his own.

"Look, Tom, let's not get into how stupid I am, or how stupid you were Friday night, shall we? If you like, we can get into a nasty little argument over the phone right now, with full-blown disclosures from all parties, and I can be late for work, and we can be angry with each other for the rest of the day. Or, we can deal with whatever it is you need from me so you can get on with the ranch business. What's it going to be?"

"I need Mel's home e-mail address," he said.

"OK, then. We'll talk about the other thing tonight, I guess," Kathy said.

"Mel's e-mail, Kathy. I need it."

"What for?" she asked.

"Look, if you really want me to get into it, I will. I thought you just said that you're going to be late for work and didn't want to get into a knock-down, drag-out conversation about who's fucking who when we aren't close enough to keep an eye on each other. So, can I just get Mel's e-mail?"

"Are you accusing me of having sex with somebody? I don't have to listen to this!" she said angrily, and hung up.

That went well, Tom said to himself, and redialed Kathy's cell phone.

"Look, I'm sorry, Kathy. That was uncalled for," Tom started.

She said nothing, but didn't hang up on him again, indicating that his comments may, or may not, have been uncalled for. It was a Mexican standoff, without the guns.

"I called you to get Mel's e-mail because you told me that he is well connected at Homeland Security. Is that right?"

"Yes."

"I need Mel to take my information to his sources. It'll be easy for him, and he'll get right to the top. All he has to say is that he's verifying the accuracy of his information before going with it in a story."

"I'm sure Mel is well aware of what he can and cannot do with his sources. He's the reporter, not you," Kathy said snottily. She's still defending herself, Tom thought.

"You asked me why I needed Mel's e-mail. You want to hear why, or do you just want to give me the address?"

"Just give me the short story, without all the stuff about how reporters work. I think I'm familiar with that subject."

"I want Mel to tip Homeland Security off in the hopes that they'll take some kind of immediate action. It doesn't have to be a raid in the middle of the night: a phone call to Jennings would probably do the trick. If Mel thinks that there's enough to write a story, all the better." Tom had summarized, and quit. "Can I have his e-mail, please."

"Hold on."

He heard her put the cell phone down and rummage through her briefcase.

"You said the home address, right?"

"That's right."

"It's 'beerknight@gwtc.net'," Kathy read from her address book. She had a PDA that her paper had issued her but never took time to learn how it worked.

"Cute. Oh … and one other thing," Tom said.

"What?"

"Will you call Mel as soon as you get to your desk and ask him to open and read my e-mail immediately? He'll take your call."

"All right, I'll do that on one condition."

"What's that?"

"That you send me a copy of what you're sending Mel."

He didn't want to do that. Not because Kathy didn't have a right to see it, but because it would scare her, and she'd want to talk to him about it. He didn't have time for that discussion this morning.

"I'll send you a copy," he conceded, "but you've got to promise me two things."

"Like what?"

"First, that you won't let your imagination run away with you and get frightened. You know that some of the things I'm doing cross the line. I'll spend as much time as you like this evening talking about what is going on. I just don't have an extra hour this morning. Agreed?"

"OK, what's the other thing?"

"You know how to permanently delete e-mail from your system?"

"Hit delete?"

"After you've deleted from your inbox, delete my e-mail from your 'deleted items' folder," Tom explained. "Print a copy of the e-mail if you like, but do it immediately and then delete everything. I'd prefer that you not make copies, but you do as you choose. Just don't leave my e-mail on your system."

"If you say so, Tom."

"I do."

He was about to tell Kathy thanks and goodbye when another thought struck him.

"There's one other thing, if you don't mind, Kathy." His tone had softened along with the realization that he wasn't going to be able to get the job done without her.

"What would that be, Tom?"

"It's about the montmorillonite, the calcium at the mineral lick," he explained.

"What do you need?"

"I think you could help me blow Jennings' cover, or at least give me an idea of what he's up to. As a reporter, you can get a lot further in less time than I can."

"I'm not going to use my position at this newspaper in a fraudulent way, if that's what you had in mind, Tom. No discussion."

"Hear me out, and if you aren't willing to do it, fine," Tom said. He knew it wouldn't be easy to convince Kathy to use her position at the paper for a personal reason. It could get her fired—and it wasn't ethical.

"I need you to call the CEO's of the ten biggest pharmaceutical companies in the country and leave a message to call you back," Tom said.

"Why am I calling them, and why will they give a shit?"

"You're calling them just to see who calls back. That's all I need to know. Assuming any of these guys return your call, I can take it from there."

"Why am I calling?"

"You aren't going to get through to any of them on the first call; we both know that. But if you call, rather than me, it's highly likely that your message will get to them immediately. Most corporate honchos know enough to take care of media business immediately—especially if the call comes from a major daily newspaper," he said.

"So you want me to use the power of my paper to get you some personal information?" Tom could see that she was positioning herself to say no.

"Yes and no." Tom replied. "The answer is 'no,' because you aren't going to get any hard information about any of these companies, because you aren't going to take or return any calls that come back to you. But, 'yes,' you are going to call me with a piece of information that I am going to use personally. Is that something you can do?"

Kathy said nothing.

"You there, Kathy?"

"I'm thinking. Tell me what message you want me to leave, and I'll tell you whether I think I can do it or not."

"Tell them that you have it from good sources that the montmorillonite they're trying to procure through Dr. Bill Jennings has been sold to someone else. My guess is that you're going to hear back from one of those CEO's, pronto. Either that, or you're going to get a surprise call from your executive editor, wanting to talk to you about a story you're developing."

"Why would my executive editor call me?" She sounded alarmed.

"Because corporate executives are all members of the same club. They expect to get—and to be asked for—favors from other members of the club. The Fitzer Chemical CEO could be the Standard Oil CEO next year, and vice versa. So, if we touch a nerve, and one of those pharma guys reacts, he might just figure that the shortest path to your silence is to call his counterpart at your company and ask him to shut you up, or just stall for time. That's one possibility. If we actually are on to something, and one of these guys calls you back, then bingo, I've got what I need to keep the ball rolling on my end."

"No. Not going to happen, Tom," she said flatly.

"Why?"

"You know why. It's unethical as hell, and if my executive editor calls me on the carpet, I'm fired. I'm not doing this."

"Look, Kathy, if your executive editor calls you, which is the least likely scenario, just tell him you've got a lead on a good story—which you do …"

"Which is not my beat," she interrupted him.

"… which you're just trying to verify before handing it over to whomever on your staff would be the appropriate person to follow up and write the piece," Tom continued, acknowledging her objection. "If your executive editor comes to talk to you, he's coming to kill the story. No big deal, you weren't going to write a story anyway. You agree and it's a dead issue. By the time your editor gets around to doing anything further about you, the Post will have run its story, and your editor won't be able to say anything to anybody. You'll have the e-mail that you send back to him saying that you won't pursue the story in Hot Springs any further at his request. Sprinkle in a few details from the e-mail I'm sending Mel, and you've got an insurance policy for as long as you work at the paper."

"I would never blackmail anyone, Tom, for any reason. What are you saying?" She was acting offended, and it was pissing Tom off.

"We're not talking blackmail here, Kathy, and you know it. It's about whether you believe that journalists have the responsibility to investigate news independently, or whether you believe that the corporation should hand you talking points for your news stories every day, like they do over at FOX. You can't have it both ways. Which is it?"

"You know which it is, Tom!"

"Then you won't have any problem with your executive editor if he calls you, will you?"

Kathy's silence told Tom she wouldn't argue that point any further.

"As to the pharma CEO's, yes, I'm asking you to use the implication that your paper is doing a story to smoke one of these guys out. I admit that it could be considered an ethical lapse. But you need to admit that, given what's at stake here—including my personal safety—that perhaps it's a marginal risk you're willing to make this one time." He'd played his best card, his own safety, and waited.

"I'll make one call to each of them and that's it. I'm not answering any callbacks from anybody, I'm not making multiple calls, and I'm not answering any questions."

"That'll do. Thanks," Tom said.

As if she hadn't heard him, Kathy continued, "And don't ever ask me to do something like this again, marginal or not."

"I promise."

"For what that's worth," she muttered.

"What did you say?"

"It doesn't matter. Now, is there anything else I can do for you on my company's time and phone bill?" she asked sarcastically.

"No. Just call me immediately if you hear back from any of those CEO's," he said.

"I'll call you," Kathy said and hung up.

"Thanks," he said to the dead line.

Tom pulled up a draft of the e-mail message he'd composed earlier and attached the photo files plus a list of the web sites Mel would need to retrieve copies of the satellite images and the abstracts from Perez Construction. He didn't make any mention of the montmorillonite or the mineral lick. Mel didn't need that information to get Homeland Security on the drill, and he didn't want any reporter sniffing around that story, at least for now. Tom sent a blind copy to his attorney and one to Kathy.

It was seven-thirty, and Tom dialed Mayor Carl Graves. Making a business call before eight in the morning might not fly in the big city, Tom thought, but there was no problem with it in Hot Springs. If a person wasn't on the job, having coffee, or in his truck by seven in the morning, you probably didn't need to be doing business with him anyway.

"Carl here."

"Morning, mayor. It's Tom Larkin. Catch you at a bad time?"

"Oh, heck no, Tom. What's on your mind?"

"Little bit of clarification on that thing we discussed yesterday. Got time for coffee? I'd just as soon not discuss it over the phone," Tom said.

"Why, sure, Tom," Carl said. His plan to save the day for Elements seemed to be on track and having coffee was always a good excuse for having a glazed donut or two. "When would be good for you?"

"Will nine o'clock work for you? At the Flat Iron?" Tom asked. "I've got to stop by the bank on my way over."

"Look forward to chatting with you, Tom, nine o'clock will be fine. Say, Tom, we don't have a problem with, you know, what we discussed, do we?"

"I don't if you don't, Carl. I just want to sit down and share a little good news with you and make sure you can deliver, that's all. Otherwise, I can get things covered in a different way. See you at nine." Tom hung up, leaving Carl guessing.

MONDAY, 8:30 A.M.

"Aren't you new around here?" the bank teller asked, her eyes dropping slowly to her nails and back again.

Tom didn't have the inclination to flirt. "Who do I see about a safety deposit box?"

"We can offer you a very nice discount if you have a relationship with us." She batted her eyes again. "Are you a customer at one of our other branches, by any chance?"

"I'll be a customer after you rent me a safety deposit box," Tom snapped at her and instantly regretted it. "Look, I don't mean to be rude, darling. I am not currently a customer, but I consider myself lucky to have such a charming representative of the bank helping me to become one."

Her wounded look morphed into a pleased one, and she busied herself getting forms filled in and putting little "x's" in the places where Tom should sign, asking all kinds of personal questions of him and, generally, making the process last as long as she could.

She was a carbon copy of all of the other fine-looking young women in the world who weren't Eva Shepherd.

She gave Tom a windy recap of the deposit protocol and escorted him into a dingy room with a reinforced outer door. The door looked to Tom as if it might withstand a determined attack, but it had been set into a stick-built wall covered with plasterboard, which made about as much sense as installing a cattle guard across a road without fences on either side.

The teller lingered by the door after showing Tom where his box was located.

"Is there anything else you need from me, Mr. Larkin?"

"No thank you, darlin'. I'll give you a whistle if I want you," he said and winked.

She blushed and, holding her hands together in front of her skirt, turned quickly so that her skirt made a little swoosh and jumped up, and she was gone.

After she left, Tom emptied the contents of his backpack into the safety deposit box. There were a digital memory card, infrared satellite photos, a copy of his contract for deed on the McPherson ranch with Jo's Last Will and Testament attached, Cody's journal, the mineral samples from the tunnel floor and the tunnel room wall, a canister marked "14.25 m," Jennings' written notes to Eva, and a crusty Parker fountain pen with the inscription "Jennings" along its clip.

Tom managed to evade the fetching teller on his way out, left his car parked at the bank, and hoofed it three blocks to the Flat Iron.

Carl was seated in a corner booth.

"Morning, Mayor," Tom said cheerfully, extending his hand.

"Morning, Tom. Rest your dogs and fill me in on the good news you was telling me about."

"It's about the ranch."

"I know," Carl replied. "It's been all over town since yesterday. Hear tell that Jo sold you the place under a contract for deed. That right?"

"That's right, Carl. Jo and I signed off on it this weekend."

"Heard about what happened to her," Carl said. "Damn shame. You know, what with Cody dying earlier this year and now she's got the ranch off her back and all; she was free to travel or whatever. Now this happens."

"I don't think Jo was looking to get the ranch 'off her back,' Carl. She seemed awfully reluctant to let the place go," Tom said.

"Still a damn shame," Carl replied. "You found her, I heard."

"I did. Went out there to go over a couple of details on my way back to St. Paul. Place was filling up with smoke, and she was unconscious. Had a stroke sometime during the night."

"Heard that," Carl said.

"Anyway, Carl, getting back to the ranch," Tom said. "I have good news on the financing. Hear anything about that, yet?"

Carl squirmed. "Nope, didn't hear nothing. What's doing?"

Tom figured it wouldn't hurt to leave Carl hanging a bit longer.

"Before I get into that, did you check with any of the city council members, or with your partners, about our proposed agreement? If you won't be able to get both sides to the table, there's no sense me discussing my financing with you."

CARL WAS COUNTING on presenting his plan during Elements' call with their lawyers later in the day. Carl had made up that whole business about the city council, assuming that Elements would provide the cash, and the council would just go along with the plan if there was something in it for them. If he wanted to be the power broker, he'd have to tell some more lies.

"Got it all covered, young Larkin," Carl said, confident he could figure out the details later. "We have a deal … with Elements and the city."

"That's good to hear," Tom said, studying his hands. "Because, if we don't have a deal, I'll have to make some phone calls this morning and get the down stroke handled differently.

"It looks like I can get the money elsewhere without any problem," Tom said, matching Carl's lie with one of his own, "but we shook on the deal, I intend to keep my word just as long as you're able to keep up your part of the bargain."

"I said we've got a deal, Tom. Just like we agreed. No problem," Carl said rapidly and defensively, nodding his head up and down.

"Well, here's the good news, then: the down payment on the contract is just ten percent, rather than the twenty percent we were looking at before. The city is only going to have to come up with a little more than six hundred thousand on the forgivable loan. I figure that'll make it a bit easier for them to approve the loan, you think?"

"I suppose so," Carl said.

"Kathy and I have gone over all the financial details and we're good to go. The proposed mining rights contract with Elements provides us with the bridge funds that, quite frankly, make the whole thing work for us. I can't tell you how grateful we are that you came to us with your proposal."

That was what Carl wanted to hear. If Larkin was over a financial barrel without Elements, they could get whatever they wanted from him. Larkin could keep the goddamn topsoil.

Carl puffed himself up. *Wait until my partners hear my plan*, he thought. *Especially that know-it-all, Shepherd.* Carl planned to wait until the very last minute, when they were out of options, to spring his idea on them. *First*, he mused, *I'll propose it as a "what if" type of deal. After Shepherd jumps in and tells everybody, "Yeah, it'd be great in la-la land, but Larkin will never go for it," I'll just lean back and tell them I already done it!* Carl couldn't wait to see the stunned look on Shepherd's face.

"I said Kathy and I are real grateful to you and your partners for your offer, Carl, except ..." Tom repeated.

Jolted back to reality, Carl stammered, "Except what, Tom? I thought we had a deal?"

"We do have a deal, Carl. What I was about to say is that we certainly are grateful, but there's a bit of not-so-good news we need to discuss."

"What's the not-so-good news, Tom?"

"This is not my doing, Carl. It's just one of the terms of the contract for deed that Jo dictated and to which we had to agree. I'm hoping it won't be a problem for you. If it is, I understand. Like I said, we'll just get the six hundred K elsewhere and negotiate the mining rights another time."

"OK, OK. It's not your doing. What are you talking about?"

"The deal has to be consummated immediately, as in this week," Tom lied again.

"What … what do you mean, this week?" Carl sputtered.

"I mean that I've got to deliver the down stroke and finalize the contract this week," Tom repeated. "I didn't think it'd be a problem on your side since you said that the loan program was already in place, and that Elements would be providing the funds. Anyway, it's what Jo McPherson stipulated. It isn't negotiable.

"So here's the thing: Since it will take at least three or four business days for me to get the money from my other sources, you're going to have to come up with the city funds by the end of business today. If you can't, I'm afraid our deal won't work out, given the timing that has been imposed on me."

Carl flushed.

"I'm sorry as hell about this, Carl," Tom said. "I wouldn't blame you a bit if you just told Kathy and me to go chase ourselves."

Carl's mind was racing.

"Of course, if you decide that the down payment deal is too cumbersome for the city, our mineral rights agreement with Elements is moot," Tom yammered on. "I'm sure that nobody in their right mind would want to pay what you offered, but if we don't go with the city loan, it'll give us time to do a full assay of the ranch and find out what's really there.

"For example, Jo suggested that I have somebody take a look at that mineral lick in the southwest corner of the ranch. Said it might be able to be commercialized for …"

"What?" Carl interrupted, visibly perturbed.

"The mineral lick, Carl. You don't know what I'm talking about, but it's a …"

"I know what it is," Carl boasted.

"You do?"

Realizing his mistake, Carl backtracked. "Of course. Of course I do. Old man Cody was always bragging about his cattle. Best in the county, or so I hear. The lick kept his herd in top form, some say. So, yeah, I know what it is."

"Anyway," Tom went on, "I was telling Jo that Kathy and I were a little short on cash flow, and Jo said maybe the stuff in the lick could be brought to market—you know, for cattle. I would never have given it a second thought, but you brought up this mining idea, and I thought, why not take a look at it ... especially if this loan from the City isn't going to work?"

"So, I'm thinking of putting that mineral lick stuff on the excluded list for the mining rights, that is, if you don't have any objection."

Carl went numb.

"Carl?"

Carl set his jaw and made a decision. He wasn't going down without a fight.

"Tom," he said, his demeanor suddenly calm and purposeful, "let's not be too hasty here. You caught me off guard on the timing, is all. I'm not going to tell you that it'll be easy to get the down payment money put together by the end of the day, but it isn't impossible, either. So, let's not be too hasty, OK?"

"Fair enough," Tom said.

"Let's just say, theoretically speaking, you understand, that we were able to get you the loan money today," Carl said. "Is everything still a go?"

"Sure," Tom agreed easily. "That would be my first choice, obviously. Hard to beat a forgivable loan, Mayor."

"I've got an idea that might make this whole thing come together for you, Tom. Well, for us, really," Carl said.

"I'm all ears, Carl."

"In order for the city to make the funds available to you by the end of the day, I'm going to have to throw them a bone that normally wouldn't be necessary. But under the circumstances ..."

"What bone?" Tom interrupted.

"I'm thinking that, if we were able to peel off that, what did you call it, that mineral lick stuff and give it over to the city in exchange for their quick action, I might be able to convince the council to go ahead today. It would be a sight easier because I could give them that mineral as collateral. Seems like an easy way to get you that down-payment money today, that is, if you're not opposed, Tom."

"Why would the council consider the mineral lick rights to be collateral, Carl? We don't know if they're worth a plug nickel," Tom countered.

"It has lots of value to Elements," Carl said.

"What do you guys want with a cow lick?" Tom asked incredulously.

"Of course Elements doesn't want that old cow lick, Tom. We just don't want anybody else—including you—digging up the ground on the ranch. Our deal for a million and a half bucks hinges on us being able to continue our tunneling operation right about where that lick sits. So, I'll tell the city council that Elements will guarantee the city their money back plus a kicker in exchange for the mineral lick rights you're going to give the council. That makes the lick a pretty sound piece of collateral, wouldn't you say?"

TOM WAS IN a real bind. Bringing up the mineral lick seemed like an advantage earlier, but the strategy backfired. Instead of being smoked out, Carl had turned the mineral lick into a bargaining chip. Tom had delivered it to him on a silver platter.

"Jo put another condition in the contract for deed relating to the mineral rights, Carl, and I'm hoping you can figure out how to deal with it; otherwise, we probably don't have anything further to talk about."

"What, Tom? Deal with what?" The color of Carl's neck was darkening at his collar.

"I probably should have brought this up first, but … it's just that … oh, hell, Carl, the contract prohibits me from selling any of the mining rights."

"What! Why didn't you tell me this right off? If you don't even have the mining rights, why …" Carl was indignant.

Tom cut him off with a wave of his hand.

"Carl … Carl … calm down. I didn't say that. I will own all the mining rights and am free to mine anything in any way I please. The contract for deed just says that the rights can't be sold; if there is any mining done, I have to do it—or it has to be done under my direct supervision. That's the issue," Tom explained.

"Well, that's an entirely different animal, Tom! Did you say that you could exercise any of the rights if the mining was done under your supervision?"

"I did. What are you thinking?"

"Well, then, I don't see a problem."

"You don't?"

"No. It's simple. You put the mineral rights into a corporation whose purpose is to oversee any mining done on the ranch. So, technically, you aren't selling your mineral rights. For the sake of discussion, let's call this new corporation Tom's Mining Company. You'll be the president of Tom's Mining, but it will be a ceremonial position; of course you'll draw a nice salary, but you won't be involved in any decision-making."

"Why wouldn't I be involved in making decisions?"

Carl explained. "Your majority ownership in Tom's Mining is non-voting, common stock. What you'll sell for $1.5 million to Elements are Series A voting shares in Tom's Mining. You'll issue Series B voting shares to the City of Hot Springs. The Series B shares carry a special privilege given in exchange for the forgivable loan: the exclusive right to any and all minerals, ores or any other materials on a parcel of your land that includes the mineral lick."

"So what of it? Under this new set-up, can you see your way clear to use the mineral lick as collateral for the forgivable loan?"

"It's a great idea at first blush, Carl, but what if things don't go according to plan? What if your partners won't pony up the extra dough to buy the Series B shares from the city? Hell, you haven't even talked to them about this."

"Well, now, don't you worry about any of that, Tom," Carl said, "I'll call my partners together at lunch today and get their blessing.

"We've already approved a million and a half bucks; another six, seven hundred thousand won't be a problem." Carl beamed reassuringly. "When the city council finds out that they are getting paid back the full amount of the loan plus a kicker, they'll love it. They won't even have to come downtown! Why, I'll just have my girl go find each of them and they can sign off in absentia."

Tom hooked his boots under the table legs and leaned back in his chair, thinking. Agreeing to Carl's proposal was as good as dropping the lick straight into Jennings' lap.

"Tell you what, Carl. I think what you've proposed is nifty, and I'm inclined to go along with it except ..."

"Except what?" Carl said.

"I'm hesitant to carve up the mineral rights before I have that $1.5 million agreement done with Elements," Tom started. "This could work out very badly for me if things somehow don't work out between the city and Elements. The $600K is great but I *need* the $1.5 million to make the math work long term."

"Well, I can assure you that our company will work it out with the city, Tom," Carl said, indignantly.

"I don't really give a shit about the city, Carl, except as it impacts my dealings with Elements. You've already said that my loan is forgivable either way. I need to be assured that we will put together a mining agreement with Elements—however it gets done—and that this forgivable loan deal with the city won't queer the proposed mining arrangement with Elements."

"I can vouch for Elements and for the city, Tom. This will all happen—you have my word on it."

"Shall we put that in writing?" Tom asked.

"Fine by me."

"My agreement with the city," Tom explained, "has to say that they can't sell or assign their Series B shares in Tom's Mining Company until after I've got my $1.5 million agreement done with Elements.

"Furthermore, the city can't sell those shares to anyone other than Elements. If they don't sell their shares to Elements Corporation, the shares revert to me. That keeps the rights from getting beyond my control. Does that work for you?"

"No problem there, Tom. If Elements doesn't give you your $1.5 million contract, you get the Series B shares back from the city," Carl repeated.

"Lastly, I want a performance term on the agreement—let's say six months. The agreements between me and Elements and between Elements and the city, have to be executed within six months, or the shares I'm granting to the city come back to me. In either case, the city loan is forgivable." Tom stopped and held his breath.

"I don't see a problem with any of that, Tom."

Carl has no idea what he's walking into, Tom thought, and relaxed for the first time in an hour.

"Great, Carl. Then we've got ourselves a deal," Tom said.

Carl nearly knocked their coffee cups to the floor in his haste to stand and shake hands.

"By the way," Tom said, "you will include a felony clause in the city's agreement to sell its shares to Elements Corporation, won't you Carl?" Tom lifted his hand to Carl's and took hold of it.

"Well, you got me on that one. What's a felony clause?" Carl stammered.

"Sorry, Carl. Being mayor, I thought you would have run across it before. I'll have my attorney fax you the paragraph. It's standard stuff. Basically, it says that the city can't sell or assign their shares to Elements if any of Elements' owners, representatives or agents is a convicted felon or is under indictment. No big deal, I assume? I mean, you aren't a felon, are you, Carl?"

"No! No. I should say not. A felon? That's a good one."

"I'm going to assume none of your partners are felons, either?"

"No, Tom, no. Not at all."

"Well, no problem, then." Tom shook Carl's hand vigorously.

Carl was sporting a smile as wide, and as murky, as the Missouri in August.

"Any questions, Carl?"

"Everything's clear as a bell, young man. And don't you worry about us getting things worked out with Elements. We'll have that piece done in a couple of weeks—at most," Carl assured him.

"That's great, Carl. I'll have my attorney send you language that covers my issues with the city so we won't have to rewrite at the last minute. No time to waste now, is there?" Tom said.

"Got that right," Carl said. "I'm on my way to the office. You can reach me there if you—or your attorney—have any questions. Got my number?"

Tom patted his breast pocket to indicate that he was carrying Carl's card with him. "What time and where shall we plan on signing the agreement?"

"Let's shoot for five-thirty at the bank," Carl said.

"That doesn't work," Tom replied. "I've got to have the funds deposited before the end of business. How about four-thirty?"

"Four-thirty it is. I'll give you a call as soon as I've got my partners' approval on the extra amount to cover the city. Then everything's a green light for getting your money today," Carl exclaimed, and headed for the door.

TOM DIDN'T LEAVE the Flat Iron. Instead, he took out his cell phone and dialed Jack Boyle, his attorney in St. Paul.

"Jack, it's Tom Larkin."

"Got your e-mail this morning, Tom. What in the devil's name have you gotten yourself into?"

"It's serious," Tom said. "I need your help."

"Start at the beginning and don't spare any details."

Tom reviewed each of the e-mail attachments, the conversation with Carl, and what Jo had said about the mineral lick and the stipulations in the contract for deed. Finally, he laid out his theory about Cody's death and the role he surmised Jennings had played in it.

"First order of business," Jack said, "is to write up the terms of your agreement with the city. You still want to set up this management company—what did you call it?"

"Tom's Mining Company. Yes, let's do it that way," Tom said.

"It's flimsy, Tom."

"I know. Just do it. And make the verbiage tighter than a bull's ass at fly-time, Jack."

"I think I've got this bit down cold, Tom. Number one, we stipulate that Elements Corporation is the only entity to whom the city can sell or assign its shares, and they can't even do that until you've executed the other, million-and-a-half dollar agreement. If you haven't gotten that agreement from Elements in six months, all shares you gave the city revert back to you, but the loan remains forgivable.

"Right."

"Second, if any person affiliated with Elements, regardless of their title or position, is a convicted felon or under indictment, the city cannot sell the shares to them, and said shares revert back to you. Is that right?"

"That's everything just as Carl and I agreed."

"Assuming that Mayor Graves will write up all of the separate agreements between the parties, and do so in short order," Jack explained, "the timing could cause some big problems.

"How so?" Tom asked.

"What if Carl sold the city's Series B shares to Elements immediately after you get your million and a half bucks from Elements? These guys could have the whole deal done in a week—in 24 hours if they chose. You want to bet that there will be an indictment in a week . . . or in 24 hours? That's beyond risk; it's insane."

"Well, I just won't sign the agreement with Elements when they present it," Tom argued.

"The city will never allow you to sit on the deal with Elements, Tom," Jack explained. "That would essentially allow you, if you wanted, to walk away with six hundred thousand of the city's dollars, no strings attached. I'm guessing that the city's attorney isn't likely to overlook a problem this obvious. They will require that you sign the agreement with Elements when it is offered. And if you didn't sign, you'd be defrauding the City of Hot Springs.

"Big, big problem, my friend. You can't sign any agreement that essentially gives unconditional control of the mineral rights to Elements—even if it is being done under the auspices of this new management company you and Carl have cooked up. That would be a breach of your purchase contract with Jo.

"Since you can't sign a document written like that, and since you've got nowhere else to go for the down payment money, you're out of the picture, and Elements gets the ranch. We both know that Jo's attorney will have to sell it to them as a responsible fiduciary.

"Game, set, match to Elements. You're the odd man out."

"You're right, Jack," Tom conceded. "It's too risky. I can't just go in there today at four-thirty and hope they're stupid.

"How do we fix it?" Tom asked quietly.

"We stipulate that the Series B shares cannot, under any circumstance, be transferred by the city to Elements until the last day of the six-month term—which we will now call a 'review period' rather than a performance period. That will slow everything down, and, because no one in their right mind wants to part with his money any sooner than he has to, it would be highly suspect if Carl objects to this clause. Next, we name all of the current Elements officers and stipulate that if any of those individuals are indicted or convicted of a felony offense at any time prior to or during the six-month review term, the city's shares revert to you and you have no further obligation to conclude any agreement of any kind with Elements. We will also state that there is no remedy for this type of breach of contract. That gives you six months, rather than six hours, to nail one of these bastards."

"That's brilliant, Jack. They can't refuse to sign off on that condition without incriminating themselves!"

Tom laughed.

"You know, I really don't pay you enough."

"That we *can* remedy, my friend. But before we get to that, allow me a personal comment, Tom."

"Sure, Jack."

"You're taking a huge risk walking this fine legal line you're asking me to draw ... not to mention the fact that it's unethical as hell—for you, not for me. It's not your style."

"Ethics isn't a word that comes to my mind in dealing with these guys," Tom shot back. "They will do anything, and I mean anything, to get that ranch, Jack. If I have to break a few rules to beat them, I won't lose any sleep over it.

"So, tell me about the risk."

"If you sign these agreements with the city and with Elements, and no felony indictments or charges are forthcoming to invalidate them, you'll have to give Elements what they want or fight them in court. If you give them what you agreed to, Jo could sue you for breach of the purchase agreement. If you try to fight Elements, they'll sue you. You would probably lose the ranch in either case."

"How can Jo sue me? I'm still the majority owner of the shell corporation that is supervising all mining on the ranch, aren't I?"

"That's just a tactic, Tom, and it's as transparent as hell. You aren't really in control of anything. My guess is that Jo would be able to take the ranch back from you."

"At least that would stop Elements," Tom replied.

"Not necessarily. Since you had the legal right to enter into a contract with Elements at the time it was signed, and since the contract for deed gives you the right to mine as long as you own the mineral rights and directly supervise the mining activity, Elements will be able to claim that you had every legal authority to sign the contracts—and therefore, they are valid.

"You could have Jo and Elements suing you at the same time, for different reasons, and you could wind up losing everything— the ranch, every cent you'd put into it, big legal fees, and your good name."

"Yeah, you're right," Tom conceded.

"And you and I both know that who and what is right will have very little to do with the outcome. The party with the most money and the best litigator will win in the end."

There was a long silence on the phone. Jack was making a lot of sense, and Tom didn't like hearing it.

"You sure you want to do this, Tom? It's marginal, at best. Maybe we ought to think about a different strategy."

"No. There's no time, Jack. The contract with Jo is in place, I've made my pitch to Carl, and he's at work on the agreements now. We just need to think of a way to put more distance between me and Elements, but still appear to be giving them what they want."

"You have any ideas, Tom?"

"What if we name Carl Graves, rather than Elements Corporation, as the only entity to whom the city can sell its Series B shares?" Tom asked. "The contract for deed only mentions Elements Corporation and Dr. Bill Jennings. What Carl does with those shares is his personal business.

"We could also add a clause that allows me, at my sole discretion, to buy those Series B shares back for the price of the loan at any time during the six-month review period. That gives me a way out of this if push comes to shove. It would be painful as hell, but it would give me an option and it puts a legal arm's length between me and Elements."

Jack mulled this over and said, "From a legal standpoint, both of those things would help. It still violates the spirit of your agreement with Mrs. McPherson—it just makes the *intent* to violate more difficult to prove."

The ranch purchase had become a nasty business, and it sickened Tom to think that he was going betray Jo's trust to get the down payment money he needed.

"What's the worst case scenario if I go ahead with this, Jack?"

"No indictment, no felony conviction, no way for you to cough up the $600K to buy back the shares, and under this structure, Elements essentially winds up with the mineral rights they want—through Carl. You will have shafted Mrs. McPherson. That plain enough language for you?" Jack said somberly.

Tom closed his eyes and damned the nature of things; he cursed the kind of people who were willing to destroy whatever lay in their path for money. He damned his financial position, and he damned himself. *Am I really any different,* he thought, *than Jennings and his crew? Look what I've already done in the name of "saving" the ranch! Saving it for whom? For me? For Cody? For Jo? Damn,* Tom cursed himself and all creation again.

"Do it," Tom instructed Jack. "Do it, and I will make it right."

"Never known you to cross a line like this, Tom," Jack said. "Are you absolutely sure you want to go down this road?"

"No, I'm not sure!" Tom barked and was immediately ashamed.

"I'm sorry, Jack. This isn't your doing. I'm frustrated and I know this isn't the right way of going about things. I just don't see another way. If I can't get one of those Elements' guys into legal trouble, I'll have done exactly what Jo asked me not to do. Believe me, I get that."

Tom stopped, but Jack didn't say anything.

"So, yeah, I'm unsure about this. I'm unsure about almost everything I'm doing right now—except that I'm sure I want the ranch, and I'm sure that I can hang something around somebody's neck. That's all I've got. I'm going with it."

"OK, Tom. I'll write it up," Jack said. "Anything else?"

"Nothing I can think of," Tom said, dully. "Can you think of anything I'm missing?"

"I think that I should review whatever they write up before you sign it."

"Good idea. How does that work?" Tom asked in the same flat tone.

"I'll put my name and contact numbers on the agreement clauses when I fax them over to Carl. I'll also write him a note saying that the final contract has to be back on my desk no later than three-thirty this afternoon, Mountain Time, in order to give me time to review it and make any necessary amendments. If you haven't heard back from me before then, give me a call when you get to the signing and we'll do this over the phone."

"Thanks, Jack. Thanks a lot."

"Happy to do it. And, by the way, you remember saying that you didn't pay me enough? Please feel free to add a bump to the invoice when you pay it." Jack laughed.

"You sure you don't want to take this job on a contingent basis?" Tom countered.

"Just exactly what settlement would I be getting a piece of, Tom?"

"How about a third of whatever's in the mineral lick in exchange for your firm handling all the legal work surrounding it?" Tom offered hopefully.

"With all due respect," Jack said, "why don't I just buy any salt blocks I need down at the farm supply store and bill you for the hours. You can keep the cow medicine, Tom."

"Your loss," Tom said, not really believing it.

He threw a twenty on the table, and left the Flat Iron to find Eva Shepherd.

MONDAY, *10:00* A.M.

Eva had awakened in the middle of the night to the sound of her phone ringing.

It was Jennings calling to say that a little birdie had told him that a big black Cadillac had been parked in front of her house all night Saturday and several hours on Sunday afternoon. He wanted to know what she'd found out.

When Eva told him she was done playing his game, he had reminded her of their arrangement involving her daughter, and when Eva maintained that she had learned nothing, Jennings had said that if she ever wanted to see her precious little Shelly again, she'd better find her memory and call him back in the morning. Otherwise, Jennings had said, the kid would be put in his sole custody, and Eva could call him if she cared to know where her brat was or how she was doing.

Eva had lain in bed for an hour, first raging and then fighting despair. At last, she was able to calm herself and think. She spent the next hour rearranging all the important details of her life in a new, and for her, unorthodox fashion. As she lay there shuffling her priorities, hopelessness gave way to resolve, and she got out of bed. She costumed herself in a pair of khaki slacks, flats, and a Ralph Lauren button-down shirt; unearthed a hidden file from the back of her closet; and drove her Mustang GT to the Rapid City Regional Airport, arriving just before dawn.

Eva now knew exactly what she had to do. Tom had sparked in her a chain reaction of gut-wrenching, astonish-

ing, painful, startling, wretched and wondrous emotions that
had somehow rekindled hope in her life. He had inspired her
to dismiss as hogwash the convoluted rules that governed her
past routines. When she was with Tom, she liked who she
was; she was no longer ashamed of being Eva. Tom hadn't
just stirred the pot; he'd helped her throw its contents out the
window. She could start over now. It was his gift to her, and
she loved him for it.

But what she needed to do wasn't for Tom.

Eva took the first Mesaba flight to Omaha, rented a car, and
pulled up to the Prairie Star, a private, long-term pediatric care
facility, at ten o'clock in the morning.

She arrived at the administration desk armed with a well-worn
file that held all the paperwork necessary to prove Shelly's parent-
age to anyone with a need to know.

"Good morning. My name is Eva Shepherd. I believe you
know me. I've come for my daughter, Shelly."

"I'm sorry, Ms. Shepherd, we didn't get word that you were
coming. How long will you be staying today?" The secretary
asked.

"I'm not staying, and neither is Shelly. I've come to take her
home."

The secretary blanched, got up from her post and returned
with the facility administrator, Chuck Emmer, who came around
the secretary's desk and extended his hand to Eva. "Hello, Ms.
Shepherd. Welcome back to Prairie Star. What has it been, two or
three weeks since we last saw you? Always a pleasure to have you
visit us and Shelly."

"Thank you, Chuck. But, as I just said, I'm not visiting, and
when I leave here today, Shelly is leaving with me. What do I have
to sign?"

"Why don't you have a chair in my office and we can go over
this privately?" He wasn't really asking. "Would you care for a cup
of coffee?"

"No," Eva said. "Let's just get through this as quickly as possible."

"Now, Ms. Shepherd," Emmer began, "this is a highly unusual request, and we have had absolutely no advance warning that you wanted . . ."

Eva cut him off sharply. "Here's the situation, Chuck. Shelly is here because I voluntarily put her here. Everything that is owed Prairie Star has been paid. All accounts are current . . . isn't that right, Chuck?"

"I'd have to check our ledgers and . . ."

Eva stood up while Emmer was talking.

"Are the bills paid, or are they not paid, Chuck?"

Eva had calculated how angry she would allow herself to be, and in what stages, during the drive from the airport to Prairie Star. Now she stood directly above Emmer, hands on her hips, and raised her voice.

"Are the bills paid, Chuck, or are they not paid, Chuck?"

"No need to get hostile, Ms. Shepherd."

"Chuck! Are the bills paid?"

"Well, yes, I suppose they are, but . . ."

"But nothing. Here's the deal. The last time I checked, this care facility was not a state prison. Responsible adults are free to come and go with their children as they damn well please. So either you pull some discharge paperwork out of your hat in the next sixty seconds, or I dial 911." To show Emmer she wasn't joking, Eva took out her cell phone and flipped it open.

"Just exactly what would you be reporting, Ms. Shepherd?" Emmer smirked.

"Kidnapping, you asshole!" Eva shouted back.

The secretary poked her head in Emmer's office to ask if everything was OK.

"Call the police," Eva ordered.

"Good grief, Ms. Shepherd. Calm down," Emmer said. "Everything is fine here. Now please shut my door." The secretary retreated.

"Are we going to do this civilly, or do I have to go to war with you to take my daughter home? Either way, Chuck, you've got about fifteen seconds left on the clock," Eva commanded, looking down at her cell phone.

"All right, Ms. Shepherd, all right. I'm sure we can get things worked out to your satisfaction. It's just that we don't get requests like this out of the blue every day. There is a procedure that needs to be followed—for the sake of the patients' safety, of course."

"Whatever. Let's just get the damn procedure underway."

Chuck Emmer brushed past Eva and rustled some papers out of a four-drawer file near his desk and returned with them. "These must be completed before we can release Shelly. There will also be the matter of the initial intake paperwork, birth documents, and a few pieces of correspondence of which you will have to produce original copies."

Eva slapped her file on Emmer's desk. "Everything you need is in there."

There is no substitute for the right paperwork in a bureaucrat's world. And if Eva had ever gotten anything right in her life, she had Shelly's discharge documents as right as rain. She didn't need to threaten anybody. She just needed to stand her ground until Emmer gave in.

"Of course, there is also the matter of the blood test," Chuck said.

"You know who I am, Chuck; can we dispense with the bullshit?" Eva asked.

Chuck the bureaucrat had eaten his crow, and he intended to make Eva eat what little he could dish up to her.

"I'm sorry, Ms. Shepherd. It's policy."

While Eva sat filling out forms in his office, Emmer left, and a few minutes later she could hear him talking to Jennings in an agitated tone. From what Eva could gather from eavesdropping, Emmer was apologizing all over himself and promising to send back any unused funds and telling Jennings that he had done everything in his power. The conversation was short, and Emmer returned to his office.

"You and Bill have a nice chat?" Eva sneered.

"He is very unhappy with what you are doing. Unfortunately, he is very unhappy with me as a result. Is this all necessary, Ms. Shepherd?"

"That is none of your business, Chuck. Where do I get the blood test?"

"I'll show you the way," a resigned Emmer sighed.

In addition to the blood test, Eva patiently answered a nasty battery of questions to which no parent had previously been subjected. She hung on like a bad cold and made herself about as welcome.

By noon, Eva was walking out to the parking lot with a blue-vested teddy bear under her arm, a Hello Kitty suitcase in one hand, with little Shelly limping along and glommed onto the other.

It took a minute to unlock the car because tears of relief and hope blurred her vision, and her hands were shaking.

"Mommy? Why are you crying?"

"Because I love you, sweetie. Because I love you so very much."

On the plane ride back to Rapid City, Eva sat with her arms around Shelly, clutching the girl like she might fly out the window if Eva were to let go even for an instant. They sat, heads together, cooing and babbling, crying and laughing in a communion so unabashed and animated that other passengers might have had reason to complain, for air travelers have a right to their silence. But no complaints were lodged.

It might have later dawned on those waiting at the gate in Rapid City how unusually pleased and happy the arriving passengers on Flight 161 from Omaha seemed that day. In particular, they might have remembered the happy chatter of a little girl who hobbled alongside her mother on one strong and one stunted spindle, in a broken skip.

It was clear to those watching her lively but uneven gait that the child was in so buoyant a mood that she couldn't be bothered by anything as paltry as her one wobbly stilt. She was going home with Mommy!

It was the best day yet in both of their lives.

Tom plugged his iPod into his cell phone, dialed a number at the Washington Post, and hit the "record" button.

"Mel Bateman."

"Mel, it's Tom Larkin."

"Good to hear your voice. Been a while."

"Yeah. Too long. You get the materials?"

"I did. Serious stuff. I've been through everything and have a good idea of what it means. What's the rest of the story?" Mel asked.

"Off the record?" Tom replied.

"Why?"

"Because that's the way I have to play it, Mel, and you don't need me as a source to write the story. In fact, if nothing should come of this, I sure as hell don't want to be on the record, and you don't want to know how I got the photos I sent you, so don't even ask me that. Anyway, I'm off the record, agreed?"

"If that's the way you want it, Deep Throat. I'm going to get all the glory. This is your last chance."

"Have at it, tiger. I don't need glory; I need action."

"What kind of action?"

"We off the record, Mel?" Tom asked again.

"We are officially off the record. Now, exactly what are you looking for? I'm a reporter, not a law enforcement official," Mel said.

"You are a reporter with high-level connections at federal agencies that can take action. Based on what you told Kathy, Homeland Security is already conducting an investigation of Elements; it just isn't on the front burner, right?"

"Correct."

"I'm asking you to contact your source and pass along the information that I sent you."

"I've got no problem doing that, Tom. In fact, I've already placed the call. What's that got to do with the 'action' you were referring to?"

"I need Homeland Security to issue an immediate indictment of Elements Corporation," Tom said.

"Look, Tom," Mel said, "based on what you sent me, I don't think there is any question but what an indictment will come down—sooner or later. What's the hurry?"

"I think Bill Jennings will either clean up his mess or flee the country, or both, when he gets wind of what's going on. For all I know, he may already be aware that there is an investigation."

"How would he know that?" Mel asked.

"Because you told Kathy, Kathy wrote it down and e-mailed it to me in Hot Springs, and I am quite certain that my communications here at the hotel have been compromised."

"Jesus Christ, Tom, what have you gotten yourself into?"

"I'll give you the back story over a beer sometime, Mel. Let me finish.

"If Homeland Security is serious about nailing Jennings, they have to act fast. And I mean right now. Today, tomorrow, end of the week, or he will be gone," Tom argued. "He's rich and he's one smart cookie. I'd say he's a flight risk if ever there was one."

"I understand these guys are in pretty deep, but I hardly think Jennings will flee. If he's got money, and he's as smart as you say, he'll probably just sit tight and fight the charges."

"No, he won't, Mel. Jennings has another problem—more serious than the things Homeland Security is looking at. If I can pry the lid off this other thing—and I'm trying—believe me, he'll be gone."

"Care to talk about this other issue?" Mel asked.

"Sorry, Mel. I can't, yet. So you need to try and get your contact at Homeland Security to promise you that he'll push for an indictment in exchange for the evidence I sent to you. Is that unethical?"

"It's not unethical, Tom, but there's no guarantee he will—or can—do anything," Mel answered.

"Just do your best to goad the Feds into action. If they know that you know, they'll be a lot more motivated to act. That's all I'm asking."

"Is that it, Tom?"

"There is one more thing, and I know this falls in the category of a favor that I don't have coming. I'd like you to call Elements' law firm in Philadelphia. Name is Perez, Farmer and something or another."

"Call them for what reason?" Mel asked.

"I know they can't and won't answer any questions about their client's business. But you could ask them if they will be defending Elements against upcoming charges of violating the Nuclear Security Act or whatever other charges your contact at Homeland Security is contemplating."

"Why would I do a stupid thing like that, Tom? We won't have to worry about Jennings getting wind of the investigation then. We'll have given him an engraved announcement," Mel said, a bit dumbfounded by Tom's request.

"I know," Tom said. "I'm hoping it will light a fire under your buddies at Homeland Security. You'll be able to tell them, with certainty, that Elements has been alerted to the investigation. If the Feds believe that any of these guys will run or hide, they're going to want to indict as quickly as possible," Tom explained. "That's why I want you to call their law firm."

"OK, Tom," Mel said, "Call me if anything else comes up. I'll do what I can on my end."

"You're a good man, Mel."

MONDAY, *11:30* A.M.

Carl dove into the fax from Tom's attorney. As he read, a small frown grew into a full-fledged scowl.

"What the hell is he trying to do?" Carl muttered aloud. "This is not what we talked about!"

Carl was a big man, and he tipped back in his chair with a caution born of experience. He'd sent himself sprawling backward just twice; once because he'd come to the office after having way too much fun, and then a second time—again after having drunk too much—because he'd forgotten about the first time.

He was mightily displeased with what had come back from Larkin's lawyer. *Typical,* he fumed silently, *goddamn lawyers get involved, and everything comes undone.* He had already assigned his personal attorney to write the agreements up and made a point of telling him that he didn't want any surprises. Apparently, Larkin had made a unilateral decision—for what reason, Carl had no idea— that the city could only transfer the Series B shares to himself, not to Elements, as agreed. The more he thought about it, the more it upset him.

"Transfer the shares to me, indeed! What makes him think my partners will go for a fool idea like that?" Carl reached for his desk phone to call Larkin.

He lodged the phone between his shoulder and his well-fed cheek and started stabbing at numbers. One of his fat fingers stopped in mid-air, and he hung up the phone. He sat in that position, motionless, with his arm outstretched and his hand still resting on the receiver, for several seconds.

The sour look on his puss slowly dissolved into a huge grin that begat a chuckle that started Carl cackling aloud in his empty office.

"Carl, something the matter?" Norma, his assistant, had materialized at his door. She looked around inside Carl's office, puzzled. "Somebody in here?"

"No. Nobody's here," Carl said. "Just a joke my buddy sent me on the Internet. Funny guy. Close my door, will you, Norma? Thank you."

When Norma had closed the door, Carl slammed his hammy fists on the desk with glee. Then he put his head down between his fists and pounded some more.

Larkin, he thought, *you wonderful, ignorant, unsuspecting fool of a godsend! Of course my partners will never agree to transfer those Series B shares to me, and that's why it's so perfect. I don't need their agreement anymore,* he chortled to himself. *This ain't a negotiation anymore. Elements has to play cards with good old Carl, and good old Carl is holding all the cards.* Carl's fantasy of simply saving the day for Elements had grown into the notion of being the kingmaker, or maybe even the king.

This is going to turn out about a hundred times better ... no ... Carl corrected his thinking and financial dreams ... about a million times better than what he originally had in mind.

"I've just got to make a somewhat different arrangement on the down payment money for Larkin," he calculated aloud. Carl knew where to find that kind of money. There was a minimum balance of one million dollars in the Elements account at all times, and he was a signatory. However, any check over a hundred thousand dollars required the signatures of two partners. Jennings could sign by himself for any amount, but Carl could not. Bill had set things up that way, and the other partners had agreed because Jennings was the reason so much money was at their disposal in the first place.

The money problem caused Carl to slump, but not lean back in his chair. There he remained for several minutes, wedged between the desk and his chair, head in hands.

With a jerk, he sat bolt upright.

"But I can write a check for under a hundred grand," he proclaimed, while prying himself out of his chair. Once standing, he pointed his index finger skyward like some God-thanking NFL receiver who has just caught the game-winning pass at the Super Bowl. "I can write a check for under a hundred grand, and there aren't any rules about how many of them I can write!"

"We've got trouble," Brady said, as soon as Jennings picked up.

"I've got fifteen minutes for you, so don't mince words," Jennings ordered.

"Homeland Security is investigating Elements, as you suspected ..."

"I know that. What's the bad news?"

"The bad news is they're serious. This isn't just exploratory, Doc. They've apparently been snooping around for quite some time. The good news, if you can call it that, is that the case is still being handled by junior staff."

"Do they have anything concrete to go on, Brady? Anything I should be worried about?"

"The partner who checked it out says that they're still chewing on scraps, but they aren't letting go. The word from the top is to keep looking; they will indict as soon as they have something solid."

"Is that all you've got?" Jennings spat back at Brady.

"That's what I've got on the Homeland Security thing, yeah."

"Well, good. That's not bad news, that's old news. What else do you have?"

"On Larkin, the Qwestead letter of credit, or the custody assignment?"

"On Qwestead," Jennings said. "That's the next most important issue."

"I kind of wanted to save the really big news for last—but you're the boss."

"I am. Is Qwestead ready to roll?"

"They're giving you carte blanche to negotiate on their behalf with respect to the ranch, the mineral rights, you know, what you asked for ... the whole nine yards. If I do say so myself, it was a pretty nice piece of lawyering on my ..."

Jennings interrupted him. "Don't bother to congratulate yourself, Brady. They came through because they fear what will happen if I take my business down the road. What about the money? Any problem with that?"

"The letter of credit is being prepared. It'll be in my office by the end of business today."

"I've changed the plan," Jennings said. "I want bearer bonds rather than a letter of credit. The bonds should be issued in 100,000-Euro denominations, drawn on the Geneva branch of Credit Suisse Bank."

"Bearer bonds are like cash, Doc. Don't you think Qwestead's going to have a problem with that? I mean, we're talking thirty million bucks here. That's not chump change, even for Qwestead," Brady protested.

"I know very well what bearer bonds are, you lamebrain," Jennings continued in rapid fire, "which is why I'm asking for them. Just do it. And be sure that the bonds are delivered to me personally, in Hot Springs."

"When would you like the thirty million delivered?"

"Tomorrow."

"Tomorrow? As in Tuesday, twenty-four hours from now? That tomorrow?"

"Do I stutter, or do you need to clean the bar napkins out of your ears? Tomorrow, Phil. And please, don't start whining and apologizing when you call Qwestead. They'll issue the bonds. If they give you any grief, get angry and threaten to move our business to Paxomed Labs. Have you got a problem with that?"

Jennings solved problems with power and operated under the assumption that he was always right and deserved whatever he could lay his hands on.

"Next item. Did you get the custody thing underway? That bitch is in Nebraska right now trying to spring her brat, so I may need this piece to move fast." Like a field general taking heavy fire, Jennings wasn't really questioning his subordinate. He simply wanted to hear that all his previous orders had been successfully carried out. "No" was not an acceptable answer.

"Everything is very straightforward stuff—unless we're challenged," Brady said. "However, there is one thing left to do, and you'll have to take care of it."

"What's that?"

"You'll need to get a blood test and fax the results to me. It's required by the state."

"I'll fax it over later today," Jennings said. To gain leverage with Eva, he had doctored the results of his blood test to convince her that, despite having had sex with her only twice, he was Shelly's biological father. All he would have to do is change the date on that paperwork.

"With your blood test in hand," Brady concluded, "we'll be ready to move whenever you pull the trigger."

"So far, you're batting a thousand," Jennings said, paying Brady the closest thing to a compliment Jennings would ever issue.

"Last item, Doc, you wanted a book on this guy Larkin."

"Right. What did you find?"

"Nothing very juicy," Brady began. "Larkin is your average, squeaky-clean suburban mutt with a few dings on his credit report. We did a full write-up, but it would bore you silly, and by my watch, you've got about five minutes before your conference call."

"I'm looking for something unsavory, Brady. Save all the Boy Scout stuff for when you need to sleep and you're not blotto."

"The IRS slapped a lien on Larkin's house twenty years ago—apparently the result of a dispute over partnership taxes. Larkin paid the taxes, but all of it was eventually refunded to him. Seems that Larkin was right and the IRS was wrong, but they still emptied his bank accounts at the time."

"That's nothing. What else is there?"

"I think you'll like this. He's got a bankruptcy."

Jennings brightened at the news. "You don't say? When?"

"Five, six years ago. Only it wasn't personal bankruptcy. It was a start-up company that he and three other guys founded. Something medical. They had to take Chapter Eleven but are still operating."

"Strike two, Brady. Everybody and their brother has been through that—including many of your esteemed clients. If it was a personal bankruptcy, I might be able to use it. Because Larkin owned stock in a start-up that didn't make it doesn't mean anything. Is that all you've got?"

Even if Brady hadn't come up with anything to use against Larkin, through dumb luck, Jennings had. Just that morning he had overheard his secretary gossiping with a friend about a Cadillac SUV that was parked outside Eva Shepherd's house until late Saturday night and for several hours again on Sunday. *If Larkin values his relationship with his wife,* Jennings thought, *he'll gladly trade something for my silence.*

Thinking about Eva in bed with Larkin angered and embarrassed Jennings. *Probably has a big dick,* he fumed silently. Jennings momentarily lost himself in a fantasy—Eva's legs stretched wide and her torso bowed with pleasure; her hands and mouth full of Tom; lying with her ass in Tom's hand and pressing herself against the arm of the sofa to keep from being driven off and onto the floor. In Jennings' mind, Tom and Eva kept at each other in every conceivable way—tormenting him—long after he tried to make them stop.

Jennings detested Larkin for fouling up his plan to purchase the McPherson place and hated the way women were drawn to Larkin.

Bill Jennings had the appearance of a garter snake. His skin was scaly; his eyes were two black beads set closely together atop his beak. For laughs, God had given Jennings a tiny little pecker to boot. Jennings knew that whatever women he attracted were after his money and power—or he had something over them, like he did with Eva Shepherd. Most women fled from him in droves after any kind of sexual encounter with him. It drove Jennings crazy.

"Doc! You still there, Doc? I said there's one other thing on Larkin. You want to hear it, or not?"

"Phil! Yeah ... of course ... what do you have?"

"As far as we can tell from recreating his financials, Larkin's net worth is no more than six, maybe seven hundred thousand bucks. Does that help?"

"How sound is that number?"

"We're being conservative on the high side—it could be a hundred grand less," Brady answered.

"Hone in on Larkin's finances, Phil. This ... this ... wannabee is playing a game of financial chicken with me, thinking I don't know how far he can go. If I can determine his absolute financial limits, then I'll know exactly where I can inflict pain or offer relief. Pay whatever you need to get the information. You know the drill."

"I'm on it, boss."

"And stay on the Qwestead money. I want those bearer bonds here tomorrow afternoon if you have to fly in with them yourself. Are we clear?"

"Crystal clear, partner," Brady said collegially.

"You're not my partner," Jennings said condescendingly, and hung up on him.

Monday Noon

"Please hold for Randy Hearst," the receptionist told everyone on the call.

Doc Jennings, Carl Graves, Jim Shepherd, and Sam Barker were there as always; John Evans, Jr., was not—as was increasingly the case.

"What is Evans' problem, anyway?" Shepherd asked. "He's never around anymore. I'm beginning to think that we'd be smart to ease him out the door before we launch the deal with Qwestead. Anybody else here got a problem with him?"

Not having any quarrel with Shepherd's opinion, but not wanting to openly support him, Carl said, "Evans called me and left a message this morning. There's a major valve malfunction at the Plunge, and he said he'd been there most of the night with a crew and couldn't leave. Sent his apologies. What's he supposed to do, let the place flood?"

"As a matter of fact, Carl, yeah, he should let it flood," Shepherd snarled. "Evans makes more money from Elements every month than he makes in a year from that outhouse. Between you and Evans, I don't know which one is thicker. Carl, you ought to stick to ... to ... to whatever it is you do at City Hall and leave the business discussions to those of us who understand the difference between making money and raising taxes."

Before Carl and Jim could get into it, Jennings interrupted. "Why don't we save this discussion for another time? Carl, I'm sure that Evans has his hands full managing his plumbing, and Jim, I certainly agree that we should re-evaluate John's contributions to our business. Meanwhile, let's hope that Hearst and his crew have some options for us, since none of you seem to have come up with anything over the weekend."

Carl said nothing because time had not ripened the situation sufficiently enough to announce his deal with Tom.

"Good afternoon, gentlemen," Randy Hearst said as he joined the conference. "Everybody here?"

"Evans couldn't make it," Shepherd sneered. "Big surprise, huh?"

"Should we wait?" Hearst asked.

"No," Jennings said. "Let's get to it. What have your people come up with?"

There was an uncomfortable moment during which no one spoke. Then Hearst began.

"As you recall, we looked into a number of different issues, including promotional fraud and professional misconduct or licensure irregularities on the part of Mr. Burley.

"My associate, Caroline Lesser, was unable to give us anything to pursue regarding the promotional fraud."

"What about Burley?" Shepherd asked.

"While Mr. Burley does have several complaints lodged against him with the South Dakota real estate board, he remains, at this moment, in good standing. Our chances of voiding the existing contract for deed on the basis of his professional standing are remote."

"What new ground did you break," Jennings said flatly.

"Our other associate, Mr. Bohr, checked South Dakota probate law. This also turned out to be a dead end. We found nothing that would contradict Jo McPherson's right to the full estate; her actions are legal and binding. We did reach the late Mr. McPherson's sisters, both of whom politely told us to mind our own business and that whatever Jo did with the ranch was Jo's business.

NATIVE GROUND

Despite our best efforts, we could not reach Mrs. McPherson's only sibling—a brother who appears to reside on the Rosebud Indian Reservation, although we couldn't be absolutely certain of this information.

"As to the McPherson marriage license, it is in perfect order—and Cody did not die intestate. Now, had there been any irregularity involving his death, such as suspicion of foul play, then we might have something ..."

Jennings cut him off. "So you've come up empty-handed on all the ideas we discussed on Friday, would that be a fair statement?"

"I'm afraid so, Dr. Jennings."

"Well," Jennings sighed, "none of us thought that any of those ideas had much merit to begin with ... so what new ideas did your team develop?"

Hearst cleared his throat and began his spiel. "Having explored a great number of other avenues, all of which led nowhere, it is our considered opinion that we should begin to focus on negotiating with Mr. Larkin, under the assumption that he will be more reasonable than Mrs. McPherson."

If he'd had a good idea, Hearst would have personally taken credit for it. A bad idea, on the other hand, was "our" opinion, and always "considered." Their idea, presumably, had been concocted by a gaggle of attorneys who were unable to be present at the meeting.

The silence that ensued was as thick and bitter as griddle smoke.

"Well, how about those two geniuses whose names are on the door? Did you get either of them involved?" Jennings asked sarcastically.

"You mean Mr. Perez and Mr. Farmer?"

"Yeah, that's them, Randy: Daddy's-Money Perez and Wifey's-Money Farmer. Did you get them involved?"

Hearst started to say why the senior partners hadn't weighed in, but Jennings stopped him.

"Don't bother covering for those chumps, Hearst. They're both as useless as tits on a boar. Consulting with them will only add to our bill, without adding anything to the conversation."

Hearst had the poor judgment to speak.

"Well, how about your team? Did you come up with any ideas?"

"We aren't a 'team,' Hearst. We're clients. We don't work for you, you work for us, and you don't seem to be working very hard."

"Amen," Shepherd interjected.

"Shut up, Jim!" Jennings ordered. "Elements and Qwestead pay you a king's ransom to solve our legal problems, not to rephrase them—or come to us for solutions. Getting hold of that ranch is our number-one problem at the moment, and you have the balls to tell us that you've got nothing?" Jennings voice was as shrill as a tea kettle.

"Dr. Jennings, we . . ." Hearst started.

"We? *We*, Hearst?" Jennings screeched. "How about you? What are you going to say to Qwestead when they ask you how things are going with the McPherson deal? Huh? Just exactly what line of bullshit are you planning to feed them to save your retainer?"

"I don't know, Bill, I haven't . . ."

Jennings cut him off.

"You don't know. That's the first intelligent thing I've heard you say. Well, all right, Randy, since you don't know, shut up and listen.

"Since you don't have anything to tell Qwestead, I strongly suggest that you say nothing until I instruct you otherwise."

"Agreed," was the only word Hearst could force himself to say.

"As to our strategy, we will target Larkin; not because he is 'reasonable', Randy, but because he is the weak link in this chain. I intend to break him," Jennings announced.

Carl was enjoying the fireworks. Things couldn't be turning out better for him if he'd planned every word and handed out scripts.

Jennings was crucifying Hearst and his firm, Shepherd had been shushed like a schoolboy, and Barker, as usual, was saying nothing because he had nothing to say.

It's just about time, Carl thought to himself. *I'll let Jennings spill his idea first, since it's about Larkin. If it's a lousy idea, I can shoot it down by telling everybody what I've already got in the works. If it's a good idea, I'll say nothing, undo the deal with Larkin after the call, or alter my plan to fit Jennings'. Either way, I can't lose.* He leaned back very carefully in his chair and waited.

"Break Larkin in what way, Bill?" Hearst asked.

"Perhaps 'break' is the wrong choice of words," Jennings continued. "Larkin's financial appetite, shall we say, exceeds his means by quite a large sum."

Got that right, Jennings, Carl thought. *Too bad you didn't figure out what to do about it like I did.*

"Larkin has signed a contract for a piece of ground that he can't afford," Jennings said.

Got that wrong, Carl thought. *For once, Jennings, you are way, way behind the eightball. And old Carl, well, old Carl is behind the cue ball and about to run the table.*

Jennings went on like a professor condescending to teach his intellectually stunted undergrads.

"That doddering old Jo McPherson made it easy for Larkin to buy the ranch with owner financing. Despite that break, Larkin still can't chew what he's bitten off. He's attached to the ranch, won't let go, but can't pay for it, either. That's his weakness.

"I intend to swap him the entire ranch for the mineral rights. We give him the six million, he gives Elements the rights we want. There's no way he can turn it down, especially after his wife gets wind of the offer," Jennings proudly concluded.

I can't wait to see the look on your face, nitwit, Carl thought. *The great Dr. Jennings offering to pay three times what I already got the rights for.* Carl figured that a chunk of the difference between what Jennings was prepared to pay and what Carl had already negotiated should go right into Carl's pocket.

"And if this Larkin fellow refuses the offer?" Hearst asked.

"If Larkin says no, he and I will have a little chat about the female company he's been keeping. His choices are to sell us the rights for six million bucks and keep the ranch and his marriage, or walk away from us and lose both. It has a kind of symmetry to it, don't you think?" Jennings said, unveiling his coup de grâce.

Instead, Shepherd, whose ears had pricked instantly at the mention of the words "female company," spoke first. "What female company you talking about, Doc?"

I told you so, dickhead, but you wouldn't listen, now, would you? Carl thought smugly.

"The 'female company' I refer to," Jennings answered, "is my card to play. The person in question is relevant only if the financial offer doesn't work."

"You're not referring to Eva, are you?" Shepherd sounded menacing.

"I'm referring to 'female company,' Jim. Make whatever you want of it."

"If you are, you're wrong!"

"Why don't you just grow up, Jim—or, at least, wise up," Jennings said.

Carl saw his opportunity.

"Ah-hem." Carl cleared his throat. "This is Carl. Carl Graves."

By jumping in between Shepherd and Jennings, Carl had given Shepherd a less dangerous target for his anger.

"We know which Carl you're referring to—unless your twin brother showed up, you know, the smart one," Shepherd fired back.

"Very funny, Jim. If you're so smart, how come you don't know nothing about the, what'd Doc say, the 'female company', Larkin has been keeping these past few days? I can't hear you, Jim, what about that?"

"You trying to say something to me, Carl? Huh? If you are, you better spit it out!"

"Let's all calm down," Jennings ordered. "What have you got to say, Carl?"

"Well, I was about to say that, since we're talking about trying to deal with Tom Larkin in some way, perhaps you'd all be interested in a little conversation I had with him about an hour before this call."

Dead silence.

"I'll take that as a 'yes'," Carl said, and continued. "After chatting with him the other day, I think it was Friday, while we were out taking a tour of the golf course, he let on that he was, let's say, a little short on the ranch financing. I didn't say nothing, just let him ramble on, and he pretty much laid himself bare, financially speaking."

Jennings broke in.

"Where are you going with this, Carl? You saying that he gave you a number, told you how much he's short, or what? And while you're at it, explain to me why you didn't come to me immediately with this information?"

Carl knew that Jennings would be furious about this.

"No, Larkin didn't give me a number, as such," Carl said, dragging out his explanation as long as possible. "It was me that gave him a number, so to speak. I suggested that perhaps, in my capacity as mayor, I might be able to persuade the city to help him out."

"Help him out? Help him out!" Jennings squawked. "Are you out of your mind, Graves? We're trying to put this son-of-a-bitch into a financial corner he can't get out of. Then we'll 'help him out'."

"If you'll kindly let me finish, Bill, I'll explain the agreement I proposed, and I think that you'll see that it's a lot less costly— and a whole lot cleaner—than your idea, and it gets us where we want to go all the same," Carl snapped.

Jennings was livid.

"Well, this is a fine time to bring up whatever hare-brained notion you've dreamed up. How many times have I told you that we don't work things out in public? We discuss things amongst ourselves first, then we make a consensus recommendation. That's how it works, Carl."

Carl wasn't about to be reprimanded for having the winning idea.

"Tell you what, Doc. I could have said the same thing about your whiz-bang idea to pay six million bucks for something we can get for a third of that. But, hey, if my idea don't work, then fine, we can go blackmail Larkin by threatening to tell his wife he's been banging Eva!"

Shepherd exploded.

"Why don't you, for once, try to keep your big, fat mouth shut, Graves!" Shepherd screamed. "And if you can't, call me. I'll come over to your office and help shut it for you."

The call had turned ugly, and Hearst tried to calm the situation. "Please, gentlemen, please. Let's try to stay on point ..."

Jennings shouted over both Hearst and Shepherd.

"Carl, not another word, do you hear me? You come to me with whatever it is you've got, and we'll work it out—in private! That's how it's going to be. You meet me for supper tonight at eight, back room at the Lucky Strike ... got it? And by the way, if you've done anything with Larkin, un-fucking do it!"

THIS IS MY DEAL, Jennings raged silently. *My deal. My deal. Nobody's going to upstage me. I found the calcium! Me! It's mine!*

Had Jennings continued to rant, perhaps saner heads may have intervened and prevailed. But Jennings clammed up after lashing out at Carl, the madness in his eyes unseen by anyone. He had the perverse survival instincts of a lunatic.

Seeing nothing to salvage from the call, Hearst said, "Why don't we make arrangements for a follow-up call tomorrow evening, say ten Eastern? I'll have my secretary call everyone in the morning to make the arrangements. I'm sure you'll have reached some agreement on your end by then. Thank you for your time, gentlemen."

Without another word, everyone hung up.

YEAH, CARL THOUGHT. *I'll meet you for supper tonight, you pompous control freak, and then we'll see who gets to undo what. By that time, I'll have the agreement in hand, and you can eat crow and kiss my ass while I have a nice, juicy fillet and decide whether I want you in on the mineral deal or not.*

Carl's dream had grown beyond a simple desire to knock Bill Jennings down a peg or two, beyond his need to upstage Jim Shepherd, and beyond his thirst for recognition and group status. He had convinced himself that he could take Jennings' crown— by force if necessary.

When Tom answered the knock at his hotel room door, Eva and the little girl from the photographs were standing in the hall. Tom must not have spoken, because Eva said, "Can we come in, Tom?"

"Good grief, where are my manners? Come on in, ladies."

The little girl was pasted to Eva's leg. Tom shut the door and knelt down so that he was more or less at eye-level with the child.

"Do you like M&M's?" he asked her. "They're my favorite."

She gave Tom a faint smile and an emphatic up and down nod of her head.

"Well, that's a good thing, because I just happen to have some right here. I always keep a box around in case of emergencies," he said, walking to the honor bar.

"Of course, it would have to be OK with your ..." and Tom looked directly at Eva, "... your mother."

Eva's eyes were calm and unafraid. She smiled at Tom and nodded her permission.

Tom found the M&M's and held them out in such a way as to force the child to let go of Eva or forfeit the M&M's. As Tom suspected, the M&M's won out.

"How about a nice soda pop to go with those M&M's?" As he asked, Tom glanced up and saw Eva shaking her head back and forth vigorously.

"Well, doggone it," Tom said, rattling bottles and pretending to search the mini fridge, "we seem to be fresh out of soda pop.

How about some orange juice? It's my second favorite." He held out the juice and the child accepted it.

"Tom," Eva reminded him, "her name is Shelly."

"Well, Shelly, I am awfully pleased to meet you, sweetheart." Shelly smiled at him, plopped herself onto one of the beds, and proceeded to tear the M&M box open.

Tom stood and faced Eva. There was an awkward distance between them that Eva bridged in two quick steps, taking up both of his hands in hers. "Eva, I ..." Tom started to explain that he'd been looking for her earlier in the day and wanted to tell her why.

Eva put her index and middle finger gently to his lips to stop him from speaking.

"Don't. Please don't say anything, Tom. Let me tell you what I've come here to say.

"I've acted very badly, very foolishly. Not just the past few days, but for a very long time. Long before you came to Hot Springs," she said.

"No, you haven't ..." Tom started again, and again she put her fingers to his lips.

"Let me. Please. I have to say this." Her eyes silenced him.

"We've only known each other a couple of days, Tom, and I know you think it's silly, but I do love you, as much as I know how to," she said, giving his hands a tender squeeze. "I would really, really love for you to just take me away from here, but ..." she struggled on, "... but that isn't ... going to ... happen ... and I know it." Bits of mascara followed the escaping tears.

"I know you don't love me, and I understand why you can't. But you care for me; I know that; I can feel it. But no matter how much you care, we'll never have a future."

Tom removed one of his hands from hers, reached to the desk and found a tissue for her. She mopped up her tears, smearing the mascara and making her look more the waif than the mother.

"After you left yesterday," Eva continued, "Jennings called me and threatened to take Shelly away and never let me see her if

I didn't tell him everything we'd talked about on Sunday afternoon."

A fire rose in Tom's eyes: Eva saw it and shook her head. Tom understood her meaning: she wanted him to listen to her words and not to the voice that was urging him to go find Jennings and beat the tar out of him.

"I am glad Jennings called, Tom. It scared me to death, but it made me think. I thought about the things that you have that I want. About having a family of my own, about coming home for supper, seeing children grow up. About having a man like you in my life, who would love me, and who I could call my own.

"You're wonderful, Tom, but you'll never be mine. Shelly will always be mine, and I will never, ever let her out of my life again. Last night, out of all the confusion and fear, my life began to sort itself out. I realized that I've been going about things all wrong. But I hope to change that—starting today," she said with determination.

"What are you going to do?" Tom whispered.

"The first thing was getting Shelly back. I've done that. We just got home a few minutes ago, and I came straight here with her."

"Do you need a safe place to stay?"

"No. At least I don't think so. I don't even know how long we'll stay in Hot Springs. I've got to tell my parents that they have a granddaughter. Depending on how that goes, Shelly and I could be gone by tonight," Eva said matter-of-factly.

"But first, I needed to clear things up with you." Eva paused. "You helped me see myself again, see the person in me that I like. The time we spent together was, well, magical. Even before we had supper at the Lucky Strike, and you were trying to be angry, all I could think about was when I'd see you next. Another time, another place, who knows? It might have gone somewhere. But we started wrong, and things got more twisted and out of shape as we went along, and I don't want to leave them that way."

"Neither do I, Eva," Tom said.

She reached up and cradled Tom's face in her hands.

"I'm going to miss you, Tom," she said, straightening his collar and smoothing his shirt across his shoulders.

"What are we going to do, Eva?" Tom asked.

"I'd like us to try and keep the connection we made, even if you never hold me in your arms again. Even if I can't have that part of you, Tom, I don't want to lose all the rest; I feel that we belong to each other in some way."

Eva's words tore at Tom's heart.

They had found in each other something far beyond what the flesh desired. Behind the made-up Eva, there was a good woman looking for some solid ground on which to build her life, a woman who longed to go back home and be welcomed there. Eva wanted everything from Tom that he wanted from the ranch.

Tom took Eva in his arms and drew her close.

"I feel like I have known you for a long, long time, Eva," Tom whispered into her hair. "You are beautiful and strong."

The remarkable four days they had spent together began to play like a film in Tom's head, and, moved by Eva's naked honesty, a confession welled up among his hot memories and he gave it to Eva as a gift.

"I love you, too."

Tom held her body fast to his.

"Before you leave, let me hold you like this for just one minute more."

Neither was capable of further thought or speech. They clung to each other desperately, each using the short time left to memorize the other's body.

With an effort, Tom peeled himself away and held Eva at arms-length.

They searched each other's eyes, looking for a way to stay together, to change the past, to cheat destiny, to move the hand of God. Driven by the certainty that such a way would never exist in their lifetimes, they fell back together in a crushing embrace and a deep kiss that, Tom knew, may have to last them forever.

They parted without speaking. Eva took Shelly by the hand and led her out of Tom's room and into their future.

Having lost the will to move, Tom stood anchored to the place where he'd last seen Eva, remembering her lips and her laughter, her hands and her bedroom, her eyes and her outline, the fit of her in his arms, and her hot, healing tears that had a wild taste of the sea.

Like an autumn afternoon of pine-washed wind, the smell of burning leaves, and the feeling that anything was possible, their moment had been brief, but perfect.

And now, it was over.

MONDAY, 3:30 P.M.

With Shelly in tow, Eva entered her parent's house the way she usually did—through the back porch, without knocking.

"Mom? Daddy? Anybody home?" she yelled.

"In here, sweetie," her mother sang out from the kitchen.

Eva and Shelly went to the kitchen door and stood there silently, hand-in-hand.

Eva's mother had her back to them, busy assembling a dish of lasagna on the far counter. Eva's fondest childhood memories were set in this kitchen: freshly-baked loaves of bread on cooling racks after school, homemade apple butter, boiled and colored Easter eggs, deep-fat-fried donuts, frosting leftovers, cherry pies, and jack-o-lanterns carved on the floor. Eva watched her mother lay mozzarella strips on lasagna noodles, on sauce, on cottage cheese, on sausage, and she remembered how happy she had been here. It made her smile to recall sitting on the marble counters that always seemed so cold at first, looking out the window on a gray or sun-washed day, reading fairy tales while her mother tended to the kitchen chores or made gingersnaps.

In the last light of this early spring day, the stained and worn marble counters seemed warm and inviting, and Eva had an urge to take a run across the kitchen and jump up on one, sprawl out with a book, and let her mother feed her mozzarella scraps.

Shelly tugged at her mother's hand, interrupting Eva's memories. Eva put one finger to her lips to signal quiet.

"We've been worried about you, dear. They called over here from the hotel and said you hadn't shown up for the morning shift. Your father had to call Nicole in, and she wasn't very happy about it," Mrs. Shepherd said, still facing her work. "Where were you?"

"I was in Nebraska, Mom."

"Nebraska! Why in the world were you in Nebraska so soon again?" Mrs. Shepherd said, wiping her hands on her gingham apron as she turned to face Eva.

Eva gave her mother the few seconds she needed to be surprised by the sight of her standing there holding a four-year-old girl's hand in hers.

Mrs. Shepherd had stopped wiping her hands when she saw the little girl, but they were still wrapped in her apron. As she stared at the child, her hands set themselves back in motion in concert with her brain.

"Why, you've brought your friend's little girl to Hot Springs for a visit, haven't you? How sweet!"

"Mom, I'd like you to meet Shelly."

Mrs. Shepherd had taken just one step toward her daughter and the child when Eva knelt by Shelly and said, "Shelly, this is your grandmother."

Eva's mother froze.

She stared intently at the child and then at her daughter. Then the child, and then again at Eva. Like the morning sun slowly but certainly pushing back the curtain of night, the truth dawned on her. Mrs. Shepherd hadn't bothered to question Eva's story about the child's pictures hung frame-to-frame on the entry wall. She hadn't dared to look at them too closely, to think too hard about the striking similarities between her daughter and the images.

She hadn't dared hope.

Grandmother!

The realization of it coursed through her like a shock and a balm, applied at once. She felt battered and rejuvenated. Some of the lines in her brow deepened, others relaxed. A struggle between the bitter and the sweet erupted in her breast, and it heaved mightily, not knowing whether to break or to burst with joy.

Eva made a step toward her mother, but the older mother moved faster. She leapt forward and took daughter and grand-daughter in her arms, kissing Eva and running her kind fingers through the child's hair.

"Oh my, Eva. Good Lord, child," was all she could muster.

"I'm sorry, Mom, I'm so sorry," Eva sobbed.

Shelly couldn't comprehend the emotion of the moment and clung to her mother for comfort. But Eva was herself a defenseless child; a child in need of acceptance, of absolution, and of love.

Eva's mother gathered the two children in her arms and held them close.

The embrace melted Eva's fears and, for the moment, answered some of her questions.

Eva lifted her face from the crook of the older woman's neck and placed her forehead on her mother's.

"I know you'll love her, Mom," she cried. "She is so good."

They both began to laugh and cry at the same time.

When they managed to get control of themselves, Mary Shepherd noticed that Shelly had retreated behind Eva, and she opened her arms to the little girl.

Eva extracted her hand from Shelly's and nudged her toward her grandmother. Shelly took three very shy—but very brave—steps to the older woman and accepted an uncomfortably long, but loving, hug.

"Where have you been hiding from Grandma, Shelly?"

Shelly looked at her mother, who nodded to her and mouthed the words, "It's OK."

"The hospiddle," the child said.

"Well, I'm so happy you're here now, Shelly. So very, very happy." And Grandma stood up, took Shelly's hand, and led her across the kitchen to one of the cupboards. Shelly didn't even bother to look back at her own mother; she just tripped along beside her grandmother like a puppy.

"Let me see, here, Shelly. Grandma's house isn't a hospital, so I don't have any medicines or things like that. But, I do have some fresh chocolate chip cookies! How would that be?"

Shelly nodded enthusiastically and got to choose her own cookie from the same big glass jar that Eva had chosen from as a child. Watching her mother and her child reenact a scene from the kitchen of her childhood caused Eva another fit of joyful sobbing, and she had to cover her face so Shelly wouldn't think something was wrong.

Mother, daughter and granddaughter sat down at the kitchen table, catching up and giggling and weeping and talking about each other for a long, long time. For Eva and her mother, it was a decade recaptured in two glorious hours. It was four cookies and two glasses of milk in Shelly-time.

The only real awkwardness came when Eva revealed the name of the man she believed to be the father of her child.

Jim Shepherd returned home from the office at half past five.

Mary Shepherd was out of the kitchen before the front door closed. She intercepted him in the front hallway.

"Eva's come home, Jim," she said in a whisper.

Before Mary could say another word, Jim Shepherd started in.

"Well, where the hell's she been? You know she was supposed to be at the hotel this morning, and I had to scramble to get the desk covered because . . ."

"Stop it right now!" she ordered. "She'll hear you.

"She has a child with her, Jim. The one from the pictures in her hallway. Her name is Shelly. She isn't the child of a friend. She's Eva's daughter. She's our granddaughter!"

Shocking news, or bad news, is best given to a man straight up, all at once and in short sentences. There are women who understand this.

"How could we not have known?" Shepherd stammered. "You can't hide something like that! There's no way that . . ."

Mary Shepherd put her index and middle fingers to her husband's lips.

"Eva will explain everything to you. First I want to tell you a few things before you go in there," she said, motioning with her head to the kitchen, "so you don't say something foolish and scare the child and make Eva leave."

Eva remained in the kitchen talking softly to Shelly, explaining to her that her grandfather had come home and was taking off his coat and boots and talking to Grandma, and that he'd be in to see her in just a couple of minutes. Eva knew that when her mother had her father prepared and calmed down, she would present him in the kitchen. Despite her confidence in her mother, Eva was nervous and steeled herself.

Mary Shepherd was holding her husband's hand when they entered the kitchen. Jim Shepherd gave his daughter a hard look, but only flexed, rather than flapped, his jaw.

"Shelly, this is your grandpa."

"Jim," Mary said softly, "this is your granddaughter."

TO SHELLY, A grandfather must be nothing more than a type of grandmother, and probably the source of more goodies. And, having no reason to think otherwise, she clumped her merry way across the kitchen and stood looking up at her grandfather with high hopes.

The cross-examination intended for Eva was forgotten for the moment.

"Well, I'll be a son-of-a . . ." he looked at Mary, who was frowning, ". . . a son-of-a-gun," he exclaimed. He swept the little girl up in his arms and held her so high that her head nearly touched the ceiling. He let her fall as if he'd dropped her and caught her just as her feet reached his knees.

Shelly thought it was a grand sport and giggled in a winsome way that reminded old Jim Shepherd of another little girl who'd loved the game, too. He looked over at Eva and gave her a smile she hadn't seen in years.

Having overcome her first, delightful shock, Shelly chanted, "Again! Again! Again!"

Grandpa picked her up in a bear hug that made her little legs dance in the air. Then he tossed her up and down, again and again, while she shrieked and egged him on.

And that was how a misbegotten child mended three very broken people.

After Shelly's wild rumpus with Grandpa ended, Mary Shepherd said to Shelly, "How'd you like to help Grandma fix up your bedroom?" Thrilled to have a new adventure, Shelly left with her grandmother, leaving Jim Shepherd alone with his daughter.

"I'm sorry about all this, Daddy. I lied to you and Mom, and I hid things from you. I know you have a right, but please don't be angry with me. Please, let's try to talk this through." She had been looking at her hands and lifted her face so she could look her father in the eye. "I really need you right now."

Eva's admission broke her father, and he reached his hand across the table in a gesture that closed the many years of distance between them.

"Don't you worry, honey," he said, almost embarrassed. "We'll work things out. There isn't anything we can't help you handle."

Eva didn't speak; she just squeezed her father's hand. She could never squeeze it hard enough to hurt him or to demonstrate her gratitude.

Jim Shepherd was fighting a fierce battle inside. Minutes ago, in the hallway, his wife had told him about Jennings. The image of his business partner screwing his daughter demanded action, violent action. It would have been far easier for Shepherd to go mix it up with Jennings than it was for him to sit quietly and empathize with his daughter.

But at that moment Eva needed his support, not his rage, and he yielded.

"Are you planning to stay here with Shelly or bring her back to your place?" Shepherd asked.

"I . . . I don't feel comfortable taking Shelly to my house just yet, Dad," Eva said.

"That's perfectly fine with your mother and me. You can stay here as long as you like. Move right back in if you want."

Eva teetered on the small platform of goodwill they had built.

"Dad?"

"Yes, honey?"

"I've got to tell you something, and you have to promise me you won't get mad and go stomping out the door. Promise?"

Shepherd hated the way women did that. They'd make you promise to act a certain way about news you hadn't yet heard. If you didn't agree, you weren't told, and then both parties would be mad at each other, the one for not being told and the other for not getting the promise. If you did agree and didn't act the way you promised, then both parties would still be angry with each other. He didn't have any illusions about changing the way women did business, but he still didn't think it was fair.

"I won't go *stomping* out the door, Eva," he said, fudging on the terms of Eva's request.

"Promise me you won't get mad, *and* you won't go stomping out the door," she repeated. "Please, Dad. I just can't deal with anything else today."

She looked weary to her father.

"All right. I'll remain calm, and I won't leave my chair. How's that?"

"You promise?"

"I promise. What is it?"

"Bill, Dr. Jennings that is, called me last night and threatened to take Shelly away and never let me see her again unless I told him things about Tom." She said it quickly to be sure that it all got out.

"Did you say 'Tom', Eva?"

"Yes, Dad. Tom Larkin."

"Didn't I hear that he bought the McPherson place?" Shepherd said, trying to hide his company's interests by playing dumb and immediately realizing how stupid he must sound to Eva. If Jennings was using his daughter to get to Larkin, then she knew good and well that Elements had an interest in the ranch.

"I'm sorry, Eva. Obviously, you know a good deal about this situation," he said.

"I may know more about it than you do, Dad," Eva admitted.

"So you have been sleeping with him?"

"Who said I was sleeping with him?"

"Let's cut the crap, Eva. You're my daughter, and I love you. But we're both adults here. How in the hell else are you going to get information from him that Jennings wants?"

"Who said I was sleeping with him, Dad?" Eva repeated in an even tone.

Shepherd stopped to think. He was between a rock and a hard place. His daughter's welfare had come smack dab up against the interests of his company. There was a brief skirmish between these conflicting interests, but in Shepherd's world, family came first. He wasn't clever enough, or perhaps hypocritical enough, to have it both ways.

"It was Jennings that said you were ... you know, sleeping with Larkin. And that jerk-off Carl Graves was making some snide remarks last week about you and Larkin.

"Goddamn it, Eva! Why can't you just leave well enough alone?"

He was frustrated and had a right to be. He was her father. He had borne the brunt of their jokes and insinuations without knowing. Now he knew that they knew. The embarrassment of it all was just hitting him that moment.

"They think you're nothing more than, than ..." he couldn't bring himself to say the word slut, and finished with, "... a tramp!"

Eva hung her head.

Neither spoke for several minutes, each trying to arrange his point of view so that it would show consideration for the other.

Having chosen whose side he was on, Jim Shepherd took aim at Jennings.

"Sleeping with Tom Larkin, or even Jennings for that matter, well, I guess that's your business. You're a grown woman. You don't need to ask anybody's permission to go to bed with a man," Shepherd said, working through the issue out loud. "But Jennings using you to further our business interests? That's wrong. Way wrong. Then he threatens to take your child, or the child that you two had together, or whatever, it doesn't matter. Threatening to take that little girl, to involve her in any way, is a low, punk-ass thing to do. And I'm here to tell you, Eva," he said, eyes unwavering, "there is no way in cold hell that son-of-a-bitch is going to take Shelly from you, or hurt you, or even get near you ever again! I promise you that."

Eva got up from her place at the table, went over to her father, and put her arms around him.

"I'm sorry that I embarrassed you, Daddy. I'm going to try and do better. I'm going to make you proud of me in the future. I promise."

Shepherd stood and returned Eva's hug. He had promised her not to get angry and stomp out the door, and he had kept his promise. *But tomorrow*, he vowed to himself, *tomorrow that motherfucker Jennings is going to find out what it means to be threatened.*

"**N**ot now, Norma!" Carl Graves growled at his secretary. "I've got a meeting at the bank in twenty minutes and I've got a half-hour's work to finish before I go."

"It's an attorney from Minnesota who says it's urgent. What do you want me to tell him?" Norma said.

"Put him through. And close my door," he snapped, and picked up the phone.

"Carl, it's Jack Boyle, Tom Larkin's attorney."

"I know, I know. What can I do for you, Jack?"

"I know that you and Tom are meeting in a short while. I hadn't heard back from you on the language I sent over this forenoon. I need to know if there are any issues." Boyle made it short and sweet, having picked up on Carl's agitation.

"No. No issues. Sorry I didn't get back to you, Jack."

"Excuse me, Carl? Did you say that you have no issues to discuss?"

"Yeah. I read the stuff you sent. So did my lawyer. Everything's fine. We're set to go on our end," Carl said. He'd lied about having his attorney review the language. He'd simply told him to include it as is, no questions asked. Carl was way past the point of debating nuances—he'd already decided that nothing was going to stand in the way of his deal with Larkin.

"Well ... that's great," Jack said hesitantly. "It isn't often we get a clean bill of health on the first go around."

"Well, you did this time. Now, I don't want to appear rude, Jack, but I've still got a slew of details to take care of here, and I'm due to meet Tom at the bank in ... well, in about ten minutes. So if you don't mind?"

"Hold on a sec, Carl! Just one other thing. Sorry I forgot to ask," Jack blurted out.

Now what? Carl thought.

"I haven't received a copy of the completed agreement as of yet. Do you think you could have your secretary fax it or e-mail it over right away?"

"It's on the way to you as we speak, Jack."

Without waiting for Jack to sign off, Carl hung up and shouted Norma into his office.

"Get these things on the fax to this number, pronto," he ordered.

"The city engineer has a forty-page fax coming through at the moment."

"Well hit the stop button, Norma, and put this out first. Whatever mumbo-jumbo the engineer is wasting paper on can wait!" Carl snapped.

"Right away, Carl," Norma said, and scurried out like a little mouse the cat had spied.

CARL WAS IN a lather when he arrived at the bank five minutes late for his meeting with Tom. Not that he minded being late for meetings. He made a regular practice of it, just so people wouldn't get in the habit of expecting him on time. He also thought that it made him seem more important if he was a little late. Busy man, and all that.

Tom was waiting at the bank president's desk, as they had agreed. Carl had asked Tom why it was so important to meet at the bank, and Tom had simply said, "Because I need to know that your check won't bounce," and given him a pat on the shoulder.

"Sorry I'm late," Carl puffed cheerfully. "City business comes first, you know." He said that to impress the bank president, who was also a voter. He was late because he'd forgotten to make up six checks for ninety-nine thousand dollars each on the Elements autopenning machine, and since he didn't want anyone at his office to know that he'd written them, he'd had to negotiate the technology by himself. Like the other office equipment that was easily understood by his clerks, the forms printer was a mystery to Carl. He could have simply written checks in longhand, but he was afraid that it would raise a red flag at the bank. Carl felt that if the checks looked like his secretary had prepared them for his signature, then he had nothing to hide.

"Actually, I've just finished opening an account here, Carl, so don't worry about being late. I had a chance to get acquainted with the president," Tom said, "and I asked him to be a witness to the signing. That is, if you have no objection, Carl."

"Oh, hell, no. Bob and I go way back, don't we, Bob?"

Bob gave Carl a weak smile, but no response.

"Have you got the agreement with you, Carl?" Tom asked.

"Right here, young man," Carl said.

Tom dialed Jack Boyle and read what Carl had handed him word-for-word.

"They're clean, Tom. Good luck," Boyle said and hung up.

Tom looked at Carl. "Did you bring the money?"

Carl flushed a bit and chuckled. "Of course, Tom. Just as we agreed." Carl opened a tattered manila file folder, produced the six checks, and handed them over to Tom.

Frowning, Tom held the checks away from his body like they were contagious.

"Ah, Carl? What are these?"

"Oh! Sorry, Tom, no time to call you. I know it's six thousand dollars short, but ..." Carl started to explain when Tom interrupted.

"Not what I meant, Carl. These are Elements' checks. I'm writing an agreement with the City of Hot Springs."

"Why, Elements money spends the same as city money, Tom."

"I'm sure that Elements money spends plenty well," Tom said. "It's just that the agreement is with the city but the money isn't from the city. I don't want there to be a problem later on." Tom turned to the bank president. "Bob, do *you* foresee this being a problem?"

Bob already had a problem with it and addressed Carl directly.

"Carl, you know that I'm sworn to uphold the covenants we've made with our customers. Now, don't get upset with me, but it's my understanding that you are not authorized to sign any checks over $100,000, is that right?"

"That's the way we set it up, Bob. What's the problem?"

"Well, this is unusual, Carl. I know you're technically within the rules, but you are not distributing six smaller amounts to six different recipients; you're satisfying a lump sum obligation. As I said, it is within the rules, but I think you'd want me to double-check this if one of your other partners was in here with this kind of transaction," Bob-the-bank-president said.

Carl was feeling uncomfortably warm. *I'm not letting this deal go south because of some pissant banker and his pissant rules,* he said to himself. *Be cool, Carl, and you'll get through this.*

Rather than tell the bank president that this wasn't any of his goddamn business, Carl turned on his "aw, shucks" small-town charm.

"You are absolutely right, Bob, and sorry I didn't give you a heads-up. Didn't mean to put you in an awkward position," Carl fawned, seeing Bob begin to relax. "You see, this thing is moving so fast, hell, I'm having trouble keeping up with it myself." He willed a casual chuckle to percolate up from his belly.

Tom glanced at his watch. Carl saw it and got to the point.

"Anyways, Tom wanted the whole she-bang wrapped up by the end of business today, and it forced our hand—at the city and with my business partners. The city is more or less a middleman in the deal, you see. Elements intended to provide the funding all along. You knew that, didn't you, Tom?"

"Yeah, we talked about that some," Tom agreed.

"Well, with the deadline you set, Tom, there was no time to get everything purtied up, bows on it and all. So, when our group got together at lunch today, we just took a voice vote, and Doc Jennings said to handle it this way 'cause there wasn't time to run a check through channels, especially since we didn't get things finalized with your attorney in St. Paul until about a half-hour ago," Carl lied.

"But if you want to hold things up until tomorrow, it's fine by me. Hell, Bob, give Doc a call right now if you think you need his approval to cash the check; it don't mean nothing to me. But Larkin is the one with the deadline and holding the checks could be a deal-killer for him. What's the verdict, Tom?"

Carl had just made the biggest bluff of his life and eased back in his chair, folded his fingers together as far as they'd go and laid them atop his belt.

Tom had no choice but to go all-in.

"It's got to happen today," Tom countered, "or I'll be forced to go elsewhere. Sorry, Carl."

That put Bob in one hell of a bind. Carl was technically within his bounds writing checks under a hundred thousand dollars each, but Bob knew Jennings and feared making any kind of mistake with Elements money. On the other hand, if he killed what was obviously a huge deal for Elements, Jennings would pull every bit of business he had with First Western and move it across town. Bob chose the safe route.

"No offense, Carl. I'd better check with Doc," he said and picked up his desk phone.

Inside Carl's skull, time slowed to a crawl. His eyes lost their focus, and his brain began to shut down. He didn't even try to think about what he would say to Jennings if Bob got him on the line. There was no point. If Jennings answered the phone, the deal, his position at Elements and his lofty dreams would all come crashing down around his head.

BOB CALLED JENNINGS' office, rather than his cell phone. It was the only thing he could do to cover his own ass on all counts. Jennings had a habit of not answering his office phone, and Bob knew it. He would be able to leave a message, thus establishing his effort to check with Jennings, and still be able to approve the transaction for Carl.

Bob could care less whether Doc Jennings had approved the checks or not, or what Carl was up to, or whether Tom Larkin got six hundred grand. Bob only cared that the money stay in his bank as long as possible, and that nobody had reason to accuse him of doing anything that was against the rules.

Bob the banker had never taken a clear stand on much of anything, and it had served him well over the years.

"Carl. Carl!" Bob repeated sharply, jolting back to life a man who had left himself for dead.

"What? What? What'd Doc say?" Carl stammered.

"Doc wasn't in his office. I left a message for him to call me. I guess we'll just have to proceed with this unless Mr. Larkin is still concerned about the origin of the funds. Mr. Larkin?"

Tom was on his cell phone and held up one finger to signify he was about through.

His flip phone clicked and Tom said, "That was Jack Boyle. No problem with the Elements checks on our end. If we can figure out what to do about the missing six K, this deal is done."

A glistening and gleeful Carl Graves already had his personal checkbook out of his jacket.

"I told you this Larkin was a tough nut," he said to Bob. "If I'd a thought of it back at the office, I'd a had Norma print out another one of our checks. But, I didn't, and it's almost five o'clock. So, here, if you don't mind a personal check, we can take care of that issue, too?"

Tom smiled. "That'll work out just fine, Mayor."

Carl and Bob began to sign their names as executor and witness, respectively, on the three copies of the agreement and passed them to Tom.

Tom stopped his pen in mid-air as he was about to put his John Hancock on the first copy and said, "Since the loan money is being paid in funds that are currently on deposit with your bank, Bob, and it is being deposited to my account here, can you assure me that these checks will clear this evening and be available to me tomorrow morning without any problem?"

Tom's signing hand was suspended, motionless.

"No problem, Tom," Bob said.

Tom's hand started toward the agreement and stopped short again.

"We're not on tomorrow's business, right?" Tom asked.

"As we agreed, Mr. Larkin. You may consider the funds at your disposal as of this minute. The deposit is what is known in the business as an on-us check You may write a check for the full amount of the deposit at this instant—and of course we'd accept it," he said with more than a touch of snootiness. Bankers don't like to be asked things twice, especially if they weren't happy about agreeing to them the first time.

"Great!" Tom said. "Then we're set." He signed all three copies, endorsed seven checks totaling $600,000, filled out a deposit slip and handed it over to Bob.

"I'll need a receipt, if you don't mind, Bob."

"Yes, Mr. Larkin. Right away."

"Buy you a drink, boys?" Tom asked when Bob returned with the deposit slip.

Bob politely declined. Carl figured that Tom was spending Elements money now, so he accepted the invite—on the condition that they do their drinking at the Lucky Strike. Together, the two bluffers left the bank for the bar, each cocksure he'd bested the other.

Monday, 7:45 p.m.

Figuring that Tom would be about as welcome as a wasp at a picnic, Carl didn't invite him along to his eight o'clock supper with Jennings. Carl believed that he was the one holding aces, but he was worried about the meeting. Jennings could be intolerable and intimidating, so Carl ordered himself another cocktail to shore up his resolve.

Jennings arrived twenty minutes late, after Carl had polished off a fourth whiskey and Coke. Jennings was smoldering when he strode into the back room Carl had reserved for their supper meeting. *Let him stew,* Carl thought, *I've got a done deal in my pocket.*

"Evening, Doc."

Carl started to wiggle out of this chair to shake Jennings' hand, but Jennings said, "Just stay put and tell me what's going on between you and Larkin."

Carl struggled to his feet anyway. He had to piss.

"Whatdayere drinkin'," Carl slurred.

Jennings gave Carl a dismissive look and said, "Glenmorangie, 30-year malaga cask, neat, if you've got any in that two-bit bar of yours. If not, Glenlivet on the rocks with a splash of water. I know you've got that—'cause there's an outside chance that one of those rail jockeys out there might have seen a TV ad for it." Jennings sneered and turned his attention to the menu.

"I'll have the 50-year Glen Morkaney, Marjaney, whatever," Carl mumbled under his breath as he made his way into the bar area, "and bring it to me in your finest crystal on a silver platter and don't touch the glass or I won't drink it. Why, yes, your highness, anything you say, your highness. Can't wait for you to read the agreement, your highness, and shove it up your highness' asshole sideways, your highness."

Jennings is done pushing me around, Carl thought. *Tonight I start calling the shots.* Carl stopped to leave a drink order with the bartender and said, "We're having supper in the back room. Put everything on one tab and give it to Jennings." Then he went to the bathroom and spent an inordinate amount of time taking a shit and washing up after.

"Your guts bothering you?" Jennings remarked, when Carl returned.

At least I've got some, you slimy bastard, Carl thought, and sat down.

Jennings was on his second whisky, and Carl was headed into the fog.

Carl figured that he'd wait for Jennings to start the discussion because he'd called the meeting. So Carl just sipped his Jack Daniels and Coke, saying nothing while he played with his stir stick and ice cubes.

"You know I hate surprises," Jennings finally said.

"Well, too bad, Doc, 'cause I got a big one for you! Mr. Tom Larkin as good as handed over the mineral rights to me today. I'd say it was about, oh …" and Carl checked his wristwatch for effect, "… about three hours ago. Surprised?"

Jennings was stunned.

"What are you talking about, Carl?"

Carl ignored him and picked up his menu. "You wanna eat sumpton, Doc?"

Jennings tore the menu from Carl's hands and threw it halfway across the room.

"Are you deaf, you fat fuck? Larkin signed what over to whom today?"

Carl was enjoying every glorious second of the meeting so far, and they hadn't even started to eat.

"Since you asked so nicely, Doc, I'm going to fill you in," Carl said, and belched.

Jennings glowered at Carl, sat back and crossed his arms. "I'm waiting!"

"While you and them attorneys was dickin' around with I-don't-know-what-all, I was out giving our boy from St. Paul a tour of the golf course, which I think I tole ya already."

"I've heard this crap two or three times before. Get to the point, Carl."

"Well, he says to me, Carl, I really need some financial help on this here deal. And so I says to him, hey, if I was able to get you some help, would you be willing to sell the mineral rights to the ranch? And he says, what kind of help, and I says, how's about a down-payment loan from the city that's forgivable—'course all that would depend on them mineral rights getting in the right hands, if ya know what I mean." Carl stopped to take a drink. Jennings sat staring at him, not blinking, and not saying a word.

"So, he says that them rights must be mighty important to Elements 'cause of what we offered to pay for the ranch, and how much would we be willing to pay for the rights?" Carl grinned from ear to ear, and some whiskey dribbled out of the corner of his mouth.

"This is where it gets real good, Doc," Carl said, and had another go at his drink.

"We was going to pay ... what ... for that ranch? Like sixteen mil or some such shit? Know what I offered Larkin for the rights, and that he thought was so damn much money he almost crapped his pants? Take a guess, Doc."

"I don't know, Carl. Why don't you just tell me," Jennings said icily.

"Buck-and-a-half!" Carl said, and grinned again, losing more whiskey out of the side of his mouth, which he quickly replaced from his nearly empty glass. "Buck-and-a-mutherfuckin'-half," he repeated. "How ya like them apples?"

"You purchased the right to mine everything and anything on the ranch for one and a half million dollars?" an astonished Jennings managed to ask.

"Well, everything except gold and silver. That dumb ass Larkin wanted to exempt them from the contract. I said, sure, take mica out if ya want, take any old thing you want, cause all we needed was to dig tunnels."

"You told him about the tunnels?" Jennings asked incredulously.

"Bet your ass I told him, Doc . . . 'cause *that's* what he thinks we want the mining rights for—digging more tunnels! Got him to sign over the goods, didn't I? What's your problem, anyway, you sourpuss?"

JENNINGS WAS IN a state of disbelief. He wondered how a bungler like Carl Graves could have gotten hold of the mineral rights for a tenth of their highest offer—and Jennings had been prepared to offer more. Even more galling to Jennings, Carl had done it without him. Jennings set his jaw, determined to reestablish his control over the situation.

"So . . . Larkin signed the mineral rights over to Elements for a million and a half bucks? Fantastic! If what you say is true, partner, you may have just pulled off the biggest deal of your life. When does Elements give Larkin the money, and when can we commence mining operations?" Jennings asked.

"Things are going to happen step-like, Doc. I had to do the deal in two pieces, you know, to keep all the parties in the dark about what we really want out of this here deal," Carl said, feeling the whiskey. "It's a wee bit complicated, if you know what I mean."

"I don't. Complicated in what way?" Jennings frowned.

"For starters, Larkin don't like you one little bit, Doc, and refused to sign anything if he was going to have to deal with you directly," Carl explained, embellishing the truth to suit his own purpose. "So he agreed to sign over them rights, but under a couple little ol' conditions."

"What conditions? Get on with it, boy!"

"First, we set everything up through a shell corp, Tom's Mining Company. He's majority owner, but we eventually get all the voting stock—so he's just a figurehead. That keeps Larkin clean on the contract for deed, you see. So, the rights to the mineral lick were actually signed over to the city in the form of Series B shares in Tom's Mining Company. Pretty slick, if I do say so myself.

"Anyways," Carl slurred, "the way it hadda work is that the city can only sell them shares to one person and one person only."

"The city got the mineral lick?" Jennings exploded. "You moron! That's the one thing we wanted out of this deal . . . and you gave it to the city?"

"Just calm down, Doc. If you'd give it more than two seconds' thought, you'd probably figure out that, if the city's making a forgivable loan, they ought to have a reason to do it—you think? So, Larkin gives the city something; I suggested it be the rights to the lick. All we've got do is pay the city back for the loan, something like six hundred K or so, and we basically get everything that's in the lick. Before that can happen, though, we got to pay Larkin his mil-five for the rights to the rest of the ranch. You following all this?"

Rather than admit to Carl that he was making a lot of sense, Jennings simply nodded his head.

"OK, then. The city's got collateral for their forgivable loan, so I'm not going to get some pinhead citizen storming into my office and lecturing me on misappropriation or whatever." Carl took a breath and another drink.

"I believe, Carl," Jennings said warily, "that you said the city may sell or assign those shares to one person, and one person only. Is that the complicated part of this?"

"It's one of them, Doc. You see, we had Larkin bring in his contract for deed, so we'd know he was the legal owner, and all that. Come to find out, that old goat McPherson writes in the purchase agreement that Larkin can't sell no land or mineral rights or nothing else to Elements Corporation. Well, that would have killed the friggin' deal right then and there. So I says just put my name in there—let the city sell to me. I already told you how we was handling the rest of the deal through the new shell corp."

Carl beamed.

The color, what there was of it, had completely drained from Jennings' face.

"When I told Larkin that he could work the deal through me and still get all his money, you know what that tinhorn says to me? He looks up at me and says, 'You're the only one I know, and I trust you.' I goddamn near split a gut. Anyway, Larkin seemed to be fine with fucking with what Jo wrote in the contract for deed—all he wanted to do was get his hands on our money, if you ask me."

"What do you mean by our money, Carl?" Jennings asked.

"What d'ya think, Doc? Paying the city back for the loan and the friggin' buck-and-a-half for the rest of the mineral rights! Calm down, Doc. Have a drink and enjoy the moment."

"I'm not feeling very comfortable at the moment, thank you very much, Carl."

"You're not feeling very comfortable, Doc? Why's that?" Carl said flippantly.

"I'm not comfortable with you getting into the middle of something that's way beyond your level, Graves. I'm not comfortable hearing about this after the fact." Jennings was getting hotter by the second. "I'm not comfortable with the idea that you've taken for yourself something that belongs to Elements and the rest of your partners. I'm not comfortable when my partners keep me in the dark!" Now Jennings was screaming, and veins stood out on both sides of his neck.

Carl had too much whiskey in him to take any more guff from Jennings, and he brought his considerable frame to a standing position.

"Let me see if I can figure this out, Doc. Give me a few seconds, OK, because I'm not able to think as fast as you—given my *level* and all. What's really eating at you? Could it be you're uncomfortable because your whipping boy just outsmarted you? Are you pissed because I was able to go out and get them friggin' mineral rights for a whole hell of a lot less than you was willing to pay? And with all your smarts and your money, you still couldn't get the deal done? Or is it just that everything's going through me, and now you're going to have to deal me into the game? Or maybe, and I know I'm really going out on a limb here, maybe it's just because you ain't in control of none of this. Which one of them things has got you most pissed off, *boss*?"

Carl laughed and lifted his glass to drain it.

Jennings sprang forward and slapped the glass from Carl's hand.

"This is my deal, Graves!" Jennings screamed. "You're not going to hose my deal! Do you hear me? This is my fucking deal!"

Jennings was still screaming when the waitress came through the door to take their order. She stood stock still as Jennings shouted his last words and stood over the table eyeball-to-eyeball with Carl.

Carl reached into his jacket pocket for a copy of the mineral rights agreement and threw it onto the table.

"Well, you arrogant prick, there's my deal. Deal with that." And Carl walked out of the back room, taking the waitress with him as he went.

Carl emerged from the back room and instructed the wait staff to ignore Jennings; he was to receive no further service, even if he came out and demanded it.

Jennings sat down at the empty table and read the contract Carl had negotiated with Larkin. In disbelief and shock, he reread it, poring over every word.

Reading the contract was torturous. Like Sisyphus, Jennings was compelled to start over and over at the beginning—but each fresh reading of the document yielded neither further insight nor solution to the quandary Carl had engineered.

After an hour of this enterprise, Jennings was mumbling things to himself. After two hours, he was alternately debating with or shrieking at any one of a number of imaginary morons, subordinates, and unworthy adversaries. He was just able to pull himself together enough to stumble out of the bar.

Those who saw Jennings leave the Lucky Strike that night would later remember that his eyes were as wild as his body was contorted. No one had spoken to him.

Jennings didn't remember leaving the Lucky Strike or driving to his office. He simply became aware that he was sitting at his desk, the apocalyptic document lying in front of him.

Carl, you idiot! he ranted silently. *You've ruined everything for me! That weasel Larkin knows everything, and he took us all for a ride! It's all your doing, Graves.*

Carl couldn't possibly have foreseen the problem in signing a document that rescinded the mineral rights in the event of a felony conviction or indictment; he didn't know anything about the Homeland Security investigation.

Jennings was the only one who knew, and he'd purposely kept it from his partners. It was his practice to tell his partners only what he thought they needed to know to do the jobs he told them to do. Everything else he kept to himself.

That Carl didn't know about the investigation was, in Jennings' mind, bad luck—as Jennings didn't consider himself capable of bad judgment. If a decision he made began to sour, Jennings rearranged the facts to conform to his decision, appropriated someone else's better idea or simply made a new decision and flatly denied that he'd ever made the bad one.

Because he believed that he was never wrong, Jennings had never learned to accept responsibility for failure and had no rational way of dealing with it. He would cheat, bamboozle, blame, threaten, whine, or hang his failure on anyone handy, rather than admit he'd made a mistake.

The idea that one can do no wrong is a common conceit of the wealthy.

Jennings picked up his phone and dialed Brady's number.

"Hello?" A groggy Brady answered.

"Brady! You passed out, or what? What are you doing in bed?"

Brady's head cleared more quickly than usual. He hadn't had a drink in five days.

"That you, Doc?"

"It's me, sweetheart. Rise and shine, we've got work to do."

"Look, Doc, in five hours I'll be on a private jet with a security goon from Qwestead and your thirty million bucks. So, I've got to be up and about around three o'clock. Can we talk about whatever it is you've got on your mind tomorrow?" Brady pleaded.

"You're saying the bearer bonds will be here tomorrow?"

"About seven-thirty your time, if we get the wheels up here at six."

"When were you planning on telling me about your little excursion? And who told you that you could take a vacation out West just when I most need your butt at your desk where you can do my work?"

Brady laid the telephone receiver off to the side of the bed and closed his eyes. He was anxious to get back to drinking himself to sleep every night when this business was over.

"Brady, I asked you a question," Jennings shouted. "You there?"

Brady picked the phone back up. "Yeah, Doc. I'm here."

"So when did you intend to tell me you were on your way out here? When you got here?" Jennings demanded.

"Actually, yeah, Doc. I thought it would be a nice surprise."

"I don't like surprises, dickhead. I don't pay for surprises."

"For Christ's sake, give me a break. I just got the call two hours ago from Qwestead. The security chief said that they had the bonds ready, they couldn't reach you, and they wanted to know what to do. I said you wanted them there tomorrow, the earlier the better, all right?"

"Does that mean you need to fly out here with them, Brady?"

"Actually, it does. Qwestead said that someone representing you needed to accompany the bonds until they were handed off, to verify that they were delivered to the right person. Being a lawyer, I suggested that I was the appropriate choice. Hell, you told me yesterday to fly out with them myself if I had to—remember? Anyway, I thought it might be kind of fun to come out there and see all those little hobbit houses in Igloo, so I volunteered to chaperone your thirty million bucks. But, if you want, I'll just call Qwestead back and cancel the whole freaking trip."

"Why didn't you call me?" Jennings asked, undeterred.

Brady couldn't hide his exasperation. "I did try to call you. Twice. Once about an hour and a half ago, and then again about a half-hour ago. You either weren't answering your cell, or you had it turned off. Why don't you try checking your messages before you fly off the handle?"

Jennings fished around inside his jacket pocket and retrieved his cell phone. He had turned the thing off when he went into the meeting with Carl and had not remembered to turn it back on after he left.

Jennings powered up the phone and saw the new message icon. Brady was right.

"Did you say that Qwestead requires someone representing me to be on the plane accompanying the bonds?" Jennings asked.

"That's what I said, Doc. But you just give me the word, and I'll be more than happy to call Qwestead back right now and tell them to hold the plane, hold the bonds, and put a hold on everything else while you sleep on it. Is that what you want?"

"No need to get sarcastic, Phil; just call my cell when you arrive. I'll come to you," Jennings continued. "There have been certain other developments today that may make your presence here quite useful."

"Shouldn't I stay here where I've got resources to deal with these 'developments'?"

"No. I want you on that plane," Jennings said. "Carl Graves signed an agreement with Tom Larkin behind my back. We may need to adjust the language of that agreement, completely rewrite it, or take other action to prevent Larkin from getting his hands on that down payment money."

"What kind of agreement is this, Doc?"

"The agreement gives the rights to the McPherson mineral lick to the City of Hot Springs in exchange for six hundred grand. The rights are ultimately deeded to Carl Graves, not to Elements."

"Jesus H. Christ. Are you kidding me?"

"I am not, Phil. We might have been able to work with it if Carl hadn't stipulated that the deal is voided by a felony conviction or indictment against anyone involved with Elements Corporation."

Brady knew that there was only one logical conclusion to be drawn.

"That son-of-a-bitch Larkin knows, doesn't he?"

"Knows what?" Jennings asked innocently.

"Knows everything, right?"

"No. I don't think so, Phil. He's obviously plugged into the Homeland Security investigation, or he wouldn't have put that language about an indictment into the agreement. He got that info from his snoopy wife. He may have an inkling about something with the mineral lick, but I don't think he's very far down the road on that."

No sense telling Brady too much, too soon, Jennings reminded himself.

"Well, what the hell is he up to, then, Doc?"

"As far as I'm concerned, he's all about the money. He pulled the wool over Carl's eyes; I'll give him that. But, he knows diddly-squat about the mineral lick or anything else. He's just looking for money and leverage," Jennings said smugly.

In truth, Jennings was worried sick. Unlike Brady, he knew that Larkin had gotten on to everything: the investigation, their doings out in Igloo and the montmorillonite. His overseers in Igloo, had called late in the day about the tunnel breach. Jennings just hoped that Larkin hadn't already tracked things back to Cody's death.

"On your way out here, Brady, be thinking about what we can do to prevent Larkin from collecting the money from the city. He's got two weeks from this past Saturday to come up with the down stroke on the ranch, and we need to do whatever is necessary to prevent him from making that payment. The best way to defuse the situation would be if the contract for deed defaults," Jennings said.

"I'll do what I can," Brady answered. "That it?"

"There's another thing, Brady. Be thinking about how I can dump my partners. I don't care how it's done; I just want them out of my way. Out of *my* deal."

"That's going to be sticky, but I'll think about it."

"Good. Then I'll see you tomorrow. Call me when you land."

"Will do, Doc. Good night."

"Wait, Phil. One other thing. Bring your passport," Jennings instructed him.

"My passport? They got immigration officers at Hot Springs International, or what?" Brady joked.

"Just bring it. I'll fill you in when you get here," Jennings said.

"Well, you needn't have worried, Doc. My passport's in my briefcase now ... in fact, it's always there ..."

"You carry a passport around?"

"Yeah. The State of New York took my driver's license away after that last DUI, so I always carry my passport for identification. Can I go to sleep now?"

Jennings needed Phil's complete loyalty and complicity for the next week or two, and Brady was never more docile—or loyal—than when he was hung over.

"Just one last thing, Phil," Jennings said in a friendly way. "You've been burning the midnight oil for days on my account, and I know you've stayed away from the sauce to do it. I don't think I've taken time to thank you for that. So, my thanks, Phil."

"Uh ... you're welcome, Doc ... ah ... always glad to be of service."

"Tell you what, counselor," Jennings said in the same agreeable tone. "There's nothing that has to be handled the moment you step off the plane, so why don't you just pack a bottle in your suitcase and plan on relaxing the first day out? How's that as thanks, Phil?"

"You serious, Doc?"

"I am. You just go right ahead with a little toot, and I'll give you the high sign when it's time to dig in. In fact, I'll make sure you get that tour of the, what did you call them? The hobbit houses out in Igloo?" Jennings said with a laugh.

"Whatever you say, Doc. Thanks."

BRADY HUNG UP the phone, got up from bed, and fixed himself a whiskey.

"One for the road," he said, and took a gulp. He didn't dare tie one on until tomorrow because he might go too far and miss the flight. *Tonight*, he thought, *I'll just have a tiny little bump to keep out the devil.*

Whiskey was the whitewash Brady used to paint over the grim reality of his situation: he had little choice in life other than to do Bill Jennings' bidding.

If Brady believed he could withstand treatment for his addiction, he could rid himself of two demons at once. Jennings may have been overbearing and cruel, but treatment, to Brady, was unthinkable.

Jennings was the roof over Brady's head and his only hope for security in the future, so Phil obeyed him. He knew that his relationship with Jennings was twisted and mean, but it was the only one he had left. Brady double-checked the bedside clock, set his wristwatch alarm for safety's sake, threw back the rest of the whiskey, and lay down to sleep. In a few hours he would be in a well-stocked limousine speeding down Route One to a well-stocked private jet.

Such was the stuff that remained of his dreams.

TUESDAY

Securing ourselves against defeat lies in our own hands,
but the opportunity of defeating the enemy is provided by the enemy himself.
Sun Tzu, The Art of War

———

6:50 A.M.

Tom awoke a troubled man. First, there were the pharma calls Kathy had presumably made and about which he'd heard nothing. Then there were his questions regarding Kathy's whereabouts the past two nights. Tom imagined all sorts of lewd acts that his wife had engaged in with a string of men, some of them nameless, others not so unrecognizable.

He tried reaching Kathy at home. No dice. Next, he tried her cell phone—to no avail. But she picked up on the first ring at her office.

"Kathleen Larkin," she said, all business.

"Kathy. It's me."

"Tom! I didn't expect your call so early," she said guiltily.

"Apparently you didn't expect it yesterday or last night, either," Tom couldn't help himself from saying.

There was no answer from Kathy.

"Sorry, Kath. Didn't mean to start out that way."

There was still no answer from Kathy.

Although he knew that he had no right to be on his high horse when it came to the question of fidelity, Tom went on the offensive anyway, hissing at Kathy. "Do you want us to start over? Or do you just want to say to hell with it, and I'll see you whenever I choose to return home from Hot Springs?"

The two of them had been married long enough to predict—with great accuracy—when they'd pushed the other as far as he or she would go. Kathy knew that this was no time for brinksmanship, and said, "Yes, I'd like to start over; no, I don't want to say to hell with it. Let's try to be civil, can we?"

"I will if you will."

"Tom, I'm sorry I didn't get back to you yesterday. The truth is, I couldn't get to the pharma calls yesterday—I was on deadline until late afternoon, and I thought it was too late to call by then. I wouldn't have had any news for you had we talked, so you haven't lost any time," she said.

"Did you plan to make the calls anytime today?" he asked bitingly.

"For your information, wise guy, I came in very early this morning to place the calls. It's an hour later on the East Coast, and I figured—rightly as it turns out—that most CEO's are up and at it bright and early," Kathy countered. "Care to hear what I know, or would you prefer to exchange insults?"

Tom brightened despite the bad blood between them.

"You found something out? Great! Well, who was it? What did they say?"

"I rolled in here around seven my time, eight o'clock on the Coast. I didn't want to make these calls on company time," she explained.

"So . . ."

"I started dialing and smiling, leaving the message about the montmorillonite and Jennings, just as you asked me to do. So I'm on the fifth or sixth call, and my line starts to beep. I figured it was either a reader I didn't need to argue with this early in the morning, or one of those CEO's calling back, so I didn't pick up," she went on.

"As soon as I'd left the message for the last CEO, I got into my voice mail. Want to guess who's behind door number three?"

"Give me a name, Kathy. It could be any of them!"

"Qwestead's Paul Stolley," Kathy announced proudly. "And by the time stamp on my voice mail, I can tell you that it only took him about ten minutes to return my call after I left the message. I'd say you have your man, Tom Larkin."

For the moment, Tom forgot all of his fantasies about Kathy's nocturnal activities. "Wow! Wow, wow, wow! Do you know how big Qwestead is, Kathy?"

"I do," she said. "According to their web site, about fifty-five billion a year. Enough to give Bill Gates a run for his money, I'd say." Kathy always did her homework.

"What did Stolley say?"

"He said, 'I received your message. My secretary has been instructed to interrupt me at any time to take your call'."

"That's it?"

"That's it," Kathy said. "Seemed pretty straightforward to me. The CEO of one of the world's largest corporations says he'll interrupt anything to take a call from a reporter? He is definitely your man, Tom. What are you going to do next?"

"I'll explain in a minute. Anybody else call back?"

"Nobody yet."

"Let me know immediately if any of the others call back," Tom said. "Meanwhile, I think it's time I placed a call to my new best friend Paul Stolley and let him know that he won't need to be dealing with Jennings anymore."

"What are you going to say?"

"I'm going to tell him that there is some kind of substance on the ranch that appears to have medicinal application. For animals and humans. Then I'm going to tell him everything I know—or suspect—about Jennings and offer to sit down and discuss the situation."

"And if he won't?"

"Simple. I tell him if he doesn't want to talk, I'm going down the list of pharmaceutical companies, and I'll offer the whole kit and caboodle to the highest bidder. If this mineral is really a big deal, Stolley won't want anybody else to get hold of it. If it's nothing, he'll tell me to go pound sand. In any case, there has got to be something here, because he immediately came out into the open," Tom said.

"Good luck, Tom. I hope you know what you're doing," Kathy said uncertainly. "Just steer clear of Jennings. Promise me that."

"Promise. Got to go," Tom said in rapid-fire. He didn't want to waste any more time, and he didn't want to think about those other questions he had for Kathy.

Tom pulled on his boots and grabbed a muffin from the free breakfast bar on his way to the car. He was waiting in front of the bank when the woman who'd helped him with a safe-deposit box the previous day opened the doors for business.

She was pleasantly surprised to see Tom again so soon and showed it by not opening the door quite wide enough for him to enter the bank without brushing into her as he squeezed by. Tom excused himself politely but stood and watched her nipples harden as she apologized for being so clumsy.

"How can I help you today, Mr. Larkin?" she purred.

"Whom do I see about a wire transfer?"

"It's your lucky day, mister," she declared. "Please follow me."

She turned her backside to Tom and sauntered over to the preferred customer desk in the exaggerated gait usually associated with runway models. Upon reaching the desk, she swung around quickly so that her skirt cartwheeled.

She struck a profile pose and offered Tom a chair.

"Can I get you some coffee?" she asked. Tom could plainly see that she planned to stretch a ten-minute wire transfer into an hour and flirt with him the whole time.

Tom had other ideas.

"Thank you, no. I am in a bit of a rush this morning, so if you wouldn't mind, I'd rather ..."

"Of course. Silly me." She strolled over to a line of cabinets and bent over from the waist to retrieve a form that was on the bottom shelf.

When she returned and sat down at the desk, she made a point of rolling the chair out and sitting next to Tom. After the papers had been filled out, with an excess of light touches to Tom's hand and knee, she announced, "Wire transfers go out at two in the afternoon. Bank policy, you know."

Tom placed his hand lightly over hers and gave her his warmest smile.

"It would mean a lot to me, darlin', if you could get this transfer done immediately. It's a large amount of money, and the funds need to be accessible in St. Paul by noon."

"Five-hundred-ninety-nine thousand dollars is a lot of money, Mr. Larkin," she said with a slow uncrossing and recrossing of her legs. "I can understand why you're anxious to have yours hard at work."

"I certainly am," Tom replied. "Perhaps I should have spoken to Bob. I completely understand that you can't override bank policy. Is he in yet?"

"I didn't say there weren't other ways," she smiled.

Here it comes, Larkin thought. *The old 'you take me to dinner' and 'I'll see what I can do about the wire transfer' bit.*

Instead, he was surprised to hear the teller say, "If you're willing to pay us two hundred fifty dollars, in addition to the regular fifty dollar transaction fee, we can arrange for the transfer right away."

"You can?"

"Just give me the green light, Mr. Larkin."

"Two-hundred-fifty is fine with me," Tom quickly responded. "When can you arrange the transfer?"

"Would you like to wait for it?"

"How long?" Tom asked.

"Let's say fifteen minutes to be safe, shall we?"

"That would be great," Tom said.

"Anything I can get for you while you wait?" she said, giving Tom another shot at her.

"Maybe I'd like that coffee after all, thanks," he said, and rummaged around on the side table for a magazine. He opened up an old copy of Popular Mechanics and waited.

The teller returned twenty minutes later with a complicated-looking receipt for the wire transfer, signed by Bob himself.

"There you are, Mr. Larkin," she said, "You're all taken care of. If you'll just sign here, and here, and here, you can be on your way." She accentuated each "sign here" with a pert bob of her torso and a sharp thrust of her pen, causing her tits to hop up and down like cheerleaders.

"Thanks for the help," Tom said and stood. "I mean, really, I didn't expect such great service. Thank you."

"Anytime, Mr. Larkin," she warbled.

Tom took her hand but was unable to shake her.

"Come to think of it, there is one other thing," she said. "Can you leave us a number where we can reach you ... in case there is any problem with the transfer?"

Tom was certain she just wanted his phone number but complied. Something could go wrong, and there was no margin for error at the pace things were moving.

He scribbled his cell phone number on a bank pad, ripped it off, and handed it to her.

He'd taken two or three steps toward the door when she said, "Goodbye, Mr. Larkin."

Tom made the mistake of looking back.

She was standing by the desk, waving her arm vigorously in the air, making her perfect boobs sway in unison. The piece of paper with his number on it was in her hand.

"Mind if I keep this once the transfer business is done?"

"Only bring you heartache, darlin'," Tom said and winked.

"I'll take that under consideration, Mr. Larkin," she said, folded the slip of paper with her lips and kissed it.

Tom tipped his hat, shook his head, and walked out of the bank. He wondered how much of that come-on he'd encouraged. He wondered where Kathy had been the last two nights. He wondered how Jo was doing. He wondered if the neighbors were looking after Boone. But mostly, Tom wondered what Qwestead's CEO Paul Stolley was going to have to say for himself.

"**M**r. Larkin? This is Paul Stolley."

"Thanks for taking my call, Mr. Stolley. I've just purchased the McPherson ranch in Hot Springs, South Dakota. I believe we have something of mutual interest to discuss."

"What would that be, Mr. Larkin?"

"That would be the montmorillonite calcium on the ranch, Mr. Stolley," Tom said, silently hoping that the term he'd found in Cody's journal was the trigger he needed.

Stolley's silence confirmed what Tom had only suspected.

"Are we talking, or are we done here?" Tom demanded. He'd gotten the upper hand in quick order and intended to play it.

"Please continue, Mr. Larkin."

Paul Stolley hadn't attained his place in life by being a fool. He may not have been holding the best hand in the game, but he had the tallest stack. Larkin had cards yet to play; Stolley had the chips to see them, and he had called.

Tom laid down the whole story: his contract for deed on the ranch, the agreement he'd made with Carl for the mineral rights, the Homeland Security investigation, Cody's journal. And, finally, being careful not to make any direct accusations, Tom suggested that there were questions surrounding Cody McPherson's death that were pertinent to the montmorillonite.

"What are you planning to do next, Tom?" Stolley's use of Tom's first name was a signal that Tom understood. Stolley was opening the door.

"What I do next, Paul, will largely be determined by you," Tom parleyed. "I intend to find out what's in that mineral lick—no matter what it takes. I'll need a partner to do that, and if your company isn't interested, well, I reckon any of the other pharmaceuticals would be more than happy to hook up with me. Am I making sense here?"

"Of course you are, and I think you know it. What do you want from Qwestead?"

"I want to ascertain the exact nature of the mineral, and from there, I intend to ..."

"That's not what I mean," Stolley interrupted.

"What do you mean?"

"Let's not be coy, Tom. How much?"

Bingo, Tom thought. *Now we're talking.*

"To tell you the truth, Paul, I really don't have a number. At the moment, I'm more concerned about who I jump in bed with and how willing he is to engage on my terms. If you can convince me that you're the right partner, then we can resolve my one pressing financial issue. If you can't convince me, I'll find somebody else to do business with," Tom said.

"Why don't you tell me what you've got in mind, and I can assure you, Tom, that I'll give you an immediate answer," Stolley said. "After you've heard what I have to say, do whatever you think is right."

"Fair enough," Tom said, warming to Stolley despite himself.

They talked for a half-hour. In closing, Stolley said that his staff would arrange for a meeting in Hot Springs the following day, provided everything he and Tom had discussed checked out.

Tom's story was fantastic by any measure, and there was only one reason for the CEO of a multinational pharmaceutical company to have taken him seriously: Stolley knew a lot more about the mineral—and about Elements—than he'd let on.

Stolley promised to call back at the end of the day and let Tom know if their meeting was a go. If the answer was yes, Stolley would stop in St. Paul and pick up Tom's attorney en route to Hot Springs.

Tom had figured Stolley for a prick—he was in league with Elements, after all—and Tom didn't trust the good impression Stolley had made. But there was no denying the sincerity Tom had felt and the straightforward way Stolley had dealt with the situation. He hadn't tried to bullshit Tom or play any games—so far.

Tom's cell phone began to chatter, signaling a message waiting.

It was from Mel Bateman at the Washington Post. The Feds had been thrilled with the material Tom provided. It gave them more than enough evidence to move forward. According to Mel, indictments for Jennings and Barker were being put in motion and were expected in less than forty-eight hours; Carl Graves and Jim Shepherd would be hearing from the grand jury in the near future. John Evans, the partner who had gone missing at so many recent company meetings, had been actively negotiating a clemency agreement with Homeland Security. In light of Tom's material, he capitulated, agreeing to testify against his partners. Elements' days were numbered.

Tom sat on the side of the bed for a long time, head in his hands, thinking. The week he'd been out West felt more like a year to him. Maybe it was forever. Tom didn't know. He wasn't absolutely sure of much anymore.

Tom lay back on the bed, and as he drifted off, Tom found himself once again in the untamed valley at the ranch's northernmost reach.

Scrub cedar crawled like lizards up the gorges, catching the morning sun and repainting the walls in dazzling shades of salmon and sage, and of copper, pitch, and coral. The wind skidded across the ground, picking up scales of terrain and red dust, before chasing bluebirds and killdeer, like tumbleweeds, out of the brush. In a long, untattered ribbon Tom saw ten thousand thousand calves and pups and kits and cubs splash onto the red earth, emerge from the swirl of prairie grass and light, then fall to the ground as predators or age took them back. He saw the sun rise, consecrate the ground, and fall into the mountains to the west over and over and over and over. The images began to come faster and blur, until they fused in one colossal and blinding light that consumed Tom and the ranch and everything above it and everything below it.

Larkin had gone West looking for land, but it was the land that found him. The ranch had snatched him from his ordered life, mixed him up with its people, its history, its purpose and its fire. He could never leave.

Tom had wandered onto a battlefield, and, rather than cut and run, had chosen sides. In the first skirmish, he'd won the ranch—at what price was still unclear.

Tom awoke with a start and rubbed his eyes. He'd come far and could feel it. Still, he had unfinished business.

It was time to see the Doc.

Tuesday, 9:30 a.m.

Jennings met the Qwestead jet, signed for the thirty million in bearer bonds, and deposited a half-drunk Brady in his hotel room. On his way out, Jennings asked at the desk if a Mr. Tom Larkin was still checked in.

"Yeah, he's been here about a week, I'd say," the kid at the front said.

"I'd like to leave a message for Mr. Larkin," Jennings said. "Get me an envelope."

The kid ducked into the office and reappeared holding an envelope with the words "Red Rock Inn" emblazoned across the flap.

Assuming Tom would be out on business by this hour of the morning, Jennings scratched out a note and said, "See to it Mr. Larkin gets this note as soon as he returns."

"He's returned already," the kid replied. "Went out early, came back early. You want me to ring his room for you?"

"No. That won't be necessary. But I'd like you to bring this to Larkin's room and hand it to him personally."

Jennings gave the kid the envelope and twenty bucks, an unheard of tip.

"Jeez, thanks, Dr. Jennings!"

Jennings may not have known all of the local folks, but they all knew him.

"You are quite welcome. Be sure that Mr. Larkin gets that note immediately," Jennings ordered.

Jennings' secretary had three messages for him when he arrived at his office ten minutes later.

The first was from Bob Mumblee, the president of First Western Bank. It was dated Monday, five p.m. The second was from Randy Hearst, Elements' corporate attorney in Philadelphia. The last one was from Mr. Tom Larkin, Red Rock Inn. No room number, no phone number. Just "Red Rock Inn," and "received your message."

Jennings went into his private office, not bothering to close his door.

Jennings' secretary heard him raise his voice and made out a few random words like "what" and "not possible" and a lot of cursing, and then the sound of a handset being slammed down violently.

Seconds later, Jennings appeared at his office door and ordered the secretary to get Carl Graves on the phone. Immediately.

"What do you want, Doc?" Carl said, feigning innocence.

"I just got off the phone with Mumblee over at First Western. Can you imagine what he told me, Carl?"

"I don't know, Doc. Let's see, did he tell you it was a bright sunny day with an expected high of fifty-eight degrees?" Carl taunted.

"He told me you stole $600,000 from me, that's what he told me, you bloated Benedict Arnold, you ... you maggot! And I want my money back. Now!"

"Mumblee said I stole six-hundred-thousand bucks? That's funny, Doc, 'cause he's the crybaby who signed off on it. So he can stick 'stole it' up his ass for all I care. I told you last night what the deal was. What is your problem, anyway?"

"My problem, you tub of sour suet, is that I want my money back! Today!" Jennings was shouting into the mouthpiece, holding it in front of his face like a microphone.

Carl was holding his handset about six inches from his ear. When Jennings was done shouting, Carl said, "We'll get the money back in the account just as soon as Larkin hands over them mineral rights to me. We'll get that and a whole hell of a lot more, so why don't you just calm down, Doc?"

"Calm down? Calm down? How am I supposed to calm down when Larkin has my six hundred K and the keys to the castle, you dipshit!" Jennings' hands were shaking and his head was beginning to hurt.

Carl said, "You keep saying it's your money. Don't you mean *our* six-hundred K, Doc? Last time I looked, it said Elements Corporation on the account."

The deal for the montmorillonite and his dream of a historic place in the world of medicine were crumbling. Jennings forced himself to get a grip, to try and salvage the situation. Carl was just a stumblebum—Larkin was the problem. *Deal with Larkin, and the rest of it can be handled,* Jennings reasoned.

Collecting himself, Jennings said, "Carl, is there any possible way to undo the transaction you and Larkin conducted yesterday afternoon?"

"Don't know, but I'd guess not. This ain't no life insurance contract or a set of encyclopedias here, Bill," Carl replied. "What's the difference anyway?"

Jennings continued, now ominously calm. "Let me share a little tidbit of information direct from the Department of Homeland Security, Carl. Maybe it will help you understand how thoroughly you may have destroyed our chances of getting the McPherson ranch."

"The hell you talking about, Doc?" Doubt shot Carl through.

"We, and by that I mean me, you and the rest of my bush league partners, are currently under investigation by Homeland Security—specifically, the Federal Bureau of Investigation."

CARL FELT HIS office walls close in as the implications began to crowd out all other thoughts. *The felony clause,* he realized.

Larkin knew all along and played me for a fool! Carl felt sick. He'd gone all-in on a king-high straight, only to be outdone.

He wanted to puke, but his guts somehow held.

"Are they planning to indict?" Carl croaked.

"I don't know the answer to that quite yet, Carl, but by the looks of things, including the message from Randy Hearst sitting on my desk, I'd say smart money was on indictment. So, prepare yourself, fat man."

Carl's massive heart sounded like a kettledrum in Copland's *Fanfare for the Common Man.* Boom-boom-boom … boom-boom-boom … boom-boom-boom … boom-boom-boom … and he felt it do something like a somersault and was sure it had broken loose. He put his hand to his chest and felt the drum pounding and at least knew that he was still alive.

"What are we going to do?"

"What are we going to do, Carl?" Jennings mocked him. "What are we going to do?

"The last time I checked, it was you that unlocked the safe for Larkin. It was you who screwed the pooch, not we," Jennings said, with all the compassion of a farmer feeding freshly-cut testicles to the hogs that had just given them up. "If I were you, lard ass, I'd start packing my bags for a trip to the big house. And don't forget your KY-Jelly. You're going to need it."

Carl's end of the line went dead.

JENNINGS NEXT CALLED Hearst, who confirmed that indictments were imminent. He and Barker were likely to be served within twenty-four hours, two days at the most.

"When did you find this out, Hearst?" Jennings demanded.

"Well, yesterday I got a call from a reporter at the Washington Post wanting to know if we were going to defend you," he started.

Jennings interrupted. "Why didn't you tell me that yesterday— when it might have done some good!"

"First, Bill, I didn't know anything except that a reporter called, and I did try to alert you yesterday on the conference call, but you and Carl were going at it tooth-and-nail, and the call ended before I could mention it," Hearst protested.

"You could've called me back," Jennings spat at him.

"We had a call set up for tonight, and I decided that the indictments would be of interest to everyone involved," Hearst replied. He was in no mood to be bitch-slapped by Jennings now that Jennings would be facing a grand jury.

"Exactly how good is this information from the Post reporter?"

"My information isn't from a reporter. As you would expect, I didn't even bother to return his call. I contacted the vice president's office and called in a favor."

"Are you referring to the Vice President of the United States?" Jennings asked, amazed.

"Don't be impressed, Bill. I called in a chit because you can be connected with Qwestead, and Qwestead can't get involved in anything like this. The favor was for them, not you."

Hearst continued, "There's more. I got a call from Paul Stolley about fifteen minutes ago—he was just briefed on the situation," Hearst said, leaving Jennings hanging.

"What'd you tell him?"

"I confirmed that there are indictments coming."

Jennings was numb.

"And by the way, Doc," Hearst said, serving up his last sentence with relish, "do not call us when you go looking for a law firm to handle your criminal case. We aren't interested."

Jennings hung up on Hearst.

Fuck Hearst, fuck Graves, fuck Eva . . . fuck 'em all, Jennings thought bitterly, staring at his desktop. Larkin's return message stared back. Jennings dialed the Red Rock Inn. Tom Larkin would be happy to meet with him. Twenty minutes. Jennings' office.

Tuesday, 11:00 A.M.

Jennings stepped out of his office to greet Tom. "Thanks for coming, Tom. Sorry about the short notice."

"Why don't we just cut the crap, Jennings," Tom said, returning Jennings' smile with an icy glare. "You don't like me. I don't like you. Let's just settle the business you mentioned and be done with each other."

Jennings smiled at his secretary and motioned Tom into his private office.

Once the door was closed, Jennings said, "You're right, Larkin. I don't like you. You've been nothing but trouble for me. But I'm hoping that, if you'll give me the chance, I can dispel some of the nasty things you must think of me."

"Your show. Have at it."

"I asked you to come over here to discuss two things. First, the mineral rights agreement you made with Carl Graves, and second, a financial proposition we have for you on the McPherson property."

"What have you got?" Tom said.

"Your agreement with Carl may hold up in a court of law, and it may not. That remains to be seen."

"And why wouldn't it?" Tom said.

"Because it stipulates a position taken by the City of Hot Springs, and the council has not yet made a decision regarding that issue. Furthermore, a consideration payment of $600,000 was drawn improperly from the Elements Corporation account.

Certain federal banking rules indicate that we may be able to demand that the money be returned, escrowed and the transaction reviewed."

Tom was listening intently. If Jennings was right, it was a setback, even if temporary. Still, Tom had eleven days to replace the money, and he was confident, now, that he could get it from Paul Stolley.

Jennings continued, "But we don't have to engage in that unpleasantness. It would be a very lengthy and costly battle that neither of us wants to pursue … you especially, Tom, now that you've got a big monthly payment to make on the ranch."

"Go on," Tom said flatly.

"I thought that perhaps we could eliminate this issue entirely," Jennings replied.

"And how would we do that?"

"With the stroke of a pen, Mr. Larkin," Jennings said. "We create an entirely new financial agreement that supercedes your current arrangement with Carl and the city. One that provides you with a much more appropriate level of compensation."

"What does Carl have to say about this? Or the city?"

"I can assure you that Carl will go along with whatever is best for Elements Corporation …" Jennings said confidently, "… and whatever is best for the City of Hot Springs. If that is your only concern …"

Tom held up his hand. "That is not, by far, my only concern."

"I understand, Tom. Please. You said you'd hear me out."

"I did. I just wanted you to know that what Carl wants is not my only concern. Clear?" Larkin didn't intend to get friendly no matter what Jennings proposed.

Jennings began to frame his pitch. "I'm not trying to make you my friend, Tom. I'm simply asking for the opportunity to maintain a civil relationship so we can talk business. I don't know what it is beyond the ranch purchase that has caused you to dislike me so intensely, but let's try and leave it out of the business discussion, all right?"

Tom said nothing, and Jennings wrongly took it as assent.

"Good. It appears that the issue, really, boils down to money."

"Money is one of the issues."

"OK. One of the big issues is money," Jennings said, and paused before continuing.

"We are prepared to offer you twenty million dollars for the exclusive mining rights to the McPherson Ranch. You keep the land."

Tom was speechless; the offer simply blew him away. Twenty million was an enormous sum; it could retire the contract for deed and free him from work for the rest of his life. It wasn't something for which Tom was even remotely prepared. He didn't want Jennings to be able to read the astonishment on his face, so Tom looked down and started picking away at the side of one boot.

Tom had courted disaster by signing the deal with Carl; if anything had gone wrong, he would have put the mineral in Elements' hands. Now that the indictments were sure to come down, he wondered if he had the *cojones* to put everything back on the line again.

An image of Jo McPherson appeared to Tom, shaking her head. "Don't listen to him, Tom. Find another way," the vision said. "Find another way."

Tom looked up and stared at Jennings. *Why?* he thought. *Why jump from two to twenty million bucks in one fell swoop? What in tarnation is in the ground out there?*

"Give me a minute, Bill. I'm a little taken back by your offer," Tom said.

"Take as much time as you want, Tom," Jennings said brightly.

Tom put his head in his hands and ran his fingers through his hair. There was no question anymore that there was something out there, and that it was worth a lot of money. Tom just didn't know what or how much.

A gambler doesn't dream of having a house in the suburbs, two kids, a snowmobile, and two weeks off to ride it. A gambler dreams of *the score*, and he's willing to accept a soup line and a Salvation Army cot as the outcome of an all-or-nothing bet that doesn't go his way.

Tom rolled the dice.

"You've made a generous offer, Jennings. Very generous. But ... I'm going to have to turn it down. If it were a hundred million bucks, it's still something Jo McPherson asked me not to do, so I just can't. It wouldn't be right."

Tom wasn't sure who was more sick about him turning down the twenty million dollars, but Jennings looked worse.

"By the way, I talked to Paul Stolley," Tom said.

"With whom?" Jennings bleated.

"Paul Stolley, why?"

"Qwestead's Paul Stolley?" Jennings looked shocked.

"Yeah, that Paul Stolley."

"What about Qwestead?" Jennings demanded, his face turning red.

"Qwestead is why I'm not taking your twenty million bucks," Tom said, upping the ante. "I think Stolley is prepared to pay a whole lot more than twenty million for those rights. Granted, I don't know why, it's just a feeling. But the bottom line is that whatever you had your sights on, Jennings, I own it now. I'll deal with Qwestead and Stolley directly. You're out of the game. From here on out, it's my ranch, and they're my minerals. I figure they're worth more than you're offering, or you wouldn't have offered so much."

JENNINGS WALKED SLOWLY to his office window, his back to Tom. Jennings knew that if Larkin had the down payment money, and Larkin had Qwestead's ear, then the only hope left was to reset the clock. Larkin could not be allowed to consummate the contract for deed. If the contract failed, Jennings mused, the legal wrangling could begin. With Jo's health the way it was, Jennings was sure that he'd have no problem convincing

Jo's attorney to make the right decision regarding her finances and sell the ranch to Elements.

Larkin has to disappear for a week or two, that's all, Jennings thought. *He doesn't have to join old Cody, but he needs to be out of commission. That can be arranged,* he thought. *Yes, that can be arranged.* Jennings turned to face Larkin.

"I'm disappointed, Tom. Sorely disappointed that you've turned down our offer. It is the best I can do."

"It was a good try, Doc," Tom said with a trace of empathy.

"My main concern, of course, was in procuring the mineral rights to the ranch, as you know. But I also said that I didn't want you to leave thinking badly of me. I would like to show you something that may help my cause in that respect."

"Show me what?" Tom asked.

"Something of grave importance to Mrs. McPherson, I believe."

"Well, show it to me."

Jennings began to spin a web of lies around a fragment of truth. "What I am prepared to show you is filed away in the sub-basement, for safekeeping. It is, I'm afraid, information that should have been put in the hands of law enforcement, but in a glaring moment of bad judgment, I withheld information to pro-tect … well, to protect one of my associates, to be quite honest."

"What does this have to do with me?"

"Well, Tom, I heard that you are close to Jo McPherson, is that right?"

"That's right."

"And I know from the contract paperwork that Jo seems to think about as poorly of me as you do, is that also correct?"

"Pretty much on target," Tom said. "What's your point?"

"I have information regarding Mr. McPherson's death, and I hope that, by giving you this information, you'll think better of me, and perhaps you'll reconsider the offer I've made this after-noon. It is a practical move on my part, I assure you."

"What you mean to say is that you would never have produced this 'information' unless it served your purpose?" Tom demanded, his eyes afire.

"I am ashamed to say that is the case."

"Well, you are a prick, then, Jennings."

"I'm hoping to change your mind on that," Jennings said evenly. "Will you at least give me a chance? I think you owe it to Jo."

Jennings had played his ace and it worked like a charm.

"OK, Doc. Show me the stuff. I'll let you know after I look at it if I think you're a Samaritan or a charlatan," Tom said.

"As I said, it's locked away in a safe place. Come with me," Jennings said and headed for the door.

"You get it. I'll wait here."

"I'm happy to do that, Tom, but getting to where it's locked away is a fifteen-minute trip each way. So, if you want to cool your heels here while I go fetch the documents, it's fine by me. I just thought that we might better use our time in discussion. But, suit yourself. Can I get you a cup of coffee while you wait for me?"

Jennings stood motionless, looking straight at Tom, waiting for an answer.

"Ah, hell," Tom said. "Forget the coffee. Let's go." A hesitant Tom got up and followed Jennings out of the inner office.

As they approached the receptionist, she said, "There is an urgent message for you, doctor."

"Not now."

"He said it was urgent," the secretary pressed, and seeing Tom lowered her voice and said, "It's Mr. Stolley from Qwestead."

"Call him back and tell him I'm with a patient and will call him back in fifteen minutes," he ordered the secretary, and in a whisper he added, "I'm just walking Mr. Larkin to his car."

"Yes, doctor," she demurred.

"Let's go, Larkin," Jennings said, and strode into the hallway.

About twenty paces from his office, Jennings turned to Tom and said, "Wait here a minute, will you Tom? I forgot to have that stupid cow cancel my next appointment," and he scampered back into his office, leaving Tom no chance to protest.

Jennings brushed past his secretary into an exam room, kicked the door shut with his foot, and unlocked a drug storage cabinet. He selected a hypodermic needle half-full of Diprivan—an anesthesia used for outpatient operations—and jammed it into the outside pocket of his lab coat. The initial dose would knock Larkin out cold, Jennings calculated, giving him several hours time to tow his car, set Tom up on a continuous sedation drip and introduce an IV feeder. He'd sleep like a baby for two weeks as long as the drug was being administered.

Returning to the outer office, he told his secretary to cancel the rest of his appointments for the day and then rejoined Tom.

"Sorry, Tom. I've got to take care of the business that feeds me," Jennings said, strode past Larkin, and headed toward a stairwell at the far end of the hallway.

"My private lab is down here," Jennings said as he held the door open for Tom.

THE STAIRWELL WAS dingy, and Tom bristled visibly. He put his hand in his jacket, feeling for his cell phone. It was gone.

After Eva had rifled his hotel room, Tom had been using his cell phone exclusively. The battery was low, and he'd left it in his car to charge.

By the time they'd reached the second floor below grade, Tom could taste metal in his mouth, like chewing on tin foil. The place felt wrong, and he wished Burley were there with him.

Jennings augered further down the stairwell.

Unlike the other doors, the one at the fifth landing was rusty. The only light was a single dreary bulb. *We're halfway to hell, and nobody knows I'm here,* Tom thought, his hackles up.

Tom stopped at the top of this last landing and watched Jennings dissolve into the shadows below. "This is as far down the rabbit hole as I go, Doc. I've got things that need doing today. Why don't you just grab the stuff and run it over to my hotel tomorrow?"

"Get down here, you pansy," Jennings mocked him from the gloom below, "You afraid of the dark, or just afraid of me?" He opened the lab door, turned on the lights and entered.

Tom's head was full of wild notions, but few of them bothered him any more than appearing weak to Jennings, so Tom descended the last flight of stairs.

The lab was brightly lit and drew Tom in like an insect to the flame.

Tom expected a room stocked to the gills with microscopes and autoclaves, transducers and incubators: an enclave of high technology. But the chamber was nearly empty. There were Petri dishes stacked like silver dollars in several small refrigerators with clear glass doors, a half-dozen filing cabinets, an office desk and chair, two empty tables, and a piece of equipment Tom didn't recognize humming away in the corner. Two ceiling fluorescents blared a nauseating green light into every corner of the room.

"Welcome to my world," Jennings said. "Please close the door, will you, Tom?"

"Right," Tom said, and closed the door carefully, noting whether or not it locked automatically. It didn't.

Tom stayed with his back to the door while Jennings rummaged around in a file cabinet. He pulled a fat manila folder from one of the drawers and threw it on the table next to the cabinet. It was the file implicating Barker in Cody's murder.

"There it is, Larkin. The truth about Cody." Jennings pointed to the lone file on the otherwise empty table. "I'll get you a chair."

Tom edged over to the table, keeping an eye on Jennings. Tom knew that he could put up a good fight under any circumstances, and he could certainly handle Jennings. Still, being so isolated from the rest of the planet was unnerving.

Tom sat down to examine the file. He felt a reckoning at hand, the moment when he might finally discover the truth about Cody's death and make good on his promise to Jo. The first document was a coroner's report, and Tom began to read. He could hear Jennings dragging a chair across the floor but was engrossed and paid no attention.

As he closed on Larkin, Jennings removed the syringe he'd secreted in his lab coat, flicked the cap off the needle, and lunged at Tom's back.

Tom didn't see the stab coming, but he felt it and moved instinctively. The needle pricked his raised arm before the syringe clattered to the floor.

Having failed to make a direct hit, Jennings' arm swung wide, and he lost his balance, crashing into the desk and rolling away from his target.

Awakened by the threat of Jennings, the sleeping beast in Tom took charge. The beast commanded Tom's eyes and legs; it infused Tom's ligaments, his muscles, and his blood.

Tom-the-beast was immediately disoriented from the single drop of Diprivan the needle had delivered; focusing was impossible. An aqua haze muddied everything. He could see no fewer than two of anything, including Jennings, who was getting to his feet.

As Jennings rose, Larkin attacked ferociously. Tom's aim was to make contact with both of the Jennings he saw so that his unreliable vision would no longer be a factor in the fight. After contact, the animal that first found his opponent's jugular would prevail.

Larkin hit before Jennings could reach the needle, and the two flew back and crashed into a file cabinet, Jennings spine absorbing entirely the brutal collision. At the instant the two bodies hit the floor, Tom raised his head and let it smash into Jennings' face.

Jennings exhaled a mist of blood, sputum and what was left of his foul breath.

Jennings was splayed and motionless. Inches away, Tom lay gasping for breath, his heart pounding furiously. The beast in Tom still held sway, and guttural sounds formed in Tom's mouth.

Tom didn't know if he'd killed Jennings, and he didn't care.

Reason had no dominion in this place—the beast took whatever it could, and killing was as natural as copulating. A brute must be vicious and strong, or learn to be cunning—or he died. A beast does not come to the aid of another in mortal trouble; he waits in a shadow for the right moment to kill—and, if he must, leave some scraps behind.

Still slumped against a file cabinet, Tom had a vision of the hairy, clawed, muscle-bound and tiny-brained fiends that were his ancestors. His line had survived by killing first and spreading their seed. These hellions were his grandmothers and grandfathers, and he was grateful to them in that hour.

Tom's breathing became less jagged, which must have satisfied the beast. It made a silent retreat, leaving Tom to deal with the consequences of being alive.

Tom rose unsteadily to his feet. Jennings was still inert.

Looking around the room, Tom spied the needle intended for him lying near the door. He stumbled over to it and back to Jennings. Putting the needle safely behind his back, Tom leaned over to test Jennings for life. Jennings' pulse was strong.

Tom rolled Jennings onto his side so that he would not drown in his own drool or blood. It was a practical consideration, not done out of compassion. Tom ripped a lumbar support from the office chair and jammed it between Jennings' neck and the floor. Then he buried the syringe in Jennings thigh and emptied it.

"There, you sick fuck!" Larkin spat at the shape on the floor and leaned back against a file cabinet for several minutes.

When his vision finally cleared, Tom stood and made the best assessment of the premises as his cloudy mind could manage. The science experiments were beyond his ken, and he had no desire to dig into anything that might be dangerous to his health. Most of the files contained medical journals and lots of background on various diseases and the clinical trials associated with them. One of the file drawers, however, was marked "personal."

"What else are you hiding, scumbag?" Tom muttered as he rifled through the folders. At the back of the drawer he found a thick file marked "Shelly Shepherd." He pulled it out and tossed it on the table with the one he'd been reading.

Finding nothing else that seemed relevant to the ranch or to him, Tom closed the drawer, picked up the McPherson file, and began reading where he had left off.

Tom thumbed through item after item, stopping to read a report completely, then scanning several more before reading another more thoroughly again. Although every detail of Cody's murder was not crystal clear, the big picture was.

Tom had seen enough.

He fished around in Jennings' lab coat until he found the key. With the two file folders tucked under his arm, Tom stumbled out, locking the door behind him.

Nauseated by the chemical and what he'd read in the files, Tom emerged from the back of Building C and dropped to the ground. He gulped the cold mountain air, filling his lungs with life and cleansing the stink of Jennings' foul world. There would be time enough to parse his newfound—and unwelcome— knowledge. For now, breathing was enough.

In the distance, Tom heard an ambulance wailing.

TUESDAY, *12:30* P.M.

Carl often ate lunch at his desk, and, lately, he hadn't been any too pleasant if Norma disturbed him when his office door was shut. So, when noontime rolled around and Carl's door was still closed, Norma left without telling Carl, went to the Flat Iron, and enjoyed a nice bowl of soup, figuring she'd leave well enough alone.

When she got back from lunch, there were two people sitting in the office waiting to see Carl. She apologized to them for making them wait, and, happy for a reason to interrupt Carl, rapped sharply on his door. When he didn't respond, she peeked in and saw him face down on a stack of papers.

Although Norma had never discovered a body before, she knew immediately that Carl was done for this world. He was slumped forward onto his desk, one arm hanging at his side, the other stretched out across the desk as if he were reaching for a pen that he'd never again need. His face had turned a strange pink color where it rested against the desk; his jaw was jutted at a crazy angle, making his mouth pucker; his eyes were fixed on God-knows-what; and his great bulk, usually huffing and puffing even if sitting, was motionless.

Norma stared at the body for a few more seconds, transfixed, then quietly closed the mayor's door and told the waiting citizens that Carl wouldn't be seeing anyone that day, ushered them out, and locked the office behind them.

She didn't intend to turn Carl's death into a circus any more than she intended to share the limelight with anyone.

Norma called the newspaper and the ambulance, in that order.

Carl's heart had finally done him a favor. It helped Carl cheat Homeland Security of its due and avoid an ignoble fall from office. Granted, it wasn't a high political office, the Mayor of Hot Springs, so the fall would be a short one. But Carl had much more at stake. A conviction and a prison term, assuming he survived it, would have cost Carl his acceptance in the town he had lived his entire life. Like a merciful enemy, his heart had spared Carl from having to pay the steep price of greed and took his life in one swift attack.

A good number of years later, the City of Hot Springs would name a street after Carl Graves: an out-of-the-way cul-de-sac in a subdivision west of town. That future council would eschew the name "Graves" and call the short little byway Carl's Way. The people who built their houses along Carl's Way never bothered to ask after their address's namesake. They just tried to mind their own business and hoped their neighbors would do the same.

Jim Shepherd was out looking for Bill Jennings on the morning Carl suffered his massive coronary. Jennings wasn't answering any of his various phone numbers, and Shepherd had gone to Jennings' office to wait him out. It was there he heard about the mayor, and he left to join several other upstanding members of the community in a vigil at Carl's house.

Still wearing the apron she had on when the sheriff had come to the door, Mrs. Graves sat in an overstuffed chair in the middle of her living room, not talking to anyone, her eyes fixed on something not in the room, while her old fingers made little creases in her apron. Over and over. Crease and fold, crease and fold. No one had the heart to tell her to take off the apron, and no one tried to speak to her again after she refused to say a word to the first several well-wishers. An untouched piece of cake—getting hard around the edges—and a full cup of cold coffee were all that sat next to Mrs. Graves as she grieved and creased and folded away.

For once, Jim Shepherd didn't mind spending time with a bereaved widow. It was a good opportunity, he thought, to rehearse everything he intended to say to Jennings when the slimy bastard emerged from whatever hole he'd found to hide in.

Nine hours after Tom stuck him with a syringe full of Diprivan, Jennings regained consciousness in the blackness of his private lab. Lying on the damp concrete floor, his memory returned in erratic flashes, sometimes gripping rationally and then slipping back into chaos. Each remembered event triggered a fresh stream of bile and opened another door to nowhere.

In the bitter dark, Jennings gagged and wailed and cursed all of creation. Venom flowed into his soul, filling all the places that were not already choked with it.

Missing Larkin with the needle was the final miscarriage of Jennings' derelict dream.

He was lost in a wilderness of misery and incrimination, without will, light, or hope. In those hours of darkness, the man Jennings once might have been was being carried away on a crazy wind, leaving behind an unsettled hatter to make what he might of Jennings' shattered legacy.

In that dark hole where light never ventured, a clarity born of madness took hold of Jennings, and a desperate plan was born.

The plan begat reason, and reason, hope. Buoyed by his new vision, Jennings willed himself to crawl, found his way to the wall switch, and flooded his mean cell with light.

Like a newborn colt, Jennings tottered to his feet, instinct driving his unstable limbs to run. Run fast and run hard. Run for shelter. Run for milk. Run from danger. Just run, run, run.

Jennings wasn't out of options. He could still run, and he started for the door.

It was locked.

Jennings had never bothered to change the key entry to a dead bolt and simply left a spare key hanging by the door. If he were, by some quirk, to misplace or damage the key he used to enter the lab, no one would find him until it was too late. He'd planned for that remote possibility.

Along with his newfound hope for the future, his distain for any intelligence other than his own came rushing back.

I'm a genius, he reminded himself. *They'll see.*

Grabbing the key, he released himself from the prison he'd built and made his way back to the world of light and shadows.

After four-thirty in the afternoon, the only denizens of the Veteran's Administration complex were in the patient areas. All other employees checked out at the bell because no one's paycheck depended on extra effort. As a result, there was no security guard or janitor in Building C to be alarmed at Dr. Jennings' appearance when he surfaced at nine o'clock.

Jennings reached his private office unseen and shut the door in relief. The leather briefcase with the bearer bonds sat undisturbed where he'd left it under his desk.

"This isn't over, not by a long shot," Jennings muttered aloud, as he extracted this and that from file drawers.

Jennings picked up the phone and dialed the Red Rock Inn.

"Phil Brady. Room 301. Put me through."

It took three tries to rouse Brady. He was in the bag, as Jennings had allowed.

"Pfil Raedeh," Brady struggled to form words.

"Wake up, you lush. We're leaving in an hour."

"Who . . . is . . . this?"

"It's your long-lost slut of a mother," Jennings spat. "Who do you think is calling? Meet me in front of the hotel in an hour."

"Doc?"

"Yeah, it's me, the boozehound's best friend!" Jennings cackled.

Brady grabbed the glass of whiskey from the side table and downed it, steadying himself.

"Doc. Why are you calling at this hour?"

"None of your business. Just do as I say."

"Tell me again what you want … slowly. Jesus, Doc, you said I could have a cocktail when I got here."

"I changed my mind. We're leaving Hot Springs—now."

Brady was drunk and couldn't be sure that Jennings was as deranged as he sounded. With the receiver still to his ear, he located a bottle and pulled deep on it. It helped him make sense of Jennings and the world.

"OK, Doc. An hour. I'm on it," he slurred.

"Drink the rest of whatever it is you're sucking down right now and be out front at ten. Got that? Out front, not in the lobby. Ten sharp!"

Jennings made one quick stop at his house after checking to see that there were no police waiting for him there, then pulled into the alley behind the hotel, parked, and walked around to the front.

Like a good dog, Brady was standing on the hotel steps.

"Brady!" Jennings called from the corner of the building. "Over here."

Brady strained to see, and failing, followed the sound of his master's voice.

"Jesus, Doc. What are you doing? I mean, it's the middle of the night, for Christ's sake!"

"You OK to drive?" Jennings asked, ignoring Brady's question.

"Yeah, if you want me to," he said loudly enough to be heard over the clamor of bottles clinking in his suitcase. "I don't have a license, but if you'll let me maintain this buzz, I can last four, maybe five hours. After that, you'll have to take over if you don't want to die."

"That'll do, Brady. Let's go."

Once they were clear of Hot Springs, Jennings said, "Give me your cell phone, Phil."

Brady tried to remember where he'd put it. "You calling your girlfriend?" Phil cracked, his strained laughter filling the car with the sour smell of alcohol.

"Just thought I'd leave a message for Mrs. Larkin," Jennings said. "I think it would be a shame if she weren't up to speed on the social scene out here, since it looks like she's going to be a ranch wife pretty soon."

"What 'social scene' are you talking about, Doc?"

"Listen up; I think you'll find this interesting," Jennings said, his eyes glowing with hate.

EVEN IN A HAZE, Brady knew that what they were doing was crazy. Sneaking out of town in the middle of the night with thirty million dollars of somebody else's money meant that Brady would never again practice law. He told himself that he had no choice but to go along with Jennings—which was not true. He had other choices; it's just that they were all, in his besotted estimation, less savory than casting his lot with a man in possession of thirty million dollars.

Since Brady was broke in every way a man can possibly be broke, he just clammed up and didn't think about what had made Bill Jennings take flight, or what they were going to do next, or what might happen if the law caught up to them.

Brady handed his cell phone to Jennings, who connected with an operator, who, in a sweet voice she'd used a million times before and would use another million times until she found a better job, recited the Larkins' home phone number.

Kathy answered Jennings' call immediately. "Tom, where have you been?"

"This is Dr. Bill Jennings, Mrs. Larkin. I have a message for you from Tom."

"Why are you calling me?" she stammered.

"Your husband wants you to know that he's busy taking care of Eva Shepherd this evening and won't be able to call. He says you'll know what that means. Same as Saturday, he told me. Have a nice evening," Jennings said, and hung up.

"What was that?" Brady said.

"Call it my housewarming gift to the Larkins. On the occasion of their new ranch," Jennings said. "Just wanted to make sure that, the next time she sees her lovey-dovey, they'll have something interesting to discuss."

The two drove on in silence for another half-of-a-fifth before Brady figured it might be safe to start a conversation.

"Ah … where we going, Doc?"

"Cheyenne."

"Cheyenne … ah …?"

"Cheyenne, Wyoming, you moron. To the airport."

"Yeah, Wyoming. Got it. And from there?" Brady ventured. "You know, the big picture?"

"South America, Brady. South America!" Jennings finally exclaimed as if the idea had just occurred to him.

"You've got to be kidding."

"Not kidding, Phil. South America. With a short stop in Geneva, Switzerland," Jennings pronounced.

"And Brady, do not speed. If we get stopped we're dead."

WEDNESDAY

You cannot own the land.
The land owns you.
Scottish ballad

———

2:30 A.M.

After the run-in with Jennings, Tom had gone back to the Red
Rock Inn and collapsed in his room.

Twelve hours later, Tom resurrected himself in complete darkness. His body felt renewed, but his mind was blank, and it took
him several minutes to reconstruct where he was and what had
happened. As memory returned, Tom panicked and jammed his
hand under the pillow he had been spooning. The files were still
there, right where he'd buried them.

He stared at the clock, rubbed his eyes, and stared again.

"Jesus Christ!" he swore. "How could I have slept so
long?"

Tom had missed his scheduled call with Paul Stolley, he desperately needed to speak to Kathy, and he had left Jennings
locked up in his lab.

Tom dressed quickly and was about to leave when he noticed
his message light blinking.

Kathy had called twice, wondering where he was and why
he wasn't answering his cell phone. Burley's message was pretty
much the same thing, except he had an update on Jo McPher-

son; said she was doing real well except that they didn't think she'd regain the use of her legs. Eva called just to see how things were going.

Tom breathed a sigh of relief when he heard the last two messages. One was from Paul Stolley saying that everything Tom had told him checked out and that he would be in Hot Springs Wednesday morning to meet. The other was from Jack Boyle, Tom's attorney, saying that he'd received a call from Qwestead's CEO about a meeting in Hot Springs. Boyle said that if he didn't hear back from Tom, he'd assume that he should drop everything and get on the jet with the Qwestead guy—they'd be arriving at ten a.m., Mountain Time.

Tom killed the messages and went to his car. His cell phone was still plugged in, and he yanked it free. The messages on it were identical to the ones in his room, except that Kathy had called again around eleven-thirty. She wanted to know where he was and sounded rattled.

Kathy and Tom Larkin had lost track of each other in many ways over the past several years. Although they weren't out of love, they weren't in love, either. They didn't exactly argue about a lot of things—the idea of moving onto a ranch being the exception—but with the children grown and gone, they found less and less either to talk about or to agree upon.

Both knew what was happening, and both sincerely wanted to do something about it. Tom felt that a move would be good for both of them. While Kathy trusted Tom's judgment, she wasn't at all keen on the idea of moving back to South Dakota, and onto a ranch, to boot. And so it went. One of them proposed an idea, and the other dragged his feet or shot it down.

While it was difficult for love to survive between them, somehow it had. It had just not prospered much lately.

"I guess you probably would like to know where I am, Kathy. Well, I'm here," he muttered to himself and dialed Kathy at home. "Where are you?"

Tom dialed and redialed their home phone number and Kathy's cell and Kathy's work numbers while he drove to the Veteran's Administration, continuing to dial her numbers for ten minutes after he'd arrived and parked behind Building C.

Finally admitting that he wasn't going to get an answer, Tom quit dialing.

Tom sat there stewing over what he'd done, and what Kathy had done, and what should have happened, and what was unfair, and who'd done him wrong and where he'd gone wrong, and what was right and what was wrong and who's to say anyhow, and up and down and back and forth, and none of it got him one step closer to feeling good or knowing what to do next.

He felt wronged and guilty, righteous and damned, damned lucky and lonely as hell.

Try as he might to make sense of everything, he couldn't make any headway. The more he figured, the more confused he got, and he finally just stepped out of the car and slammed the door.

There were no security guards to be found in Building C, and since Tom wasn't about to go back underground alone, he walked over to the main building. It took some explaining, but he convinced the guard to leave his post, and the two of them went to retrieve Jennings from the lab in sub-level six.

At the fourth landing below ground, Tom asked the guard if he might be willing to let him have the nightstick, as a safety measure. The guard gave Tom a skeptical look, but handed the nightstick over anyway.

In order to open the last stairwell door, the guard used the pry bar Tom had suggested they bring along.

When they got to the lab it was dark—and empty.

Jennings had managed to free himself and slither away. Tom was relieved. Not because he feared a confrontation, but because he hadn't killed Jennings. No amount of blood on Jennings' hands could justify Tom bloodying his own without good reason.

Tom relocked the lab door and told the guard that he'd keep the key until things got squared away. The guard didn't like that idea much, but Tom told him there was evidence in the lab that was material to an upcoming federal investigation, and that if he were to hand over the key, and anything were to go missing, it'd be the guard who'd have to answer.

After surfacing, the guard made Tom fill in forms for over an hour, but he let Tom keep the lab key.

On his way back to the hotel to shower and change into a clean set of clothes for the morning's meeting with Boyle and Paul Stolley, Tom tried Kathy's numbers again.

He didn't reach her on any of them.

WEDNESDAY, 6:30 A.M. CENTRAL TIME

Groggy after just three hours' sleep, Kathy awoke in a strange bed. She prayed that she wouldn't reach out and feel a man's body next to hers. Her head cleared, and she remembered that she had arrived at Tom's sister Mary's house, halfway between St. Paul and the Black Hills, in the middle of the night.

The call from Jennings had scared her.

Fifteen minutes after Jennings hung up, she had a suitcase packed and was headed westbound out of the city. She didn't know what else she was going to find when she got to the Black Hills, but she needed to find Tom.

You son-of-a-bitch! She cursed Tom silently, rolled over, and began to cry into her pillow. *Why did you make me do it? Why, why, why?* It was all his fault, she told herself. If she hadn't felt sure that Tom slept with that hotel clerk, she'd never have gone looking to get laid herself. The thought of it all made her sick.

After she'd met him at the bar the previous night, it hadn't been difficult for Kathy to convince her colleague Greg to take her out for drinks again. They had flirted on and off for years, and she knew that he'd screw her in a New York minute—given the opportunity. After several cocktails and some dancing at a downtown hotel bar, he suggested they have a nightcap at his apartment. Kathy knew what that meant, and she had agreed.

When they got in bed, Kathy discovered that Greg had a nice fat dick, and she thought that at least she'd get a decent fuck out of the deal. She wanted him to hammer her as hard as she felt like pounding Tom, but it didn't happen.

There was no retribution and no orgasm.

Kathy had urged him to do her any way he wanted; she had gone down on him like a whore in an army tent and oohhed and aahhed about how big his dick was. Despite a performance quite worthy of a standing ovation, Greg's dick never did get hard. With considerable effort, Kathy got the jellyfish to give a few soft strokes, after which Greg ejaculated, rolled off her, and was soon snoring.

Yesterday, she'd received an e-mail from Greg saying it was the best sex he'd ever had, and he wanted to get together for drinks again that evening—that is, if Tom was still out of town.

Kathy wondered how many showers it would take before the memory of his big flaccid penis and big soft belly would be washed from her body's memory.

Tom, you lousy son-of-a-bitch! Where are you?

She buried her head deeper in the pillow and cried.

Kathy was angry but sick with worry. Angry and worried about another woman, worried about money, angry with herself for sleeping with another man to spite Tom, and worried about how much more damage they had done to their marriage. She was angry at Jennings for confirming her suspicions. But mostly, Kathy was worried about Tom.

He'd put himself in the middle of a firestorm over a piece of ground that he seemed to love more than her.

Kathy fretted for several more minutes before deciding that she'd never get back to sleep and might just as well get back on the road.

Downstairs, the coffee was brewing. Tom's sister Mary was usually at the hospital by seven but had stayed home today.

"Morning, Kathy," Mary said, when Kathy shuffled into the kitchen. "Coffee?"

"Uh-huh," Kathy managed.

"You were fit to be tied when you rolled in last night," Mary said.

Kathy started to tear up.

"You and Tom OK?" Mary asked. Being Tom's sister, she had the right to ask.

Grateful to have someone to talk to who knew Tom well, and who cared how things turned out, Kathy replied quietly, "I don't know, Mary. I really don't."

"You want to tell me what's going on?"

"All I know is that Tom went to the Hills to buy a ranch and fell in love with a place that we can't afford and signed a purchase agreement for it," Kathy said.

"Sounds like my brother," Mary said, to give Kathy time to get a grip. "I'd have thought that, by now, you'd be used to his grand plans."

Kathy and Mary exchanged knowing smiles; the ranch deal was vintage Tom.

"I think he's over his head this time, Mary. Tom's crosswise with this doctor out there, and I'm worried that something seriously bad has happened to him."

"What kind of 'bad' do you mean? Like they might have hurt him, that kind of bad?" Mary asked, alarmed.

"That's possible—I haven't been able to get hold of Tom since early yesterday."

"Well, Kathy, if it's just that he isn't answering his phone, I wouldn't get my shorts in a bunch. He has a tendency to disappear, if you know what I mean, even when he's right under your nose."

"It's more than that, believe me. Tom is determined to have that ranch, Mary—you know how dogged he is when his mind is made up—and he may have done something to piss these guys off. And believe me, they are not the kind of people you want for enemies."

"Won't be the first time my brother's pissed the wrong people off," Mary chuckled.

"It's not funny. He's made this personal, and he seems to be prepared to do anything to get that ranch. He's just so, so blinded, that I seem to have completely lost touch with him on this."

"Lost touch how, Kathy?"

"It's like he's somebody else—like somebody flipped a switch, and I'm married to a stranger." Kathy put her head in her hands. "I guess I don't know Tom as well as I've always believed. I don't know, Mary, I just don't seem to know much about anything anymore." Tears were falling onto the tablecloth.

After a considerable silence, Mary said, "Did Tom ever talk to you about when we were kids?"

"Well, yeah, of course," Kathy answered, wiping her eyes on a napkin. "What are you getting at?"

"When we lived on the farm, Tom was always gone. Out on the land somewhere. During the winter he was up before light and down at the creek with his dog and his rifle, checking traps. Then he'd come home and do his skinning before we got on the bus; after school, he'd go straight to the barn to check the horses, or fuss with his calves, or screw around with the tractor. One year, he sent away for a bunch of chemicals and whatnot for taxidermy and set up a table in the basement where he could practice on all sorts of animals he'd found or shot. You know, pheasants, gophers, muskrat, and the like. Once he bought a couple of big rabbits and gassed them, just to see what they looked like inside and see if he could preserve them."

"I knew he trapped," Kathy said. "He was running a trap line when I met him in high school. He brought a dead mink into your living room one Saturday before a date and scared the crap out of me. That was the last time he pulled that stunt, I can tell you!"

They both laughed, and Mary continued. "In the summer, when he wasn't working for a neighbor, he'd always be out with his dog. He'd get up and leave the house before the rest of us woke up and be gone all day, often until after dark. Nobody knew where he went, and nobody asked him. Dad was in town, and Mom didn't even try to control him. He'd do his chores and just leave. He and that cockeyed appaloosa of his would splash around in the creek and chase around all over the county; our mangy dog followed him around like he was a god."

Kathy understood that Mary wasn't just talking about old farm memories.

"I've heard Mom say it was the same when Tom was little, and we were living on the edge of town. He'd just up and leave in the morning and be gone until dark, or after. God, Kathy, he was just six or seven years old, and he had hideaways up and down the Sioux River—and some in town, too! If something had happened to him ... if some sicko had gotten hold of him, or if he'd fallen into a gully and cracked his head open, or been pulled under while swimming in the river, we might never have known. But none of that ever fazed Tom. He was a pretty wild boy in most ways, and I don't think that he's changed all that much."

As she listened to Mary go on about Tom, Kathy began to realize that, for her husband, the horses, the trapping, the long absences, the hikes and hideaways, the rivers, the dogs, and the mysteries weren't just old memories—they were a way of life that he could reclaim. Tom hadn't gone to the Black Hills for a change of scenery or a new adventure. He'd gone looking for a part of himself that he'd lost. He'd gone home.

It dawned on Kathy for the first time that Tom must have found what he had gone looking for, and that he had no intention of ever leaving it. He was home and would fight for it to the end if necessary. That much she did know about her husband. He would never give up until he had won or been broken.

"That helped me," Kathy whispered, "understand some of this craziness."

"There's something else, though," Mary said. "Am I right?"

"I think Tom slept with a woman out there ... hell, I know for a fact that he did. Some clerk at the hotel where he's staying."

"That's another thing about my brother. He never had any problem getting a date, if you catch my drift."

"Unfortunately, yes, I know exactly what you mean."

"If Tom did sleep with that clerk, or whatever," Mary reassured Kathy, "he knows it's wrong. I'm not saying you don't have a right to be furious—I would be. But I'd try to keep it in perspective as best you can."

"What kind of perspective is there for something like that?" Kathy asked, her anger beginning to rise.

"Well, how about 'shit happens,' for starters?"

"Tell me about it," Kathy said, and big round tears began to fall again. One made a bull's-eye in her coffee.

"Coffee too strong for you?" Mary joked.

"It isn't just Tom. I might have strayed a bit far off of the reservation, too," Kathy confessed.

"Might have?"

"Did," Kathy said.

Mary broke out laughing.

"Well, good for you, sister! We can't let Tom have all the fun!"

Kathy laughed, too. Mary had a way of seeing what was silly in other people's seriousness. Kathy guessed that was one of the things that made her such a damn fine nurse.

"Don't let it ruin your life, sweetie, or your marriage," Mary said soberly. "What you're talking about can happen to anybody; hell, it happens to the best of us. So buck up, girl. It isn't the end of the world, and it sounds like you've got bigger fish to fry.

"Best thing for you, I think, is to get something in your belly and get back on the road and find that brother of mine. He needs you—he just doesn't know how to admit it."

Mary went over to Kathy and gave her a hug and kissed the top of her head.

There are times when a woman needs another woman a lot more than she needs her man. Sometimes she needs another woman just to understand her man. Sometimes, even, it's another woman that drives her man back home.

After breakfast, Kathy was off.

"Damn!" Kathy said as she dug in her purse for a cigarette and found her cell phone instead. "I've got to remember to turn this frigging thing on." It took Kathy a second to locate the power button, and once on, the phone began to chirp its message waiting tone. Kathy opened the phone and said, "Hello?" She hoped it was Tom.

"Hello? Hello, hello? Hello!" she shouted.

Kathy used her phone so seldom that it didn't immediately occur to her that the ringing wasn't an incoming call, but a reminder to check messages. She dialed the voice mail access number and, instead, got a low-battery warning message and a different beeping tone. In her mind she saw the wall charger still plugged into a kitchen outlet, where she'd left it in her hurry to leave town last night.

"Screw it," she fumed, and dropped the phone back into her purse without bothering to switch the power off.

Paul Stolley and his entourage arrived in Hot Springs a half-hour late because Stolley decided at the last minute to bring counsel of his choosing, rather than the Perez-Farmer attorney. Tom was waiting for them at the airstrip, and they immediately piled into the car and headed out to the ranch; Tom and Paul Stolley sat in front; Boyle, the Qwestead attorney and a secretary squeezed themselves into the back seat.

"I appreciate you coming all this way, Paul," Tom said once they were on their way, "and on such short notice."

"It's me who should be thanking you, Tom," Stolley replied. "You've done me a big favor by giving Qwestead the first shot at the montmorillonite, despite the reservations you must have about us at the moment."

"It's true. I've got my doubts. But I figured you were already down the road on this project and could make decisions quickly. Quite frankly, I called you because it was the most practical choice; timing is my biggest concern," Tom said.

"We have had serious reservations about Elements Corporation for months, Tom, and the information you gave me yesterday helped confirm our worst suspicions. Although we have made a modest investment in Elements thus far, it's not something that will get in the way of our discussion with you," Stolley said. "And I hope you will believe me when I say that Qwestead is washing its hands of the Elements Corporation as of today. Although we have a few small matters to clear up with Dr. Jennings, they don't concern you."

"That's what I wanted to hear you say first," Tom answered. "Now tell me why you came out here in person."

"I came out here to meet you."

"Mind telling me why?"

"Of course, we haven't bet the farm on the montmorillonite," Stolley began, "but if it proves out, we will be faced with enormous financial and ethical decisions that could alter the course Qwestead Pharmaceuticals takes in the future.

"Our scientists believe that the substance in the ground on your ranch will eliminate the need for several of our blockbuster compounds ..."

"Like Prezitran?" Tom interrupted.

"Exactly like Prezitran. Prezitran earns several billions of dollars per year for our firm. Blockbusters like that are the grand slams our research teams are constantly trying to hit."

"So you're saying the montmorillonite has the potential to make or break your company?" Tom asked.

"Yes and no," Stolley said. "No, we don't believe that the montmorillonite will put any of the large pharmas, including us, out of business. We are big companies, and we have very diverse businesses. But it could cripple several smaller companies, depending upon how well the montmorillonite works and how many disease groups it might address.

"On the other hand, the montmorillonite has the potential to catapult Qwestead to the top of the pharmaceutical industry. I don't think I'm telling you anything you haven't already guessed when I say that the montmorillonite may be the most exciting compound in the history of modern pharma. As of right now, you own the compound. That makes you extremely important to Qwestead."

"Sounds good for me," Tom said without smiling.

"As important as you are to our company because you own this mineral, that's not why I came out here today. We have attorneys who are excellent negotiators.

"I wanted to meet you and determine for myself what kind of person we would be getting into business with. It may sound a little hokey to you, Tom, but I can't make that kind of decision after talking to someone on the phone. I need to look the man in the eye and shake his hand. I made the mistake of not meeting Bill Jennings until we'd been working with Elements for several years. I don't intend to make that mistake twice."

Tom was impressed.

"I also wanted to give you an opportunity to size me up. You must have some very negative feelings about us and about our motives. I'd like to think I can change your mind on those counts."

As had happened on the phone, Tom warmed quickly to Paul Stolley.

During the rest of the ride, Tom told everyone the story about Jennings and the lab. Stolley's brow was deeply furrowed by the time Tom finished.

"That certainly explains why our people haven't been able to get hold of Jennings," Stolley said.

"What do you want with him, now?" Tom asked.

"Do you recall my mentioning that we have a few matters to discuss with Dr. Jennings?" Stolley directed his question to Tom.

"I do."

"As you know, our plan was to acquire the mineral rights through the Elements Corporation. Mr. Cody had rebuffed all of our previous attempts to negotiate. Two days ago we advanced Dr. Jennings a small amount of cash for the purpose of obtaining those rights, and it seems that both the doctor and the cash are unaccounted for at the moment."

"A 'small' amount?" Tom couldn't help but pry.

"Thirty million," the Qwestead attorney piped up from the back seat, drawing a steely-eyed but silent rebuke from Stolley.

Thirty million! Tom thought. *No wonder Jennings' offer was so generous. He was prepared to go higher. Much higher.*

"I take it we're getting a tour of the ranch first," Stolley said, quickly changing the subject before his attorney could further damage their negotiating position.

"I'm more than happy to give you the tour; in fact, I'd love to give you a tour if you've got the time. But that's not my purpose," Tom said. "I thought we'd hold our meeting at the ranch because it's quiet—and confidential. I figured that our meeting didn't need to be the talk of the town."

"Good move," Stolley said.

"However, I thought you'd probably want to see the mineral lick before we sit down. I'm sure you don't have any doubts as to its existence, given what so many people have done to get their mitts on it, but I thought you might like to go out there and kick the tires just the same. So we'll make a quick stop out at the lick and then head back to the house."

The rest of the trip to the lick was consumed with talk, mostly from Tom, about Hot Springs, the land and its flora and fauna, some well-embellished local stories, and an ode to southern Black Hills weather.

They arrived at the lick after rattling over twelve miles of gravel and bouncing down a couple miles of two-track on the ranch. The car doors burst like a ripe milkweed pod, spilling three guys and a gal in suits, and one man in a cowboy hat, across the lick.

Judging by the way two of these besuited seeds were prancing around, Tom guessed it had been too long between pit stops for them.

"I'd suggest you mosey on back of that little rise over there if you're thinking of taking a piss," Tom said unceremoniously.

Tipping his hat to Stolley's secretary he said, "You'll excuse my language, miss?"

She gave Tom an extra-nice smile.

The two attorneys beat a hasty path in the direction Tom had pointed, trying, unsuccessfully, to look dignified and nonchalant.

The secretary giggled when she caught Tom's eye, and he invited her to join him on the lick. She just nodded her head "no," and stayed glued to the Cadillac.

Stolley was already walking around on the lick.

"Ever seen this stuff before?" Tom asked.

"Of course we required Dr. Jennings to send samples," Stolley said. He dropped to his knees and began to sift through the grainy earth.

"Want to take some of this stuff back with you?" Tom offered.

"If you don't mind," Stolley said.

"I don't mind in the least, Paul, but that ground is whole hell of a lot harder than it looks. I've got a Buck knife and some plastic garbage bags in the back of the Caddy," Tom said. "Why don't I grab them for you?"

"That would be perfect. Thank you," Stolley said, standing up. There were two dusty splotches of mineral chalk on the knees of his silk Armani suit.

Tom looked at the spots and grinned. "If I didn't know better, I'd say you've got a little bit of country boy in you, Stolley."

"Fourth-generation Appalachian," Stolley said.

" 'Taint nary no use fer it down yonder wit them city fellers," he drawled, his esses whistling like teakettles and his words crawling out of the side of his mouth like they had to first get round a chaw of tobacco.

Both men laughed.

"My hillbilly background isn't something you'll find on my curriculum vitae, Tom," Stolley said while brushing off the front of his pants, "but I'm not ashamed of it, either." He was a Princeton grad and pronounced the word "either" with a long "i": eye-thur.

"I'll be goddamned." Larkin shook his head and headed back to retrieve the knife and plastic bags.

You've got to love a guy that looks like a million bucks and sounds like Clem Kadiddlehopper, Tom thought. *I'd bet a silver dollar to a donut that Qwestead's board doesn't know their rainmaker is a hayseed.*

Stolley further ingratiated himself with Tom by insisting that his secretary sit in the front seat on the way back to the ranch house, relegating himself to the back seat like he was just one of the boys.

Stolley's secretary had slender legs that she folded up and pointed toward Tom, allowing her to turn and face Stolley should she be asked a question. She fiddled with the hem of her skirt all the way back to the ranch house, smoothing it, lifting it, running her fingers along its edge next to her skin, and stealing a glance at Tom every so often.

She reminded Tom of a doe, grooming herself like that.

Tom gave her a good long look just once, touched the brim of his hat, and nodded to her in silence. Then, he returned his eyes to the two-track and his mind to the impending mineral deal with Qwestead.

When they arrived at the house, Pat Burley stepped off the porch and approached the group, saying, "Looks like a party. Am I invited?"

"You know you are, Burley," Tom said. "You bring the moonshine?"

Introductions were made outside; then they stepped inside and sat down at the dining room table.

"Where would you like to begin, Tom?" Stolley said.

"I'm going to be right up front with you, Paul." Tom noticed that Jack Boyle was frowning. "Despite the concerns my attorney might have about me running off at the mouth, I'm just going to lay my cards on the table, and I'll ask you to do the same when I'm done."

"Please proceed, Tom," Stolley said.

"I'm at a disadvantage, here," Tom began, "because I don't really know what's in the ground out there. I know it's damned important, that's about all. Cody McPherson left a journal saying that the mineral might be able to heal humans as well as cattle, and it appears that he was right."

Tom looked at Stolley and Stolley nodded back.

"I came to the Black Hills to live on the land, not to tear it up for profit," Tom said. "Mrs. McPherson, who sold me the place, has strong feelings along the same lines, and I'd have asked her to this meeting if she weren't laid up in a hospital bed at the moment.

"My feelings about the ranch haven't changed just because there's something out there that folks are anxious to get their hands on. But if there is some kind of medicine in the ground that'll be of benefit to people"—Tom looked squarely at Stolley—"and not just another way to milk a couple of billion dollars a year out of the healthcare system, it should be explored by reasonable people in a reasonable way.

"So here's what I'm thinking. Your company, Paul, has as many resources and as many top-notch scientists as any other in the world. If we've got something here, and if you're willing to put your scientists—not your marketing department—in charge of the development, I'm willing to work with you to see if this mineral has applications in human medicine."

"You've taken a very level-headed position, Tom," Stolley said, "and if there are new and viable ways to treat human disease using the mineral, Qwestead is prepared to undertake development and to do it responsibly. You have my word on that."

Two days ago, Stolley's word wouldn't have been worth a hill of beans to Larkin. After seeing the man who stood at the helm of one of the country's biggest corporations on his knees in the dirt, Stolley's word was as good as gold.

"I like what I see in you, Paul, but I can't—and won't—turn the reins over to anybody."

"How would you propose we go forward, then?" Stolley asked.

"My lawyer's going to have a fit because I haven't had a chance to discuss it with him," Tom said, turning to address Boyle. "We create a corporation to develop the montmorillonite. Qwestead will fund one hundred percent of the development costs, which will be laid off against future earnings. I'll own fifty-two percent of the new corporation, and Qwestead will own forty-eight percent.

"Those aren't negotiable percentages, Paul. The contract for deed does not allow me to relinquish control of any mineral rights, and even though I anticipate being able to retire the note shortly, I don't intend to violate the spirit of my agreement with Mrs. McPherson," Tom said.

Stolley's secretary was furiously taking notes, as were both attorneys. Stolley, who seemed relaxed and completely at ease, smiled and said, "You only need fifty-one percent for control, Tom."

"There's the matter of a minority owner," Tom said, grinning at Burley. "That ornery-looking cowboy over there is going to be a one-and-one-half-percent owner, and it comes out of my end."

Burley, as unaware of Tom's plan as anyone else in the room, looked dumbfounded. It was a gift that, if things worked out even modestly well, would make Pat Burley—and his children—wealthy beyond their wildest dreams.

"Of course, we don't want to be having him on the board, or anything like that," Tom added, "because he's a bit too rough around the edges for the Harvard types. Besides that, there aren't spittoons in the boardroom, last time I checked. You don't mind not being on the board, do you Pat?" Tom looked over at Burley and saw that he was studying his boots.

"Anything else we need to know about this joint venture, Tom?" Stolley asked.

"A couple of things, yes. Jo McPherson will have a lifetime appointment to the board of directors."

"I like that idea," Stolley said.

"If the mineral shows significant market potential—say, several billions of dollars per year—then Qwestead will fund and build a research institute dedicated to exploring and applying all manner of natural medicines and cures."

"How about Qwestead building the institute, with the annual operating funds of the clinic coming from the joint-venture profits?" Stolley suggested.

"I'll readily agree to that if the institute is built right here on the ranch," Tom countered, "and is named after Cody McPherson."

"Agreed," Stolley said, "Anything else?"

"There is one last item. It's the matter of an up-front payment to me in consideration for our exclusive relationship," Tom said.

"Will our relationship be exclusive in perpetuity?" Stolley asked in a level tone.

"It will," Tom replied.

Boyle spoke up for the first time. Unlike Stolley's man, Boyle knew when it was time to insert himself and when it was time to take notes.

"Perhaps, Mr. Stolley," Boyle began, "you may want to have your counsel discuss that matter with our firm? We would be more than happy to take that matter up outside the context of this meeting."

Jack Boyle was a good negotiator, but Paul Stolley was a master.

"I completely understand why you'd want to keep this delicate matter from ending our meeting on a sour note, Mr. Boyle. I share your concern. But I was hoping that, if I were to give Tom a dollar figure right here and now, we could leave this meeting and everything would be in motion.

"Tom," Stolley said addressing himself only to Larkin, "would you be willing to listen to an offer from me right now? Strictly for the up-front consideration, that is?"

Boyle moved to intercept, but Tom put his hand up and stopped him.

"I know you'd do a bang-up job negotiating this payment, Jack, but I also feel that if Paul is willing to make a serious enough offer today, we shouldn't fret about anything we left on the table. We could move forward in a neighborly way," Tom said, throwing the ball back into Stolley's court.

The stakes were high for Stolley. If there wound up being further negotiations, they would start at the figure he was about to name.

Everyone at the table sat in silence, waiting on Stolley. The big clock on the wall ticked away thunderously, tick-tock, tick-tock, tick-tock, tick-tock, tick-tock. While Stolley mulled over a number, Tom clenched his jaw, and the rest looked at their toes.

Without the slightest hint of an expression, Stolley finally spoke. "Given the circumstances, Tom, I think something in the range of sixty or seventy million would be fair consideration."

Tom didn't know whether to burst out laughing, shit his pants, or fall off his chair.

As hard as Tom tried to hide it, Stolley caught Tom's expression and smiled for the second time in the meeting.

"I take it, Tom, that you are favorably impressed?"

"Is this for real, or did you say that just to impress me?"

"Our attorneys are present," Stolley said matter-of-factly. "Seventy million is a firm offer from Qwestead. Do we have a deal?"

Tom looked at Boyle for confirmation and Boyle nodded.

"Well, then, Mr. Stolley," Tom said as slowly as he could make the words come out, "it looks like we're going be seeing a lot of each other in the next few years. Welcome to Trail's End!"

Tom pushed his chair back and stood up, extending his hand.

Tom Larkin, rancher, and Paul Stolley, captain of industry, men whose words still meant something in a world full of shysters, sealed the deal with a handshake.

WEDNESDAY, 4:30 P.M.

She's probably in bed with somebody, Tom thought, as he listened to Kathy's voice-mail greeting. *Serves me right.* He heaved the cell phone over his shoulder and heard it explode as it hit the back window.

Jo was recovering, Tom was rich, Carl was dead and, as far as Tom could ascertain, so was his marriage. Tom jammed the brakes, skidded to a stop in the middle of the road, and got out. The sweet smell of the air couldn't mask the bitterness in his heart.

What have I done? he asked himself. *What have I done?*

He collapsed onto the shoulder and began to kick at the loose gravel with one boot, idly watching stones tumble into the ditch. He was too tired to think, too tired to move, too tired to be angry.

When the road was gone in a hundred years, or a hundred thousand years, the land would still be there. Thoughts of the land comforted Tom, but he was tormented by what he feared had been given in exchange for it.

His head dropped. "Where am I?"

While his thoughts chased each other around in endless circles, a herd of clouds rumbled past, sometimes blocking the sun and sometimes just missing; the prairie grass bowed and righted itself in the wind; and a bluebird sang for a moment and then was off with more purpose than Tom thought he'd ever have again in his life.

Tom could find no shelter from the storm raging in his soul.

After a time, though, the storm passed, and a calm washed up like night waves that stroll into shore and leave with a murmur. Swash and whoosh. Swash ... and whoosh. Swash ... whoosh. Swash ... and ...

Nothing.

Stillness.

His spirit took flight, climbing over a hill, drifting through a draw, and floating down the crested road that separated Tom and the land. This specter, this ghost of Tom Larkin heeded no laws of gravity or men and simply went home. Home to the land that would dirty Tom's fingernails and quicken his dreams. Home to the land that would delight his grandchildren, and their children, and their cousins, and their lovers. Home to the land that harbored pain. Home to the land that could heal him.

Tom felt the sun sinking and looked up. After a journey of 100 million miles, its cryptic rays burned his eyes. Like a stone, Tom stared back.

From the East, he heard an eagle call and looked away from the dying light. Circling in a purple sky, the bird cried to Tom over and over, "Come home! Come home! Come home!"

Tom looked down at his hands. *They've aged*, he thought, *since I got here. They've calmed Eva's tears and lifted Jo's frail body and done business with scoundrels and good men alike, and trespassed, and held the phones that called the number that no longer answers.*

Weary as he was, there was a last chore to be done before he could pack up, return to St. Paul, and see what had become of his future with Kathy.

Tom struggled to bring himself upright. Twice it was more than he could manage, and he fell back into the gravel like some already-dead beast refusing to stay down. On the third try, Tom gained his feet. He would finish his work before the light died. *For Jo*, he vowed.

Tom had retrieved the contents of the safe-deposit box. To that sad collection he had added a copy of everything in Jennings' McPherson file, sealing it all in a length of polyvinyl irrigation pipe. *Pandora's pipe,* Tom thought ruefully, *a dowry for the devil.* The PVC would withstand ground conditions for seventy-five or a hundred years. In the arid climate of the southern Hills, it might even be good for 500 years—unless the polar caps melted.

The autopsy report he'd saved out would send Sam Barker to the gallows for Cody's death. Jennings had set that up flawlessly. Jennings' fountain pen, the damning evidence that Barker had not acted alone, was sealed in the pipe. Perhaps God cared, but the states attorney wouldn't want to know about Jennings' involvement. Jennings would never return to Hot Springs, so the prosecutor would have no reason to bring him into Barker's trial. It would only confuse the jury and work to Barker's advantage.

Tom swore that he would never tell Jo about Jennings—ever. If Jo thought that one of Cody's murderer's had slipped the noose, it would only make her miserable, and she deserved what little peace she'd find in seeing somebody—anybody—brought to justice.

Evidence of his Igloo break-in and burglary was sealed alongside the proof of Jennings' guilt. Best place for both, Tom reasoned, was in the ground. Tom had decided to bury his secrets alongside Cody's ashes, up on the high ridge above the ranch house, under the big red boulder. It was an ugly offering to lay in such sacred ground, but maybe, Tom hoped, just maybe Cody could deal with it.

Tom's spirits rose as he neared the ranch. He had spent most of his adult life traveling a long arc that led to this land, and he would never leave it. Kathy could leave him. The land wouldn't. His children would grow old and die. The land wouldn't. Nations would rise and fall. The land would continue racing through time until time gave up.

He drove as far as he could and had to climb fifteen or twenty yards up a low rise to reach the red boulder overlooking the ranch house and all the rest of creation. When he got there, Tom stood with his foot on the shovel, listening to the wind.

Then, he started digging. Digging and thinking.

The first slice of steel into the red earth grated sharply and sounded foreign. Was it the shovel ringing from a blow struck hard and true, or the earth crying out? Tom was tearing into Cody's ground. Maybe it was wrong, Tom considered, maybe sacrilege. He stopped after another brutal stab at the dirt, shovel half-buried, and rested one boot on the shovel's lip, the other planted under the earth he'd already disturbed.

In that moment, it caught up to him; anguish overran hope, remorse bore down on his dreams.

In desperation, Tom began to stab at the ground: babbling and sobbing and creating havoc with the earth. The perverse nature of things descended on him like harpies, biting and scratching and attacking everything he held to be true. The only solid thing remaining was the ground, so he went on stabbing at it, looking for his heart.

He landed blow after vicious blow, making the dirt leap and crumble, and then fly away in clods and dust. Tom hacked his way back through time and unintended circum-stances, looking for an answer without knowing the question; he was looking to hide something or find something, and he couldn't figure out which. His only hope was to keep going, finish the digging, finish the burying, and see about every-thing else tomorrow.

The dust from his efforts clung to the trail of his tears. In another time, Tom might have been mistaken for a primitive and simple creature, painted in gritty stripes to please God.

Tom stopped clawing at the ground and looked up.

The light was dim now, but the gathering cloud of dust mak-ing its way toward him was unmistakable. No ghost or errant whirlwind, it was the billow of dirt made by a vehicle too low slung for a two-track road and moving fast.

A glint from the Caddy's windshield was a beacon, giving Tom's position away; the cloud gained on the ridge where he stood. It snaked through a gully where some cows were holed up and advanced toward him with purpose. The plume poured over the lick and began to climb. It was coming for him.

A hundred yards out, Tom saw that it was Kathy. She was a slow and deliberate driver on the freeway and had probably been on her way to him since before dawn. Perhaps since before he was born.

Not knowing which of his emotions to trust, Tom held his breath and kept his boot to the shovel, his head bowed.

Fifteen yards beyond the boulder where Tom stood frozen at his task, the car stopped.

He didn't turn or move as footfalls advanced from below. Crunch, silence, crunch. Crunch, silence, crunch. All other sound in the universe ceased. Crunch, silence, crunch, silence, crunch, crunch, crunch.

The march stopped short of his back, but close enough for Tom to hear the sound of her breathing. It was calm and familiar.

Tom could not unbow his head. He waited so, and she continued to breathe so, but she did not speak.

The light that remained was warm, like the glow of embers from a great bonfire spent.

Two more footfalls rang out, and Kathy's arms went around him in a fierce embrace. She wept into his back, making their souls quake, although they made no more sound than snowflakes landing on a pond. She drew him even closer, to remind him and to keep him alive and to keep him with her and to hold him to the land for which he'd paid such a terrible price.

"What are you doing, Tom?"

"Trying to bury the past," he sobbed.

"I'm here now. Let's do it together."

THE END

ACKNOWLEDGEMENTS

Native Ground was propelled in the early going by the exceptional Nicole Lockwood, who showed me around Hot Springs and shared her invaluable insights about the people and places in the Black Hills. Many thanks to my reading committee, whose contributions made the book stronger and otherwise reined me in when the writing wandered off track: Patrick Brown, Alex Friedrich, Rich Brisbois, Gita Sitaramiah, Jeff Ouellette and my son, Joseph O'Connor. Later, consummate reader and my friend, Fred Weiner, helped me see that changes were needed to deepen the relationship between Tom and Kathy, and craft their dialog in a more compelling way. My editor, and *New York Times* bestselling author Lou Aronica (founder of The Fiction Studio) mercilessly cut away at my unnecessary "telling." His hand in the process made *Native Ground* a much better novel. My daughter, Anne O'Connor was instrumental in the final jacket design—a sea change compared to what I originally had in mind. The photo of me on the back cover was taken by Franz Brown. Finally, and most importantly, I could not have completed this first novel without the unflagging support, love, literary intuition, and expert copy editing of my wife, Debra.

Native Ground is the first book in a planned Tom Larkin trilogy. The second book is scheduled to be available for purchase in late 2014. If you would like to be notified when the second book is available, please send an e-mail to moconnor@mynewasset. com with the words "Book 2 Discount, Please" in the subject line. Approximately two weeks before the second book becomes available, you will receive a coupon via e-mail that will entitle you to a discounted price on the book.